## Praise for *Boy Swallows Universe*

'I've always looked out for Trent's work because he has a magic about him; what he sees, how he explains things. He can describe a kitchen table in a way that makes you want to throw your arms around it. After reading *Boy Swallows Universe* I realise that his genius isn't really just about writing so much; it's about hope, and his instinctive and infectious "Yes" to one of the most plaguing questions of the human night: Can tenderness survive brutality? This novel confirms Trent Dalton as a genuine treasure of Australian letters.'
Annabel Crabb

'As a brilliant journalist, Trent Dalton has always intimately understood how fact is often stranger than fiction. Perhaps it took someone like him to produce a novel so humming with truth. Call it a hunch, but I think he might've just written an Australian classic.' Benjamin Law

'*Boy Swallows Universe* is one of those stories that defies expectations, shatters genre boundaries and beguiles from start to finish'
*Good Reading*

'This book will light up the dimmest days' *Sydney Morning Herald*

'A towering achievement. It is the *Cloudstreet* of the Australian suburban criminal underworld' *Herald Sun*

'Glorious' *Adelaide Advertiser*

'It is a story in thrall to the potential the world holds for lightness, laughter, beauty, forgiveness, redemption and love.' *The Australian*

'a wonderful, unexpectedly beautiful portrayal of boyhood and destiny' *Better Reading*

'Goosebumps good' *Queensland Times*

'I cannot recommend this novel highly enough and I can't wait to read what Dalton produces next' *NZ Herald*

'It'll break your heart and r
the same sentence'

D1323642

Trent Dalton is a staff writer for *The Weekend Australian Magazine* and a former assistant editor of *The Courier-Mail*. He's a two-time winner of a Walkley Award for Excellence in Journalism, a three-time winner of a Kennedy Award for Excellence in NSW Journalism and a four-time winner of the national News Awards Features Journalist of the Year. *Boy Swallows Universe* is his first book.

# BOY
# SWALLOWS
# UNIVERSE

# TRENT
# DALTON

FOURTH ESTATE

**Fourth Estate**
An imprint of HarperCollins*Publishers*

First published in Australia in 2018
by HarperCollins*Publishers* Australia Pty Limited
ABN 36 009 913 517
harpercollins.com.au

**HarperCollins*Publishers***
Level 13, 201 Elizabeth Street, Sydney NSW 2000, Australia
Unit D1, 63 Apollo Drive, Rosedale, Auckland 0632, New Zealand
A 53, Sector 57, Noida, UP, India
1 London Bridge Street, London, SE1 9GF, United Kingdom
Bay Adelaide Centre, East Tower, 22 Adelaide Street West, 41st floor, Toronto,
  Ontario M5H 4E3, Canada
195 Broadway, New York NY 10007, USA

A catalogue record for this book is available from the National Library of Australia.

ISBN 978 1 4607 5389 7 (paperback)
ISBN 978 1 4607 0841 5 (ebook)

Cover design by Darren Holt, HarperCollins Design Studio
Cover images: Splendid fairywren by Michael Leach / Getty Images; all other images by
shutterstock.com
Author photo by Lyndon Mechielsen
Typeset in Bembo Std by Kirby Jones
Printed and bound in Australia by McPherson's Printing Group
The papers used by HarperCollins in the manufacture of this book are a natural, recyclable
product made from wood grown in sustainable plantation forests. The fibre source and
manufacturing processes meet recognised international environmental standards, and carry
certification.

*For Mum and Dad.*
*For Joel, Ben and Jesse.*

# Boy Writes Words

Your end is a dead blue wren.

'Did you see that, Slim?'

'See what?'

'Nothing.'

Your end is a dead blue wren. No doubt about it. Your. End. No doubt about it. Is. A. Dead. Blue. Wren.

*

The crack in Slim's windscreen looks like a tall and armless stickman bowing to royalty. The crack in Slim's windscreen looks like Slim. His windscreen wipers have smeared a rainbow of old dirt over to my passenger side. Slim says a good way for me to remember the small details of my life is to associate moments and visions with things on my person or things in my regular waking life that I see and smell and touch often. Body things, bedroom things, kitchen things. This way I will have two reminders of any given detail for the price of one.

That's how Slim beat Black Peter. That's how Slim survived the hole. Everything had two meanings, one for *here*, here being where he was then, cell D9, 2 Division, Boggo Road Gaol, and another for *there*, that boundless and unlocked universe expanding in his head and his heart. Nothing in the *here* but four green concrete walls and darkness upon darkness and his lone and stationary body. An angle iron and steel mesh bed welded to a wall. A toothbrush and a pair of cloth prison slippers. But a cup of old milk slid through a cell door slot by a silent screw took him *there*, to Ferny Grove in the 1930s, the lanky young farmhand milking cows on the outskirts of Brisbane. A forearm scar became a portal to a boyhood bike ride. A shoulder sunspot was a wormhole to the beaches of the Sunshine Coast. One rub and he was gone. An escaped prisoner here in D9. Pretend free but never on the run, which was as good as how he'd been before they threw him in the hole, real free but always on the run.

He'd thumb the peaks and valleys of his knuckles and they would take him *there*, to the hills of the Gold Coast hinterland, take him all the way to Springbrook Falls, and the cold steel prison bed frame of cell D9 would become a water-worn limestone rock, and the prison hole's cold concrete floor beneath his bare feet summer-warm water to dip his toes into, and he would touch his cracked lips and remember how it felt when something as soft and as perfect as Irene's lips reached his, how she took all his sins and all his pain away with her quenching kiss, washed him clean like Springbrook Falls washed him clean with all that white water bucketing on his head.

I'm more than a little concerned that Slim's prison fantasies are becoming mine. Irene resting on that wet and mossy emerald boulder, naked and blonde, giggling like Marilyn Monroe, head back and loose and powerful, master of any man's universe, keeper of dreams, a vision there to stick around for here, to let the anytime blade of a smuggled shiv wait another day.

'I had an adult mind,' Slim always says. That's how he beat Black Peter, Boggo Road's underground isolation cell. They threw him in that medieval box for fourteen days during a Queensland summer heatwave. They gave him half a loaf of bread to eat across two weeks. They gave him four, maybe five cups of water.

Slim says half of his Boggo Road prison mates would have died after a week in Black Peter because half of any prison population, and any major city of the world for that matter, is filled with adult men with child minds. But an adult mind can take an adult man anywhere he wants to go.

Black Peter had a scratchy coconut fibre mat that he slept on, the size of a doormat, or the length of one of Slim's long shinbones. Every day, Slim says, he lay on his side on the coir mat and pulled those long shinbones into his chest and closed his eyes and opened the door to Irene's bedroom and he slipped under Irene's white bedsheet and he spooned his body gently against hers and he wrapped his right arm around Irene's naked porcelain belly and there he stayed for fourteen days. 'Curled up like a bear and hibernated,' he says. 'Got so cosy down there in hell I never wanted to climb back up.'

Slim says I have an adult mind in a child's body. I'm only twelve years old but Slim reckons I can take the hard stories. Slim reckons I should hear all the prison stories of male rape and men who broke their necks on knotted bedsheets and swallowed sharp pieces of metal designed to tear through their insides and guarantee themselves a week-long vacation in the sunny Royal Brisbane Hospital. I think he goes too far sometimes with the details, blood spitting from raped arseholes and the like. 'Light and shade, kid,' Slim says. 'No escaping the light and no escaping the shade.' I need to hear the stories about disease and death inside so I can understand the impact of those memories of Irene. Slim says I can take the hard stories because the age of my body matters nothing compared to the age of my soul, which he has gradually narrowed down to somewhere between the early seventies and dementia. Some months ago, sitting in this very car, Slim said he would gladly share a prison

3

cell with me because I listen and I remember what I listen to. A single tear rolled down my face when he paid me this great roommate honour.

'Tears don't go so well inside,' he said.

I didn't know if he meant inside a prison cell or inside one's body. Half out of pride I cried, half out of shame, because I'm not worthy, if worthy's a word for a bloke to share a lag with.

'Sorry,' I said, apologising for the tear. He shrugged.

'There's more where that came from,' he said.

Your end is a dead blue wren. *Your end is a dead blue wren.*

\*

I will remember the rainbow of old dirt wiped across Slim's windscreen through the shape of the milky moon rising into my left thumbnail, and forever more when I look into that milky moon I will remember the day Arthur 'Slim' Halliday, the greatest prison escapee who ever lived, the wondrous and elusive 'Houdini of Boggo Road', taught me – Eli Bell, the boy with the old soul and the adult mind, prime prison cellmate candidate, the boy with his tears on the outside – to drive his rusted dark blue Toyota LandCruiser.

Thirty-two years ago, in February 1953, after a six-day trial in the Brisbane Supreme Court, a man named Judge Edwin James Droughton Stanley sentenced Slim to life for brutally bashing a taxi driver named Athol McCowan to death with a .45 Colt pistol. The papers have always called Slim 'the Taxi Driver Killer'.

I just call him my babysitter.

'Clutch,' he says.

Slim's left thigh tenses as his old sun-brown leg, wrinkled with seven hundred and fifty life lines because he might be seven hundred and fifty years old, pushes the clutch in. Slim's old sun-brown left hand shifts the gearstick. A hand-rolled cigarette burning to yellow, grey and then black, hanging precariously to the spit on the corner of his bottom lip.

'Noootral.'

I can see my brother, August, through the crack in the windscreen. He sits on our brown brick fence writing his life story in fluid cursive with his right forefinger, etching words into thin air.

*Boy writes on air.*

Boy writes on air the way my old neighbour Gene Crimmins says Mozart played piano, like every word was meant to arrive, parcel packed and shipped from a place beyond his own busy mind. Not on paper and writing pad or typewriter, but thin air, the invisible stuff, that great act-of-faith stuff that you might not even know existed did it not sometimes bend into wind and blow against your face. Notes, reflections, diary entries, all written on thin air, with his extended right forefinger swishing and slashing, writing letters and sentences into nothingness, as though he has to get it all out of his head but he needs the story to vanish into space as well, forever dipping his finger into his eternal glass well of invisible ink. Words don't go so well inside. Always better out than in.

He grips Princess Leia in his left hand. Boy never lets her go. Six weeks ago Slim took August and me to see all three *Star Wars* movies at the Yatala drive-in. We drank in that faraway galaxy from the back of this LandCruiser, our heads resting on inflated cask wine bags that were themselves resting on an old dead-mullet-smelling crab pot that Slim kept in the back near a tackle box and an old kerosene lamp. There were that many stars out that night over south-east Queensland that when the Millennium Falcon flew towards the side of the picture screen I thought for a moment it might just fly on into our own stars, take the light-speed express flight right on down to Sydney.

'You listenin'?' barks Slim.

'Yeah.'

No. Never really listenin' like I should. Always thinkin' too much about August. About Mum. About Lyle. About Slim's Buddy Holly spectacles. About the deep wrinkles in Slim's forehead. About the way he walks funny, ever since he shot himself in the leg in 1952. About the fact he's got a lucky freckle like me. About how he believed me when I told him my lucky freckle had a power to it, that it meant something to me, that when I'm nervous or scared or lost, my first instinct is to look at that deep brown freckle on the middle knuckle of my right forefinger. Then I feel better. Sounds dumb, Slim, I said. Sounds crazy, Slim, I said. But he showed me his own lucky freckle, almost a mole really, square on the knobby hill of his right wrist bone. He said he thought it might be cancerous but it's his lucky freckle and he couldn't bring himself to cut it out. In D9, he said, that freckle became sacred because it reminded him of a freckle that Irene had high up on her inner left thigh, not far at all from her holiest of holies, and he assured me that one day I too would come to know this rare place on a woman's high inner thigh and I too would know just how Marco Polo felt when he first ran his fingers over silk.

I liked that story, so I told Slim how seeing that freckle on my right forefinger knuckle for the first time at around the age of four, sitting in a yellow shirt with brown sleeves on a long brown vinyl lounge, is as far back as my memory goes. There's a television on in that memory. I look down at my forefinger and I see the freckle and then I look up and turn my head right and I see a face I think belongs to Lyle but it might belong to my father, though I don't really remember my father's face.

So the freckle is always consciousness. My personal big bang. The lounge. The yellow and brown shirt. And I arrive. I am here. I told Slim I thought the rest was questionable, that the four years before that moment might as well never have happened. Slim smiled when I told him that. He said that freckle on my right forefinger knuckle is home.

*

Ignition.

'For fuck's sake, Socrates, what did I just say?' Slim barks.

'Be careful to put your foot down?'

'You were just staring right at me. You looked like you were listenin' but you weren't fuckin' listenin'. Your eyes were wanderin' all over my face, lookin' at this, lookin' at that, but you didn't hear a word.'

That's August's fault. Boy don't talk. Chatty as a thimble, chinwaggy as a cello. He can talk, but he doesn't want to talk. Not a single word that I can recall. Not to me, not to Mum, not to Lyle, not even to Slim. He communicates fine enough, conveys great passages of conversation in a gentle touch of your arm, a laugh, a shake of his head. He can tell you how he's feeling by the way he unscrews a Vegemite jar lid. He can tell you how happy he is by the way he butters bread, how sad he is by the way he ties his shoelaces.

Some days I sit across from him on the lounge and we're playing *Super Breakout* on the Atari and having so much fun that I look across at him at the precise moment I swear he's going to say something. 'Say it,' I say. 'I know you want to. Just say it.' He smiles, tilts his head to the left and raises his left eyebrow, and his right hand makes an arcing motion, like he's rubbing an invisible snow dome, and that's how he tells me he's sorry. *One day, Eli, you will know why I am not speaking. This is not that day, Eli. Now have your fucking go.*

Mum says August stopped talking around the time she ran away from my dad. August was six years old. She says the universe stole her boy's words when she wasn't looking, when she was too caught up in the stuff she's going to tell me when I'm older, the stuff about how the universe stole her boy and replaced him with the enigmatic A-grade alien loop I've had to share a double bunk bed with for the past eight years.

Every now and then some unfortunate kid in August's class makes fun of August and his refusal to speak. His reaction is always the same: he walks up to that month's particularly foul-mouthed school bully who is dangerously unaware of August's hidden streak of psychopathic rage and, blessed by his established inability to explain his actions, he simply attacks the boy's unblemished jaw, nose and ribs with one of three sixteen-punch boxing combinations my mum's long-time boyfriend, Lyle, has tirelessly taught us both across endless winter weekends with an old brown leather punching bag in the backyard shed. Lyle doesn't believe in much, but he believes in the circumstance-shifting power of a broken nose.

The teachers generally take August's side because he's a straight-A student, as dedicated as they come. When the child psychologists come knocking, Mum rustles up another glowing testimony from another school teacher about why August's a dream addition to any class and why the Queensland education system would benefit from more children just like him, completely fucking mute.

Mum says when he was five or six August stared for hours into reflective surfaces. While I was banging toy trucks and play blocks on the kitchen floor as Mum made carrot cake, he was staring into an old circular make-up mirror of Mum's. He would sit for hours around puddles looking down at his reflection, not in a Narcissus kind of way, but in what Mum thought was an exploratory fashion, like he was actually searching for something. I would pass by our bedroom doorway and catch him making faces in the mirror we had on top of an old wood veneer chest of drawers. 'Found it yet?' I asked once when I was nine. He turned from the mirror with a blank face and a kink in the upper left corner of his top lip that told me there was a world out there beyond our cream-coloured bedroom walls that I was neither ready for nor needed in. But I kept asking him that question whenever I saw him staring at himself. 'Found it yet?'

He always stared at the moon, tracked its path over our house from our bedroom window. He knew the angles of moonlight. Sometimes, deep into the night, he'd slip out our window, unfurl the hose and drag it in his pyjamas all the way out to the front gutter where he'd sit for hours, silently filling the street with water. When he got the angles just right, a giant puddle would fill with the silver reflection of a full moon. 'The moon pool,' I proclaimed grandly one cold night. And August beamed, wrapped his right arm over my shoulders and nodded his head, the way Mozart might have nodded his head at the end of Gene Crimmins's favourite opera, *Don Giovanni*. He knelt down and with his right forefinger he wrote three words in perfect cursive across the moon pool.

*Boy swallows universe*, he wrote.

It was August who taught me about details, how to read a face, how to extract as much information as possible from the non-verbal, how to mine expression and conversation and story from the data of every last speechless thing that is right before your eyes, the things that are talking to you without talking to you. It was August who taught me I didn't always have to listen. I might just have to look.

*

The LandCruiser rattles to chunky metal life and I bounce on the vinyl seat. Two pieces of Juicy Fruit that I've carried for seven hours slip from my shorts pocket into a foam cavity in the seat that Slim's old and loyal and dead white bitzer, Pat, regularly chewed on during the frequent trips the two made from Brisbane to the town of Jimna, north of Kilcoy, in Slim's post-prison years.

Pat's full name was Patch but that became a mouthful for Slim. He and the dog would regularly sift for gold in a secret Jimna backwoods creek bed that Slim believes, to this day, contains enough gold deposits to make King Solomon raise an eyebrow. He still goes out there with his old pan, the first Sunday of every month. But the search for gold ain't the same without Pat, he says. It was Pat who could really go for gold. The dog had the nose for it. Slim reckons Pat had a genuine lust for gold, the world's first canine to suffer a case of gold fever. 'The glittery sickness,' he says. 'Sent ol' Pat round the bend.'

Slim shifts the gear stick.

'*Be careful to push the clutch down*. First. Release the clutch.'

Gentle push on the accelerator.

'And steadily on the pedally.'

The hulking LandCruiser moves forward three metres along our grassy kerbside and Slim brakes, the car parallel to August still writing furiously into thin air with his right forefinger. Slim and I turn our heads hard left to watch August's apparent burst of creativity. When he finishes writing a full sentence he dabs the air as though he's marking a full stop. He wears his favourite green T-shirt with the words *You Ain't Seen Nothin' Yet* written across it in rainbow lettering. Floppy brown hair, borderline Beatle cut. He wears a pair of Lyle's old blue and yellow Parramatta Eels supporter shorts despite the fact that, at thirteen years of age, at least five of which he has spent watching Parramatta Eels games on the couch with Lyle and me, he doesn't have the slightest interest in rugby league. Our dear mystery boy. Our Mozart. August is one year older than me but August is one year older than everybody. August is one year older than the universe.

When he finishes writing five full sentences he licks the tip of his forefinger like he's inking a quill, then he plugs back into whatever mystical source is pushing the invisible pen that scribbles his invisible writing. Slim rests his arms on the steering wheel, takes a long drag of his rollie, not taking his eyes off August.

'What's he writin' now?' Slim asks.

August's oblivious to our stares, his eyes only following the letters in his personal blue sky. Maybe to him it's an endless ream of lined paper that he writes on in his head, or maybe he sees the black writing lines stretched across the sky. It's mirror writing to me. I can read it if I'm facing him at the right angle, if I can see the letters clear enough to turn them round in my head, spin them round in my mirror mind.

'Same sentence over and over this time.'

'What's he sayin'?'

The sun over August's shoulder. White hot god of a thing. A hand to my forehead. No doubt about it.

'Your end is a dead blue wren.'

August freezes. He stares at me. He looks like me, but a better version of me, stronger, more beautiful, everything smooth on his face, smooth like the face he sees when he stares into the moon pool.

Say it again. 'Your end is a dead blue wren.'

August gives a half-smile, shakes his head, looks at me like I'm the one who's crazy. Like I'm the one who's imagining things. *You're always imagining things, Eli.*

'Yeah, I saw you. I've been watching you for the past five minutes.'

He smiles wide, furiously wiping his words from the sky with an open palm. Slim smiles wide too, shakes his head.

'That boy's got the answers,' Slim says.

'To what?' I wonder.

'To the questions,' Slim says.

He reverses the LandCruiser, takes her back three metres, brakes.

'Your turn now.'

Slim coughs, chokes up brown tobacco spit that he missiles out the driver's window to our sun-baked and potholed bitumen street running past fourteen low-set sprawling fibro houses, ours and everybody else's in shades of cream, aquamarine and sky blue. Sandakan Street, Darra, my little suburb of Polish and Vietnamese refugees and Bad Old Days refugees like Mum and August and me, exiled here for the past eight years, hiding out far from the rest of the world, marooned survivors of the great ship hauling Australia's lower-class shitheap, separated from America and Europe and Jane Seymour by oceans and a darn pretty Great Barrier Reef and another 7000 kilometres of Queensland coastline and then an overpass taking cars to Brisbane city, and separated a bit more still by the nearby Queensland Cement and Lime Company factory that blows cement powder across Darra on windy days and covers our rambling home's sky-blue fibro walls with dust that August and I have to hose off before the rain comes and sets the dust to cement, leaving hard grey veins of misery across the house front and the large window that Lyle throws his cigarette butts out of and I throw my apple cores out of, always following Lyle's lead because, and maybe I'm too young to know better, Lyle's always got a lead worth following.

Darra is a dream, a stench, a spilt garbage bin, a cracked mirror, a paradise, a bowl of Vietnamese noodle soup filled with prawns, domes of plastic crab meat, pig ears and pig knuckles and pig belly. Darra is a girl washed down a drainpipe, a boy with snot slipping from his nose so ripe it glows on Easter night, a teenage girl stretched across a train track waiting for the express to Central and beyond, a South African man smoking Sudanese weed, a Filipino man injecting Afghani dope next door to a girl from Cambodia sipping milk from Queensland's Darling Downs. Darra is my quiet sigh, my reflection on war, my dumb pre-teen longing, my home.

'When do you reckon they'll be back?' I ask.

'Soon enough.'

'What'd they go see?'

Slim wears a thin bronze-coloured button-up cotton shirt tucked into dark blue shorts. He wears these shorts constantly and he says he rotates between three pairs of the same shorts but every day I see the same hole in the bottom right-hand corner of his rear pocket. His blue rubber thongs are normally moulded to his old and callused feet, dirt-caked and sweat-stunk, but his left thong slips off now, caught on the clutch, as he slides awkwardly out of the car. Houdini's getting on. Houdini's caught in the water chamber of Brisbane's outer western suburbs. Even Houdini can't escape time. Slim can't run from MTV. Slim can't run from Michael Jackson. Slim can't escape the 1980s.

'*Terms of Endearment*,' he says, opening the passenger door.

I truly love Slim because he truly loves August and me. Slim was hard and cold in his youth. He's softened with age. Slim always cares for August and me and how we're going and how we're going to grow up. I love him so much for trying to convince us that when Mum and Lyle are out for so long like this they are at the movies and not, in fact, dealing heroin purchased from Vietnamese restaurateurs.

'Lyle choose that one?'

I have suspected Mum and Lyle are drug dealers since I found a five-hundred-gram brick of Golden Triangle heroin stowed in the mower catcher in our backyard shed five days ago. I feel certain Mum and Lyle are drug dealers when Slim tells me they have gone to the movies to see *Terms of Endearment*.

Slim gives me a sharp look. 'Slide over, smartarse,' he mumbles from the corner of his mouth.

Clutch in. First. Steadily on the pedally. The car jolts forward and we're moving. 'Give it some gas,' Slim says. My bare right foot goes down, leg fully extended, and we cross our lawn all the way to Mrs Dudzinski's rosebush on the kerbside next door.

'Get onto the road,' Slim says, laughing.

Hard right on the wheel, off the gutter onto the Sandakan Street bitumen.

'Clutch in, second,' Slim barks.

Quicker now. Past Freddy Pollard's place, past Freddy Pollard's sister, Evie, pushing a headless Barbie down the street in a toy pram.

'Should I stop?' I ask.

Slim looks in the rearview mirror, darts his head to the passenger side mirror. 'Nah, fuck it. Once round the block.'

Slip into third and we're rumbling at forty kilometres an hour. And we're free. It's a breakout. Me and Houdini. On the run. Two great escapologists on the lam.

'I'm *driiiiving*,' I scream.

Slim laughs and his old chest wheezes.

Left into Swanavelder Street, on past the old World War II Polish migrant centre where Lyle's mum and dad spent their first days in Australia. Left into Butcher Street where the Freemans keep their collection of exotic birds: a squawking peacock, a greylag goose, a Muscovy duck. Fly on free, bird. Drive. Drive. Left into Hardy, left back into Sandakan.

'Slow her down,' says Slim.

I slam the brakes and lose footing on the clutch and the car cuts out, once again parallel to August, who is still writing words on thin air, lost in the work.

'Did ya see me, Gus?' I holler. 'Did ya see me driving, Gus?'

He doesn't look away from his words. Boy didn't even see us drive away.

'What's he scribblin' now?' Slim asks.

The same two words over and over again. The crescent moon of a capital 'C'. Chubby little 'a'. Skinny little 'i', one descending stroke in the air with a cherry on top. August sits in the same spot on the fence that he usually sits on, by the missing brick, the space two bricks along the fence from the red wrought-iron letterbox.

August is the missing brick. The moon pool is my brother. August is the moon pool.

'Two words,' I say. 'A name starting with "C".'

I will associate her name with the day I learned to drive and, forever more, the missing brick and the moon pool and Slim's Toyota LandCruiser and the crack in Slim's windscreen and my lucky freckle, and everything about my brother, August, will remind me of her.

'What name?' Slim asks.

'Caitlyn.'

Caitlyn. There's no doubt about it. Caitlyn. That right forefinger and an endless blue sky sheet of paper with that name on it.

'You know anyone named Caitlyn?' asks Slim.

'No.'

'What's the second word?'

I follow August's finger, swirling through the sky.

'It's "spies",' I say.

'Caitlyn spies,' Slim says. 'Caitlyn spies.' He drags on his cigarette, contemplatively. 'What the fuck does that mean?'

Caitlyn spies. No doubt about it.

Your end is a dead blue wren. Boy swallows universe. Caitlyn spies.

No doubt about it.

These are the answers.

The answers to the questions.

# Boy Makes Rainbow

This room of true love. This room of blood. Sky-blue fibro walls. Off-colour paint patches where Lyle has puttied up holes. A made-up queen bed, tightly tucked white sheet, an old thin grey blanket that wouldn't have been out of place in one of those death camps Lyle's mum and dad were escaping from. Everybody running from something, especially ideas.

A framed Jesus portrait over the bed. The son and his jagged crown, reasonably calm for all the blood dripping down his forehead – so cool under pressure that guy – but frowning like always because August and I aren't supposed to be in here. This still blue room, the quietest place on earth. This room of true companionship.

Slim says the mistake of all those old English writers and all those matinee movies is to suggest true love comes easy, that it waits on stars and planets and revolutions around the sun. Waits on fate. Dormant true love, there for everybody, just waiting to be found, erupting when the thread of existence collides with chance and the eyes of two lovers meet. Boom. From what I've seen of it, true love is hard. Real romance has death in it. It has midnight shakes and flecks of shit across a bedsheet. True love like this dies if it has to wait for fate. True love like this asks lovers to cast aside what is meant to be and work with what is.

August leads, boy wants to show me something.

'He'll kill us if he finds us in here.'

Lena's room is out of bounds. Lena's room is sacred. Only Lyle enters Lena's room. August shrugs. He grips a flashlight in his right hand, passes Lena's bed.

'This bed makes me sad.'

August nods knowingly. *It makes me sadder, Eli. Everything makes me sadder. My emotions run deeper than yours, Eli, don't forget it.*

The bed sags on one side, weighed down on one half for the eight years that Lena Orlik slept alone on it without the balancing weight of her husband, Aureli Orlik, who died of prostate cancer on this bed in 1968.

Aureli died quiet. Died as quiet as this room.

'Reckon Lena's watching us right now?'

August smiles, shrugs his shoulders. Lena believed in God but she didn't believe in love, or at least the kind written in stars. Lena didn't believe in fate because if her love of Aureli was meant to be then the birth and the whole unholy and deranged head-fuck adulthood of Adolf Hitler was also meant to be because that monster, 'that filthy *potwor*', was the only reason they met in 1945 in an American-run displaced persons holding camp in Germany where they stayed for four years, long enough for Aureli to collect the silver that formed Lena's wedding ring. Lyle was born in the camp in 1949, spent his first night on earth sleeping in a large iron wash bucket, wrapped in a grey blanket like the one right here on this bed. America wouldn't take Lyle and Great Britain wouldn't take Lyle, but Australia would and Lyle never forgot this fact, which is why, during a wildly misspent youth, he never burned or vandalised property marked *Made in Australia*.

In 1951 the Orliks arrived at the Wacol East Dependants Holding Camp for Displaced Persons, a sixty-second bike ride from our house. For four years they lived among two thousand people sharing timber huts with a total of three hundred and forty rooms, with communal toilets and baths. Aureli landed a job pegging sleepers for the new rail line between Darra and neighbouring suburbs, Oxley and Corinda. Lena worked in a timber factory in Yeerongpilly, in the south-west, cutting sheets of plywood alongside men twice her size and with half her pluck.

Aureli built this room himself, built the whole house on weekends with Polish friends from the railway line. No electricity for the first two years. Lena and Aureli taught themselves English by kerosene lamp light. The house spread, room by nailed room, short stump by short stump, until the smell of Lena's Polish wild mushroom soup and potato and cheese *pierogi* and cabbage *golabki* and roasted lamb *baranina* filled three bedrooms, a kitchen, a living room, a lounge room, a laundry off the kitchen, a bathroom and a stand-alone flushable toilet beneath a wall hanging of Warsaw's white three-nave Church of the Holiest Saviour.

August stops, turns to the room's built-in wardrobe. Lyle built this wardrobe himself using all those woodcraft skills he learned watching his dad and his dad's Polish friends piece this house together.

'What is it, Gus?'

August nods his head right. *You should open the wardrobe door.*

Aureli Orlik lived a quiet life and was determined to die quietly too, with dignity, not to the sound of heart monitors and rushing medical staff. He wouldn't make a scene. Every time Lena returned to this death room with an empty pisspot or a fresh towel to wipe her husband's vomit from his chest, Aureli would apologise for causing such trouble. His last word to Lena was 'Sorry', and he didn't stick around long enough to clarify what exactly he was sorry for, and Lena could only be sure he did not mean their love because she knew there was hardship in this true love and endurance and reward and failure and renewal and, finally, death, but never regret.

I open the wardrobe. An old ironing board standing up. A bag of Lena's old clothes on the wardrobe floor. A hanging row of Lena's dresses, in single colours: olive, tan, black, blue.

Lena died loud, a violent cacophony of crashing steel and a Frankie Valli high note, returning from Toowoomba's Carnival of Flowers along the Warrego Highway at twilight, eighty minutes out of Brisbane, her Ford Cortina meeting the front steel grille of a semitrailer hauling pineapples. Lyle was down south in a Kings Cross drug rehab with his old girlfriend, Astrid, on the second of three attempts to kick a decade-long heroin habit. He was jonesing all the way through a subsequent meeting with police officers from the highway town of Gatton who attended the scene. 'She wouldn't have suffered,' said a senior officer, which Lyle took as the officer's tender way of saying, 'The truck was fuckin' huuuuge.' The officer handed over the only possessions of Lena's they were able to prise from the Cortina's wreckage: Lena's handbag, a set of rosary beads, a small round pillow that she sat on to see better above the steering wheel and, miraculously, a cassette tape recording ejected from the car's modest stereo system, *Lookin' Back* by Frankie Valli and The Four Seasons.

'Fuck,' Lyle said, holding the tape, shaking his head.

'What?' said the officer.

'Nothing,' Lyle said, realising an explanation would delay the smack fix that was dominating his thoughts, the physical need for drugs and their beautiful daydream – for what I heard Mum once call 'the siesta' – creating an emotional levee that would break a week later, flooding him with the notion that there was no longer a single person left on earth who loved him. That night, on a small sofa bed in the Darra basement of his childhood best friend Tadeusz 'Teddy' Kallas, he shot his left arm up to the thought of how romantic his mum was, how deeply she loved her husband, and how the soaring high notes of Frankie Valli made every human on earth smile except his mother. Frankie Valli made Lena Orlik weep. In a heroin haze, Lyle placed The Four Seasons cassette into Teddy's basement tape deck. He pressed play because he wanted to hear the song that was playing when she smashed into the semitrailer full of pineapples. It was 'Big Girls Don't Cry', and in that moment Lyle remembered, as sure as Frankie Valli's first high note, that accidents never happened to Lena Orlik.

True love comes hard.

*

'What is it, Gus?'

He puts a forefinger to his lips. He silently shifts aside the bag of Lena's clothes, slides Lena's dresses across the wardrobe's hanging pole. He pushes against the rear wall of the wardrobe space and a sheet of white painted timber, a metre by a metre, clicks against a compression mechanism behind the wall and falls forward into August's hands.

'What are you doing, Gus?'

He slides the timber sheet along the back of Lena's hanging dresses.

A black void opens behind the wardrobe, a chasm, a space of unknown distance beyond the wall. August's eyes are wide, elated by the hope and possibility in the void.

'What is that?'

*

We met Lyle through Astrid, and Mum met Astrid in the Sisters of Mercy Women's Refuge in Nundah, on Brisbane's

north side. We were all dipping bread rolls into beef stew —
Mum, August and me — in the refuge dining room. Mum says
Astrid was at the end of our table. I was five years old. August
was six and kept pointing at a purple crystal tattooed beneath
Astrid's left eye, shaped so it looked like she was crying crystals.
Astrid was Moroccan and beautiful and permanently young
and always so bejewelled and mystical that I'd come to think of
her and her exposed coffee-coloured belly as a character from
*Arabian Nights*, a keeper of magical lamps and daggers and flying
carpets and hidden meanings. At the refuge dining table Astrid
turned and stared into August's eyes and August stared back,
smiling for long enough that it inspired Astrid to turn to Mum.

'You must feel special,' she said.

'For what?' Mum asked.

'Spirit chose you to watch over him,' she said, nodding at
August.

Spirit, we would later discover, was an all-encompassing
term for the creator of all living things who visited Astrid
on occasion in three manifestations: a mystical white-robed
goddess spirit, Sharna; an Egyptian Pharaoh named Om
Ra; and Errol, a farting, foul-mouthed representation of all
the universe's ills, who spoke like a small drunk Irishman.
Lucky for us, Spirit liked August and Spirit soon made some
miraculous communication with Astrid about how her path to
enlightenment included arrangements to have us stay for three
months in the sunroom of her grandmother Zohra's house in
Manly, in Brisbane's eastern suburbs. I was only five years old
but I still called bullshit, but Manly's a place where a boy can
run barefoot across the low-tide mudflats of Moreton Bay for
so long he can convince himself he's running all the way to
the edge of Atlantis, where he might live forever, or until the
smell of crumbed cod and chips calls him home, so I made like
August and shut my trap.

Lyle came to Zohra's house to see Astrid. He soon came to Zohra's house to play Scrabble with Mum. Lyle's not book smart but he's street smart and he reads paperback novels endlessly so he knows plenty of words, like Mum. Lyle says he fell in love with Mum the moment she landed the word 'quixotic' on a triple word score.

Mum's love came hard. There was pain in it, there was blood and screams and fists against fibro walls, because the worst thing Lyle ever did was get my mum on drugs. I guess the best thing Lyle ever did was get her off drugs, but he knows I know that the latter could never make up for the former. He got her off drugs in this room. This room of true love. This room of blood.

\*

August turns on the flashlight, shines it into the black void beyond the wardrobe wall. The dead white light illuminates a small room almost as big as our bathroom. The torchlight shines on three brown brick walls, a cavity deep enough for a grown man to stand in, like some kind of fallout shelter but unstocked and empty. The floor is made of the earth that the room was dug out from. August's torch shines on the empty space until it finds the only objects in the room. A wood stool with a cushioned circular seat. And upon this stool is a push-button box telephone. The telephone is red.

\*

The worst kind of junkie is the one who thinks they're not the worst kind of junkie. Mum and Lyle were woeful for a while there, about four years ago. Not in the way they looked, just the way they behaved. Not forgetting my eighth birthday, as such, just sleeping through it, that kind of thing. Booby-trap syringes and shit. You'd creep into their bedroom to wake them up and tell them it was Easter, hop onto their bed like the joyful seasonal bunny and cop a junk needle in your kneecap.

August made me pancakes on my eighth birthday, served them up with maple syrup and a birthday candle that was actually just a thick white house candle. When we finished the pancakes, August made a gesture that said because it was my birthday we could do whatever I wanted. I asked if we could burn several things with my birthday candle, starting with the fungus-green loaf of bread that had been sitting in the fridge for what August and I had tracked at forty-three days.

August was everything back then. Mum, dad, uncle, grandma, priest, pastor, cook. He made us breakfast, he ironed our school uniforms, he brushed my hair, helped me with my homework. He started cleaning up after Lyle and Mum as they slept, hiding their drug bags and spoons, responsibly disposing of their syringes, with me always behind him saying, 'Fuck all that, let's go kick the footy.'

But August cared for Mum like she was a lost forest fawn learning to walk because August seemed to know some secret about it all, that it was all just a phase, a part of Mum's story that we simply had to wait through. I think August believed she needed this phase, she deserved this drug rest, this big sleep, this time out of her brain, this time out from thinking about the past – her thirty-year slideshow of violence and abandonment and dormitory homes for wayward Sydney girls with bad dads. August combed her hair while she slept, pulled blankets over her chest, wiped drool from her mouth with tissues. August was her guardian and he'd clean me up in a flurry of pushes and punches if ever I stood in judgement and disgust. Because I didn't know. Because nobody knew Mum but August.

These were Mum's Debbie Harry 'Heart of Glass' years. People say junk makes you look horrific, that too much heroin tears your hair out, leaves scabs all over your face and your wrists from your anxious fingers and your anxious fingernails that keep filling with blood and rolled skin. People say the gear sucks the calcium out of your teeth and your bones, leaves you couch-bound like a rotting corpse. And I'd seen all that. But I also thought junk made Mum look beautiful. She was thin and pale white and blonde, not as blonde as Debbie Harry but just as pretty. I thought junk made Mum look like an angel. She had this fixed dazed look on her face, there but not there, like Harry in that 'Heart of Glass' clip, like something from a dream, moving in the space between sleeping and waking, between life and death, but sparkling somehow, like she had a mirror ball permanently spinning in the pupils of her sapphire eyes. And I remember thinking that's how an angel really would look if they found themselves in suburban Darra, south-east Queensland, down all this way from heaven. Such an angel really would be dazed like that, puzzled, glassy, flapping her wings as she studied all those dishes piling up in the sink, all those cars passing by the house beyond the cracks in the curtains.

There's a golden orb-weaver spider that builds a web outside my bedroom window so intricate and perfect that it looks like a single snowflake magnified a thousand times. The orb-weaver spider sits in the middle of the web like it's parachuting sideways, suspended in the quest it keeps wanting to finish without needing to know the reason why, blown but not beaten by wind and rain and afternoon summer storms so strong they fell power poles. Mum was the orb-weaver spider in those years. And she was the web, and she was the butterfly too, the blue tiger butterfly with sapphire wings being eaten alive by the spider.

*

'We need to get outta here, Gus.'

August hands me the flashlight to hold. He turns around and kneels down, sliding his legs backwards through the space in the wardrobe and into the void of the room. He drops into the room and his feet find footing. He turns back around to me and, standing on his toes for extra height, he nods at the sliding wardrobe door. I close it behind us and we're in total darkness but for the light from the torch. August nods me into the void, reaches up to take the flashlight from my hands. I shake my head.

'This is insane.'

He nods me in again.

'You're an arsehole.'

He smiles. August knows I'm just like him. August knows that if someone told me there was a hungry Bengal tiger on the loose behind a door I'd open it to be sure they weren't lying. I slip down into the room and my bare feet land on the cold damp earth of the room's floor. I run a hand along the walls, rough brick and dirt.

'What is this place?'

August stands staring at the red telephone.

'What are you looking at?'

He keeps staring at the telephone, excited and distant.

'Gus, Gus ...'

He raises his left forefinger. *Wait a second.*

And the telephone rings. A rapid ring that fills the room. Ring, ring. Ring, ring.

August turns to me, his eyes wide and electric blue.

'Don't answer it, Gus.'

He lets it ring three more times and then his hand reaches for the receiver.

'Gus, don't pick up that fucking phone!'

He picks it up. Phone to his ear. He's already smiling, seemingly amused by someone on the other end of the line.

'Can you hear something?'

August smiles.

'What is it? Gimme a listen.'

I grab for the phone but August pushes my arm away, his left ear squeezing the phone to his left shoulder. He's laughing now.

'Is someone talking to you?'

He nods.

'You need to put the phone down, Gus.'

He turns away from me, listening intently, the phone's twisting red cord wrapping over his shoulder. He stands with his back turned to me for a full minute, then he turns back around with a vacant look across his face. He points to me. *They want to speak to you, Eli.*

'No.'

He nods his head and passes the phone to me.

'I don't want it now,' I say, pushing the phone away.

August snarls, eyebrows raised. *Don't be such a child, Eli.* Then he throws the phone at me and, instinctively, I catch it. Deep breath.

'Hello?'

The voice of a man.

'Hello.'

A real man type man, deep voice. A man in his fifties maybe, sixties even.

'Who is this?' I ask.

'Who do you think this is?' the man replies.

'I don't know.'

'Of course you do.'

'No, I really don't.'

'Yes, you do. You have always known.'

August smiles, nodding his head. I think I know who it is.

'You're Tytus Broz?'

'No, I am not Tytus Broz.'

'You're a friend of Lyle's?'

'Yes.'

'You're the man who gave Lyle the Golden Triangle heroin I found in the mower catcher?'

'How do you know it was Golden Triangle heroin?'

'My friend Slim reads *The Courier-Mail* every day. When he's finished with the paper he passes it to me. The crime desk has been writing stories about heroin spreading through Brisbane from Darra. They say it comes from the main opium-producing area of South-East Asia that overlaps Burma, Laos and Thailand. That's the Golden Triangle.'

'You know your stuff, kid. You read a lot?'

'I read everything. Slim says reading is the greatest escape there is and he's made some great escapes.'

'Slim's a very wise man.'

'You know Slim?'

'Everybody knows the Houdini of Boggo Road.'

'He's my best friend.'

'You're best friends with a convicted killer?'

'Lyle says Slim didn't kill that cab driver.'

'Is that right?'

'Yes, that's right. He says Slim was verballed. They stitched him up for it because he had history. They do that, you know, the cops.'

'Has Slim told you himself that he didn't do it?'

'Not really, but Lyle says there's no way in hell he did it.'

'And you believe Lyle?'

'Lyle doesn't lie.'

'Everybody lies, kid.'

'Not Lyle. He's physically incapable of it. That's what he told Mum, anyway.'

'You don't really believe that, do you?'

27

'He called it a full-blown medical condition, "Disinhibited Social Engagement Disorder". It means he can't mask the truth. He can't lie.'

'I don't think that means he can't lie. I think it means he can't be discreet.'

'Same thing.'

'Maybe, kid.'

'I'm sick of adults being discreet. Nobody ever gives you the full story.'

'Eli?'

'How do you know my name? Who are you?'

'Eli?'

'Yes.'

'You sure you want the full story?'

There's the sound of the wardrobe door sliding open. Then August sucks in a deep mouthful of air and I feel Lyle looking through the wardrobe space well before I hear him.

'What the fuck are you two doing in there?' he barks.

August drops to the ground and in the dark I can only see flashes of his torchlight frantically making lightning bolt shapes on the walls of this small dank underground earth room as his hands feel desperately for something and he finds it.

'Don't you fucking dare,' Lyle hollers through clenched teeth.

But August does fucking dare. He finds a square brown metal door flap at the base of the right wall, the size of the cardboard base in a large banana box. A bronze latch keeps the flap fixed to a strip of wood in the floor. August loosens the latch, flips the door up and, slipping quickly onto his belly, uses his elbows to crawl through a tunnel running off the room.

I turn to Lyle, stunned.

'What is this place?'

But I don't wait for an answer. I drop the phone.

'Eli!' screams Lyle.

I dive to my belly and follow August through the tunnel. Soil on my stomach. Damp earth and hard dirt walls against my shoulders, and darkness, save for the shaky torch bouncing white light from August's hand. I have a friend at school, Duc Quang, who visited his grandparents in Vietnam and when he was there his family visited a tunnel network built by the Viet Cong. He told me how scary it was crawling through those tunnels, the suffocating claustrophobia, the dirt that falls on your face and into your eyes. That's what this is, goddamn it, full North Vietnamese army madness. Duc Quang said he had to stop halfway through a tunnel, frozen stiff with fear, and two tourists who were crawling behind him had to drag him out of the tunnel backwards. There's no going back for me. Back in that room is Lyle and, more significantly, Lyle's open right palm which I have no doubt whatsoever he is priming with a series of finger flexes and muscle clenches in readiness to smack the bounce out of my poor white arse. Fear stopped Duc in his tunnelling tracks, but fear of Lyle keeps me elbow-crawling like a seasoned VC explosives expert – six, seven, eight metres into darkness. The tunnel takes a slight left turn. Nine metres, ten metres, eleven metres. It's hot in here, effort and sweat and dirt mix into mud on my forehead. The air is thick.

'Fuck, August, I can't breathe in here.'

And August stops. His torchlight shines on another brown metal flap. He flips it open and a foul sulphur stench fills the tunnel and makes me gag.

'What is that smell? Is that shit? I think that's shit, August.'

August crawls through the tunnel's exit and I follow him hard and fast, taking a deep breath when I spill into another square space, smaller than the last but just big enough for the two of us to stand up in. The space is dark. The flooring is earth again, but there's something layering the earth and cushioning my feet. Sawdust. That smell is stronger now.

'That's definitely shit, August. Where the fuck are we?'

August looks up and my eyes follow his to a perfect circle of light directly above us, the radius of a dinner plate. Then the circle of light is filled with the face of Lyle looking down at us. Red hair, freckles. Lyle is Ginger Meggs grown up, always in a Jackie Howe cotton singlet and rubber flip-flops, his wiry but muscular arms covered in cheap and ill-conceived tattoos: an eagle with a baby in its talons on his right shoulder; an ageing staff-wielding wizard on his left shoulder who looks like my Year 7 teacher at school, Mr Humphreys; pre-Hawaii Elvis Presley shaking his knees on his left forearm. Mum has a colour picture book about The Beatles and I've always thought that Lyle looks a bit like John Lennon in the wide-eyed 'Please Please Me' years. I will remember Lyle through 'Twist and Shout'. Lyle is 'Love Me Do'. Lyle is 'Do You Want to Know a Secret?'.

'You two are in so much shit,' Lyle says through the circular hole above us.

'Why?' I say defiantly, my confusion turning to anger.

'No, I mean you're actually standing in shit,' he says. 'You just crawled inside the thunderbox.'

Fuck. The thunderbox. The abandoned rusty tin outhouse at the end of Lena's backyard, cobwebbed home to redback spiders and brown snakes so hungry they even bite your arse in your dreams. Perspective's a funny thing. The world seems so different looking up at it from six feet under. Life from the bottom of a shithole. The only way is up from here for August and Eli Bell.

Lyle removes the thick sheet of wood with the hole in it that stretches across the thunderbox and acts as the toilet seat that once cushioned the plump backsides of Lena and Aureli and every one of Aureli's workmates who helped build the house we just miraculously crawled away from through a secret underground tunnel.

Lyle reaches his right arm down into the void, hand extended for grabbing.

'C'mon,' he says.

I move back from his hand.

'No, you're gonna give us a floggin',' I say.

'Well, I can't lie,' he says.

'Fuck this.'

'Don't fuckin' swear, Eli,' Lyle says.

'I'm not going anywhere until you give us some answers,' I bark.

'Don't test me, Eli.'

'You and Mum are using again.'

Got him. He drops his head, shakes it. He's tender now, compassionate and regretful.

'We're not using, mate,' he says. 'I promised you both. I don't break my promises.'

'Who was the guy on the red phone?' I shout.

'What guy?' Lyle asks. 'What the hell are you talking about, Eli?'

'The phone rang and August picked it up.'

'Eli ...'

'The man,' I say. 'Deep voice. He's your drug boss isn't he? He's the man who gave you the bag of heroin I found in the mower catcher.'

'Eli ...'

'He's the big bad mastermind, the puppet master behind it all, the kingpin who sounds all sweet and nice and boring like a high school Science teacher but is actually a murderous megalomaniac.'

'Eli, damn it!' he screams.

I stop. Lyle shakes his head. He takes a breath.

'That phone doesn't get calls,' he says. 'Your imagination's getting the better of you again, Eli.'

I turn to August. I turn back up to Lyle.

'It rang, Lyle. August picked it up. A man was on the other end. He knew my name. He knew us all. He knew Slim. I thought for a minute it was you but then …'

'That's enough, Eli,' Lyle barks. 'Whose idea was it to go into Lena's room?'

August puts a thumb to his chest. Lyle nods his head.

'All right, here's the deal,' he says. 'Come up now and get what's coming to you, and after everyone's settled down a bit I'll update you on a few things we got goin' on.'

'Fuck that,' I say. 'I want answers now.'

Lyle replaces the wood toilet seat back on the thunderbox.

'Let me know when you find your manners again, Eli,' he says.

Lyle walks away.

\*

Four years ago I thought he was going to walk away forever. He stood at the front door with a duffle bag over his right shoulder. I clutched his left hand and leaned back on it with all my weight and he dragged me with him out the door.

'No,' I said. 'No, Lyle.'

Tears in my eyes and tears in my nose and mouth.

'I gotta get myself better, mate,' he said. 'August is gonna look after your mum for me. And you gotta look after August, all right.'

'No,' I howled and he turned his head and I thought I had him because he never cries but his eyes were wet. 'No.'

Then he shouted at me: 'Let me go, Eli.' And he pushed me back through the door and I fell to the linoleum floor of the front sunroom, friction taking skin from my elbows.

'I love you,' he said. 'I'll be back.'

'You're lying,' I shouted.

'I can't lie, Eli.'

Then he walked out the front door and out along the path to the front gate and out further past the wrought-iron letterbox and the brown brick fence with the single missing brick. I followed him all the way out to the gate and I was screaming so loud it hurt my throat. 'You're a liar,' I screamed. 'You're a liar. You're a liar. You're a liar.' But he didn't even turn around. He just kept walking away.

But then he came back. Six months later. It was January and it was hot and I was in the front yard, shirtless and tanned, with my thumb on the garden hose directing arcing sheets of vapour spray to the sun to make my own rainbows and I saw him walking through the wall of water. He opened the front gate and closed it behind him and I dropped the hose and ran to him. He had navy blue work pants on and a navy blue denim work shirt covered in grease. He was fit and strong and when he kneeled on the pathway to meet my height I thought he kneeled like King Arthur and I had never loved another man more in my short life. So rainbows are Lyle and grease is Lyle and King Arthur is Lyle. I ran at him so hard he nearly fell backwards with my impact, because I hit him like Ray Price, steel-hard lock forward for the triumphant Parramatta Eels. He laughed and when my fingers clutched at his shoulders to draw him closer, he dropped his head on my hair and kissed the top of my head and I don't know why I said what I said next but I said it all the same. 'Dad,' I said.

He gave a half-smile and he straightened me up with his hands on both my shoulders, stared into my eyes. 'You've already got a dad, mate,' he said. 'But you got me, too.'

Five days later Mum was locked in Lena's room, punching the thin fibro walls with her fists. Lyle had nailed wooden boards across the room's two sets of windows. He'd dragged out Lena's old bed and taken the Jesus picture off the wall, removed Lena's old vases and framed photographs of distant relatives and close friends from the Darra Lawn Bowls Club. The room was bare but for a thin mattress with no sheets or blankets or pillows. For seven days Lyle kept Mum locked in that sky-blue room. Lyle, August and I would stand outside her locked door, listening to her screams, long and random banshee howls, as if beyond that locked door was a Grand Inquisitor overseeing some wicked variety of torture involving pulley systems and Mum's outstretched limbs. But I knew for certain there was no one else in that room but her. She howled at lunch, she wailed at midnight. Gene Crimmins, our next-door neighbour on the right side, a retired and likeable postman with a thousand tales of misdirected mail and suburban kerbside happenstance, came over to check on things.

'She's almost there, mate,' was all Lyle said at the front door. And Gene simply nodded like he knew exactly what Lyle was talking about. Like he knew how to be discreet.

On the fifth day, Mum singled me out because she knew I was the weakest.

'Eli,' she cried through the door. 'He is trying to kill me. You need to call the police. Call them, Eli. He wants to kill me.'

I ran to our phone and I dialled three zeroes on the long rotary dial until August gently put his finger down on the receiver. He shook his head. *No, Eli.*

I wept and August put a gentle arm around my neck and we walked back down the hallway and stood staring at the door. I wept some more. Then I walked to the lounge room and I slid open the sliding bottom doors of the wood veneer wall unit that held Mum's vinyl records. *Between the Buttons* by the Rolling Stones. The one she played so much, the one with the cover where they're standing in their winter coats and Keith Richards is all blurred like he's stepped halfway into a time portal that will take him to his future.

'Hey, Eli, go to "Ruby Tuesday",' Mum always said.

'Which one's that?'

'Side one, third thick line from the edge,' Mum always said.

I unplugged the record player and I dragged it down the hall, plugged it in close to Lena's door. Dropped the needle down, third thick line from the edge.

That song about a girl who never said where she came from.

The song echoed through the house and Mum's sobbing echoed through the door. The song finished.

'Play it again, Eli,' Mum said.

\*

On the seventh day, at sunset, Lyle unlocked the door. After two or three minutes, Lena's bedroom door creaked open. Mum was thin and gaunt and waddling slowly like her bones were tied together with string. She tried to say something but her lips and her mouth and throat were so dry and her body was so spent that she couldn't get the words out.

'Gr ...' she said.

She licked her lips and tried again.

'Gr ...' she said.

She closed her eyes, like she was faint. August and I watched and waited for some sign she was back, some sign that she was awake from the big sleep, and I guess that sign was the way she fell into Lyle's arm and then collapsed onto the floor, clinging to the man who might have saved her life, and waving in the boys who believed he could do it. We huddled around her and she was like a fallen bird.

And in the cave of our bodies she chirped two words.

'Group hug,' she whispered. And we hugged her so tight we might have all formed into rock if we'd stuck around long enough. Formed into diamond.

Then she staggered, clinging to Lyle, to their bedroom. Lyle closed the bedroom door behind them. Silence. August and I immediately stepped softly into Lena's room like we were treading lightly into a minefield in one of those North Vietnamese jungles of Duc Quang's grandparents' homeland.

There were scattered paper plates and food scraps across the floor amid clumps of hair. There was a bedpan in the corner of the room. The room's sky-blue walls were covered in small holes the size of Mum's fists and emanating from these holes were streaks of blood that looked like tattered red flags blowing in battlefield winds. A long brown streak of dried-up shit wound like a dirt road to nowhere along two walls. And whatever the battle was that Mum had been waging in that small bedroom, we knew she had just won it.

My mum's name is Frances Bell.

*

August and I stand in silence in the hole. A full minute passes. August pushes me hard in the chest in frustration.

'Sorry,' I say.

Another two minutes pass in silence.

'Thanks for taking the hit on whose idea it was.'

August shrugs. Another two minutes pass and the smell and the heat in this shithole grip my neck and my nose and my knowing.

We stare up to the circle of light, up through Lena and Aureli Orlik's backyard wooden arse void.

'Do you think he's coming back?'

# Boy Follows Footsteps

Wake up. Darkness. Moonlight through the bedroom window bouncing off August's face. He's sitting by my lower bunk bed, rubbing sweat from my forehead.

'Did I wake you again?' I ask.

He gives a half-smile, nodding. *You did, but that's all right.*

'Same dream again.'

August nods. *Thought so.*

'The magic car.'

The magic car dream where August and I are sitting in the back tan vinyl seat of a Holden Kingswood car the same colour as Lena's sky-blue bedroom walls. We're playing corners, leaning hard against each other, laughing so hard we might piss our pants, as the man driving the car makes sharp lefts and rights around bends. I wind the window down on my side and a cyclonic wind blows me along the car seat pinning August to his side door. I push with all my strength against the wind funnelling through the window and I lean my head out to discover we're flying through the sky and the driver of this mystery vehicle is ducking and weaving through clouds. I wind the window back up and it turns grey outside. Everywhere grey. 'Just a rain cloud,' August says. Because he talks in this dream.

Then it's grey and green outside the car window. Everything grey and green outside, and wet. Then a school of bream swim past my window and the car passes a forest of waving seaweed ferns. We're not driving through a rain cloud. We're driving to the bottom of an ocean. The driver turns around and that driver is my father. 'Close your eyes,' he says.

My dad's name is Robert Bell.

*

'I'm starving.'

August nods. Lyle didn't give us a flogging for finding his secret room. I wish he had. The silence is worse. The looks of disappointment. I'd take ten open-palm smacks across my arse over this feeling that I'm getting older, that I'm getting too old for smacks across my arse and too old for creeping into secret rooms I was never supposed to know about; too old for squawking about finding dope bags in mower catchers. Lyle hauled us out of the thunderbox this afternoon in silence. He didn't have to tell us where to go. We went to our bedroom out of common sense. Rage was coming off Lyle like a bad cologne. Our room was the safest place to be, our cramped sanctuary decorated by a single long-faded McDonald's promotional poster showing team photos from the 1982–83 Benson & Hedges World Series Cup one-day cricket competition between Australia, England and New Zealand, with a special cock and balls ink tribute August has added to the forehead of David Gower in the front row for the Poms. We didn't get dinner. We didn't get a single word, so we just went to bed.

'Fuck this, I'm gettin' somethin' to eat,' I say a couple of hours later.

I tiptoe down the hall in darkness, into the kitchen. Open the fridge, a corridor of light filling the kitchen. There's an old wad of plastic-wrapped deli luncheon meat, a tub of ETA 5 Star margarine. I close the fridge door and turn left towards the pantry and bump into August, already laying four slices of bread on a cutting board on the bench. Luncheon meat sandwiches with tomato sauce. August takes his to the front window of the living room so he can stare up at the moon. He reaches the window and immediately hunches down in a panicked effort to stay out of sight.

'What is it?' I ask.

He waves his right hand downwards. I duck down and join him beneath the window. He nods his head upwards, raises his eyebrows. *Have a look. Slowly.* I raise my head to the bottom of the window and peek out to the street. It's past midnight and Lyle is out on the kerbside, resting on the brick fence by the letterbox, smoking a Winfield Red. 'What's he doing?'

August shrugs, peeks out alongside me, puzzled. Lyle wears his thick roo-shooting coat, the thick woolly collar up, breaking the midnight chill against his neck. He blows cigarette smoke that floats against the dark like a grey ghost.

We both drop down again, chomp into our sandwiches. August drips tomato sauce onto the carpet beneath the window.

'Sauce, Gus,' I say.

We're not allowed to eat food on this carpet now that Lyle and Mum are all drug-free and house-proud. August wipes the drops of sauce up from the carpet with his thumb and forefinger, licking the recovered red sauce from his fingers. He spits on the red stain left on the carpet and rubs it in, not enough for Mum not to notice.

Then a loud popping sound echoes across our suburb.

August and I immediately hop up, eyes peeking out through the window. In the night sky, about a block away, a purple firework whizzes into the darkness above the suburban houses, rising and fizzing with a corkscrew velocity before reaching its peak elevation and exploding into ten or so smaller firework strands that umbrella-pop into a briefly luminous and vivid purple sky fountain.

Lyle watches the firework flare out then he takes one more long drag of the Winfield and drops it at his feet, stubbing it out beneath his right boot. He puts his hands into the pockets of his roo-shooting coat and starts walking up the street in the direction of the firework.

'C'mon, let's go,' I whisper.

I stuff the rest of my luncheon meat and tomato sauce sandwich into my mouth so it must look like I'm eating two large marbles. August stays beneath the window eating his sandwich.

'C'mon, Gus, let's go,' I whisper.

He still sits there, processing like always, running the angles like always, weighing the options like always.

He shakes his head.

'C'mon, don't you want to know where he's going?'

August gives a half-smile. The right forefinger that he just used to wipe up tomato sauce slashes through the air, scribbling the invisible lines of two words.

*Already know.*

\*

I've been following people for years. The key elements to a successful follow are distance and belief. Distance enough from the subject to remain undetected. Belief enough to convince yourself you're not actually following the subject, even though you are. Belief means invisibility. Just another invisible stranger in a world of invisible strangers.

Cold out here. I give Lyle a good fifty-metre start. I'm just past the letterbox when I realise I'm barefoot in my winter pyjamas, the ones with the large hole over my right arse cheek. Lyle marches on, hands in his coat, drifting into the darkness beyond the streetlights that line the entrance to the Ducie Street Park across the road from our house. Lyle turns into a shadow, crossing the cricket pitch at the centre of the black oval, climbing up a hill that leads to a kids' playground and the council barbecue that we had a sausage sizzle on for August's thirteenth birthday last March. I'm creeping softly across the oval grass like a phantom, walking on air, ninja quiet, ninja quick. Snap. A thin dry stick breaks beneath my bare right foot. Lyle stops beneath a streetlight at the other side of the park. He turns and looks back into the park darkness engulfing me. He's staring right at me but he can't see me because I have distance and I have belief. I believe I am invisible. And Lyle does too. He turns from the park and walks on, head down, along Stratheden Street. I wait until he turns right into Harrington Street before I sprint out of the park darkness and into the exposed streetlights of Stratheden. A sprawling mango tree on the corner of Stratheden and Harrington provides the visual protection I need to watch Lyle, clear as day, take a left into Arcadia Street and into the driveway of Darren Dang's house.

\*

Darren Dang is in my grade at school. There's only eighteen of us Year 7 students at Darra State School and we all agree that handsome Vietnamese-Australian Darren Dang is by far the most likely of us to become famous, probably for killing all eighteen of us in a classroom machine-gun massacre. Last month while we were working on projects about the First Fleet, making British ships out of Paddle Pop sticks, Darren passed by my desk. 'Hey, Tink,' he whispered.

Eli Bell. Tinkerbell. Tink.

'Hey, Tink. Bottle bins. Lunchtime.'

That translated to, 'You best come by the large yellow metal bottle recycling bins behind groundsman Mr McKinnon's tool shed at lunchtime if you are at all interested in continuing your modest Queensland state school education with both of your ears.' I waited for thirty minutes by the bottle bins and was thinking, with false hope, that Darren Dang might not make our impromptu rendezvous when he crept up behind me and gripped the back of my neck between his right forefinger and thumb. 'If you saw ninjas, you're seeing ghosts,' he whispered. It's a line from *The Octagon*. Two months earlier, during a Physical Education class, I'd told Darren Dang that I, like him, believed the Chuck Norris movie about a secret training camp for terrorist ninjas was the best movie ever made. I had lied. *Tron* is the best movie ever made.

'Ha!' laughed Eric Voight, Darren's roly-poly empty-headed muscle from a family of roly-poly empty-headed mechanics who run the Darra Auto Transmission and Window Tinting shop across the road from the Darra brickworks. 'Tinkerbell the fairy just shit his little fairy pants.'

'Shat,' I said. 'Tinkerbell the fairy just *shat* his pants, Eric.'

Darren turned to the bottle bins and dug his hands into a collection of Mr McKinnon's empty spirits bottles.

'How much does this guy drink?' he said, clutching a Black Douglas bottle and sucking down half a capful of liquor resting at the bottom. He did the same with a small bottle of Jack Daniels, then a bottle of Jim Beam bourbon. 'You good?' he said, offering me the dregs of a Stone's Green Ginger Wine.

'I'm good,' I said. 'Why did you want to meet me?'

Darren smiled and slung a large canvas duffle bag off his right shoulder.

He reached into the duffle bag.

'Close your eyes,' Darren said.

Such requests from Darren Dang always end in tears or blood. But, like school, once you start with Darren Dang there's no realistic way of avoiding Darren Dang.

'Why?' I asked.

Eric pushed me hard in the chest: 'Just close your eyes, Bell End.'

I closed my eyes and instinctively cupped my hands over my balls.

'Open your eyes,' Darren said. And I opened my eyes to see a close-up view of a large brown rat, its two front teeth nervously buzzing up and down like a council jackhammer.

'Fuckin'ell, Darren,' I barked.

Darren and Eric howled with laughter.

'Found him in the storeroom,' he said.

Darren Dang's mum, 'Back Off' Bich Dang, and his stepdad, Quan Nguyen, run the Little Saigon Big Fresh supermarket at the end of Darra Station Road, a one-stop super shop for Vietnamese imported vegetables, fruits, spices, meats and whole fresh fish. The storeroom at the rear of the supermarket, next to the meat locker, is, much to Darren's joy, home to south-east Queensland's longest and most well fed dynasty of obese brown rats.

'Hold him for a second,' Darren said, foisting the rat into my reluctant hands.

The rat trembled in my palms, inactive with fear.

'This is Jabba,' Darren said, reaching into his duffle bag. 'Grab his tail.'

I half-heartedly gripped the rat's tail with my right forefinger and thumb.

Darren then pulled a machete from his duffle bag.

'What the fuck is that?'

'Granddad's machete.'

The machete was longer than Darren's right arm. It had a

tan wooden handle and a large wide blade, rusting at its flat sides but oiled and silver and gleaming on its cutting edge.

'No, you really gotta get a good grip on his tail or you'll lose him,' Darren said. 'Really wrap your fist around the tail.'

'You gotta hold it tight like you were holding your dick, Bell End, because he'll take off,' Eric said.

I gripped the tail tight in my fist.

Darren pulled a red cloth like a large handkerchief from his duffle bag.

'Okay, now place him on the septic but don't let him go,' he said.

'Maybe Eric should hold him?' I said.

'You're holding him,' Darren said, something unhinged in his eyes, something unpredictable.

There was a concrete underground septic tank with a heavy red metal lid by the bottle bins. I placed Jabba gently on the tank, my right hand gripping his tail.

'Don't move a muscle, Tink,' Darren said.

Darren rolled the large red handkerchief into a blindfold and wrapped it around his eyes, resting on his knees like a Japanese warrior about to drive a blade into his own heart.

'Oh, for fuck's sake, Darren, seriously,' I said.

'Don't move, Tink,' barked Eric, standing over me.

'Don't worry, I've done this twice already,' Darren said.

Jabba, poor dumb rat, was as fear-stiff and meek as I was. He turned to me with his teeth rattling up and down, confused and terrified.

Darren gripped the machete handle with both hands and raised it slowly and methodically above his head, the unsubtle instrument's cutting blade sparkling for a moment in the full sun that was lighting this hellish stage.

'Wait, Darren, you're gonna chop my hand off,' I stammered.

44

'Bullshit,' Eric said. 'He's ninja blood. He can see your hand better in his mind than he can with his actual eyes.'

Eric put a secure hand on my shoulder to keep me in place.

'Just don't fuckin' move,' he said.

Darren took a deep breath. Exhaled. I took one last look at Jabba, his body cringing with fear, motionless, like he thought if he just stayed still we might forget he was even there.

Darren's machete dropped down in a swift and violent whoosh and the oiled and gleaming blade dug into the septic tank lid with a brief yellow spark a centimetre from my closed fist.

Darren slipped his blindfold off in triumph to gaze upon the bloody remains of Jabba the Rat. But there was nothing to see. Jabba had vanished.

'What da fark, Tink?' Darren shouted, his Vietnamese accent more evident in anger.

'He let him run!' Eric screamed. 'He let him run!'

Eric wrapped his arm around my neck, the foul stench of his armpit like an old swamp. I caught sight of Jabba scurrying to freedom through a gap beneath the mesh school fence into the thick scrub running alongside Mr McKinnon's tool shed.

'You dishonour me, Tink,' Darren whispered.

Eric spread his belly weight over my back, forcing me flat onto the septic tank.

'Blood for blood,' Eric said.

'You know the warrior's code, Eli Bell,' Darren said formally.

'No, I really don't know the code, Darren,' I said. 'And besides, I believe that ancient code was more of a loose guide than anything else.'

'Blood for blood, Eli Bell,' Darren said. 'When the river of courage runs dry, blood flows in its place.' He nodded at Eric. 'Finger,' he said.

Eric reefed my right arm back out across the septic tank.

'Fuck, Darren,' I hollered. 'Think about this for a second. You'll get expelled.'

Eric yanked my right forefinger out of my closed fist.

'Darren, think about what you're doing,' I begged. 'They'll put you in juvenile.'

'I accepted my path long ago, Eli Bell. How about you?'

Darren slipped the blindfold over his eyes once more and raised the machete with both hands high over his head. Eric twisted my wrist to breaking point and pushed down hard, clamping my outstretched and exposed finger to the septic tank lid. I screamed in agony under the pressure. My finger was the rat. My finger was the rat wanting to disappear. My right forefinger, the one with my lucky freckle on its middle knuckle. My lucky freckle. My lucky finger. I stared at that lucky freckle and I prayed and I prayed for good fortune. And that's exactly when Mr McKinnon, early-seventies drunk Scotch-loving Irish groundsman, rounded the corner of his tool shed and stood, perplexed, by the scene of the Vietnamese boy in a red blindfold about to sacrificially sever the forefinger of the boy with the lucky freckle who was spread out across the septic tank.

'What the hell's going on here!' Mr McKinnon barked.

'Run!' Eric screamed.

Darren fled, indeed, with the stealthy reaction powers of his beloved ninja. Eric was slower to lift his burdensome belly fat off my left shoulder but he evaded the clutches of Mr McKinnon's thick sweeping left arm, which eventually found a hold on the back pocket of my maroon cotton school shorts, making me look like Wile E. Coyote running on air as I tried to beat a useless getaway.

'Where do you think you're going?' Mr McKinnon said, his breath reeking of Black Douglas.

*

Creeping now, hunched down, to the Dang family's fence made of tall brown timber palings with pointed ends. Lyle padding down Darren Dang's long driveway. Darren Dang's house is one of the biggest in Darra. Three thousand yellow bricks bought half-price direct from the Darra brickworks, shaped into a three-storey house with Italian mansion ambitions but bad-taste cheap-suburbia realities. The front lawn is the size of half a football field and lined with maybe fifty tall palm trees. I slip briefly down the long concrete driveway then peel off right among the front lawn palms to stay out of sight. Closer to the house is a trampoline surrounded by plastic princess castles belonging to Darren's three younger sisters, Kylie Dang, Karen Dang and Sandy Dang. I scurry to the trampoline, duck behind the largest of the princess castles, a pink plastic fairytale kingdom with a brown drawbridge fashioned into a children's slide, with castle walls big enough for me to hide behind as I watch Lyle sitting with Darren's mum and stepdad, Bich and Quan, on a lounge suite through the sliding glass doors of their living room.

'Back Off' Bich Dang earned her nickname with acts of unspeakable savagery. As well as the Little Saigon supermarket, she owns a large Vietnamese restaurant and the neighbouring hairdressing salon where I get my hair cut, across from Darra train station. Quan Nguyen is more her humble loyal servant than her husband. Bich is famous in my town as much for her selfless sponsorship of Darra community events – dances, historical society show days, fundraising flea markets – as she is for the time she stabbed a Year 5 Darra State School girl, Cheryl Vardy, in the left eye with a steel ruler for teasing Karen Dang about having steamed rice every day for school lunch. Cheryl Vardy needed surgery after the incident. She nearly went blind and I never understood why Bich Dang didn't go to prison. That's when I realised Darra had its own rules and laws and codes and maybe it was 'Back Off' Bich Dang who had selflessly drafted them into existence. Nobody knows what happened to her first husband, Darren's dad, Lu Dang. He disappeared six years ago. Everybody says Bich poisoned him, laced his prawn and pork rice paper rolls with arsenic, but I wouldn't be surprised if she stabbed him in the heart with a steel ruler.

Bich wears a light purple dressing gown, her mid–fifties face made up even at this hour. All the Vietnamese mums in Darra have the same look: big black hair in a bun so heavily treated it can bounce light beams, white powdery foundation on their cheeks and long black eyelashes that make them look permanently startled.

Bich has her hands folded, elbows resting on her knees, giving instructions, pointing her forefingers occasionally the way the great Parramatta Eels coach Jack Gibson used to give instructions to his on–field brains trust, Ray Price and Peter Sterling, from the sideline. Bich nods her head at something Lyle is saying and then she points at her husband, Quan. She directs him away somewhere and he nods obediently, waddles out of view and then returns with a large rectangular Styrofoam ice box, the same kind the Dangs keep their whole fresh fish in at the Little Saigon supermarket. Quan places the box at Lyle's feet.

Then a sharp and cold metal blade presses against my neck.

'Ring, ring, Eli Bell.'

Darren Dang's laugh echoes through the palm trees.

'Jeez, Tink,' he says, 'if you're trying to stay invisible you might want to think about changing out of your old pyjamas. I could see that pale Aussie arse all the way from my letterbox.'

'Good advice, Darren.'

The blade is long and thin and presses hard into the side of my neck.

'Is that a samurai sword?' I ask.

'Fuck yeah,' he says proudly. 'Bought it at the pawn shop. Been sharpening it for six straight hours today. Reckon I could take your head off in one slice. Wanna see?'

'How would I see it if I don't have a head?'

'Your brain still works even after it gets chopped off. It'd be cool. Your eyeballs looking up from the ground, me waving at you, holding your headless body. Fuck. What a funny way to go out!'

'Yeah, I'm laughing my head off.'

Darren howls.

'That's good, Tink,' he says. Then, on a dime, he turns serious, pushes the blade harder against my neck.

'Why are you spying on your dad?'

'He's not my dad.'

'Who is he?'

'He's my mum's boyfriend.'

'He good?'

'Good at what?'

The blade isn't pushing so hard against my neck now.

'Good to your mum.'

'Yeah, he's real good.'

Darren relaxes the sword, walks over to the trampoline, parks his backside on the edge of the trampoline, his legs hanging over the steel springs connected to the black bounce canvas. He's dressed all in black, his black sweater and tracksuit pants as black as his bowl haircut.

'You want a smoke?'

'Sure.'

He moves his sword, spears it into the ground, to make room for me on the trampoline's edge. He takes two smokes from a soft white packet with no branding, lights them in his mouth and hands me one. I suck a tentative drag and it burns my insides, makes me cough hard. Darren laughs.

'North Vietnam durries, Tink,' he smiles. 'Kick like a mule. Good buzz, though.'

I nod heartily, my head spinning with the second drag.

We look up through the living room sliding doors at Lyle and Bich and Quan talking over the Styrofoam ice box.

'Won't they see us?' I ask.

'Nah,' Darren says. 'They don't notice shit when they're doing business. Fuckin' amateurs. It'll be their undoing.'

'What are they doing up there?'

'You don't know?'

I shake my head. Darren smiles.

'C'mon, Tink. You must know. You might be full Aussie but you're not that fuckin' dumb.'

I smile.

'The box is full of heroin,' I say.

Darren blows cigarette smoke into the night.

'And ...' he says.

'And the purple firework was some kind of secret alert system. It's how your mum lets her clients know their orders are ready.'

Darren smiles.

'Order up!' he says.

'Different coloured fireworks for different dealers.'

'Very good, Flathead,' Darren says. 'Your good man up there is running for his boss.'

'Tytus Broz,' I say. Tytus Broz. The Lord of Limbs.

Darren drags on his cigarette, nodding.

'When did you work all this out?'

'Just now.'

Darren smiles.

'How do you feel?'

I say nothing. Darren chuckles. He hops off the trampoline, picks up his samurai sword.

'You feel like stabbing something?'

I dwell on this curious opportunity for a moment.

'Yes, Darren. I do.'

\*

The car is parked two blocks from Darren's house in Winslow Street outside a small low-set box of a home with its lights out. It's a small jelly-bean dark green Holden Gemini.

Darren pulls a black balaclava from the back of his pants and slips it over his head.

From his pants pocket he pulls a stocking.

'Here, put this on,' he says, creeping low towards the car.

'Where'd this come from?'

'Mum's dirty clothes basket.'

'I'll pass, thanks.'

'Don't worry, they slip on fine. She's got fat thighs for a Vietnamese woman.'

'This is Father Monroe's car,' I say.

Darren nods, hopping quietly onto the car's bonnet. His weight makes a dent in the car's old, rusting metal.

'What the fuck are you doing?' I ask.

'Ssssshhh!' Darren whispers, one arm down on Father Monroe's windscreen to prop his weight as he crawls up and stands in the centre of the car's roof.

'C'mon, don't fuck with Father Monroe's car.'

Father Monroe. Earnest and ageing Father Monroe, softly spoken retired priest from Glasgow via Darwin and Townsville and Emerald, in Queensland's Central Highlands. Butt of jokes, keeper of sins and frozen paper cups of orange and lime cordial that he keeps in his downstairs freezer and gives to permanently thirsty local kids like August and me.

'What did he ever do to you?'

'Nothing,' Darren says. 'He did nothing to me. It was Froggy Mills he did something to.'

'He's a good man, let's just get out of here.'

'Good man?' Darren echoes. 'That's not what Froggy says. Froggy says Father Monroe pays him a tenner every Sunday after mass to show him his dick while he whacks off.'

'That's bullshit.'

'Froggy doesn't bullshit. He's religious. Father Monroe told him it's a sin to bullshit but it's not a sin, of course, to show a seventy-five-year-old man your bat and balls.'

'You won't even get it through the metal.'

Darren taps his shoe on the car roof.

'That's thin metal. Half rusted out. This blade has been sharpened for six hours straight. Finest Japanese steel all the way from—'

'The Mill Street Pawnbrokers.'

Through the holes in his balaclava, Darren closes his eyes. He raises the blade high with both fists gripping the handle, concentrating on something inside, like an old warrior about to ritually end the life of his best friend, or his favourite Australian suburban getabout motorcar. 'Shit,' I say, frantically pulling Bich Dang's unwashed stocking over my head.

'Wake up, time to die,' Darren says.

He drives the sword down and it stabs into the Gemini with a shriek of metal on metal. The first third of the blade pierces the car roof like Excalibur in stone.

Darren's mouth drops open.

'Fuck, it went through.' He beams. 'You see that, Tink!'

A light goes on in Father Monroe's house.

'C'mon, let's go,' I bark.

Darren reefs at the sword handle but the lodged shaft doesn't move. He tugs hard three times with both hands. 'It won't come.' He bends the top end of the blade shaft back towards himself, then forward, but the bottom end won't move.

A window opens in Father Monroe's living room.

'Hey, hey, what are you doing?' Father Monroe bellows through a half-open window.

'Come on, let's go,' I urge.

Father Monroe opens his front door and steams down his pathway to his gate.

'Get off my car!' he screams.

'Fuck,' Darren says, leaping off the back of the car.

Father Monroe reaches his car and sees the samurai sword twanging back and forth, its mystical shaft speared inexplicably through the top of the parked car.

Darren turns around at a safe distance, joyously waving around the Vietnamese cock he's pulled from his pants.

'Just ten dong for this donger, Father!' he screams.

*

Still night air and two boys smoking on a gutter. Stars up there. A cane toad down here has been flattened by a car tyre on the bitumen road a metre from my right foot. Its pink tongue has exploded from its mouth so it looks like the toad was flattened halfway through eating a raspberry lolly snake.

'Sucks, doesn't it?' Darren says.

'What?'

'Growing up thinking you were with the good guys, when all along you were running with the bad guys.'

'I'm not running with the bad guys.'

Darren shrugs. 'We'll see,' he says. 'I remember when I first found out Mum was in the game. Cops burst through our door when we were living over in Inala. Turned the place upside

53

down. I was seven years old and I shit my pants. I mean, I actually shit my pants.'

The cops stripped Bich Dang naked, threw her against fibro walls, smashed household items with relish. Darren was watching *The Partridge Family* on a large National television that detectives tipped over looking for drugs.

'It was fuckin' mad, stuff breaking everywhere, Mum screaming at them, kicking her legs, scratchin' 'em and shit. They dragged Mum away out the front door and left me alone on the floor of the lounge room crying like a bitch, huge big dump in my dacks. I was so stunned I just sat watching that Partridge mum talking to her kids upside down on the telly.'

I shake my head.

'That's insane,' I say.

'That's the game,' Darren shrugs. "Bout two years later Mum gave it to me straight. We were key players. I felt like you're feeling now.'

He says this sinking feeling inside me is the realisation that I'm with the bad guys but I'm not the baddest of the bad guys.

'The baddest guys just work for you,' he says.

Paid killers, humourless and mad, he says. Ex-army, ex-prison, ex-human. Single men in their thirties and forties. Mysterious bastards, weirder than the kind who squish avocadoes between their fingers at fruit and veg markets. The kind who will squeeze a man's neck until it squishes. All the villains operating between the cracks of this quiet city. Thieves and cons and men who rape and kill children. Assassins, of a kind, but not the kind we love from *The Octagon*. These men wear flip-flops and Stubbies shorts. They stab people not with samurai swords but with the knives they use to slice Sunday roast when their widowed mothers drop in. Suburban psychopaths. Darren's mentors.

'They don't work for me,' I say.

'Well, they work for your dad,' Darren says.

'He's not my dad.'

'Oh, forgot, sorry. Where's your real dad?'

'Bracken Ridge.'

'He good?'

Everybody wants to measure the adult men in my life by goodness. I measure them in details. In memories. In the times they said my name.

'Never found out,' I say. 'What's with you and men being good?'

'Never met a good one, that's all,' he says. 'Adult men, Tink. Most fucked-up creatures on the planet. Don't ever trust 'em.'

'Where's your real dad?' I ask.

Darren stands up from the gutter, spits a jet of saliva through gritted teeth.

'He's right where he should be,' he says.

\*

We walk back down Darren's driveway, resume our places at the edge of the trampoline. Lyle and Bich are still deep into a seemingly endless conversation.

'Don't sweat it, man,' Darren says. 'You just won the lottery. You've landed smack bang inside a growth industry. The market for that shit up there in the ice box never dies.'

Darren says his mum told him a secret recently about Australians. She said this secret would make him a rich man. She said the greatest secret about Australia is the nation's inherent misery. Bich Dang laughs at the ads on telly with Paul Hogan putting another shrimp on the barbie. She said foreign visitors should rightfully be advised about what happens five hours later at that Australian shrimp barbecue, when the beers and the rums mix with the hard sun headaches and widespread Saturday night violence spreads across the country behind closed front doors. Truth is, Bich said, Australian childhoods are so idyllic and joyous, so filled with beach visits and backyard games of cricket, that Australian adulthoods can't possibly meet our childhood expectations. Our perfect early lives in this vast island paradise doom us to melancholy because we know, in the hard honest bones beneath our dubious bronze skin, that we will never again be happier than we were once before. She said we live in the greatest country on earth but we're actually all miserable deep down inside and the junk cures the misery and the junk industry will never die because Australian misery will never die.

'Ten, twenty years, I'll own three-quarters of Darra, maybe half of Inala, a good chunk of Richlands,' Darren says.

'How?'

'Expansion, Tink,' he says, eyes wide. 'I got plans. This area won't always be the city's shithole. Some day, man, all these houses round here will be worth somethin' and I'll buy 'em all when they're worth nothin'. And the gear is like that too. Time and place, Tink. That gear up there ain't worth shit in Vietnam. Put it on a boat and sail it to Cape York, it turns to gold. It's like magic. Stick it in the ground and let it sit for ten years, it'll turn to diamond. Time and place.'

'How come you don't talk this much in class?'

'There's nothing I'm passionate about in class.'

'Dealing drugs is your passion?'

'Dealing? Fuck that. Too much heat, too many variables. We're strictly imports. We don't make deals. We just make arrangements. We let you Aussies do the real dirty work of putting it on the street.'

'So Lyle's doing your dirty work?'

'No,' Darren says. 'He's doing Tytus Broz's dirty work.'

Tytus Broz. The Lord of Limbs.

'Hey, a man's gotta work, Tink.'

Darren puts his arm around my shoulder.

'Listen, I never thanked you for not ratting on me about Jabba,' he says. He laughs. 'You didn't rat about the rat.'

The school groundsman, Mr McKinnon, marched me by the collar to the principal's office. Mr McKinnon was too blind, or too blind drunk, to identify the two boys who were intending to slice my right forefinger off with a machete.

All McKinnon could say was, 'One of 'em was *Vietnamese.*' And that could have been half our school. It wasn't out of loyalty that I didn't name names, more self-preservation, and one week's detention writing number facts in an exercise pad was a small price to pay for my hearing.

'We could use a guy like you,' Darren says. 'I need men I can trust. Whaddya reckon? You want to help me build my empire?'

I stare for a moment up at Lyle, still discussing business with fierce Bich Dang and her humble husband.

'Thanks for the offer, Darren, but, you know, I never really considered heroin empire building as part of my life plan.'

'Is that right?' He flicks his cigarette butt into his sister's fairy castle. 'The man with the plan. So what's Tink Bell's grand life plan?'

I shrug.

'C'mon, Eli, smart Aussie mud crab like you, tell me how you're gonna crawl out of this shit bucket?'

I look up at the night sky. There's the Southern Cross. The saucepan, the set of white stars shimmering, shaped like the small stovetop pot Lyle boils his eggs in every Saturday morning.

'I'm gonna be a journalist,' I say.

'Ha!' Darren howls. 'A journalist?'

'Yep,' I say. 'I'm gonna work on the crime desk at *The Courier-Mail*. I'm gonna have a house in The Gap and I'm gonna spend my life writing crime stories for the paper.'

'Ha! One of the bad guys making a living writing about the bad guys,' Darren says. 'And why in fuck you wanna live in The Gap?'

We'd bought our Atari games console through the *Trading Post*. Lyle drove us out to a family in The Gap, a leafy suburb eight kilometres west of Brisbane's CBD, who had recently purchased a Commodore 64 desktop computer and no longer needed their Atari, which they sold to us for $36. I'd never seen so many tall trees in one suburb. Tall blue gums that shaded kids playing handball in suburban cul-de-sacs. I love cul-de-sacs. Darra doesn't have enough cul-de-sacs.

'The cul-de-sacs,' I say.

'What the fuck is a cul-de-sac?' Darren asks.

'It's what you're on here. A street with a dead end. Great for playing handball and cricket. No cars going through.'

'Yeah, I love a no-through road,' he says. He shakes his head. 'Man, you want to get some joint in The Gap, that shit ain't gonna happen for twenty, thirty years in some journalising bullshit. You need to go get some degree, then ya gotta go beg for some job from some arsehole who'll boss you around for thirty years and you'll have to save your pennies and by the time you're done savin' there'll be no more houses in The Gap left to buy!'

Darren points up into the living room.

'You see that Styrofoam box beside your good man's feet up there?' he asks.

'Yeah.'

'There's a whole house in The Gap inside that,' he says. 'Us bad guys, Tink, we don't have to wait to buy houses in The Gap. In my game, we buy them tomorrow if we want to.'

He smiles.

'Is it fun?' I ask.

'What?'

'Your game.'

'Sure it's fun,' he says. 'You meet lots of interesting people. Lots of opportunities to build your business knowledge. And when the cops are sniffin' around, you really know you're alive. You pull off some huge import right under their noses and you make the sales and you bank the profits and you turn around to your family and friends and say, "Goddamn, look at what you can achieve when you act as a team and you really stick to it."'

He breathes deep.

'It's inspiring to me,' he says. 'It makes me believe that in a place like Australia, anything really is possible.'

We sit in silence. He flicks the flint on his lighter, hops off the trampoline. He walks to the house's front staircase.

'C'mon, let's go up,' he says.

I'm puzzled, mute.

'What are you waiting for?' he asks. 'Mum wants to meet you.'

'Why does your mum want to meet me?'

'She wants to meet the boy who didn't rat about the rat.'

'I can't go up there.'

'Why not?'

'It's nearly 1 a.m. and Lyle will kick my arse.'

'He won't kick your arse if we don't want him to.'

'What makes you so sure?'

'Because he knows who we are.'

'And who are you?'

'We're the bad guys.'

*

We enter through the sliding glass doors off the balcony. Darren marches confidently into the living room, ignoring Lyle sitting in the armchair to his left. His mum sits, elbows resting on her knees, on the long brown leather lounge suite, her husband resting back on the lounge beside her.

'Hey Mum, I found this guy spying on you all in the yard,' Darren says.

I enter the living room in my pyjamas with the hole in the arse.

'This is the kid who didn't rat about Jabba,' Darren says.

Lyle turns to his right and he sees me, face filling with rage.

'Eli, what the hell are you doing here?' he asks, soft and intense.

'Darren invited me,' I say.

'It's 1 a.m. Go. Home. Now.'

I turn around immediately and walk back out the living room doors.

Bich Dang releases a gentle laugh from the couch.

'Are you really going to give up that easily, boy?' she asks.

I stop. Turn around. Bich Dang smiles, the porcelain white foundation on her face cracking around the wrinkles of her widening mouth.

'Plead your case, boy,' she says. 'Please tell us why exactly you are out at this time in your pyjamas flashing that cute white tush?'

I look at Lyle. He looks at Bich and I follow his gaze.

She takes a long white menthol cigarette from a silver case, lights it, leans back into her lounge as she draws in her first puff, then blows it out, her eyes sparkling as though she's looking at a newborn baby.

'Well?' she prompts.

'I saw the purple firework,' I say. Bich nods knowingly. Fuck. I never realised how beautiful she is. She might be in her mid-fifties, early sixties even, but she's so exotic and so cold-blooded exciting she has the presence of a serpent. Maybe she's so attractive at this age because she sheds her skin, slips out of her own body when she finds a new one to wriggle through life in. She keeps me in her gaze with that smile until I have to look away from it, drop my head to fiddle with the drawstring on my loose pyjama bottoms.

'And ...?' she says.

'I ... ummm ... I followed Lyle here because ...'

My throat thickens. Lyle's fingers dig into his chair's armrests.

'Because of all the questions.'

Bich leans forward on the lounge. Studies my face.

'Come closer,' she says.

I move two steps towards her.

'Closer,' she says. 'Come to me.'

I shuffle closer and she places her cigarette in the corner of a glass ashtray and she takes my hand to draw me so close that her kneecaps rub against mine. She smells of tobacco and citrus-scented perfume. Her hands are pale white and soft and her fingernails are long and fire-engine red. She studies my face for twenty seconds and she smiles.

'Oh, busy young Eli Bell, so many thoughts, so many questions,' she says. 'Well, go ahead, ask away, boy.'

Bich turns to Lyle, a seriousness across her face.

'And, Lyle, I trust you'll answer truthfully,' she says.

She fixes her hands on my thigh and turns me towards Lyle.

'Go right ahead, Eli,' she says.

Lyle sighs, shakes his head. I keep my head down.

'Bich, this is—'

'Have courage, boy,' Bich says, cutting off Lyle. 'You better use that tongue before Quan here cuts it out and drops it in his noodle soup.'

Quan beams, raises his eyebrows at the prospect.

'Bich, I don't think this is necessary,' Lyle says.

'Let the boy decide,' she says, enjoying this moment.

I have a question. I always have a question. I always have too many.

I lift my head, stare into his eyes.

'Why are you dealing drugs?' I ask.

Lyle shakes his head, looks away, offers nothing.

Bich sounds like my school principal now. 'Lyle, the boy deserves an answer, doesn't he?'

He takes a deep breath, turns back to me.

'I'm doing it for Tytus,' he says.

Tytus Broz. The Lord of Limbs. Lyle does everything for Tytus Broz.

Bich shakes her head: 'The truth, Lyle.'

He dwells on this for a long moment, digs his fingernails deeper into the armrest. He stands, picks the Styrofoam ice box up from the living room carpet.

'Tytus will be in touch about the next order,' he says. 'Let's go, Eli.'

He walks out the sliding doors. And I follow him because there was care in his voice just then, his love was in it and I will follow that feeling anywhere.

'Wait!' barks Bich Dang.

Lyle stops, so I stop too.

'Come back here, boy,' she says.

I look at Lyle. He nods his head. I shuffle cautiously back to Bich. She looks me in the eye.

'Why did you not rat on my son?' she asks.

Darren is now sitting up on a kitchen benchtop running off the living room, eating a muesli bar as he silently observes the conversation unfolding before him.

'Because he's my friend,' I say.

Darren seems shocked by the admission. He smiles.

Bich studies my eyes. Nods her head.

'Who taught you to be so loyal to your friends?' Bich asks.

I throw my thumb immediately to Lyle.

'He did.'

Bich smiles. She's still staring into my eyes when she says, 'Lyle, if I might be so bold ...'

'Yes,' Lyle says.

'You bring young Eli back again some time, you hear, and maybe we talk about a few opportunities that have emerged. Let's see if we can't consider doing business between ourselves.'

Lyle says nothing. 'Let's go Eli,' he says. We walk out the door, but Bich Dang still has one more question. 'You still want your answer, Eli?' she asks.

I stop and turn around.

'Yes.'

She leans back into the lounge, dragging on her long white cigarette.

She nods, blowing out so much smoke from her mouth that a cloud of grey masks her gaze. The cloud and the serpent and the dragon and the bad guys.

'It's all for you.'

# Boy Receives Letter

*Dear Eli,*

*Greetings from B16. Thanks, as ever, for your correspondence. Your letter was the best thing about a month I was glad to see the back of. Worse than Northern Ireland in here lately. Few blokes have gone on hunger strike, protesting about cramped conditions, overpopulation in the cells, not enough activities for rec days. Yesterday, Billy Pedon got his head dumped in the 4 Yard shit bucket for giving a bit too much lip to Guigsy, who was bitching about the cold outside. Now they've put a little rim inside all of the shit buckets so they're too small to fit a human head inside. I guess that's what ya call progress? Big scrap broke out in the caf on Sunday. Old Harry Smallcombe drove a fork into Jason Hardy's left cheek because Hardy took the last of the rice pudding. All hell broke loose and, as a result, the screws took away the television from 1 Yard. No more* Days of Our Lives. *Take a Boggo con's freedom, take his rights, take his humanity, take his will to live, but for God's sake, please don't take his* Days of Our Lives! *As you can imagine, the boys went apeshit over that and started dropping shits throughout the prison like they were apes. I wonder if that's where apeshit comes from? Anyway, all the boys are keen on hearing any updates outworlders might have on* Days, *so any insights would be greatly appreciated. Last we saw, Liz looked like doing a lag for shooting Marie – dumb slut she* is – even though it was an accident. She still hadn't found the silk 'C' scarf that I reckon will be her undoing. My shitter broke on Tuesday because Dennis had the runs from a bad batch of lentils they fixed us. Dennis used up his toilet paper ration and he had to start using pages from an old copy of Sophie's Choice we had lying around. Of course the pages didn't break down and just choked the shitter so the whole of One Division could smell Dennis's inner demons. Did I tell you about Tripod in the last letter? Fritz found a cat creeping through the yard a while back. Fritz has been behaving well lately so the screws let him look after the cat during day rec. We all started keeping a bit of food from lunch to feed the cat and now it skips on through our cells at its leisure during day rec. Then one of the screws accidentally closed a cell door on the cat and the poor blighter had to be taken to a vet who gave Fritz's little kitty a troubling ultimatum: expensive surgery to have a leg removed or it was a bullet between the eyes (not quite what the surgeon said, but you get the picture). Word spread round about the crippled cat and we passed a hat around and we all put our month's wages into surgery for Fritz's bloody kitty. It had the op and came right back to us walking around on three legs. Then we had a lengthy discussion about what we were gonna name the cat whose life we all saved and we all settled on the name of Tripod. That cat's become bigger than The Beatles in here. Glad to hear you and August are doing so well at school. Don't slack off on your studies. You don't want to end up in a shithole like this because you don't want to find yourself all souped up on chloral hydrate and butt-fucked through the laundry fence by the Black Stallion because that's what can happen to kids who don't keep on top of their studies. I've told Slim to keep me posted on yours and August's report cards, good and bad. In answer to your question, I guess the best way to know if a bloke is wanting to knife you is by the speed of their steps. A man with a killin' on his mind starts to show it in his eyes, there's an intent to them. If they're carrying, you'll see them approach their victim slowly, eyeballing them like a hawk from afar, then, when they get closer, they'll quicken their steps. Shuffle, shuffle,

*shuffle. You want to be coming at the victim from behind, shove the shiv in as close as you can to the kidneys. They'll drop like a bag of spuds. The key is to shove the shiv in hard enough to get your point across, but soft enough to avoid a murder charge. A fine balance indeed.*

*Tell Slim his garden has never looked better. The azaleas are so pink and fluffy it looks like we're growing fairy floss for the Royal Show.*

*Thanks for the picture of Miss Haverty. She's even prettier than you described. Nothing sexier than a young schoolteacher in spectacles. You're right about that face, like a dawn sunrise. I guess you won't tell her if you know what's good for you, but the boys from D wing send their regards. Well, gotta go, matey. Grub's up and I better get my share of bolognese before it goes the way of the dodo. Climb high, kid, tread lightly.*

*Alex*

*P.S. Have you phoned your dad yet? I'm not the best man to judge father–son relationships but I reckon if you've been thinking about him so much, there's a fair chance he's been thinking about you.*

*

Saturday morning letter writing with Slim. Mum and Lyle are out at the movies again, keen film buffs that they are. They're going to see *Octopussy*. August and I asked to go. They said no again. Funny that. Fucking amateurs.

'What's *Octopussy* about?' Slim asks, his right hand furiously crafting his letter in a remarkably neat longhand cursive.

I pause from my letter to respond.

'James Bond fights a sea monster with eight vaginas.'

We're at the kitchen table with glasses of Milo and sliced oranges. Slim's got the Eagle Farm horse races playing through a wireless by the kitchen sink. August has an orange quarter skin stuck across his teeth like Ray Price's mouth guard. Hot and sticky outside because it's summer and it's Queensland. Slim's got his shirt off and I can see his POW-chic ribcage, like he's slowly dying in front of me from his diet of cigarettes and sorrow.

'You been eatin' Slim?'

'Don't get started,' he says, a rolled cigarette in the corner of his mouth.

'You look like a ghost.'

'A friendly ghost?' he asks.

'Well, not unfriendly.'

'Well, you're no bronze statue yourself, ya little runt. How's your letter going?'

'Almost done.'

\*

Slim spent a total of thirty-six years in Boggo Road. He wasn't allowed letters for much of his lag in D9. He knows what a well-written letter means to a man inside. It means connection. Humanity. It means waking up. He's been writing letters to Boggo Road inmates for years, using false names on the envelopes because the screws would never pass a letter on from Arthur 'Slim' Halliday, a man who knows how to escape their red-brick-wall fortress better than anyone.

Slim met Lyle in 1976 when they both worked at a Brisbane car repair shed. Slim was sixty-six then. He'd served twenty-three years of his life sentence and was on a 'release-to-work' scheme, working in a supervised environment outside by day and returning to Boggo Road by night. Slim and Lyle worked well on engines together, had a shorthand for motor mechanics like they had a shorthand for their misspent youths. Some Friday afternoons Lyle slipped long handwritten letters into Slim's daypack so he could find them over the weekend and they could carry on their chats via Lyle's piss-poor handwriting. Slim once told me he'd die for Lyle.

'Then Lyle went and asked for something more troubling than dyin'.'

'What's that, Slim?' I asked.

'He asked me to babysit you two rats.'

Two years ago I found Slim writing letters at the kitchen table.

'Letters to cons who don't receive letters from family and friends,' he said.

'Why don't their family and friends write to them?' I asked.

'Most of these blokes don't have any.'

'Can I write one?' I asked.

'Sure,' he said. 'Why don't you write to Alex?'

I took a pen and paper and sat beside Slim at the table.

'What do I write about?'

'Write about who you are and what you've been doing today.'

*Dear Alex,*

*My name is Eli Bell. I'm ten years old and I'm in Year 5 at Darra State School. I have an older brother named August. He doesn't talk. Not because he can't talk, but because he doesn't want to talk. My favourite Atari game is* Missile Command *and my favourite rugby league team is the Parramatta Eels. Today August and I went for a ride to Inala. We found a park that had a sewage tunnel running off it that was big enough for us to crawl into. But we had to come out when some Aboriginal boys said the tunnel was theirs and we should get out if we didn't want to cop a flogging. The biggest one of the Aboriginal boys had a big scar across his right arm. That was the one that August bashed before they all ran away.*

*On our way home we saw a dragonfly on the footpath being eaten alive by green ants. I said to August that we should put the dragonfly out of its misery. August wanted to leave it be. But I stood on the dragonfly and squashed it dead. But when I stood on it I killed thirteen green ants in the process. Do you think I should have just left the dragonfly alone?*

*Yours sincerely,*

*Eli*

P.S. *I'm sorry nobody writes to you. I'll keep writing to you if you want.*

I was overjoyed two weeks later when I received six letter pages back from Alex, three of which were devoted to memories of the times in Alex's childhood when he'd been intimidated by boys in sewage tunnels and of the violence that ensued. After the passage in which Alex detailed the anatomy of the human nose and how weak it is in comparison to a swiftly butted forehead, I asked Slim just who it was exactly I had become pen pals with.

'That's Alexander Bermudez,' he said.

Sentenced to nine years in Boggo Road Gaol after Queensland Police found sixty-four illegally imported Soviet AK-74 machine guns in the backyard shed of his home in Eight Mile Plains, which he was about to disperse among members of the Rebels outlaw motorcycle gang, of which he was once Queensland sergeant-at-arms.

*

'Don't forget to be specific,' Slim always says. 'Details. Put in all the details. The boys appreciate all that detailed daily life shit they don't get any more. If you've got a teacher you're hot for, tell 'em what her hair looks like, what her legs look like, what she eats for lunch. If she's teaching you geometry, tell 'em how she draws a bloody triangle on the blackboard. If you went down the shop for a bag of sweets yesterday, did you ride your pushy, did you go by foot, did you see a rainbow along the way? Did you buy gobstoppers or clinkers or caramels? If you ate a good meat pie last week, was it steak and peas or curry or mushroom beef? You catchin' my drift? Details.'

Slim keeps scribbling across his page. He drags on his smoke and his cheeks compress and I can see the shape of his skull, and his short back and sides with a flat top haircut makes him look like Frankenstein's monster. It's alive. But for how long, Slim?

'Slim.'

'Yes, Eli.'

'Can I ask you a question?'

Slim stops writing. August stops too. They both stare at me.

'Did you kill that taxi driver?'

Slim offers a half-smile. His lip trembles and he adjusts his thick black spectacles. I've known him long enough to know when he's been hurt.

'I'm sorry,' I say, dropping my head, placing my pen's ballpoint back on the letter page. 'There's a feature in today's paper,' I say.

'What feature?' Slim barks. 'I didn't see anything on me in *The Courier* today?'

'Not *The Courier-Mail*. It was in the local rag, the *South-West Star*. They had one of those "Queensland Remembers" yarns. Huge piece it was. It was about the Houdini of Boggo Road. They talked about your escapes. They talked about the Southport murder. It said you could have been innocent. It said you might have gone away for twenty-four years for a crime you didn't—'

'Long time ago,' Slim says, cutting me off.

'But don't you want people to know the truth?'

Slim drags on his cigarette.

'Can I ask you a question, kid?'

'Yes.'

'Do you think I killed him?'

I don't know. What I know is nothing killed Slim. What I know is he never gave up. The darkness didn't kill him. The cops didn't kill him. The screws didn't kill him. The bars. The hole. Black Peter didn't kill him. I guess I've always figured if he was a murderer then his conscience might have been the thing that killed him during those black days down in the hole. But his conscience never killed him. The loss, the life that might have been, never killed him. Almost half his life spent inside and he can still smile when I ask if he's a murderer. Houdini was locked in a box for thirty-six years altogether and he came out alive. The long magic. The kind of magic trick that takes thirty-six years for the rabbit to stick his head up out of the hat. The long magic of a human life.

'I think you're a good man,' I say. 'I don't think you're capable of killing a man.'

Slim takes his smoke from his mouth. He leans across the table. His voice is soft and sinister.

'Don't you ever underestimate what any man is capable of,' he says.

He leans back in his chair.

'Now show me this article.'

## QUEENSLAND REMEMBERS: NO CHANCE TOO SLIM FOR THE HOUDINI OF BOGGO ROAD

He was regarded as the most dangerous prisoner in the British Commonwealth, the master escapologist they called 'The Houdini of Boggo Road Gaol', but Arthur 'Slim' Halliday's greatest trick would be walking out of prison a free man.

A church orphan who lost both his parents at the age of 12, Slim Halliday began his predestined life of crime when he was imprisoned for four days for jumping trains en route to the shearing job in Queensland that might well have kept him on the straight and narrow. Halliday was a seasoned 30-year-old conman and housebreaker by 28 January 1940, when he made his first escape from Boggo Road Gaol's notorious Number 2 Division.

## SLIM'S PICKINGS

Houdini Halliday conjured his first magic escape by scaling a section of the prison wall that became known as 'Halliday's Leap', an observation blind spot invisible to guards in surrounding watchtowers. Despite public criticism over the strength of prison security after the one-man escape, this section of the prison wall remained unchanged.

It was little surprise to the Brisbane public, then, when it was revealed that in a subsequent escape, on 11 December 1946, Halliday climbed over a corner wall of the prison workshops, a mere 15 yards from the now mythical 'Halliday's Leap'. Beyond the prison fence, he stripped off his cell garb to reveal the smuggled civilian clothes he was wearing underneath and caught a taxi to Brisbane's northern suburbs, giving the driver a tip for his trouble.

After a frantic and widespread police manhunt, Halliday was recaptured four days later. Asked why he made the bold second escape, he replied: 'A man's liberty means everything to him. You can't blame a man for trying.'

## CYCLE OF A LIFER

Released in 1949, Halliday moved to Sydney where he worked for the Salvation Army before he began a roof repair business using sheet-metal skills he'd learned in Boggo Road. He changed his name to Arthur Dale and returned to Brisbane in 1950, where he fell in love with the daughter of a Woolloongabba snack bar operator. Halliday married Irene Kathleen Close on 2 January 1951, and the couple moved into a flat in Redcliffe, on Brisbane's northern seaside, in 1952, mere months before

Halliday made national headlines again when he was convicted and sentenced to life imprisonment for the Southport Esplanade murder of taxi driver Athol McCowan, 23.

The case's chief investigator, Queensland Police Detective Inspector Frank Bischof, claimed Halliday fled the scene of the McCowan murder and rushed to Sydney, where he was captured by police after shooting himself in the leg when his own .45 calibre handgun went off during a violent wrestle with a valiant Guildford storekeeper he was attempting to rob.

In a packed court, Bischof testified that Halliday confessed to the McCowan murder while recovering from his bullet wound in a Parramatta Hospital bed. Bischof claimed Halliday's confession detailed how he slipped into McCowan's cab in Southport that fateful night of 22 May 1952 and later held up the young taxi driver at a secluded spot at the Currumbin Lookout, further south. When McCowan resisted, Bischof claimed, Halliday battered the driver to death with his .45 calibre handgun. Bischof testified that Halliday recited a poem during his confession: 'Birds eat, and they're free. They don't work, why should we?'

Slim Halliday, meanwhile, has vehemently maintained Bischof framed him for McCowan's murder; the detailed confession – from its precise place names to its poetry – was, Halliday claimed, a figment of Bischof's imagination.

*The Courier-Mail* reported on 10 December 1952, Mr Halliday 'caused a stir in court when Bischof said Halliday had told him, "I killed him."

'Halliday sprang to his feet,' the report stated. 'And, leaning over the dock rail, shouted, "That's a lie."'

Halliday maintained that on the night of McCowan's murder he was in Glen Innes in the Northern Tablelands of New South Wales, some 400 kilometres away.

Frank Bischof would go on to become Queensland Police Commissioner from 1958 to 1969, resigning amid widespread allegations of corruption. He died in 1979. Before being sentenced to life in prison, Halliday declared from the dock: 'I repeat, I am not guilty of this crime.'

Outside court, Halliday's wife, Irene Close, vowed to stand by her man.

## BLACK DAYS IN THE BLACK PETER

In December 1953, after another failed escape attempt, Halliday was dropped inside Boggo Road's notorious Black Peter, an underground solitary confinement cell, a relic harking back to Brisbane's barbaric and bloody penal colony past. Halliday survived 14 days in searing December heat, sparking fierce public debate over modern methods of prisoner rehabilitation.

'So Halliday has been given solitary confinement,' wrote L.V. Atkinson of Gaythorne to *The Courier-Mail* on 11 December 1953. 'The miserable caged wretch, for instinctively seeking his freedom, is to be penalised to the fullest, foulest extent of our medieval prison system? The principle of modern legal punishment cannot allow the infliction of human torture.'

Halliday emerged from Black Peter an urban legend. The schoolyard kids of 1950s Brisbane didn't whisper tales of Ned Kelly and Al Capone over their morning tea Anzac biscuits, they told tales of 'The Houdini of Boggo Road'.

'His knowledge of buildings, rooftops and tools, combined with his viciousness and daring, make him the jail's most closely watched prisoner,' wrote the *Sunday Mail*. 'Detectives who have known him through his years of housebreaking say he can climb walls like a fly. Probably, Halliday will never stop trying to escape. Police who know him say he will have to be watched every minute of his life sentence, which, if he lives to be an old man, means another 40 years at least of maddening existence behind the red brick walls of Boggo Road.'

For the next 11 years of his sentence, Halliday was strip-searched three times a day. The only clothing allowed in his cell was his pyjamas and slippers. Two officers escorted him everywhere. His studies were cancelled. Additional locks were fitted to his cell, D9, and additional locks were fitted to D wing. Boggo Road's Number 5 yard was converted to a maximum security yard where Halliday could move at daytime within the confines of a steel mesh cage. Only on weekends was a single prisoner allowed inside the cage with him to play a game of chess. He was not allowed to speak to other prisoners for fear he would pass on his endless escape strategies.

On 8 September 1968, Brisbane's *Truth* newspaper reported on Halliday nearing the age of 60 with an article headlined: 'BROKEN KILLER TALKS TO NO ONE'.

'The gleam has gone out of the eyes of Queensland killer and Houdini jailbreaker, Arthur Ernest Halliday,' the report read. 'After years under constant double guard and the most elaborate security precautions ever taken with any prisoner in this State, 60-year-old Slim Halliday has become a walking vegetable inside the grim walls of Boggo Road.'

But Halliday possessed an 'indomitable spirit', the prison's superintendent told media at the time, 'which rigorous punishment failed to break, and he was never known to complain about his treatment no matter how harsh or uncomfortable it may have been'.

As his lengthy sentence diminished, so did Halliday's obsession with escape. By his late 60s, he was simply too old to scale the red brick walls of Boggo Road. After years of good behaviour he was given the role of prison librarian, which allowed him to share his love of literature and poetry with increasingly interested inmates. They would gather regularly in the yard to hear Houdini Halliday recite the poems of his beloved

Persian philosopher-poet Omar Khayyám, whose work he had discovered in a prison library in the 1940s.

His favourite poem was Khayyám's *The Rubáiyát*, which he'd recite over the chessboard and pieces he meticulously crafted out of machine-turned metal in the prison workshop.

'Tis all a Chequer-board of Nights and Days
Where Destiny with Men for Pieces plays:
Hither and thither moves, and mates, and slays,
And one by one back in the Closet lays.

## REPORTER STRIKES GOLD

In the end the greatest trick Houdini Halliday ever pulled was surviving Boggo Road Gaol. He eventually escaped the prison by walking out the front gate after serving 24 years for the murder of Athol McCowan, with smiles of congratulations from inmates and prison officers alike.

In April 1981, Brisbane *Telegraph* reporter Peter Hansen found the long-reclusive Slim Halliday puddling for gold in a creek near Kilcoy where he had paid $5 to the Forestry Department to live lawfully on forestry land as a prospecting hermit.

'I never confessed,' he said of his controversial murder conviction. 'Bischof simply made up the confession he produced in court. Bischof was a ruthless man, you know. It was my case that made him Commissioner of Police.

'I left Brisbane two days before the murder … I was convicted because my name was Arthur Halliday.'

Halliday said he would not fear returning to Boggo Road as an old man. 'I practically own the place,' he said. 'In the end they were using me as a security consultant.'

Two years on, Arthur 'Slim' Halliday appears to have dropped off the face of the earth. He was last seen living out of the back of his truck in Redcliffe, on Brisbane's north side. But the legend

of Slim Halliday lives on inside the red brick walls of Boggo Road
Gaol, where Houdini's cell, number nine in the D wing, remains
empty. Simple logistics, prison officials say. Though inmates are
convinced they're yet to find a prisoner worthy enough to fill it.

'Slim?'

'Yeah, kid?'

'It says Irene said she would stand by her man?'

'Yeah.'

'Well, she didn't, did she?'

'Yes she did, kid.'

Slim hands the article back to me, his long tanned arms
reaching across the kitchen table.

'You don't always have to be standing by someone to stand
by them,' he says. 'How's your letter going?'

'Almost done.'

*Dear Alex,*

*Do you think Bob Hawke is doing a good job as prime*
*minister? Slim says he has just the right amounts of guile and*
*guts to be a good leader for Australia. Slim says he reminds him*
*of Roughie Regini, the old Jewish German fella who ran the*
*Number 2 Division tote with Slim in the mid-1960s. Roughie*
*Regini was a diplomat and a standover man all in one. He took*
*bets for anything: horseraces, football, boxing matches, fights in*
*the yard, chess games. Once he set up bets for what the boys*
*were going to have for Easter lunch 1965. Slim says it was*
*Roughie Regini who developed the cockroach courier system.*
*Do you guys still use the cockroach courier system? Winnings*
*were paid in White Ox tobacco mostly but cons started kicking*
*up a stink about delays in getting their rightful winnings on*
*night-time lockdown, just when they appreciated a cigarette*
*the most. To separate himself from other potential bookies,*

*Roughie Regini developed the cockroach courier system. He kept a collection of fat and well-fed cockroaches in a pineapple tin beneath his bed. Bloody strong those cockroaches were. Using threads of cotton from his blanket and bedsheet, Roughie learned to tie up to three thin rolled White Ox cigarettes to the back of a cockroach and slip it under his cell door, send it off on its way to his intended punter. But how would he make sure the cockroach went where he wanted it to go? A cockroach has six legs, three on either side. Roughie started doing experiments on his little couriers. He soon realised the cockroaches would go in certain directions according to which of their six legs had been removed. Take a front leg off and a cockroach will start moving in a north-east or north-west direction. Take a middle left leg off, the cockroach will start leaning to his left so hard he'll start doing circles, anti-clockwise. Take a middle right leg off, he'll start doing clockwise circles. Put that cockroach against a wall he'll follow it right along a straight line and be grateful to do so. If Roughie needed to get a package to Ben Banaghan, seven cells down the aisle to his left, he'd remove a cockroach's left middle leg and send it off on its great adventure, its top cigarette scrawled with the name of its destination cell, 'Banaghan'. The brave cockroach would slip under every cell along its journey and honour-bound cons would dutifully send it off again on its great odyssey along the wall. I keep thinking about how gentle their hands must have been. All those killers and robbers and crooks. I guess they had time to be gentle. All the time in the world.*

*I've been thinking lately, Alex, that every problem in the world, every crime ever committed, can be traced back to someone's dad. Robbery, rape, terrorism, Cain putting a job on Abel, Jack the Ripper, it all goes back to dads. Mums maybe too, I guess, but there ain't no shit mum in this world that wasn't first the daughter of a shit dad. Don't tell me if you don't want to, but I'd love to hear about your dad, Alex. Was he good? Was he decent? Was he there? Thanks for your thoughts about calling my dad. You make a fair point. Two sides to every story, I guess.*

*I asked Mum for an update on* Days of Our Lives. *She said to tell you Marie was showing signs of improvement in hospital. Liz went to ICU to confess but when Marie woke she said it was too dark to identify her assailant so Liz kept her mouth shut and she seems to be able to live with the guilt. The first word Marie said when she woke was 'Neil', but despite Neil being her true love, she said she could never be his wife and gave him consent to go be with Liz and their child.*

*Talk real soon,*

*Eli*

P.S. *I've enclosed a copy of Omar Khayyám's poem,* The Rubáiyát. *Slim says it got him through prison. It's about the ups and downs of life. The downside is life is short and has to end. The upside is it comes with bread, wine and books.*

'Slim?'

'Yeah, kid?'

'Arthur Dale. That new name you took.'

'Yeah.'

'Dale.'

'Yeah.'

'That was the name of that screw, Officer Dale.'

'Yeah,' Slim says. 'I needed the name of a gentleman and Officer Dale was about as close as I ever got to a gentleman.'

Officer Dale stretched back to Slim's first lag in Boggo Road, early 1940s.

'See, kid, there's all kinds of bad inside,' he says. 'Blokes who start good and turn bad; blokes who seem bad but aren't bad at all; and then there's the blokes who are bad in blood and bone because they're born that way. That about describes half of those screws in Boggo. They took those jobs inside because they were drawn to their own kind, all those rapists and killers and psychopaths they were pretending to help rehabilitate when all they were doing was feeding their own evil beasts that lay dormant inside the cells of their own fucked-up heads.'

'But not Officer Dale.'

'Nah, not Officer Dale.'

After his first escape attempt, the Boggo Road screws came down hard on Slim, vigorously strip-searched him several times a day. During these searches it was customary for the officers to bash Slim across the side of the head to instruct him to turn around; kick him in the arse when they wanted him to bend over; elbow him in the nose when they wanted him to step back. One day Slim reacted, exploded in his cell, started throwing chunks of slop from his cell room slop bucket at the officers. They returned with the pressure hose treatment. One officer then came with two buckets of scalding water from the coppers that sat boiling in the prison kitchen. Another officer began shoving a red hot poker through the cell bars at Slim.

'Them officers were terrorising me like I was some rooster they were priming for a cockfight,' Slim says. 'I had a prison-issue knife I'd been sharpening under my pillow and I grabbed it and I stabbed one of those pricks in the hand. I was waving the knife at them, spittin' and frothin' like I was a sick dog. All hell broke loose after that, but amid all the madness there was this bloke, Officer Dale, he was standing up for me. He was shouting at these sick bastards, telling them to leave me be, that I'd had enough. And I remember looking at him like it was all going in slow motion and I was thinking that true character surely is best shown in hell, that true goodness must surely be best displayed in an underworld where the very opposite is the norm, when evil is living and goodness is an indulgence, you know what I'm saying?'

Slim smiles, looks at August. August nods at Slim, one of those knowing August nods, like he thinks he did a lag right alongside Slim, his neighbour in cell D10.

'You know,' Slim says, 'you dive that far down into hell that a wink from the devil starts to feel like a fuckin' hand job from Doris Day, you catch my drift?'

August nods again.

'Piss off, Gus, you don't even know who Doris Day is,' I say.

August shrugs.

'Doesn't matter,' Slim says. 'Point is, I was in this daydream amid all this chaos, looking at Officer Dale, watching him trying to get these guys to lay off. I was so bloody touched by the gesture I think I got a tear in my eye. Then I got a whole lotta fucking tears in my eyes because a second wave of screws came with masks and threw teargas bombs in my cell. They kicked the shit out of me good and proper and dragged me to Black Peter there and then. My clothes were still wet from the hose. Right in the middle of winter that one was. No blanket. No mat on that one. Everybody goes on about the fourteen days in Black Peter in the heatwave. But I'd take the fourteen days in the heatwave over that one night with Black Pete wet as a beaver in the middle of winter. Spent the whole night shiverin', just thinking one thing ...'

'That everybody has goodness in them?' I ask.

'Nah, kid, not everyone, just Officer Dale,' Slim says. 'But it got me thinking that if Officer Dale still had some goodness working among those other bastards for so long, then I might still have some goodness left in me when I was done with Black Peter; or when I was done with the joint forever.'

'New name, new man,' I say.

'Seemed like a good idea in the hole,' Slim says.

I pick up the *South-West Star*. One of the supporting pictures in the 'Queensland Remembers' spread shows Slim in 1952, sitting in the backroom of the Southport Court House. He's smoking a cigarette in a cream-coloured suit, over a white shirt with a thick collar. He looks like he belongs in Havana, Cuba, not the cell where he was going to live for the next twenty-four years of his life.

'How did you do it?' I ask.

'Do what?'

'How did you survive for so long without ...'

'Swallowing a rubber-band ball filled with razor blades?'

'Well, I was gonna say "givin' up", but ... yeah, that too.'

'That article is half right about that Houdini magic crap,' he says. 'What I did in that joint was a kind of magic.'

'What do you mean?'

'I mean I could do things with time in there,' Slim says. 'I got so intimate with time that I could manipulate it, speed it up, slow it down. Some days all you wanted was to speed it up, so you had to trick your brain. You get yourself so busy you can convince yourself there's not enough hours in the day to achieve everything you want to achieve. By "achieve", I don't mean learning how to play the violin or getting a degree in economics. I mean realistic midday prison cell goals. I mean collecting enough black balls of cockroach shit in a day that you can spell your name with them. Some days, bitin' your fingernails down to the quick became a leisure activity to look forward to like an Elvis double bill. So much to do, so little time. Make your bed, read chapter 30 of *Moby Dick*, think about Irene, whistle "You Are My Sunshine" from start to finish, roll a smoke, have a smoke, play yourself at chess, play yourself at chess again because you're pissed off you lost the first game, go fishing off Bribie Island in your mind, go fishing off Redcliffe jetty in your mind, scale your fish, gut your fish, cook that fat flathead on some hot coals on Suttons Beach and watch the sun go down. You race that bastard clock so hard you get surprised when the day is over and you're so tired from your daily schedule of bullshit head games that you yawn when you put your head on the pillow at 7 p.m. and tell yourself you're mad for staying up so late and burning the candle at both ends. But, then, in those good hours, those sunshine hours in the yard, you could make them slow, you could pull them up like they were well-trained horses and you could turn an hour in the flower garden into half a day, because you were living time in five dimensions and the dimensions were the things you were smelling and the things you could taste and touch and hear and the things you could see, things within things, small universes in the stamen of a flower, layers upon layers, because your vision was so enhanced by the inactivity of all that concrete-wall watching that every single time you walked into that garden yard it was like Dorothy walking into technicolour.'

'You learned to see all the details,' I say.

Slim nods. He looks at us both.

'Never forget, you two, you are free,' he says. 'These are your sunshine hours and you can make them last forever if you see all the details.'

I nod loyally.

'Do your time, hey Slim?' I say.

He nods proudly.

'Before it does you,' he says.

That's Slim's favourite nugget of porridge wisdom.

*Do your time before it does you.*

*

I remember when I first heard him say it. We were standing in the engine room of the clock tower of the Brisbane City Hall, the old and glorious brown sandstone building in the

83

heart of the city, towering over King George Square. Slim took us in on the train from Darra. He said there was an old elevator inside the high clock tower that took people right up to the top of the tower and I didn't believe him. He knew the old lift operator, Clancy Mallett, from his farmhand days and Clancy had said he would let us go up inside the elevator for nothing, but when we arrived the lift was undergoing repairs, out of order, and Slim had to sweet-talk his old friend with a put-your-dog-on-it tip for race 5 at Eagle Farm to convince him to lead us up a secret set of stairs that only the City Hall staff knew about. The dark stairwell up that clock tower went forever and Slim and old Clancy the lift operator wheezed the whole way up, but me and August laughed the whole way up. Then we gasped when Clancy opened a thin door that led into an engine room of spinning steel pulleys and cogs – the city's clockwork – that powered the four clock faces on the tower. North, south, east and west, each with giant black steel hands tracking the minutes and the hours of each Brisbane day. Slim stared mesmerised at those hands for ten straight minutes and he told us that time is the ancient enemy. He said time was killing us slowly. 'Time will do you in,' he said. 'So do your time before it does you.'

Clancy the lift operator walked us up another set of secret stairs off the engine room that led up to an observation deck where Slim said Brisbane kids used to throw coins over the rail and seventy-five metres down to the roof of City Hall as they made a wish.

'I wish I had more time,' I said as I tossed a copper two-cent piece over the rail.

Then time struck.

'Block your ears,' Clancy smiled, turning his eyes up to a giant steel blue bell I hadn't seen above us. And this bell rang loudly eleven times and near burst my eardrums and I changed my wish to one where time had to stop in that moment for the wish to come true.

*

'You seeing all the details, Eli?' Slim asks across the table.

'Huh?' I say, snapping back to now.

'You catchin' all the details?'

'Yeah,' I say, puzzled by the testing look in Slim's eye.

'You catching all that periphery stuff, kid?' he asks.

'Sure. Always, Slim. The details.'

'But you missed the most interesting thing about that article you have there.'

'Huh?'

I study the article, scan the words again.

'The byline,' he says. 'Bottom right-hand corner.'

The byline. The byline. Bottom right-hand corner. Eyes scanning down, down, down across ink words and pictures. There it is. There's the byline.

'What the fuck, Gus!'

I will associate this name with the day I learned how to manipulate time.

This name is Caitlyn Spies.

Slim and I look sharply at August. He says nothing.

# Boy Kills Bull

Here's Mum through a half-open bedroom door. She stands in her red going-out dress in front of the mirror hanging on the inside door of her wardrobe, fixing a silver necklace around her neck. How could any sane man not be happy in her presence, not be content, not be grateful for what he's got to come home to?

Why would my father fuck that up? She's so fucking wondrous my mum that it fills me with rage. Fuck any and all of those fuckers who stood within a foot of her without first seeking permission from Zeus.

I pad into her bedroom, sit on the bed near her at the mirror.

'Mum?'

'Yes, matey.'

'Why did you run from my father?'

'Eli, I don't want to talk about this now.'

'He did bad things to you, didn't he?'

'Eli, that's a conversation—'

'We'll have when I'm older,' I say. The go-to line.

She gives a half-smile into the wardrobe mirror. Half apologetic. Half touched I give a shit.

'Your father wasn't well,' she says.

'Is my father a good man?'

Mum thinks. Mum nods.

'Is my father more like me or more like Gus?'

Mum thinks. Mum says nothing.

'Does Gus ever scare you?'

'No.'

'Sometimes he scares the shit out of me.'

'Watch your language.'

Watch my language? *Watch my language?* This is what really shits me, when the clandestine heroin operation truth meets the Von Trapp family values mirage we've built for ourselves.

'Sorry,' I say.

'What scares you?' Mum asks.

'I don't know, the stuff he says, the stuff he writes in the air with his magic finger wand. Sometimes it doesn't make sense and sometimes it makes sense only two years later or a month later when it's impossible for him to have known it would make sense.'

'Like what?'

'Caitlyn Spies.'

'Caitlyn Spies? Who's Caitlyn Spies?'

'That's just the thing. We have no idea whatsoever, but ages ago Slim and I were messing around in the LandCruiser and we were watching August write his little messages in thin air and we caught him writing that name over and over. Caitlyn Spies. Caitlyn Spies. Caitlyn Spies. Then, last week, we read this big article in the *South-West Star*, this big "Queensland Remembers" spread, and it's all about Slim, it's the whole story of the Houdini of Boggo Road and it's a really interesting piece and then we see the name of the woman who wrote it squeezed down in the bottom right-hand corner of the page.'

'Caitlyn Spies,' Mum says.

'How'd you know?'

'You were kinda setting it up for that, buddy.'

She moves to her jewellery box on a white chest of drawers. 'He's obviously been reading her pieces in the local rag. He probably just liked how her name sounded in his mind. He does that, latches on to a name or a word and runs it over and over again in his mind. Just because he doesn't speak words doesn't mean he doesn't love them.'

She clutches two green gem earrings in her hand and leans down to me, talking softly and carefully.

'That boy loves you more than he loves anything in this universe,' she says. 'When you were born ...'

'Yeah, I know, I know.'

'... he watched over you so carefully, guarded your crib like all of human life depended on it. I couldn't drag him away from you. He's the best friend you will ever have.'

She stands and turns to the mirror.

'How do I look?'

'You look beautiful, Mum.'

Keeper of lightning. Goddess of fire and war and wisdom and Winfield Reds.

'Mutton dressed up as lamb,' she says.

'What does that mean?'

'I'm an old mutton dressing up as a young lamb.'

'Don't say that,' I say, frustrated.

She sees my mood in the mirror.

'Hey, I'm just joking,' she says, fixing her earrings in.

I hate it when she puts herself down, self-worth being, I believe, a fairly major root cause of everything from our living in this street to my outfit tonight, a yellow polo shirt and a pair of black slacks all purchased from the St Vincent de Paul Society opportunity shop in the neighbouring suburb of Oxley.

'You're too good for this place, you know,' I say.

'What are you talking about?'

'You're too good for this house. You're too smart for this town. You're too good for Lyle. What are we doing here in this shithole? We shouldn't even fucking be here.'

'All right, thanks for the heads-up, matey. I think you can go finish getting ready now, huh?'

'All those arseholes got the lamb because she always thought she was mutton.'

'That's enough now, Eli.'

'You know you should have been a lawyer. You should have been a doctor. Not a fucking drug dealer.'

Her hard slap hits my shoulder before she's even turned around.

'Get out of my room,' she barks. Another slap on my shoulder with her right hand, then another with her left on the other shoulder.

'Get the hell out of my room, Eli!' she screams. Her teeth are gritted so tight I see the creases in her top lip, breathing hard, breathing deep.

'Who are we kidding?' I shout. 'Watch my language? Watch my language? We're fucking drug dealers. Drug dealers fucking swear. I'm sick of all these bullshit airs and graces you and Lyle go on with. Do your homework, Eli. Eat your fuckin' broccoli, Eli. Tidy this kitchen, Eli. Study hard, Eli. Like we're the fucking Brady Bunch or somethin' and not just a dirty bunch of smack pushers. Give me a fucking bre—'

Then I'm flying. Two hands grip my underarms from behind and I'm flying, hurled off Mum and Lyle's bed, shoulders first, head second, into their bedroom door. I bounce off the door and drop to the polished wooden floorboards in a bone heap. Lyle looms above me and kicks me in the arse so hard with his Dunlop Volleys – his going-out shoes, one step up from his rubber flip-flops – that I belly slide two metres across the hallway floor to the bare feet of August who gives a curious *This again? So soon?* look to Lyle.

'Fuck you, druggo cunt,' I scream, rabid and groggy, trying to get to my feet.

He kicks me in the arse again and I dive this time across the living room floor.

Mum's screaming behind him. 'Stop it, Lyle, that's enough.'

Lyle's got the red-mist rage I've had the misfortune of encountering thrice before. Once when I ran away from home and slept a night in an empty bus in a wrecker's yard in Redlands. Another time when I stuck six cane toads in the freezer to die a humane death and those hardy and uneasy-on-the-eye amphibians survived in that sub-zero coffin all the way through to Lyle's after-work rum and Coke and he opened the freezer to find two toads blinking on his ice tray. A third time when I joined a schoolmate, Jock Whitney, on a neighbourhood doorknock fundraising drive for the Salvation Army, except we were really fundraising to buy *ET the Extra Terrestrial* on Atari – I still feel rotten about that, the game was a piece of shit.

August, dear, pure-of-heart August, stands in front of Lyle as he approaches for a third arse punt. He shakes his head, holding Lyle's shoulders.

'It's all right, mate,' Lyle says. 'It's time Eli and I had a little talk.'

Lyle brushes past August and he hauls me up by the collar of my opportunity shop polo, then pushes me out the front door. He hauls me down the front stairs and along the path, through the gate, still holding my collar, his big streetfightin' fists pushing against the back of my neck. 'Keep walkin', smartarse,' he says. 'Keep walkin'.'

He takes me across the street, under the streetlight outshining the moon above us, into the park opposite our house. All I can smell is Lyle's Old Spice aftershave. All I can hear is our footsteps and the sound of cicadas rubbing their legs, like they're excited by the tension in the air, rubbing their legs the way Lyle rubs his hands before an Eels preliminary final.

'What the fuck's got into you, Eli?' he asks, forcing me on across the cricket oval grass, unmown so my shoes keep kicking up the black fur of the tall paspalum grass shoots onto my pant legs. He walks me to the centre of the cricket pitch and he lets me go. He paces back and forth, fixing the buckle on his belt, breathing in, breathing out. He's wearing his cream-coloured slacks with his blue cotton button-up shirt with the white tall ship cutting full mast across it.

Don't cry, Eli. Don't cry. Don't cry. Fuck. You pussy, Eli.

'Why are you crying?' Lyle asks.

'I don't know, I *really* didn't want to. My brain doesn't listen to me.'

I cry some more with this realisation. Lyle gives me a minute. I wipe my eyes.

'You all right?' Lyle asks.

'Me arse stings a bit.'

'Sorry about that.'

I shrug. 'I deserved it,' I say.

Lyle gives me another moment.

'You ever wonder why you cry so easy, Eli?'

'Because I'm a pussy.'

'You're not a pussy. Don't you ever be ashamed of crying. You cry because you give a shit. Don't ever be ashamed of giving a shit. Too many people in this world are too scared to cry because they're too scared to give a shit.'

He turns and looks up at the stars. He sits down on the cricket pitch for a better angle, looks up and takes in the universe, all that scattered space crystal.

'You're right about your mum,' he says. 'She's way too good for me. Always has been. Far as I'm concerned, she's too good for anyone. She's too good for that house. She's too good for this town. Too good for me.'

He points to the stars. 'She belongs up there with Orion.'

I park my tender arse down beside him.

'You want to get out of here?' he asks.

I nod, stare up at Orion, the cluster of perfect light.

'So do I, mate,' he says. 'Why do you think I been doing the extra work for Tytus?'

'That's a nice way of putting it. Extra work. I wonder if Pablo Escobar calls it that.'

Lyle drops his head.

'I know it's a hell of a way to make a buck, mate.'

We sit in silence for a moment. Then Lyle turns to me.

'I'll make you a deal.'

'Yeah ...'

'Gimme six months.'

'Six months?'

'Where you wanna move to? Sydney, Melbourne, London, New York, Paris?'

'I want to move to The Gap.'

'The Gap? Why the fuck ya wanna move to The Gap?'

'Nice cul-de-sacs in The Gap.'

Lyle laughs.

'Cul-de-sacs,' he says, shaking his head. He turns to me, deeply serious. 'It'll get good, mate. It'll get so good you'll forget it was even bad.'

I look up at the stars. Orion fixes his target and he draws his bow and he lets his arrow fly, straight and true through the left eye of Taurus and the raging bull is silenced.

'Deal,' I say. 'Under one condition.'

'What's that?' Lyle asks.

'You let me work for you.'

*

We can walk to Bich Dang's Vietnamese restaurant from home. The restaurant is called Mama Pham's, named in honour of the stocky cooking genius, Mama Pham, who taught Bich how to cook in her native Saigon in the 1950s. The *Mama Pham's* sign on the front is written in blinking lime green neon against an eastern red backdrop, but the neon 'P' is busted and dulled so the restaurant, for the past three years, has looked to passers-by more like a pork and bacon–based restaurant named 'Mama ham's'. Lyle holds a six-pack of XXXX Bitter in his left hand and opens the Mama Pham's front glass door for Mum, who slips past him in the red dress and the black heels from beneath her bed. August walks past next with his hair combed back carelessly and his pink Catchit T-shirt tucked into shiny silver-grey slacks, bought from the Darra Station Road opportunity shop seven or eight shops past the TAB down from Mama Pham's.

The inside of Mama Pham's is as big as a cinema hall. There are more than twenty round dining tables with lazy Susans spinning for eight, ten, sometimes twelve people per table. Beautiful Vietnamese mums with made-up faces and immovable hair and normally quiet Vietnamese dads loosened and laughing heartily on beer and wine and tea. There are great beasts of the ocean lying sideways in the centre of each table, glazed and oiled and boiled and crumbed and salted and peppered, and whole deep-sea leviathans from the Mekong and beyond, Neptune maybe; big fat awkward bottom lips and slimy tentacle whiskers in colours of green and moss green and blue green and grey green and brown, black and red. Bich Dang owns acres of land at the back of Darra, beyond the Polish migrant centre, with soil like chocolate cake where her old and wrinkled and wise farmers grow the piles of rau ram coriander, shiso leaf, hung cay mint, basil, lemongrass and Vietnamese balm that guests pass between themselves tonight like they're playing some children's party game called Hands Across the Table. An oversized mirror ball twinkles above us and a Vietnamese lounge singer twinkles on stage, purple glitter make-up on her cheeks and a turquoise sequined dress that shimmers the way a mermaid's scales might shimmer beached on the banks of the Mekong. She sings 'Calling Occupants of Interplanetary Craft' by The Carpenters, sways to the crackly backing track, alien somehow, like she just flew into Darra on the kind of craft she's calling through that old microphone. Red tinsel lines the walls, running above fish tanks with catfish and cod and red emperor and fat snapper fish with balls on their heads that look like someone's clubbed them with a cricket bat. There's two more tanks dedicated to the crayfish and the mud crabs who always seem so resigned to the fact they'll form tonight's signature dish. They sit beneath their tank rocks and their cheap stone underwater novelty castle decorations, so breezy bayou casual all they're missing is a harmonica and a piece of straw to chew on. They're so unaware of their importance, so oblivious to the fact they're the reason people drive from as far away as the Sunshine Coast to come taste their insides baked in salt and pepper and chilli paste.

A staircase to the right of the restaurant runs up to a second balcony level with ten more round tables where 'Back Off' Bich Dang seats her VIP guests, and tonight there's only one VIP and his name is stretched across the birthday banner running across the balcony rail of the top level: *Happy 80th Tytus Broz*.

'Lyle Orlik, son of Aureli!' Tytus Broz says grandly, his arms raised welcomingly in the air, standing over the balcony rail. 'It seems Bich has pulled out all the bells, all the whistles and all the stops to celebrate my eighth decade on this good planet!'

Tytus makes me think of bones. He wears a bone-white suit over a bone-white shirt and a bone-white tie. His shoes are brown polished leather and his hair is as bone white as his suit. His body is all bone, tall and thin, and he smiles like a skeleton frame would smile if it hopped off a Biology classroom hook and started to dance like Michael Jackson in the 'Billie Jean' clip August and I love like lemonade. Tytus's cheekbones are round like the protruding balls on the heads of Bich Dang's tank snapper, but his actual cheeks have been slowly sucked inwards over eighty years on earth and when his lips tremble – and they tremble all the time – it looks like he's permanently sucking on a pistachio nut, or a vampire bat sucking on a human liver.

Tytus Broz makes me think of bones because he's made a fortune out of bones. Tytus Broz is Lyle's boss at Human Touch, the Queensland prosthetics and orthotics sales centre and manufacturing plant he owns and runs in the suburb of Moorooka, ten minutes' drive from our house. Lyle is a mechanic there, works maintenance on the machines that build artificial arms and legs for amputees across the State. Tytus Broz is the Lord of Limbs, whose vast natural arm reach has stretched across my and August's lives for the past six years, ever since Lyle landed the Human Touch maintenance job through his best friend, Tadeusz 'Teddy' Kallas, the man with the thick black moustache seated four plastic white chairs to the right of Tytus at the VIP dining table. Teddy is also a maintenance mechanic at Human Touch. Teddy is also, I have long suspected, a man with a lucrative on-the-side stream of Tytus Broz's 'extra work' that Lyle spoke of earlier this evening. The man sitting next to Teddy in a grey suit and maroon tie with black hair like a newsreader's looks a hell of a lot like our local council member, Stephen Bourke, the man who sends us magnetised calendars each year that keep Mum's shopping lists pinned to the refrigerator. He sips from a glass of white wine. Yeah, in fact, I'm certain that's our local member. 'Stephen Bourke –

Your Local Leader' the calendar reads. Stephen Bourke, right here at the table of Tytus Broz, 'Your Local Dealer'.

The thing about Tytus Broz that reminds me most of bones is that every time I see him – and this is only my second sighting of him – I get a shiver down my spine. He smiles at me now and he smiles at Mum and he smiles at August, but I don't buy that pistachio-nut-sucker smile for a second. I don't know why. Just something in my bones.

\*

The first time I met Tytus Broz was two years ago when I was ten years old. Lyle was taking me and August to the roller-skating rink in Stafford, on the north side of Brisbane, but on the way he had to drop in to his work at Moorooka to fix a faulty lever on the machine that shaped the artificial arms and legs that paid for Tytus Broz's bone-white suits. It was the old warehouse back then, before the business was overhauled into the whole Human Touch modern manufacturing plant of today. The warehouse was an aluminium shed the size of a tennis court, with giant ceiling fans to fight the suffocating heat of all that sun-baked metal housing a thousand fake limbs spread across hooks and shelves that led past plaster-makers casting body shapes and mechanics turning screws into fake bent knees and fake bent elbows.

'Don't touch anything,' Lyle ordered as he led us past endless leg limbs standing in a row like a Moulin Rouge can-can troupe miraculously dancing without their torsos. We walked through rows of arms hanging on hooks from the ceiling and these arms had plastic hands that touched my face as we passed and I pictured those arms connected to the bodies of dead Arthurian knights impaled and hanging from long spears in the ground and their hands were reaching out for help that August and I could not give because Lyle insisted we didn't touch anything, not even the reaching hand of the great Sir Lancelot du Lac. I saw those arms and legs coming alive, reaching at me, clutching for me, kicking at me. That warehouse was the end of a hundred bad horror movies, the start of a hundred nightmares I was yet to have.

'These are Frances's boys, August and Eli,' Lyle said, ushering us into Tytus Broz's office at the back of the warehouse. August was the taller and the older so he walked into the office first and it was August who captivated Tytus from the start.

'Come closer, young man,' Tytus said.

August looked up at Lyle for assurance and an exit out of that moment, but Lyle didn't give it, he just nodded at August like he should do what was polite and walk closer to the man who was putting the meat and three veg on our table every night.

'Give me your hand,' Tytus said from a swivel chair at a red-brown antique work desk. There was a framed painting of a giant white whale above this desk. It was Moby Dick, from what Lyle told me later was Tytus Broz's favourite book, the one about the elusive whale hunted by an obsessive-compulsive amputee who could have benefited from having a Human Touch prosthetics and orthotics sales centre and warehouse in downtown Nantucket. I asked Slim soon after that if he'd ever read *Moby Dick* and he said he'd read it twice because it's worth reading a second time, though he said second time around he skipped the bit where the writer goes on about all the different species of whales found across the world. I asked Slim to tell me the whole story from start to finish and for two hours while we washed his LandCruiser he told me that thrilling adventure tale so enthusiastically I wanted Nantucket fish chowder for lunch and white whale steaks for dinner. When he described Captain Ahab, with his wild-eyed face and his age and his thinness and his whiteness, I pictured Tytus Broz on that whale ship barking at his spotters high up in raging wind, demanding to see his prey, his white whale as white as Tytus Broz himself. Slim turned the LandCruiser into Moby Dick and the garden hose was the harpoon that he stabbed into the whale's side and we grabbed onto the hose rubber for dear life as the whale dragged us into the abyss and the hose water became the ocean that would take us down, down, down to Poseidon, god of seas and garden hoses.

August offered his right hand and Tytus cupped it gently in his own two hands.

'Mmmmmmm,' he said. With his forefinger and thumb he squeezed each of the fingers of August's right hand, moving his way along the hand, thumb to pinkie.

'Oh, there is a strength in you, isn't there?' he said.

August said nothing.

'I said, "There is a strength in you, boy, isn't there?"'

August said nothing.

'Well ... would you care to respond, young man?' Tytus said, puzzled.

'He doesn't talk,' Lyle said.

'What do you mean he doesn't talk?'

'He hasn't spoken a word since he was six years old.'

'Is he simple?' Tytus asked.

'No, he's not simple,' Lyle said. 'Sharp as a tack, in fact.'

'He's one of those autistic boys, is he? Can't function in society but he can tell me how many grains of sand are in my hourglass?'

'There's nothin' wrong with him,' I said, frustrated.

Tytus turned his swivel chair to me.

'I see,' he said, studying my face. 'So you're the talker of the family?'

'I talk when there's somethin' worth talkin' about,' I said.

'Wisely talked,' Tytus said.

He reached out his hand.

'Give me your arm,' he said.

I held out my right arm and he gripped it with his soft and old hands, his palms so smooth it felt like they were covered in the Glad Wrap Mum kept in the third drawer down beneath the kitchen sink.

He squeezed my arm hard. I looked at Lyle, he nodded assurance.

'You're scared,' Tytus Broz said.

'I'm not scared,' I said.

'Yes, you are, I can feel it in your marrow,' he said.

'Don't you mean my bones?'

'No, your marrow, boy. You are weak-boned. Your bones are hard but your bones are not full.'

He nodded at August. 'Marcel Marceau's bones are hard and they are also full. Your brother possesses a strength that you will never have.'

August shot a smug and knowing smile at me. 'But I've got great finger bone strength,' I said, flipping August the bird.

That was when I spotted the human hand resting on a metal prop on Tytus's desk.

'Is that real?' I asked.

The hand looked real and unreal at the same time. Severed and capped cleanly at the wrist, all five fingers looked like they were made of wax or wrapped in Glad Wrap like Tytus's felt.

'Yes, it is, in fact,' Tytus said. 'That is the hand of a sixty-five-year-old bus driver named Ernie Hogg who kindly donated his body to the Anatomy students of the University of Queensland whose recent investigations into plastination have been most enthusiastically sponsored by yours truly.'

'What's plastination mean?' I asked.

'It's where we replace water and body fats inside the limb with certain curable polymers – plastics – to create a real limb that can be touched and studied up close and reproduced, but the dead donor limb does not smell or decay.'

'That's gross,' I said.

Tytus chuckled. 'No,' he said with a strange and unsettling wonder in his eyes, 'that's the future.'

There was a pottery figurine of an ageing man in chains on his desk. The ageing man was wearing an Ancient Greek man dress, and had oil paint blood streaks across his exposed back. He was mid-stride, favouring a leg that was missing a foot and bandaged roughly.

'What's that?' I asked.

Tytus turned to the figurine.

'That's Hegesistratus,' he said. 'One of history's great amputees. He was an Ancient Greek diviner capable of profound and dangerous things.'

'What's a diviner?' I asked.

'A diviner is many things,' he said. 'In Ancient Greece the diviners were more like seers. They could see things others could not see by interpreting signs from the gods. They could see things coming, a valuable skill in war.'

I turned to Lyle. 'That's like Gus,' I said.

Lyle shook his head. 'All right, that'll do, mate.'

'What do you mean, boy?' Tytus asked.

'Gus sees things, too,' I said. 'Like Hegesistaramus or whatever here.'

Tytus cast a new eye over August, who gave a half-smile, shaking his head, moving backwards to stand beside Lyle.

'What things exactly?'

'Just crazy things that sometimes turn out to be true,' I said. 'He writes them in the air. Like when he wrote *Park Terrace* in the air and I wondered what the hell he was talking about, then Mum came home and told us she was standing at a set of traffic lights while she was shopping in Corinda when she saw an old woman just step right out into traffic. Right out there into the middle of it all, not giving a shit—'

'Watch your language, Eli,' Lyle said, cross at me.

'Sorry. So Mum drops all her grocery bags and takes two steps forward and reaches for this old woman and yanks her back hard to the footpath just as a big council bus is about to clean her up. She saved the old lady's life. And guess what street that happened on?'

'Park Terrace?' Tytus said, eyes wide.

'No,' I said. 'It happened on Oxley Avenue, but then Mum walks this old lady back to her house a few blocks down the road and this old woman doesn't say a word at all, just has this dazed look on her face. Then they come to this woman's house and the front door is wide open and one of the old casement windows is banging hard in the wind and the old woman says she can't go up the front stairs and Mum tries to guide her up there but she goes crazy, "No, no, no, no," she screams. And nods to Mum like she should go up those stairs, and because Mum has hard and full bones too, she climbs those stairs and she walks into the house and all the casement windows on all four sides of this old Corinda Queenslander are banging in the wind and Mum paces through this house and into the kitchen where there's a ham and tomato sandwich being eaten by flies and this whole house stinks of Dettol and something darker underneath, something fouler, and Mum keeps walking through the living room, down a hallway, all the way to the house's main bedroom and the door is closed and she opens it and she's almost knocked out by the smell of the old dead guy sitting in an armchair by a king-size bed, his head wrapped in a plastic bag and a gas tank by his side. And guess what street this house was on?'

'Park Terrace,' Tytus said.

'No,' I said. 'The cops came to the house and they pieced together the whole story and they told Mum how the old woman had found her husband like that in the bedroom a month before and she was so cross at him because he told her he was going to do it but she demanded he didn't and he defied her and she was so pissed off with him and shocked by the situation that she simply pretended he wasn't there. She closed the door on the main bedroom for a month, spreading Dettol around the house to mask the smell as she went about her daily business like making ham and tomato sandwiches for lunch. Finally, when the smell got too much, reality kicked in and she opened all the windows in the house and walked straight down to Oxley Avenue to throw herself in front of a bus.'

'So where did Park Terrace come in?' Tytus asked.

'Well, that had nothing to do with Mum. That was Lyle who copped a speeding fine on Park Terrace while driving to work that same day.'

'Fascinating,' Tytus said.

He looked at August, leaned forward in his swivel chair. There was something sinister in his eye then. He was old but he was threatening. It was the sucked-in cheekbones, the white hair, the something I felt in my weak bones. It was Ahab.

'Well, young August, you budding diviner, do please tell me,' he began, 'what do you see when you look at me?'

August shook his head, shrugged off the whole story.

Tytus smiled. 'I think I'll keep my eye on you, August,' he said, leaning back in his swivel chair.

I turned back to the figurine.

'So how did he lose his foot?' I asked.

'He was captured by the bloodthirsty Spartans and put in bonds,' he said. 'But he managed to escape by cutting his foot off.'

'Bet they didn't see that coming,' I said.

'No, young Eli, they did not,' he said. He laughed. 'So what does Hegesistratus teach us?' he asked.

'Always pack a hacksaw when you travel to Greece,' I said.

Tytus smiled. Then he turned to Lyle.

'Sacrifice,' he said. 'Never grow attached to anything you can't instantly separate yourself from.'

*

On Mama Pham's upper floor dining area, Tytus places a hand on each of Mum's shoulders and kisses her right cheek.

'Welcome,' he says. 'Thank you for coming.'

Tytus introduces Mum and Lyle to the woman seated directly to his right.

'Please meet my daughter, Hanna,' he says.

Hanna stands from her seat. She's dressed in white like her father, her hair is blonde-white, a kind of non-colour, as if all life has been sucked from it. She's thin like her father.

Her hair is straight and long and hangs over the shoulders of a white button-up top with sleeves running to the hands that she keeps below the table as she stands. Maybe she's forty. Maybe she's fifty, but then she speaks and maybe she's thirty and shy.

Lyle has told us about Hanna. She's the reason he's got a job. If Hanna Broz hadn't been born with arms that ended at her elbows then Tytus Broz would never have been motivated to turn his small Darra auto-electrics warehouse into the home of his fledgling orthotics manufacturing shop which, in turn, grew into the Human Touch, a godsend for local amputees like Hanna, and a source of several community awards given to Tytus in the name of disability awareness.

'Hi,' Hanna says softly, giving a smile that would light small towns if it only had more time in use. Mum puts out a hand for shaking and Hanna meets it with a hand of her own raised from beneath the table, and this hand is no hand at all but an artificial limb beneath the white sleeve, and Mum doesn't skip a beat as she grips that skin-coloured plastic hand and shakes it warmly. Hanna smiles, a little longer this time.

Tytus Broz reminds me of bones because I am all bones and the other man who just caught my eye is stone. He's all stone. A man of stone, staring at me. He wears a black short-sleeved button-up cotton shirt. He's old but not as old as Tytus. Maybe he's fifty. Maybe he's sixty. He's one of those hard men Lyle knows, muscular and grim – you could chop him in half and measure his age by the growth rings in his insides. He's just staring at me now this guy. All this activity around this circular dining table and here's this stone man staring at me with his big nose and his thin eyes and his silver hair that is long and pulled back into a ponytail but the hair only starts halfway along his scalp so it looks like this long silver hair is being sucked from his cranium with a vacuum cleaner. Slim's always talking about this, the little movies within the movie of your own life. Life lived in multiple dimensions. Life lived from multiple vantage points. One moment in time – several people meeting at a circular dining table before taking their seats – but a moment with multiple points of view. In these moments time doesn't just move forward, it can move sideways, expanding to accommodate infinite points of view, and if you add up all these vantage point moments you might have something close to eternity passing sideways within a single moment. Or something like that.

Nobody sees this moment the way I see it, defined as it will be for the rest of my life by the silver-haired creep with the ponytail.

'Iwan,' calls Tytus Broz, his left hand on Lyle's shoulder, pointing at August, who is standing beside me. 'This is the boy I was telling you about. He doesn't talk, like you.' The man Tytus calls Iwan shifts his focus from me to August.

'I talk,' says the man Tytus calls Iwan.

The man Tytus calls Iwan shifts his eyes to a glass of beer before him, which he then grips tightly with his right hand and brings slow as a chairlift to his lips. He drinks half the glass in a single sip. Maybe the man Tytus calls Iwan is actually two hundred years old. Nobody's ever been able to cut him in half to be sure.

Bich Dang approaches the table, calling from afar. She wears a sparkling emerald gown that hugs her torso and legs all the way to her hidden feet so when she walks across Mama Pham's upper-floor dining area it looks like she's hovering over to our table. Darren Dang shuffles over in her wake, visibly troubled by the smart black coat and pants he's not so much wearing as enduring.

'Welcome people, welcome, welcome, sit, sit,' she says. She puts an arm around Tytus Broz. 'Now I hope you have brought your appetites. I have prepared more hot dinners for tonight than this one has had hot dinners.'

*

Points of view. Vantage points. Angles. Mum in her red dress, laughing with Lyle as she drops chunks of crispy tilapia onto her plate. The tilapia has been drowned in a garlic and chilli and coriander sauce, so many exposed white bones in its charred and thorny dorsal fin that they look like the ivory keys in the warped piano organ the devil plays in hell.

Tytus Broz resting an arm over his daughter, Hanna, as he talks to our local member, Stephen Bourke, who wrestles with a chopstick clump of Vietnamese lemongrass beef noodle salad.

Lyle's best friend, Teddy, staring across the table at my mum.

Bich Dang bringing another dish to the table.

'Braised snakehead!' she beams.

Darren Dang is seated on my left and August is on my right. The three of us are eating spring rolls. The man Tytus calls Iwan is across the table, sucking the flesh from a bright orange chilli crab claw.

'Iwan Krol,' Darren says, keeping his head down as he chomps into a spring roll.

'Huh?' I say.

'Stop staring at him,' Darren says, his head darting anywhere but in the direction of the man Tytus calls Iwan.

'He gives me the creeps,' I say.

It's loud at this table. The restaurant noise, between the lounge singer on the dining floor below us and the drink-fuelled chat of our table guests and the cackling howl of Bich Dang's laughter, has caused a kind of invisible sound booth to form around Darren and me, allowing us to talk freely about the people sitting around us.

'That's what he's paid to do,' Darren says.

'What?'

'Give people the creeps.'

'What do you mean? What does he do?'

'By day, he runs a llama farm in Dayboro.'

'Llama farm?'

'Yeah, I been there. He's got all these llamas on his farm. Crazy fuckin' animals, like a donkey had sex with a camel. They got these big yellow bottom teeth, like the worst case for braces you ever saw. The teeth are so bad you give 'em half an apple they can't bite into it, they just have to roll it around their tongue like it's a gobstopper or somethin'.'

'And by night …?'

'By night, he gives people the creeps.'

Darren spins the lazy Susan on our table and brings a bowl of salt and pepper baked mud crab to our places. He takes a claw and three crispy crab legs and lays them in his small bowl of rice.

'That's his job?' I ask.

'Shit yeah it is,' Darren says. 'He's got one of the most important jobs in the whole operation.' Darren shakes his head. 'Jeez, Tink, you're one green-arse drug dealer's son.'

'I told you, Lyle's not me dad.'

'Sorry, forgot he's your temp dad.'

I take a salt and pepper crab claw and bite it with my big back teeth, and the baked crab shell breaks like an eggshell breaks under pressure. If Darra had a flag that we residents could wave in solidarity then a soft-shelled salted and peppered mud crab would have to feature on it somewhere.

'How does he give people the creeps?' I ask.

'Reputation and rumours, Mum says,' Darren explains. 'Anyone can get a reputation, of course. Just walk outside and stick a knife in the neck of the next poor bastard you see in the street.'

Darren turns the lazy Susan again, stops it spinning at a bowl of fishcakes.

I can't stop staring at Iwan Krol, picking crab shell gristle from his big straight tobacco-stained teeth.

'Sure, Iwan Krol has done his share of bad shit that everybody knows about,' Darren says. 'A bullet in the back of a head here, a hydrochloric acid bath there, but it's the shit we don't know about that scares people. It's the rumours that build up around a guy like Iwan Krol that do half the work for him. It's the rumours that give people the creeps.'

'What rumours?'

'You haven't heard the rumours?'

'What rumours, Darren?'

He looks over at Iwan Krol. He leans in close to me.

'Dem bones,' Darren whispers. 'Dem bones, dem bones.'

'The fuck ya talkin' 'bout?'

He takes two crab legs, makes them dance on his table like human legs.

'The toe bone's connected to the foot bone,' he sings. 'The foot bone's connected to the ankle bone, the ankle bone's connected to the leg bone, now shake dem skeleton bones.'

Darren bursts into laughter. He reaches out a sharp hand and grips my neck, squeezes hard. 'Neck bone's connected to the head bone,' he sings. He puts a fist on my forehead. 'Head bone's connected to the dick bone.'

He howls and Iwan Krol looks up from his plate, runs his dead brown eyes over the scene. Darren straightens up, collects himself immediately. Iwan drops his head back down to his plate of massacred crab.

'Dickhead,' I whisper. I lean closer to him this time. 'What are you talking about, the bones?'

'Forget about it,' he says, digging his chopsticks into his rice.

I slap his shoulder with the back of my hand. 'Don't be a prick,' I say.

'Why do you care so much anyway? You gonna write about it one day in *The Courier-Mail*?' he asks.

'I need to know this shit,' I say. 'I'm workin' for Lyle for a bit.'

Darren's eyes light up.

'What doin'?'

'I'm gonna watch out for things,' I say proudly.

'What?' Darren howls. He leans back in his chair, belly-laughing. 'Ha! Tinkerbell is gonna watch out for things. Well, praise the Lord and kiss my balls! Tinkerbell is on watch! And what exactly will you be watching out for?'

'Details,' I say.

'Details?' he barks, slapping his knees now. 'What sort of details? Like, today I'm wearing green jocks and white socks?'

'Yep,' I say. 'Everything. All the tiny little details. Details is knowledge, Slim says. Knowledge is power.'

'This is a full-time gig Lyle's gonna put you on?' Darren asks.

'Watching never stops,' I say. 'It's a 24/7 concern.'

'What have you been watching tonight?'

'Tell me about dem bones and I'll tell you what I've been watching.'

'Tell me about the watching and I'll tell you about dem bones, Tink.'

I take a deep breath. I look across the table. Lyle's best friend, Teddy, is still staring across the table at my mum. I've seen men look at my mum like that before. Teddy has big black curly hair and olive skin, a thick black moustache, the kind Slim says are worn by men with big egos and small pricks. Slim says he wouldn't want to share a cell with Teddy. He never says why. Teddy's got some Italian in him, some Greek maybe, from his mum's side. He catches me staring at him staring at her. He smiles. I've seen that smile before.

'How you boys goin'?' Teddy asks, shouting across the noise of the dinner table.

'Good thanks, Teddy,' I say.

'How you goin', Gussy?' Teddy says, raising a beer glass to August. August holds a cup of lemonade up in toast to Teddy, raises a half-hearted left eyebrow.

'That's the way, boys,' Teddy smiles, giving a hearty wink.

I lean back to Darren. 'The tiny little details,' I say. 'A million and one details in a single setting. The way you hold your chopsticks with that kink in your right forefinger. The smell of your armpits and the bong water stain on the bottom of your button-up shirt. The woman sitting over there with the birthmark on her shoulder shaped like Africa. The way Tytus's daughter, Hanna, hasn't eaten anything but a few forkfuls of rice tonight. Tytus hasn't taken his hand off her left thigh in more than thirty minutes. Your mum slipped an envelope to our friendly local member and then our friendly local member went to the toilet and when he came back he sat in his chair and raised his wineglass to your mum who was standing by the drinks fridge. She smiled and nodded then went downstairs to talk to the old and large Vietnamese man sitting by the stage watching that awful singer work her way through "New York Mining Disaster 1941" by the Bee Gees. There's a kid over by the trout tank poking fish with a sparkler. And that kid's big sister is Thuy Chan and she's in Year 8 at Jindalee High and she's looking so fucking beautiful tonight in that yellow dress and she's looked over here at you four times so far tonight and you're too much of a stoned arsehead to even notice.'

Darren looks down at the bottom-floor dining area and Thuy Chan catches his eye and smiles, pulls a clump of her straight black hair away from her face. He immediately turns away. 'Shit, Bell,' he says. 'You're right.' He shakes his head. 'I thought it was just a bunch of arseholes having dinner.'

'Tell me 'bout dem bones,' I say.

Darren chugs a lemonade, straightens his jacket and pants. He leans in close to me again and we stare across at the subject of our discussion, Iwan Krol.

'Thirty years ago his brother disappeared,' Darren says. 'His older brother was a bloke named Magnar and, you know, even his name meant "tough cunt" in Polish or somethin' like that. Toughest bastard in Darra. Real sadistic prick. He picked on Iwan constantly. Burnt him and shit, tied him to railways and whipped him with jumper leads. So apparently one day Magnar is drinking some Polish whisky, fifty per cent rocket fuel, and passes out in the family shed where the two brothers were working on some smash repairs. Iwan grabs his brother by the arms and drags him down to the back of the family paddock, a hundred metres away, and leaves him there. Then, cool as a cucumber, he hooks up two power leads running to the back of the paddock and then he grabs a circular power saw and lights it up and he saws off his brother's head as calmly as he'd cut the roof off a Ford Falcon.'

We stare at Iwan Krol. He looks up, like he senses us staring at him. He wipes his mouth with a napkin from his lap.

'That shit true?' I whisper.

'Mum says rumours about Iwan Krol aren't always accurate,' Darren says.

'Thought so,' I say.

'Nah, man,' Darren says. 'You're not gettin' me. She means the rumours about Iwan Krol never tell the full truth because the full truth is shit most sane people can't even wrap their heads around.'

'So what did he do with Magnar, or what was left of Magnar?'

'Nobody knows,' Darren says. 'Magnar just disappeared. Vanished. Never seen again. All the rest is just whispers. And that's his genius. That's why he's so brilliant at what he does today. One day his mark is walking the streets some place. The next day his mark is not walking any place at all.'

I keep staring at Iwan Krol.

'Does your mum know?' I ask.

'Know what?'

'What Iwan did with his brother's body?'

'Nah, Mum doesn't know shit,' he says. 'But I know.'

'What did he do with it?'

'The same thing he does with all his marks.'

'What's that?'

Darren spins the lazy Susan, stops it at a plate filled with chilli crab. He takes a whole cooked sand crab and drops it on his plate.

'Watch closely,' he says.

He grips the crab's right claw, wrenches it off violently and sucks its insides. He grips the crab's left claw, rips it from the body carapace as easy as a stick pulled from the shoulder socket of a snowman.

'The arms,' he says. 'Then the legs.'

He tears off three legs on the right of the shell. Three legs off the left.

'All them marks just disappear, Tink. Snitches, blabbermouths, enemies, competitors, clients who can't pay their debts.'

Then Darren removes the crab's rear swimmer legs, four jointed leg segments each shaped like a small flat sinker. He sucks the meat out of all these legs and places the intact leg shells back beside the carapace, exactly where they're supposed to be anatomically, but not actually touching the shell. He puts the crab claws back in place, like the legs, a millimetre from the crab's chilli-sauced body.

'Dismemberment, Eli,' Darren whispers.

Darren looks across at me to see the dumb look on my dumb face. Then he piles up all the crab's legs and claws and drops them into the upturned shell of the crab's carapace. 'Much easier to transport a body in six pieces,' he says, dropping the piled carapace in a bowl already filled with a mountain of sucked and discarded crab shells.

'Transport where?'

Darren smiles. He nods his head towards Tytus Broz.

'To a good home,' he says.

To the Lord of Limbs.

Tytus stands at that moment and taps his wineglass with a fork.

'Excuse me, ladies and gentlemen, but I believe it's time to mark this extraordinary evening with a brief note of thanks.'

*

On the walk home, a thick cloud has covered up Orion. August and Mum walk ahead of Lyle and me. We watch them balancing on the green log fences that border Ducie Street Park. These log fences – each made of one long light green treated pine log resting on two stumps – have acted as our Olympic Games gymnastics balance beams for roughly six years now.

Mum bounces up gracefully and sticks a two-foot landing on a balance pole.

She nails a daring midair scissor kick and lands it too. August claps enthusiastically.

'Now the great Comăneci prepares for the dismount,' she says, cautiously approaching the edge of the pole. She makes a flurry of straight-arm peacock-hand waves for effect and acknowledges her imaginary crowd of Montreal judges and 1976 Olympics diehards. August puts his arms out in front, braces himself low with his bent knees. And Mum springs into his waiting arms.

'Perfect ten!' she says. August spins her around in celebration. They walk on and August jumps up onto a pole of his own.

Lyle watches on from afar, smiling.

'So, you thought about it?' I ask.

'Thought about what?' Lyle replies.

'My plan,' I say.

'Tell me more about this taskforce.'

'Taskforce Janus,' I say. 'You really need to read the paper more. The police are waging war on drugs imported from the Golden Triangle.'

'Bullshit,' Lyle says.

'It's true. It's all through the paper. You ask Slim.'

'Well, the taskforce might be true, but their intentions are bullshit. It's a smokescreen. Half the senior cops around here have their Christmas holidays funded by Tytus. No bastard round here wants to stop the drugs coming because no bastard round here wants to stop Tytus's gravy train.'

'Taskforce Janus isn't cops round here,' I say. 'It's the Australian Federal Police. They're focusing on the borders. They're catching them out at sea, before they even reach the beach.'

'So …'

'So soon supply won't meet demand,' I say. 'There'll be a thousand junkies running around Darra and Ipswich looking to score but the only people with the gear will be the AFP and they won't be sellin'.'

'So?' Lyle says.

'So we buy up now. Buy up once and buy up big. Stick that gear in the ground, bury it for a year, two years, let the AFP turn that stash into diamond.'

Lyle turns to me, looks me up and down.

'I think you need to stop hanging around with Darren Dang,' he says.

'Bad move,' I say. 'Darren's our in with Bich. You keep dropping me around Darren's house and then you keep chatting to Bich like the responsible, loving guardian you are and she eventually trusts you enough to sell you ten kilograms of heroin.'

'You've lost the plot, kid,' Lyle says.

'I've been asking Darren about market prices. He says ten kilos of heroin sold even at current prices of $15 a gram would earn us $150,000. You let that stash sit for a year or two, I guarantee you'd fetch sale prices of $18, $19, $20 a gram. You can buy a decent house in The Gap for $71,000. We'd have enough for two houses with change left over to put in-ground swimming pools in both.'

'And what happens when Tytus finds out I'm running a little operation on the side and he sends Iwan Krol out for some answers?'

I have no reply to that. I keep walking. There's an empty can of Solo soft drink sitting in the gutter that I kick with my right shoe. It bounces into the middle of the bitumen street.

'You wanna pick that up?' Lyle says.

'What?'

'The can, the fucking can, Eli,' Lyle says, frustrated. 'Look at this place. Fuckin' abandoned trolleys sittin' in the park, chip wrappers and fuckin' used nappies lyin' all over the joint. When I was a kid these streets were clean as a whistle. People gave a shit about these streets. This place was just as pretty as your precious Gap. I tell ya, that's how it starts, mums and dads in Darra start dropping used nappies in the street, next thing you know they're lightin' tyres up outside the Sydney Opera House. That's how Australia turns to shit, with you just kicking that Solo can into the middle of the street.'

'I reckon widespread suburban heroin use might be a quicker road to ruin,' I suggest.

'Just pick up the can, smartarse.'

I pick up the can.

'The drop in the lake,' I say.

'The what?' Lyle says.

'The ripple effect,' I say, raising the Solo can. 'What do I do with it?'

'Put it in that bin there,' Lyle says.

I drop it in a black bin on the kerbside that's stuffed full of Silvio's pizza boxes and empty beer bottles. We walk on.

'What's the drop in the lake?' Lyle asks.

Just a theory about my life. We watch Mum and August now zig-zagging through the segmented pole fences lining the park.

'The drop in the lake was Mum's old man leaving her when she was a kid,' I say. 'That's what starts every ripple of her life. The old man takes off, leaves Grandma to look after six kids in a shoebox in Sydney's western suburbs. Mum's the eldest so she drops out of school at fourteen to get a job and help Grandma pay the bills and put food on the table. Then after two or three years she gets pissed off at Grandma because she had dreams, you know. She wanted to be a lawyer or some shit and help all those poor rat kids of Sydney's west stay out of Silverwater. She takes off hitchhiking around Australia, gets all the way across the Nullarbor, all the way to Western Australia where she waits tables in the Rose and Crown Hotel and some sick fuck holds a knife up to her neck on her way home one night and he throws her into his car and drives off up some dark highway and who knows what the fuck he's going to do to her but he slows his car at some roadworks along this highway where a road gang is widening the road at night and Mum, bravest woman in the world, just dives out of this car that's goin' at fifty clicks and she breaks her right arm on the bitumen and cuts her legs up but she's smart enough to get up and sprint like she sprinted when she was a girl who won every school sprint she ran in and she runs towards the lights of this road gang as this sick fuck in the car starts reversing back down the dark highway but Mum makes it to a mobile tea room where three roadworkers are inside having a smoko and Mum screams in hysterics about what just happened and one bloke bolts out the door to find the sick fuck's car screeching up the highway and this bloke comes back into the tea room and says, "You're safe now, you're safe," and that road gang bloke is Robert Bell, my old man.'

Lyle stops on the spot.

'Fuck,' he says.

'She never told you about the drop in the lake?'

'No, Eli, she never told me.'

We walk on.

'You really think Tytus would send Iwan Krol after us?' I ask.

'Business is business, kid,' Lyle says.

'That true, all that stuff about him?' I ask.

'What stuff?'

116

'Darren told me about what he does with the bodies. Is it true?'

'I've never cared to find out, Eli, and if you know what's good for you, you'll stop asking questions about what Iwan Krol likes to do with the bodies of dead criminals.'

We walk on.

'So where we going tomorrow?' I ask.

Lyle takes a deep breath, sighs.

'You're going to school,' he says.

'So what are we doing Saturday?' I say, unwavering, unsinkable.

'Teddy and I have some runs through Logan City.'

'Can we come?'

'No,' Lyle says.

'We'll just sit in the car.'

'What the hell you want to do that for?'

'I told you, I can watch things.'

'And what do you expect to see, Eli?'

'The same things I saw tonight. The things that you can't see.'

'What things?'

'Things like Teddy falling in love with Mum.'

# Boy Loses Luck

A drop in the lake. Mum is asked to be on the organising committee for the school fete that must meet every Saturday for the next month. She wants to do it because she never does that stuff. She hates all those Parents and Friends cows but that doesn't mean she doesn't want to feel like one of them every so often. Then Slim's chest starts playing up and his piss turns the colour of rust and his doctor tells him he has pneumonia. He's holed up resting in a small rental unit in Redcliffe on the other side of Brisbane to us. Mum and Lyle don't have a babysitter to watch over August and me on Saturdays.

Spring, 1986. I'm a high school kid. As opposed to looking out the windows of Darra State School, I take the bus each day with August now to look out the windows of Richlands State High School in Inala. I'm thirteen years old and like any self-respecting Queensland teenager with a deeper voice and bigger balls I want to experience new things, like spending this next month of Saturdays with Lyle on his heroin runs. I subtly remind Mum about August's and my burning fascination with burning things whenever we don't have adult supervision. Why, just the other day, I mention, I'd watched August set fire to a petrol-covered globe we found dumped beside a Lifeline charity bin in Oxley. 'Gonna set the world on fire!' I hollered as August held his magnifying glass over Australia and a hot apocalyptic dot of magnified sunlight descended over the city of Brisbane.

'I'll take 'em to Jindalee pool,' Lyle says. 'They can have a swim for a few hours, Teddy and I will make the run, then we'll grab them on the way home.'

Mum looks at August and me. 'What do you have left on your homework?'

'Just the Maths,' I say.

August nods. *Same as Eli.*

'You should have done the Maths first, got the hard stuff out of the way first,' Mum says.

'Sometimes life doesn't work like that, Mum,' I say. 'Sometimes you just can't get the hard stuff out of the way first.'

'Tell me about it,' she says. 'All right, you can go to the pool but you two better have your homework done by the time I get home.'

No problem. But we get to Jindalee pool and it's closed because the owner is laying a new lining across the empty fifty-metre pool.

'Fuck,' Lyle barks.

Teddy is in the driver's seat because he owns this 1976 olive green Mazda sedan, a mobile kiln even in spring, with hot brown vinyl passenger seats that stick to the undersides of my thighs, August's too, because he's wearing the same grey Kmart shorts.

Teddy looks at his watch.

'We gotta be at Jamboree Heights in seven minutes,' he says.

'Fuck,' Lyle says, shaking his head. 'Let's go.'

We pull up outside a two-storey house in Jamboree Heights. The house is made of yellow brick with a large aluminium garage door and a staircase running up the front of the house to a landing where a young shirtless Maori boy, maybe five years old, is furiously skipping on the spot with a pink plastic jump rope. It's so hot outside that the road bitumen through my car window shimmers with glassy mirage pockets of hot air.

Lyle and Teddy pause for a moment to scan the landscape, look into the car's rearview and side mirrors. Teddy pops the boot. They exit the Mazda at the same time and walk to the back of the car. Close the boot.

Lyle walks back to his front passenger door carrying a blue plastic chill box and leans into the car.

'You two just sit here and behave yourselves, all right?' he says. He goes to shut the door.

'You gotta be kidding, Lyle.' I say.

'What?'

'It must be fifty degrees in here,' I say. 'We'll be fried in ten minutes flat.'

Lyle sighs, takes a deep breath. He looks around, spots a small tree by the footpath.

'All right, wait under that tree over there,' he says.

'And what do we say when the neighbour comes out and asks us why we're sitting under his tree?' I ask. '"Just makin' a quick drug deal, mate. Don't mind us."'

'You're really startin' ta piss me off, Eli,' he says, shutting his door hard.

Then he opens the door on August's side.

'C'mon,' he says. 'But not a fucking word.'

We pass the kid with the skipping rope and he watches us, yellow snot resting at the bottom of his nose.

'Hey,' I say, passing.

The kid says nothing. Lyle knocks his knuckle against a security screen door frame. 'That you, Lyle?' comes a call from the dark living room. 'Come on in, bro.'

We enter the house. Lyle, then Teddy, then August, then me.

Two Maori men are resting on brown armchairs beside an empty three-seat couch. Smoke fills the living room. The men have full ashtrays on the armrests of their chairs. One man is skinny, with Maori tattoos across his left cheek; the other is the fattest man I've ever seen in my life, and he's the one who speaks.

'Lyle, Ted,' he says by way of greeting.

'Ezra,' Lyle says.

Ezra wears black shorts and a black floppy shirt and his legs are so big that the fat around his thighs spills over his kneecaps so the middle of his legs look like the faces of walruses without tusks. It's not the size of the man that I dwell on, though, it's the size of his black T-shirt, big enough to be a shade cover for Teddy's Mazda parked outside in the sun.

The skinny man is leaning forward in his armchair, peeling the jackets off a bowl of potatoes on a portable tray.

'Fuck, Lyle,' Ezra says, smiling as he looks at August and me. 'That's some prize parenting right there, my friend, bringing your kids to a drug deal.'

Ezra slaps his leg, looks at his skinny tattoo-faced friend who says nothing: '*Papara* of the Year, 'ey cuz!'

'They're not my kids,' Lyle says.

A woman enters the living room. 'Well, I'll take 'em then if they're not yours, Lyle,' she says, smiling at August and me as she sits down on the couch. She's barefoot, in a black singlet. A Maori woman with a tribal tattoo ringing her upper right arm. A line of tattooed dots runs across her right temple. She carries a portable tray of her own filled with carrots and sweet potatoes and a quarter of a pumpkin.

'Sorry Elsie,' Lyle says. 'They're Frankie's kids.'

'Thought they were too handsome to be your *tamariki tane*,' she says.

She gives August a wink. He smiles back.

'How many years you been looking after these boys, Lyle?' Elsie asks.

''Bout eight, nine years I've known them,' Lyle says.

Elsie looks at August and me.

'Eight, nine years?' she echoes. 'Whaddya reckon, boys? Reckon it's fair enough to say you're his kids now?'

August nods his head. Elsie turns to me for a response.

'Reckon that's fair enough,' I say.

Ezra and the skinny man are engrossed in a movie on TV featuring a hulking bronzed warrior at the head of a great ancient feast.

'What is best in life?' says a man on the screen dressed like Genghis Khan.

The bronzed warrior has his legs crossed, muscles like iron, a headband like a crown.

'Crush your enemies,' says the bronzed warrior. 'To see them driven before you and to hear the lamentation of their women.'

August and I are temporarily spellbound by this man.

'Who's that?' I ask.

'That's Arnold Schwarzenegger, bro,' Ezra says. '*Conan the Barbarian.*'

Arnold Schwarzenegger is mesmerising.

'This motherfucker's gonna be huge,' Ezra says.

'What's it about?' I ask.

'It's about warriors, bro, and wizards and swords and sorcery,' Ezra says. 'But most of all it's about revenge. Conan's travelling the world trying to find the bastard who fed his dad to dogs and chopped off his mum's head.'

I spot the video cassette recorder sitting beneath the television.

'You got a Sony Betamax?' I gasp.

'Of course, mate,' Ezra says. 'Better resolution, high-fidelity sounds, no fuzz, improved contrast, improved luminance noise.'

August and I dive immediately to the carpet to stare at the machine.

'What's luminance noise?' I ask.

'Fucked if I know,' Ezra says. 'That's what they wrote on the box.'

By the television is a bookshelf filled with black Betamax tapes with white sticky labels marked with movie titles. Hundreds of them. Some titles have been crossed out with blue ballpoint pen and other titles have been scribbled in beside them. *Raiders of the Lost Ark. ET the Extra Terrestrial. Rocky III. Time Bandits. Clash of the Titans.* August points his finger at one cassette in particular.

'You got *Excalibur*?' I holler.

'Shit yeah, bro?' Ezra beams. 'Helen Mirren, man. Smokin' hot that crazy witch.'

I nod heartily.

'Merlin,' I say.

'Crazy bastard,' Ezra rejoices.

I scan the videos. 'You got all the *Star Wars*!'

'What's the best *Star Wars*?' Ezra asks, with a tone that suggests he already knows the answer.

'*Empire*,' I say.

'Correct,' he says. 'Best bit?'

'Yoda's cave in Dagobah,' I say without contemplation.

'Oh, shit, Lyle, you got a deep one here,' Ezra says.

Lyle shrugs, rolls a cigarette from a packet of White Ox in his pocket.

'Dunno the fuck yer talkin' 'bout,' he says.

'Luke finds Vader in the cave and kills him and then the mask blows open and Luke's looking at himself,' Ezra says mystically. 'Strange shit, bro. What's this one's name?'

Lyle points at me.

'That's Eli,' he says. Points at August. 'That's August.'

'Hey Eli, what's up with that cave shit?' he asks. 'What's that shit mean, little bro?'

I keep looking at the video movie titles as I talk.

'The cave's the world and it's like Yoda says, the only thing in the cave is what you take in there with you. I reckon Luke already senses who his old man is. He already knows deep down. He's shit-scared of meeting his dad because he's shit-scared of the stuff that's already inside him, the dark side that's already in his blood.'

The living room goes quiet for a moment. August shoots me a long look. He nods knowingly, raising his eyebrows.

'Cool,' Ezra says.

Lyle places the blue chill box down by Ezra's chair.

'Got you boys some beers,' Lyle says.

Ezra nods his head to the skinny man, which is communication enough to cause the skinny man to hop up from his armchair and open the chill box. He digs his hand deep into the box filled with beer bottles and ice. He pulls out a rectangular block wrapped in a thick black plastic bag. He passes it immediately to Elsie. She screws up her face.

'You can check it, Rua, for fuck's sake,' she says.

The skinny man looks at Ezra for guidance. Ezra is engrossed in the movie but he allows time for one eye to dart towards Elsie, followed by a head nod towards the kitchen. Elsie hops up from the couch in a storm of sharp movements and snatches the black block from Rua's hand. 'Fuckin' dumb fucks,' she says.

She summons a smile for August and me. 'You boys want to come choose a soft drink?' she asks.

We look at Lyle. He nods approval. We follow her into the kitchen.

Rua passes beers to Ezra, Lyle and Teddy.

'When you Queenslanders going to get another beer other than bloody XXXX Bitter?' Ezra asks.

'We do have another beer,' Teddy says, sitting back in the three-seat couch to watch *Conan the Barbarian*. 'We got XXXX Draught.'

*

It's almost 1 p.m. when we're eating potato scallops at a snack bar along the Moorooka Magic Mile, the stretch of road in Moorooka fifteen minutes' drive from Jamboree Heights, where people across Brisbane come to buy their cars from a strip of dealerships that range in quality and prestige from 'All our cars have airbags!' to 'All our cars have windscreens!'

We sit around a white round plastic table eating from a ripped-open brown paper parcel of battered potato scallops, beef croquettes, seafood sticks, large bright yellow dim sims and hot chips made from old oil so they look like bent cigarette butts and taste about as good.

'Who wants the last beef croquette?' Teddy asks.

Teddy's the only one who's been eating the beef croquettes. Teddy's always the only one who eats the beef croquettes.

'All yours, Teddy,' I say.

August and I sip from purple cans of Kirks Pasito, our second favourite soft drink. Slim put us onto Pasito. He drinks nothing but Kirks soft drinks because they're from Queensland and he says he knew an old bloke who worked for the original Kirks company, which was actually the Helidon Spa Water Company, which made a name for itself in the 1880s bottling the restorative spring waters of Helidon, near Toowoomba, which local Aboriginals said gave them the strength they needed to fend off any greedy souls who might want to exploit the benefits of their personally significant spring water supplies. I've never tasted the natural spring waters of Helidon, but I doubt they match the sweet, restorative powers of an ice cold sarsaparilla.

'Elsie had Big Sars,' I say, selectively biting my potato scallop in an attempt to create the shape of Australia. August's biting his so it looks like a ninja star. 'She had a whole shelf of small soft drink cans. She had the whole Kirks range. Lemon Squash. Creaming Soda. Old Stoney Ginger Beer. You name it.'

Lyle's rolling himself another White Ox.

'You see anything else, Captain Details, when you went with Elsie into the kitchen?' he asks.

'Yeah, saw heaps,' I say. 'She had a whole pack of unopened Iced VoVo biscuits in the fridge on the shelf above the vegetable trays. I reckon they must have had Ribbetts last night because there was a silver takeaway box on the shelf above the Iced VoVos and even though the takeaway box had a lid on it and I couldn't see inside it I knew it was Ribbetts because I could see the Ribbetts barbecue sauce spilling over the edge of the box and there is no barbecue sauce like Ribbetts barbecue sauce.'

Lyle lights his rolled smoke.

'Any details you picked up that weren't related to what Elsie had in her fridge?' he asks, turning his head to the right to avoid blowing smoke over the potato scallops.

'Yeah, saw heaps,' I say, shoving three chips into my mouth, cold now and losing their crunch. 'There was a Maori weapon hanging on the wall above the kitchen bench and I asked Elsie what it was and she said it was called a *mere*. It was a big club shaped like a leaf and made of something called greenstone and it was passed down through generations in her family. And she stood at the sink carefully cutting the wrapping on your heroin block on the kitchen sink bench and levelling a set of kitchen scales and as she did this she told me about the horrible things her great-great-great-great-grandfather, Hamiora, did with this club. Like once there was this chief named Marama from another tribe who was always bullying and intimidating Hamiora's tribe and when Hamiora visited this rival chief's HQ ...'

'I don't know if ancient Maori chiefs had HQs,' Teddy says.

'His hut, the big rival chief's hut,' I clarify. 'When Hamiora visited Marama's hut the rival chief began to laugh at the size and shape of Hamiora's *mere* because it looked so unthreatening, like a stone rolling pin or something you might use to roll out your biscuits and Hamiora was in the centre of all these rival warriors as Marama was making jokes about him and encouraging his people to laugh and joke about Hamiora's family weapon and Hamiora started laughing along with them and then Hamiora, quicker than you can say "jam drop biscuit", struck Marama across the head with his ancient family weapon they'd all been laughing about.'

I pick up a small dim sim.

'Ol' Hamiora could wield this greenstone club the way Viv Richards wields a cricket bat and he specialised in this forearm thrust move where he hit someone in the temple but at the point of impact he gave the club a sharp twist.'

I break the top third of the small dim sim off in one tear.

'He knocked Marama's whole skullcap off in one blow and the rest of the tribe was so stunned by the scene that they didn't have time to draw their weapons when the rest of Hamiora's men – all distant relatives of Elsie's as well – sprang from some bushes and attacked the dumbstruck rival tribesmen.'

I drop the skullcap end of the dim sim in my mouth.

'And as Elsie's tellin' this story she's carefully unwrapping the gear and not really looking at where my eyes are and I'm saying things like, "Yeah, really?" and, "No wayyyyy!", like I'm really engrossed in the story but at the same time my eyes are looking all over the kitchen for details. The right eye's where it should be but I got that loose left eye darting about all over the place, taking things in.'

Lyle and Teddy sneak a brief look at each other. Lyle shakes his head.

'When August and I duck down to look inside the fridge at Elsie's collection of Kirks soft drinks she doesn't realise I've actually got a busy eye looking at her at the bench with the gear and she takes a sharp knife and slices a few edges off the smack block like she's shaving thin slices of cheddar from a block of Coon. And she gathers these shavings into a little one-gram ball and she scrapes it into a small black plastic photographic film canister with a grey lid. She puts this canister into the pocket of her jeans and then she wraps the block back up and takes it out to you guys in the lounge room and you guys have got your heads glued to *Conan the Barbarian* and she says, "All good", and nobody says shit back to her.

'Then she comes back into the kitchen and she finishes telling me this ancient yarn about great-great-great-great-grandfather chief Hamiora and dumb, dumb, dumb, dumb chief Marama and I'm seeing all these details, like there's a bunch of mail by their phone, letters from the council and bills from Telecom and then there's a piece of paper with all these names and numbers on it and your name and number is on there, Lyle, and Tytus's name was on there and then there was a Kylie and a Mal and a number next to someone named Snapper and another number next to a Dustin Vang …'

'Dustin Vang?' Teddy says, turning to Lyle, who nods his head, raising his eyebrows.

'Makes sense,' Lyle says.

'Who's Dustin Vang?' I ask.

'If Bich Dang was Hamiora, then Dustin Vang would be her Marama,' Lyle says.

'He's good news,' Teddy says.

'Why?' I ask.

'Healthy competition,' Teddy says. 'If Bich isn't the only importer on the block, it's good news for Tytus because Bich will have to start offering more competitive prices and maybe she won't take such pleasure any more from fucking us in the arse.'

'Not good news for Tytus, though, if Ezra is thinking about going direct to a new supplier,' Lyle says. 'I'll have a chat to Tytus.'

Teddy chuckles.

'Not bad, Captain Details.'

\*

Nothing connects a city quite like South-East Asian heroin. This glorious month of Saturdays with the Jindalee pool shut for renovations find Lyle, Teddy, August and me crisscrossing the city of Brisbane between every cultural minority, every gang, every obscure subculture my sprawling and hot city nurses in its sweaty bosom.

The Italians in South Brisbane. The collar-up rugby crowd in Ballymore. The drummers and guitarists and the buskers and the busted bands of Fortitude Valley.

'You can't say a word about this to yer mum, ya hear,' Lyle says as we pull up outside the Highgate Hill–based State headquarters of a national neo-Nazi group, White Hammer, led by a softly spoken and thin twenty-five-year-old man named Timothy who is open enough to tell Lyle during a genial exchange of cash and drugs that he does not actually shave his skinhead but is, in fact, naturally bald, which makes me silently consider what struck him first along his unique philosophical journey, the notion of white supremacy or that of white male pattern baldness.

I don't know what I expected from drug dealing. More romance, perhaps. A sense of danger and suspense. I realise now that the average street grunt suburban drug dealer is not too far removed from the common pizza delivery boy. Half these deals Lyle and Teddy are making I could make in half the time riding through the south-west Brisbane suburbs on my Mongoose BMX with the gear in my backpack. August could probably do it even faster because he rides faster than me and he's got a ten-speed Malvern Star racer.

\*

August and I do our Maths homework in the back of Teddy's Mazda as we cross the Story Bridge from north to south and south to north, the bridge of stories, stories like the one about the boys who beat the fire, stories like the one about the mute boy and his little brother who never asked for anything but the answers to the questions.

August holds a ten-digit scientific pocket calculator he got for his birthday, tapping numbers and turning the calculator upside down to form words. 7738461375 = SLEIGHBELL. 5318008 = BOOBIES. He taps another bunch of numbers. Proudly shows me the calculator screen. ELIBELL.

'Hey, Teddy,' I ask. 'At a school carnival twenty out of eighty tickets sold were early admission tickets. What percentage of early admission tickets were sold?'

Teddy looks into the rearview mirror. 'C'mon mate, for fuck's sake, how many twenties go into eighty?'

'Four.'

'So ...'

'So twenty is a quarter of the tickets?'

'Correct.'

'Quarter of a hundred is ... twenty-five per cent?'

'Yes, mate,' Teddy says, shaking his head, stunned. 'Fuck me, Lyle, don't leave your tax return up to these two, all right.'

'Tax return?' Lyle says, feigning puzzlement. 'That one of those algebra principles?'

The drug runs must be done on Saturdays because most of the third-tier drug dealers Lyle sells to have day jobs during the week. Tytus Broz is first tier. Lyle is second tier. Lyle sells to the third-tier drug dealers who, in turn, sell to the man or woman on the street or, in Kev Hunt's case, the man or woman out at sea. Kev is a trawler fisherman who has a side business as a third-tier drug dealer supplying many of the users in the Moreton Bay prawn trawling scene. He's out at sea most weekdays. So we make a drive out to his place in Bald Hills on a Saturday just as he likes it. It's good business. Lyle adapts to his clients' needs. Shane Bridgman, for example, is a lawyer in the city who has a side business as a third-tier drug dealer for the George Street legal set. He's always at work and never at home during the week but he sure doesn't want any drug deals taking place in his office, three buildings down from the Queensland Supreme Court. So we make a drive out to his place in Wilston, in the inner northern suburbs. He makes the deal in his sunroom while his wife bakes blueberry muffins in the kitchen and their son bowls medium pacers at a black bin in the backyard.

Lyle is masterful in these Saturday deals. He's a diplomat, a cultural ambassador, a representative of his boss, Tytus Broz, a conduit between the king and his people.

Lyle says he approaches a drug deal in the same way he approaches Mum when she's in a bad mood. Stay on your toes. Stay alert. Don't let them stand too close to the kitchen knives. Be flexible, patient, adaptable. The buyer/angry Mum is always right. Lyle bends his emotions to the buyer's/Mum's feelings at any given moment. When a Chinese property developer bitches about council red tape, he nods his head empathetically. When the head of the Bandidos motorcycle gang bitches about the poor quality of the revving in his Harley-Davidson motorcycle, Lyle nods with what looks to me like genuine concern, and this is the same look he gave Mum the other night when she was bemoaning the fact that Mum and Lyle never make an attempt to befriend any of the other parents at our school. Just make the deal, kiss the woman you love, take your wages and get out of the room alive.

*

On our last Saturday drug run Lyle tells August and me about the underground room with the red phone. Lyle built the room himself, dug it out from the bottom up, dug a hole deep in the ground beneath the cramped space under the house that August and I were never allowed to crawl into, and up into the house. A secret space built from thirteen hundred bricks bought from the Darra brickworks. The secret room where Mum and Lyle could store large boxes of weed in their formative dope-dealing days.

'What do you use it for now you're not running weed?' I ask.

'It's for a rainy day when I need to run away and hide,' he says.

'From who?'

'From anyone,' he says.

'What's the phone for?' I ask.

Teddy looks across at Lyle.

'It's connected to a line that goes straight to another red phone just like it in Tytus's house in Bellbowrie,' Lyle says.

Lyle looks into the back seat to gauge our reactions.

'So it was Tytus we were speaking to that day?'

'No,' he says. 'No, Eli.' We share a long look in the rearview mirror. 'You weren't speaking to anyone at all.'

He steps on the gas, speeds on to our last job.

*

'I felt something today I never felt before,' Mum says, forking spaghetti onto our dinner plates at the dinner table, the same laminated green Formica table with metal legs that Lyle ate cherry *babka* at as a boy.

Today was the school fete. For eight hours beneath a hot Saturday sun Mum was in charge of three sideshow alley stalls on the Richlands State High School oval. She ran the fishpond game where, for fifty cents, kids were tasked with hooking flat Styrofoam fish with a curtain rod and string; underneath these fish was a colour-coded sticker that corresponded with a colour-coded novelty toy prize worth approximately the value of the pony shit I stepped on today by the 'Uncle Bob's Barnyard' animal display. The most popular game of the whole sideshow alley, by some way, was an original game that Mum developed herself, piggybacking on the irresistible pull of *Star Wars* to raise much-needed funds for the Richlands State High School Parents and Friends Association. Her 'Han Solo Master Blaster Challenge' asked potential saviours of the galaxy to dislodge three of August's and my Imperial stormtroopers balanced on stands placed at increasingly ambitious distances, using a large water pistol she painted black to resemble Han's trusty blaster. She placed the target stormtroopers masterfully, putting the first two at more than achievable distances, thus filling her largely five- to twelve-year-old customers up on the addictive lustre of early success, but placing the third and final stormtrooper at such a distance that a child would need to access and bend the powers of the Force to land a long and arcing single prize-winning water pistol shot. Mum was also, however, in charge of the fete's least popular attraction, 'Pop Stick Pandemonium', one hundred pop sticks – ten marked with prize-winning stars – in a wheelbarrow full of sand. She could have promised the very meaning of life at the end of every one of those pop sticks and she still would have made $6.50 over eight hours.

'I felt like part of the community,' Mum says. 'I felt like I belonged, ya know.'

I watch Lyle smiling at her. He has his right fist to his chin. All she's doing is dumping large spoonfuls of her bolognese sauce with extra bacon and rosemary onto our plates, but Lyle is looking at her, wide-eyed and awed, like she's playing 'Paint It Black' on a golden harp with strings made of fire.

'That's great, hon,' Lyle says.

Teddy calls from the kitchen: 'Beer, Lyle?'

'Yeah, mate,' Lyle says. 'In the door shelf.'

Teddy's staying for dinner. Teddy's always staying for dinner.

'That's real great, Frankie,' Teddy says, entering the living room from the kitchen. He wraps an arm around Mum's shoulder unnecessarily. Holds her unnecessarily. 'We're proud of ya, matey,' he says. All buddy buddy like. I mean, like, gimme a fucking break, Ted. Right here at Lena and Aureli's table?

'I might be mistaken, but is there a new little twinkle in those blue eyes?' he says. He rubs his right thumb across Mum's cheekbone.

Lyle and I share a glance. August shoots a look at me. *Get a load of this shit. Right here in front of his best friend. I've never trusted this fuckin' guy. Comes across all nice as pie but it's those nice as pie fucks you really gotta watch out for, Eli. I can't tell who he's in love with more: Mum, Lyle or himself.*

I nod. *Hearing you, brother.*

'I don't know,' Mum shrugs, a little embarrassed by her sunny disposition. 'It just felt good to be part of something so ...'

'Boring?' I offer. 'Suburban?'

Mum smiles, holding a spoonful of bolognese mince in midair as she thinks.

'So normal,' she says.

She dumps the mince on top of my pasta and gives me one of those quick and beautiful half-smiles that she can send down a one-way corridor of devotion directly to the person she is aiming at, a tunnel of lifelong love invisible to all others, yet I know August has a tunnel just like it, and Lyle does too.

'It's great, Mum,' I say. And I've never been more serious in my life. 'I reckon normal suits ya.'

I reach for the Kraft parmesan cheese that smells like August's vomit. I sprinkle cheese flakes across my spaghetti and I dig my fork into Mum's pasta and twirl the fork twice.

Then Tytus Broz walks into our living room.

The top of my spine knows him best. The top of my spine recognises all that white hair and that white suit and the gritted white teeth in his forced smile. The rest of me is frozen and confused but my spine knows that Tytus Broz really is walking into our living room and it shivers from top to bottom and I shudder involuntarily like I do sometimes when I'm taking a piss in the troughs of Lyle's favourite pub, the Regatta Hotel in Toowong.

Lyle's mouth is full of pasta when he sees Tytus, watches him, stunned, as he paces into our house, somehow finding his way in from the back door beyond the kitchen past the toilet.

Lyle says his name like a question. 'Tytus?'

August and Mum are facing Lyle and me across the table and they turn their bodies around to see Tytus walking in, followed by another man, bigger than Tytus, darker eyes, darker mood. Oh fuck. Oh fuck, fuck, fuck me. What's he doing here?

Iwan Krol. And two more of Tytus's muscle goon thugs walking in behind Iwan. They wear rubber flip-flops like Iwan Krol, tight Stubbies shorts and tucked-in button-up collared cotton shirts; one of them is wiry and bald and the other is heavy with an upturned smile and three chins.

'Tytus!' Mum says, slipping immediately into host mode. She hops up from her chair.

'Please don't hop up, Frances,' Tytus says.

Iwan Krol rests a hand gently on Mum's shoulder and something in the gesture tells her to sit back down. It's now that I see he's carrying an army-green duffle bag, which he drops silently onto the living room floor by the table.

Teddy is holding a fork in his right hand. He has two paper towels stuffed into the neckline of his dark blue Bonds shirt, and his lips are red with bolognese sauce, like a clown who smudges his lipstick. 'Tytus, is everything okay?' Teddy asks. 'You want to join us for ...'

Tytus isn't even looking at Teddy when he puts a forefinger to his mouth and says, 'Sssshhh.'

He's looking at Lyle. Silence. Maybe a whole minute of silence or maybe it's just thirty seconds but it feels like thirty days of thunderclap-loud-as-fuck silent staring between Tytus and Lyle. Vantage points and details, a single moment stretched to infinity.

A tattoo on the wiry goon's left arm. Bugs Bunny in a Nazi uniform. August gripping his pasta spoon, nervously thumbing the handle. This moment from Mum's point of view, sitting confused in a loose peach-coloured singlet, her head darting between faces, searching for answers and finding none but the answer on the face of the only man she has ever really loved. Fear.

Then Lyle mercifully cuts the silence.

'August,' he says.

August? August? What the fuck does this moment have to do with August?

August turns back around and stares at Lyle.

And Lyle starts writing something in the air. His right forefinger flows swiftly through the air like a quill and August's eyes track the flurry of words that I can't make out because I'm not facing him and I can't spin them around properly in my mirror mind.

'What's he doing?' Tytus spits.

Lyle keeps writing words in the air, swiftly and surely, and August reads them, nodding his head in understanding with every word.

'Stop that,' spits Tytus.

Tytus screams. 'Stop that shit!' He turns to the heavy goon and through gritted teeth, he furiously screams, 'Please stop him doing that fucking shit.'

But Lyle, trance-like, keeps on scribbling words that August registers. Word after scribbled word until the heavy three-chinned goon thug's right forearm connects with Lyle's nose and he is thrown back off his chair onto the floor of the living room, his nose erupting with blood that runs down his chin.

'Lyle,' I scream, rushing down to him, hugging his chest. 'Leave 'im alone.'

Lyle gags on a glob of blood in his mouth.

'Jesus Christ, Tytus, what's—' Teddy stammers, stopped immediately by the blade point of a sharpened silver Bowie knife that Iwan Krol whips to his chin. This blade is a monster with teeth, it's alien-like and gleaming, hissing on one sharp slicing side and shrieking with a serrated opposite edge, evil metal teeth for hacking things I can only imagine – necks mostly.

'You shut the fuck up, Teddy, and you might survive this night,' Iwan says.

Teddy recoils cautiously in his seat. Tytus looks at Lyle on the ground.

'Get him outta here,' Tytus says.

The wiry thug joins the heavy thug standing over Lyle and they drag him along the living room floor for two metres with me hanging onto him around his chest.

'Leave him alone,' I scream through tears. 'Leave 'im alone!'

They pull Lyle to his feet and I drop off him, hard to the ground.

'I'm sorry, Frankie,' Lyle says. 'I love you so much, Frankie. I'm so sorry, Frankie.'

The wiry thug drives a fist into Lyle's mouth and Mum rounds the living room table with a bowl of her spaghetti bolognese that she cracks over the head of the sucker-punching goon.

'Let him go,' she screams. The caged animal that's spent a lifetime inside her and has only seen daylight three or four times wraps its arms around the neck of the heavy thug, Mum's monster digging its full-moon wolf fingernails deep into his cheeks and face, so deep the thug's skin comes off in scratches of fury and blood. She's howling now like she did when she was locked away for all those days in Lena's room. Banshee wails, terrifying and primal. I've never been so scared in my life, of Mum, of Tytus Broz, of Lyle's blood on my hands and face as he's dragged on down the hallway of the house.

'Stop that bitch,' Tytus says calmly.

Iwan Krol rushes around the kitchen table, Bowie knife in his right hand, and August rushes around the table from the opposite side and meets Iwan Krol at the start of the hallway. He raises his fists like an old 1920s boxer. Iwan Krol instantly swipes the blade at August's face and August ducks this attack, but it was only a diversion for Iwan Krol's swift left leg kick that sweeps August's feet off the ground so he lands heavily on his back. 'Don't you two dare fuckin' move,' Iwan Krol barks at us as he rushes down the hall behind Mum.

'Mum, behind you,' I shout. But she's too rabid to register, desperately clutching at Lyle's arms, trying to drag him back down the hallway. Iwan Krol switches the Bowie knife into his left hand and, with two impossibly quick and hard backhand thrusts, drives the knife's handle butt into Mum's left temple. She drops to the floor, her head hanging loosely over her left shoulder, her right calf bent back behind her right thigh like she's a crash test dummy who's hit one too many walls.

'Frankie,' Lyle screams as he's dragged out the front door. 'Frankiiiieeeee!'

August and I rush to Mum but Iwan Krol meets us in the hallway and drags us back to the dinner table, our spindly thirteen- and fourteen-year-old legs not powerful enough to get a firm grip on the ground to fight back against the force of the killer's furious dragging. He's pulling me so hard my shirt's popping up over my head and all I can see is the orange cotton blanket of the shirt front, and darkness.

He throws us onto our dining table chairs. Our backs are turned to Mum, who's lying in the hallway unconscious, or worse, I don't know.

'Sit the fuck down,' Iwan Krol says.

I'm struggling to breathe in the fear and the violence and confusion. Iwan Krol takes a rope from the army-green duffle bag. In a flurry of movement he wraps the rope around August three times and ties him tight to his dining chair.

'What are you doing?' I spit.

Tears and snot are pouring through my nose and I can barely stay upright on my seat, but August just sits quietly on his seat with a closed-mouth snarl directed at Tytus Broz, who is staring back at August.

I'm heaving deep gasps of air between tears and I can't seem to get enough in my lungs and Tytus is bothered by it.

'Breathe, for fuck's sake, breathe,' he says.

August reaches his right foot out and rests it on my left foot. It calms me but I don't know why. I breathe.

'That's it,' Tytus says. He snaps a sharp look at Teddy, sitting stunned at the head of the table. 'Leave.'

'They don't know shit these boys, Tytus,' Teddy offers urgently.

Tytus is already staring back at August when he addresses Teddy's words.

'I won't say it again,' he says.

Teddy hops to his feet, rushes out of the living room and down the hallway, stepping over Mum's unconscious body along the way. Even through all my fear and concern for Mum in the hallway and for Lyle, who's been dragged to hell knows where, there's still room enough in my thoughts for the notion that Teddy is a gutless prick.

With August tied to his chair, unable to move his arms, Iwan Krol stands directly behind me, the Bowie knife in his right hand by his waist. I can feel him behind me, smell him behind me.

Tytus breathes deep himself. He shakes his head, frustrated.

'Now, boys, please allow me to fully illuminate the unfortunate situation you two find yourselves in,' he says. 'If, through the course of this discussion, it appears I am going too fast for your youthful ears it is only because, in roughly fifteen minutes, and as soon as I exit this miserable house, two senior police detectives will enter this house through the front door to arrest your mother, supposing, of course, she remains in the land of the living, for her significant role as a courier for the head of a growing outer-western Brisbane heroin supply ring run by Lyle Orlik, who, as of approximately two minutes ago, has mysteriously vanished off the face of the planet.'

'Where are you taking him?' I shout. 'I'm gonna tell the police everything. It's you.' I'm standing up now and I don't even realise it. I'm spitting now. I'm pointing now. 'It's you. You're behind everything. You're fucking evil.'

A hard slap from Iwan Krol across my cheek drops me back into my chair.

Tytus turns and paces across the living room. He comes to a cabinet and picks up an old figurine of Lena's, a Polish salt miner made out of salt from a cavernous salt mine Lena's ancestors helped build in southern Poland.

'You are right and you are wrong, young man,' Tytus says. 'No, you will not tell the police everything because they will not speak to you. But, yes, I am indeed as you describe. I came to terms with that fact long ago. But I am not so evil as to drag children into the works of evil men. I'll leave that to men like Lyle.'

He places the salt mine figurine back on the cabinet.

'Do you boys know what loyalty is?' Tytus asks.

We don't answer. He smiles.

'That's a kind of loyalty in itself, your not answering,' he says. 'You remain loyal to a man you do not know, a man whose disloyalty to me has placed you in the position you now find yourselves in.'

He turns on the spot, clears his throat, thinks some more.

'Now, I have a question to ask you boys and before you answer it, or choose not to answer it, I simply ask that you briefly consider not putting the loyalty you have for Lyle before the loyalty you have to yourselves because, as cruel fate has so tragically determined, yourselves are precisely all you two appear to have now.'

I look across at August. He doesn't look across at me.

Tytus nods at Iwan Krol and, in an instant, Iwan Krol has a firm and immovable grip on my right hand. His forceful arms plant my palm on the green top of Lena's dining table, right next to the bowl of spaghetti I was eating before the world collapsed in on itself, before the mountains crumbled into the sea, before the stars fell from the sky and formed this terrifying evening.

'What the fuck are you doing?'

I can smell his underarms. I can smell his Old Spice cologne and his clothes smell like cigarettes. He's leaning over me with his weight on my right forearm and his big hands have bones of iron and they are trying to spread my right forefinger out, my lucky forefinger with my lucky freckle on my lucky middle knuckle. My hand instinctively makes a fist but he's so strong and he's wild on the inside and I can feel that through his hands, his black electricity, his lack of reason, no emotion other than rage. He squeezes my fist hard and my forefinger pops out, rests flat on the table.

I'm going to be sick.

August looks across at my finger flat on the table.

'What did he say, August?' Tytus says.

August looks back at Tytus.

'What did he just write, August?' Tytus asks.

August feigns a puzzled look, confused.

Tytus nods at Iwan Krol behind me and then the blade of the Bowie knife is touching my forefinger, just above the bottom knuckle.

Vomit. In my stomach. In my throat. Time slowing.

'He scribbled a message in the air,' Tytus spits. 'What did he say, August?'

The blade comes down harder into the finger, draws blood and I draw breath.

'He doesn't talk, Tytus,' I scream. 'He doesn't talk. He couldn't tell you even if he wanted to.'

August keeps staring at Tytus and Tytus keeps staring at August.

'What did he say, August?' Tytus asks.

August looks at my finger. Iwan Krol presses the blade down harder, so hard now it's cut through all my skin and flesh and is lodging into my finger bone.

'We don't know, Tytus, please,' I scream. 'We don't know.'

Dizzy now. Frantic. Cold sweat. Tytus stares deep into August's eyes. He nods again at Iwan Krol and he pushes the Bowie knife down harder. Old Spice and his breath and that blade, that endless blade digging into my bone marrow. My marrow. My weak marrow. My weak fingers.

I howl in pain, a wail so unbridled and raw it rounds out with a high-pitched squeal, from white pain and shock and disbelief.

'Please don't,' I howl through tears. 'Please don't do this.'

The blade goes deeper still and I roar with agony.

Then a voice joins the sounds in the room from a place I can't register.

A voice to my left that I couldn't hear properly over my screams but this voice makes Iwan Krol ease the pressure on the knife. A voice I've never heard before in my conscious life. Tytus leans closer to the table, closer to August.

'Come again?' Tytus says.

Silence. August licks his lips and clears his throat.

'I have something to say,' August says.

And the only thing to tell me I'm not dreaming this is the blood running from my lucky forefinger.

Tytus brightens. Nods his head.

August looks across at me. And I know that look. That slightly upturned half-smile, the way his left eye squints. That's the way he says sorry without saying sorry. That's the way he says sorry for something bad that is about to happen that he is no longer in control of.

He turns to Tytus Broz.

'Your end is a dead blue wren,' August says.

Tytus smiles. He looks at Iwan Krol, puzzled. He chuckles. A face-saving chuckle designed to mask something I never expected to see on his face in this moment. There is fear across his face in this moment.

'I'm sorry, August, could you please repeat that?' Tytus asks.

August speaks and he sounds like me. I never knew he would sound like me.

'Your end is a dead blue wren,' he says.

Tytus scratches his chin, takes a deep breath, thin eyes studying August. Then he nods at Iwan Krol and the blade of the Bowie knife smacks against Lena's table and my lucky forefinger is no longer attached to my hand.

My eyelids close and open. Life and the blackness. Home and the blackness. My lucky finger with the lucky freckle resting on the table in a pool of blood. Eyelids close. The blackness. And they open. Tytus picks up my finger with a white silk handkerchief, folds it up carefully. Eyelids close. The blackness. And they open.

My brother, August. Eyelids close. And open. My brother, August. Eyelids close.

The blackness.

# Boy Busts Out

The magic car. The magic flying Holden Kingswood. The magic sky, light blues and pinks, outside the window. A cloud so fluffy and big and misshapen it's a prime candidate for August's game of 'What's that one look like to you?'

'That's an elephant,' I say. 'There's the big ears, left and right, and the trunk going down the middle.'

'Nah,' he says, because he talks in the magic car dream. 'That's an axe. There's the blades, left and right, and the axe handle going down the middle.'

The car turns in the sky and we roll along the tan vinyl back seat.

'Why are we flying?' I ask.

'We always fly,' August says. 'But don't worry, it won't last long.'

The car dips sharply in the air and takes a leftward arcing drop through the clouds.

I look into the car's rearview mirror. The deep blue eyes of Robert Bell. The deep blue eyes of my father.

'I don't want to be here any more, Gus,' I say, the force of the plummeting car pushing us back hard against our seats.

'I know,' he says. 'But we always end up here. No matter what I do. It makes no difference.'

There's water below us. But this is like no water I've seen. This water is silver and it glows, throbbing with silver light.

'What is that?' I ask.

'It's the moon,' says August.

The car slams into the glowing silver surface and the surface breaks into liquid as the car plunges into the suffocating green of a world beneath the sea. The magic Holden Kingswood fills with water and bubbles flow from our mouths as we stare at each other. August isn't bothered about being underwater like this, not phased in the slightest. He lifts his right hand and points his right forefinger out and slowly writes three words in the water.

*Boy swallows universe.*

And I raise my right hand up because I want to write something back and I go to extend my right forefinger but it's not there any more, just a blood-filled knuckle hole leaking red blood into the sea. I scream. Then the redness. Then the blackness.

\*

I wake. Blurred vision focusing into a white hospital room. The throbbing pain in my right hand sharpens everything. Everything inside me, all my cells and all my blood molecules, rushing and then smashing against the dam wall of the heavily bandaged and taped forefinger knuckle that once connected to my lucky forefinger with the lucky freckle. But wait, the pain isn't so bad now. There's a warm feeling in my belly. A floaty feeling, something fuzzy and giddy and cosy.

A liquid drip pulses from the centre of the top of my left hand. So thirsty. So sick. So surreal here. A hard hospital bed and a blanket over me and the smell of antiseptic. A curtain that looks like Lena's old olive green bedsheets is connected to a U-shaped rod surrounding the hospital bed. The ceiling is made up of square tiles with hundreds of tiny holes in them. A man sitting on my right in a chair. A tall man. A slender man. A slim man.

'Slim.'

'How you doin', kid?'

'Water,' I say.

'Yeah, matey,' he says.

He takes a white plastic cup from a trolley beside my bed, puts the cup to my lips.

I drink the whole cup. He pours me another and I drink that one too and lean back, weak and exhausted by the small effort. I look again at my missing finger. A right thumb, a bandaged knuckle and three other fingers sticking from my hand like an uneven cactus.

'I'm sorry, kid,' Slim says. 'It's gone.'

'It's not gone,' I say. 'Tytus Broz ...'

Movement makes my hand throb in agony. Slim nods.

'I know, Eli,' he says. 'Just lie back.'

'Where am I?'

'Royal Brisbane.'

'Where's Mum?' I ask.

'She's with the cops,' Slim says. He drops his head. 'You won't be seeing her for a while, Eli.'

'Why?' I ask. And the tears inside me rush to my eyes the way the blood inside me is rushing to the nub of my forefinger, but there's no dam stopping the tears and they pour out of me. 'What happened?'

Slim moves his chair closer to the bed. He stares at me silently.

'You know what happened,' he says. 'And any minute now a woman named Dr Brennan will come in here and she'll want to know what happened too. And you need to decide what you want to tell her because she will believe you. She does not believe what the ambulance officers told her, which is what your mother told them moments before the police arrived.'

'What did she tell them?'

'She told them you and August were horsing around with an axe. She told them you were holding one of your Star Wars figurines against a log and you asked August to chop it in half and he chopped Darth Vader in two, along with your finger.'

'An axe?' I say. 'I was just dreaming about an axe. A cloud that looked like an axe. It felt so clear it could have been a memory.'

'They're the only dreams worth having, the ones you remember,' Slim says.

'What did August tell the cops?'

'The same he says about anything,' Slim says. 'Sweet fuck all.'

'Why'd they take Lyle away, Slim?' I ask.

Slim sighs. 'Forget about that, mate.'

'Why, Slim?'

Slim takes a deep breath.

'He was making his own side deals with Bich Dang,' he says.

'Side deals?'

'He was operatin' behind the boss's back, kid,' Slim says. 'He was building towards something. He had a whole plan.'

'What plan?'

'He was going to get out. He called it the "nest egg". Slowly build your stash, sit on it for a year or two. Let time and the market double its value. Somehow Tytus got wind of it and reacted as expected. He's now severed ties with Bich Dang. He'll use Dustin Vang now as his supplier. And when Bich Dang finds out about Lyle it's gonna be World War III in the streets of Darra.'

Nest egg. World War III. Find out about Lyle. Fuck.

'Fuck,' I say.

'Don't fuckin' swear.'

I weep, drag the right sleeve of my hospital gown across my eyes.

'What is it, Eli?'

'It's my fault,' I say.

'What?'

'It was my idea, Slim. I told him about the market. I told him about supply and demand, what we talked about, you know, Taskforce Janus 'n' that.'

Slim pulls his White Ox from a top shirt pocket, rolls a cigarette that he'll keep in his packet and light as soon as he exits the hospital. This is how I know Slim is anxious, by his rolling a cigarette he cannot light.

'When did you tell him that?' Slim asks.

'Few months ago,' I say.

'Well, he's been doin' it for six months, kid, so it sure as shit ain't your fault.'

'But ... that's ... impossible ... He lied to me.'

Lyle lied to me. The man who said he couldn't lie. He lied to me.

'There's a big difference between lying to a kid and not telling him something for his own good,' Slim says.

'What did they do with him, Slim?'

He shakes his head. 'I don't know, mate,' he says, tender. 'I don't want to know and maybe you shouldn't either.'

'There's no difference between lying and not telling, Slim,' I say. 'They're both weak as piss.'

'Careful,' warns Slim.

Maybe it's the pain in the knuckle where my finger once was that's putting this rage in me, or maybe it's the memory of Mum knocked out in Lena and Aureli Orlik's hallway.

'They're monsters, Slim. They're fucking psychopaths running the suburbs. I'm gonna tell 'em everything. I'm gonna tell 'em every bit of it. Iwan Krol and all the bodies he's cut up. How saintly Tytus Broz and "Back Off" Bich Dang and fucking Dustin Vang supply half the heroin across Brisbane's west. They came into our house while we were eatin' spaghetti and they took Lyle away. They just took him away from us, Slim.'

I sit up on my right elbow to get closer to Slim and a sharp pain localises around my knuckles.

'You gotta tell me, Slim,' I say. 'Where were they taking him?'

Slim shakes his head. 'I don't know, kid, but you can't be thinking about that now. You need to be thinking very carefully about what reasons your mother had for making up that story. She's protecting you boys, mate. She'll swallow that shit for you two and you'll swallow that shit for her.'

My left hand on my forehead. I rub my eyes, wipe tears from my eyes. I'm dizzy. Confused. I want to get out. I want to play *Missile Command* on Atari. I want to stare for ten minutes at Jane Seymour in Mum's *Women's Weekly*. I want to pick my fucking nose with my lucky fucking forefinger.

'Where's August?' I ask.

'The cops took him to your father's house.'

'What?'

'He's your guardian now, mate,' Slim says. 'He'll look after you boys now.'

'I'm not going to his house.'

'It's the only place you can go, kid.'

'I could stay with you.'

'You can't stay with me, kid.'

'Why not?'

This is Slim losing patience. It's not loud what he says but it's pointed.

'Because you're not my fucking kid, mate.'

Unplanned. Unwished. Unwilled. Untested. Underdeveloped. Undernourished. Undone. Unwanted. Unloved. Undead. Shoulda coulda woulda never been here in the first place if that creep hadn't dragged Mum into his car way back in the way back when. If she hadn't run away from home. If her old man hadn't run away from her.

I see my mum's dad in my head and he looks like Tytus Broz. I see the creep who tried to drag Mum into his car and he looks like Tytus Broz with thirty years shaved off that zombie face, a switchblade knife for a tongue. I see my father and I can't remember what his face looks like, so he looks like Tytus Broz too.

Slim drops his head. Breathes. I lay my head back in tears on the pillow, staring up at the square tiles. I'm counting the holes in the ceiling tiles starting from the left. One, two, three, four, five, six, seven ...

'Look, Eli, you're in the hole,' he says. 'You know what I mean. This is a low. But it only goes up, mate. This is your Black Peter. It only goes up, mate.'

I keep staring at the ceiling. I have a question.

'Are you a good man, Slim?'

Slim is puzzled by this.

'Why you askin' that for?'

Tears spill from my eyes, run down across my temples.

'Are you a good man?'

'Yeah,' Slim says.

I turn my head towards him. He's looking out my room window. Blue sky and cloud.

'I'm a good man,' Slim says. 'But I'm a bad man too. And that's like all men, kid. We all got a bit o' good and a bit o' bad in us. The tricky part is learnin' how to be good all the time and bad none of the time. Some of us get that right. Most of us don't.'

'Is Lyle a good man?'

'Yeah, Eli,' he says. 'He's a good man. Some of the time.'

'Slim ...'

'Yeah, kid.'

'Do you think I'm good?'

Slim nods.

'Yeah, kid, you're all right.'

'But am I good?' I ask. 'Do you think I'm gonna be a good man when I grow up?'

Slim shrugs. 'Well, you're a good boy,' he says. 'But I guess bein' a good boy doesn't guarantee bein' a good man.'

'I think I need to be tested,' I say.

'Whaddya mean?'

'I need to be tested. A test of character. I don't know what's inside me, Slim.'

Slim stands up and looks at the writing on my drip bag.

'I think they souped you up on some wacky juice, mate,' Slim says, sitting back down again.

'I do feel good,' I say. 'I feel like I'm still in a dream.'

'That's the painkillers, mate,' Slim says. 'Why do you need to be tested? Why don't you just know that you're a good kid? You got a good heart.'

'I don't know that,' I say. 'I'm not certain of that. I've thought some horrible things. I've had some very evil thoughts that couldn't be the thoughts of someone good.'

'Thinking evil thoughts and doing evil deeds are two very different things,' Slim says.

'Sometimes I imagine two aliens coming to planet earth and they have faces like piranhas and they drag me away in their spaceship and we're flying through space as earth comes into view in the spaceship's rearview mirror and one of the aliens turns to me from their driver's seat and says, "It's time, Eli", and I take one last look at earth and I say, "Do it", and the other alien presses a red button and in the rearview mirror earth doesn't explode like it was the Death Star blowing up, it just silently vanishes from space – it's there, then not there, like it was just deleted from the universe more than destroyed.'

Slim nods.

'Sometimes, Slim, I wonder if you're not an actor and Mum is too, and Lyle as well and Gus, oh man, Gus, he's like the best actor who ever lived, and you guys are all just acting around me and I'm being watched by those aliens in some grand production of my life.'

'That's not evil,' Slim says. 'That's just batshit crazy, and a little self-centred.'

'I need a test,' I say. 'Some moment where my true character can reveal itself naturally. I could do something noble, without a second's thought, I just do it because doing good things is in me, and I'll know for certain then that I am truly good inside.'

'We all get that test eventually, kid,' Slim says, looking out the window. 'You can do something good every single day, kid. And you know what today's good deed is going to be?'

'What?'

'Backin' up your mother's version of events,' Slim says.

'And what were they again?'

'August chopped your finger off with an axe,' he says.

'Gus is good,' I say. 'I don't remember a single time when he did something bad against someone who didn't deserve it.'

'Them rules of good and bad don't apply to that boy, I'm afraid,' he says. 'He's walkin' a different path, I reckon.'

'Where to, ya reckon?'

'Dunno,' Slim says. 'Some place only Gus knows how to get to.'

'He talked, Slim,' I say.

'Who talked?'

'Gus,' I say. 'Just before I blacked out. He talked.'

'What did he say?'

'He said—'

A woman pulls the olive green curtain along the U-shaped rod. She wears a blue woollen jumper with an image of a kookaburra resting on a branch beside a gum leaf. She wears dark green slacks the colour of the gum leaf on the jumper. Her hair is red and she's pale, late fifties maybe. She's looking at my eyes the second she pulls back the curtain. She carries a clipboard. She swings the curtain back for privacy.

'How's our brave young soldier?' she asks.

She has an Irish accent. I've never in person heard a woman speak with an Irish accent.

'He's doing good,' Slim says.

'Well, let's have a look at that dressing,' she says.

I love her Irish accent. I want to go to Ireland right now with this woman and lie in rich green grass by a cliff's edge and eat boiled potatoes with salt and butter and pepper and speak with an Irish accent about how anything is possible for thirteen-year-old boys with Irish accents.

'My name is Caroline Brennan,' she says. 'And you must be brave Eli, the young man who lost his special finger.'

'How did you know it was special?'

'Well, the right forefinger is always special,' she says. 'It's the one you use to point at the stars. It's the one you use to point out the girl in your class photo who you secretly love. It's the one you use to read a really long word in your favourite book. It's the one you use to pick your nose and scratch your arse, right?'

Dr Brennan says the surgeons upstairs couldn't do much about my missing finger. She says modern reattachment surgeries in teenagers are roughly seventy to eighty per cent successful but these complex reattachments rely heavily on one key element: a fucking finger to stick back on. After twelve or so hours without replantation of the amputated finger, that seventy to eighty per cent success rate bottoms out to 'Sorry, you poor rotten son of a smack dealer.' Sometimes, she says, finger replantations often cause more problems than they're worth, especially when the lone severed finger is an index or pinkie finger, but this just sounds to me like saying to a starving man floating out at sea on a plank of wood, 'Look, it's probably a good thing you don't have a leg of ham with you because it probably would make you constipated.'

Amputations like mine, she says, at the base of the finger, are more complex still, and even if my teenage runaway finger suddenly emerged on a bucket of ice, it is unlikely nerve function would recover enough to make the finger anything more useful than something I could shove into a bed of hot coals as a neat party trick.

'Now hold out your tall man,' she says, twiddling her middle finger.

I hold up my tall man.

'Now shove him up your nostril,' she says.

She sticks her own middle finger in her nostril, raising her eyebrows.

Slim beams. I follow suit, shove that tall man up my nose.

'See,' Dr Brennan says. 'There ain't nothing that forefinger could do that tall man can't, you hear me, young Eli? The tall man can just go deeper.'

I nod, smiling.

She carefully unwraps the dressing around my fingerless knuckle and the air on the exposed flesh makes me wince. I sneak a look at it and turn immediately away with the image of a bald white knuckle bone exposed in flesh, like one of my back teeth lodged inside a pork sausage.

'It's healing well,' she says.

'How long will he be in for, Doc,' Slim asks.

'I'd like to keep him here two or three more days at least,' she says. 'Just monitor him for infection in the early stages.'

She gives the wound a new dressing. She turns to Slim.

'Can I speak to Eli alone, please?' she says.

Slim nods. He stands, his old bones cracking as he rises. He coughs twice, a chesty, nasty, wheezy cough like he's got a hissing rhinoceros beetle lodged in his larynx.

'You had that cough seen to?' Dr Brennan asks.

'Nah,' Slim says.

'Why not?' she replies.

'Because one of you bright quacks might do something silly like stop me from dyin',' he says. He gives me a wink as he passes Dr Brennan.

'Has Eli got a place to go?' Dr Brennan asks.

'He's going to his dad's house,' Slim says.

Dr Brennan shoots a look at me.

'Is that okay with you?' she asks.

Slim watches for my response.

I nod. And he nods too.

He hands me a $20 note. 'When you're done 'ere, you get yourself a cab back to your old man's, all right?' he says. He points to a cupboard beneath my hospital bed. 'I brought your shoes and a fresh set of clothes for ya.'

Slim hands me a slip of paper and walks for the door. An address and a phone number on the paper.

'Your old man's address,' he says. 'I'm not far from you boys, just past the Hornibrook Bridge. You call this number if you need me. It's the number of a hock shop beneath the flat. Ask for Gill.'

'Then what do I say?' I ask.

'Say you're best friends with Slim Halliday.'

Then he's gone.

*

Dr Brennan reads a chart on a clipboard. She sits on the side of the bed.

'Give me your arm,' she says. Around my left bicep she wraps a velvet cuff attached to a black pump shaped like a grenade.

'What's that?'

'Checks your blood pressure,' she says. 'Just relax now.'

She squeezes the grenade several times.

'So, you like *Star Wars*?'

I nod.

'So do I,' she says. 'Who's your favourite character?'

'Han. Boba Fett, maybe.' A long pause. 'No, Han.'

Dr Brennan gives me a sharp eye.

'You sure about that?'

Pause.

'Luke,' I say. 'It's always been Luke. Who's yours?'

'Oh, Darth Vader all the way for me,' she says.

I see where she's going with this. Dr Brennan should join the fuzz. I'll bite.

'You like Vader?'

'Oh yeah, I always enjoy the bad guys,' she says. 'You don't have much of a story if you don't have some bad guys. Can't have a good, good hero without a bad, bad villain, right?'

I smile.

'Who doesn't want to be Darth Vader?' she laughs. 'Someone pushes in front of you when you're lining up for a hot dog and you give them the ol' silent Force choke.' She makes a pincer grip with her thumb and forefinger.

I laugh, making the same grip in midair. 'I find your lack of mustard disturbing,' I say and we laugh together.

Out of the corner of my eye I catch sight of a boy standing in the doorway of my hospital room. He wears a light blue hospital gown like me. He has a shaved head but for a long brown rat's tail stretching from the back of his scalp and draping over his right shoulder. His left hand grips a mobile IV stand holding the drip bag that's plugged into his hand.

'What is it, Christopher?' asks Dr Brennan.

Maybe he's eleven years old. He's got a scar across his top lip that makes him look like the last eleven-year-old boy with a mobile drip I'd ever want to come across in a dark alley. He scratches his arse.

'Tang's too weak again,' he spits.

Dr Brennan sighs. 'Christopher, there's twice as much powder in it than last time,' she says.

He shakes his head and walks away.

'I'm fuckin' dyin' and yer givin' me weak Tang?' he says on his way up the corridor outside.

Dr Brennan raises her eyebrows. 'Sorry about that,' she says.

'What's he dying from?' I ask.

'Poor bugger's got a tumour the size of Ayers Rock in his brain,' she says.

'Can you do anything about it?'

'Maybe,' she says, writing my blood pressure numbers onto a sheet on the clipboard. 'Maybe not. Sometimes medicine's got nothing to do with it.'

'What do you mean? … God?'

'Oh, no, not God. I'm talkin' about Gog.'

'Who's Gog?'

'He's God's cranky, more impatient younger brother,' she says. 'While God's off building the Himalayas, miserable ol' Gog is off puttin' tumours in the heads of young Brisbane lads.'

'Gog's got a lot to answer for,' I suggest.

'Gog walks among us,' she says. 'Anyway, where were we?'

'Vader.'

'Oh yeah, so you don't like Darth Vader, do you?' she says. 'You and your brother wanted to chop him in half with an axe, I understand?'

'We were pissed he killed Obi-Wan.'

She stares into my eyes, rests her folder on the bed.

'You ever heard the saying, Eli, "Can't bullshit a bullshitter"?'

'Slim loves that one,' I say.

'I bet he does.'

'I see some shit in this place,' she says, her Irish accent making that sentence sound like she's talking about a fine dawn sunrise. 'I've seen green shit and yellow shit and black shit and purple shit with polka dots and shit so thick you could plop it over your mother-in-law's head and fairly knock her out. I've seen shit come out of holes you didn't know existed. I've seen shit tear the arseholes out of women and men, but rarely have I seen shit so dangerous as the bullshit pouring out of your mouth right now.'

She speaks with love and compassion in all that shit-speak and it makes me laugh.

'I'm sorry,' I say.

'There are things you can do,' she says. 'There are places you can go to be safe, people you can trust. There are still people in this city more powerful than the police. There's still a few Luke Skywalkers left in Brisbane, Eli.'

'Heroes?' I ask.

'Can't have all those villains walking around without a few heroes too,' she says.

\*

*Dear Alex,*

*Greetings from the children's ward of Royal Brisbane Hospital. Firstly, please forgive my messy handwriting. I recently lost my right forefinger (really long story) but I can grip a Bic ballpoint pen just fine between my tall finger, my thumb and my right ring finger. My doctor, Dr Brennan, wants me to start using my hands and she said writing a letter might be a way to start practising my writing as well as getting the blood circulating in my hands. How are you and the boys and Tripod the cat? Sorry I can't give you any updates on* Days of Our Lives, *they only have one TV in the children's ward and it's always on* Play School. *You ever been in hospital? It's not bad here. Dr Brennan is real nice and speaks with an Irish accent that I think the boys in 2 Division would love. Dinner's a bit rough with the roast lamb but breakfast (Corn Flakes) and lunch (chicken sandwiches) are spot on. I could stay a bit longer here but I can't because I've got work to do. See, I've been thinking about heroes, Alex. You ever have a hero? Someone who saved you. Someone who kept you safe. What makes someone a hero? Luke Skywalker didn't set out to be a hero. He just wanted to find Obi-Wan. Then he just decided to step outside his comfort zone. He just decided to follow his heart. So maybe that's all it takes to be a hero, Alex. Just follow your heart. Step outside. You might not be able to get hold of me for a while because I'm going away for a bit. I'm off on a quest, going on a bit of an adventure. I have established my goal and I have the will to achieve it. Remember what Slim always says about the four things: timing, planning, luck, belief. I reckon that's like life. I reckon that's like living. I'll write to you when I can, but if you don't hear from me for a bit, I want to say thanks for all the letters and thanks for being my friend. So much more to say but I'll have to leave all that to another day because my moment is almost here and my time is slipping away. Like sand through the hourglass. Ha!*

*Your friend always,*

*Eli*

\*

Slim always had this self-belief thing about escaping prison. It went something along the lines of, 'If you truly believe the guards can see you then the guards can truly see you. But if you truly believe that you're invisible then the guards will believe you're truly invisible.' I think that's what he was saying. It was something about confidence. The Houdini of Boggo Road wasn't as magical as he was sneaky and confident and a confident sneak can make his own magic. His first successful escape from Boggo Road was in broad daylight. A blistering Sunday afternoon, 28 January 1940. Slim and his fellow D Wing prisoners were being walked around the central circle towards Number 4 yard. Slim fell back among the group and he believed he was invisible, so he was.

Four factors to a clean escape: timing, planning, luck, belief. Timing was right, between 3 p.m. and 4 p.m. on a Sunday when the majority of the prison guards were off guarding the majority of prisoners at prayer service in Number 4 yard, on the opposite side of the compound to Slim's D Wing. Simple plan. Effective plan. Confident plan. On the way to Number 4 yard, Slim simply went invisible, slipped like a ghost from the single line of prisoners and ducked into Number 1 yard, adjacent to D Wing, nearest yard to his ultimate destination, the prison workshops.

Then he believed he could scale a three-metre wooden fence and so he did. He climbed the fence bordering Number 1 exercise yard and leaped down to a track below, a sterile zone that ran along the inside of the prison walls to form a square shape. He crossed the track into the workshops area that was usually patrolled by guards but wasn't during Sunday prayer service. Sweating, hot, quiet, stealthy, he ran to the back of the workshops and, invisible to the guards, climbed onto an outhouse that allowed him to climb further and up to the roof of the workshops.

Here, potentially visible to the guards in the prison watchtowers, he produced a pair of stolen and smuggled pliers and rapidly cut through the wire netting covering the workshop ventilation windows. Timing, planning, luck, belief. And a slim build. The Houdini of Boggo Road squeezed his thin frame through the ventilation windows and dropped down into the boot-making section of the workshops.

Each workshop section was separated by wire meshing. Slim cut and slipped his way through the wire from the boot shop to the mattress shop, from the mattress shop to the carpenter's shop, from the carpenters' shop to the loom shop, from the loom shop to paradise – the brush shop in which he had been working in recent weeks and in which he had hidden his escape kit.

Timing is right for my escape. It's 3 p.m. in the children's ward play area, a polished wood floor communal space shaped like half an octagon. The area is bordered by white wood-framed latch windows like the windows in my school. Same time in the afternoon Slim made his escape. A time in the ward when most of these kids – about eighteen kids, aged four to fourteen, battling everything from appendicitis to broken arms to concussions to knife wounds to fingers chopped off by artificial limb specialists – are on a Tang and green cordial high from afternoon tea, their tongues still buzzing with the sweet elixir of the cream inside a Monte Carlo biscuit.

Kids pushing trucks and finger-painting butterflies and pulling their underpants down and playing with their dicks. Older kids reading books and five kids watching *Romper Room* and hoping gentle Miss Helena inside the television will see them through her magic mirror. A red-haired boy spinning a top made into the shape of a yellow and black tin bumblebee. A girl maybe my age gives me a half-smile the way factory workers might smile at each other across conveyor belts of bumblebee spinning tops. Prints of exotic animals across the walls. And Christopher with the mobile drip. The boy with Ayers Rock inside his melon.

'You watching this?' I ask Christopher.

He's sitting in an armchair in front of the communal television, licking the cream off a split orange-cream biscuit.

'No,' he says, indignant. 'I don't watch *Romper Room*. I asked them to put on *Diff'rent Strokes* but they reckon there's more young kids than old kids so we have to watch this shit. Fuckin' bullshit if you ask me. These little pricks can spend the rest of their lives watchin' *Romper Room*. I'm gonna be a corpse in three months and all I want to do is watch some *Diff'rent Strokes*. Nobody gives a shit.'

His tongue licks a slab of orange cream. His light blue hospital gown is as misshapen and crinkled as mine.

'My name's Eli,' I say.

'Christopher,' he says.

'Sorry to hear about your brain,' I say.

'I'm not sorry,' he says. 'I don't have to go to school no more. And Mum's been buying me Golden Gaytimes whenever I feel like one. I just say the word and she stops the car and she runs into a shop and gets me one.'

He spots my bandaged right hand.

'What happened to your finger?'

I move closer.

'A drug kingpin's hitman chopped it off with a Bowie knife,' I say.

'Faaark,' says Christopher. 'Why'd he do that?'

'Because my brother wouldn't tell the drug kingpin what he wanted to know.'

'What did he want to know?'

'I don't know.'

'Why didn't your brother tell him?'

'Because he doesn't talk.'

'Why were they asking someone who doesn't talk to talk?'

'Because he did end up talking.'

'What did he say?'

'Your end is a dead blue wren.'

'Whaaaaat?' asks Christopher.

'Forget about it,' I say, leaning in close to his chair, whispering, 'Listen, see that builder over there?'

Christopher follows my gaze to the other side of the ward floor where a builder is adding an extra section of storage cupboards beside the administration desk in the centre of the ward. Christopher nods.

'He's got a toolbox at his feet and inside that toolbox is a box of Benson & Hedges Extra Mild and a purple cigarette lighter,' I say.

'So?' Christopher says.

'So I need you to go over there and ask him a question while he's facing away from the toolbox,' I say. 'You'll create a diversion while I sneak in from behind and steal his cigarette lighter from his toolbox.'

Christopher looks puzzled. 'What's a diversion?'

It's what Slim created in December 1953, after being sentenced to life. In the mattress workshop in Number 2 Division he built up a mountain of mattress fibre and tree cotton and set it alight. The burning mountain of mattress was a diversion for arriving guards who didn't know whether to attend to the fire or to Boggo Road's most notorious prisoner, who was already climbing a makeshift ladder towards the workshop's skylight. Slim's diversion, however, was his undoing because the fire's flames rose to the roof where he was bashing out the skylight mesh before severe smoke inhalation saw him plummet five metres to the ground. But the lesson remains: fire makes people panicky as fuck.

'It's a distraction,' I say. 'See my fist.'

I wave my right fist high and in circles and Christopher's green eyes follow the fist so dutifully he doesn't see my left hand reach to his ear and tug his earlobe.

'Yoink,' I say.

He smiles, nodding.

'So what do you need the lighter for?' Christopher asks.

'To set fire to that copy of *Anne of Green Gables* sitting over there by the bookcase.'

'A diversion?'

'You learn fast,' I say. 'That brain of yours still works fine. A big enough diversion that will make those nurses at the administration desk come over here as I make my triumphant escape out through that entry door they're always eyeing off.'

'Where you gonna go?'

'Places, Christopher,' I say, nodding. 'I'm going places.'

Christopher nods.

'You want to come with me?' I ask.

Christopher considers the offer for a moment.

'Nah,' he says. 'These retards still think they can save me, so I better stick around here for a bit longer.'

He stands, pulls the drip needle out of the top of his hand that's connecting him to his metal drip trolley.

'What are you doing?' I ask.

He's already walking towards the television when he turns his head briefly.

'Diversion,' he says.

The television is a standard size and if it was tipped on its side it would reach up to Christopher's waist. He leans over it and grips the rear side of the television with his left hand and places his right hand at the base and, in one mighty and clean jerk, his wire-thin arms haul the television above his shoulders. The kids lying down on a rainbow-coloured mat on their bellies watching *Romper Room* stare in confusion and disbelief as Miss Helena inside the television is tilted on a sharp diagonal as Christopher raises the television in teeth-gritting fury.

'I said I wanted to watch *Diff'rent Strokes!*' he screams.

I step slowly backwards towards the administration desk as four nurses rush from there to surround Christopher in a panicked semicircle. One younger nurse pulls the youngest children away from Christopher as a senior nurse approaches him the way a police negotiator might approach a man in a dynamite vest.

'Christopher ... put ... the ... television ... down ... now.'

I'm already at the entry door when Christopher staggers backwards with the television above his head, the television's power cord pulled tight and about to be reefed from the power point. He's singing something.

'Christopher!' the senior nurse screams.

He's singing the theme song to *Diff'rent Strokes*. It's a song about understanding and inclusion and difference; about how some are born with less than others and more than others at the same time. It's a song about connection.

He steps back three, four, five steps, like Frankenstein's monster steps, and he turns his hip for a stronger thrust and he throws the television and gentle Miss Helena smiling inside it straight through the glass of his nearest latched white wood-framed window to an unknown destination. The nurses gasp and Christopher turns back with his arms raised not in a 'D' for Diversion but in a 'V' for Victory. He screams in triumph and as the nurses crash-tackle him as a group, his gaze somehow finds me at the entry door in all the diversionary madness. He gives a sharp wink with his left eye and the best I can give him back is a full-blooded fist pump before I slip through the door to freedom.

\*

Timing, planning, luck, belief. Planning. After Slim had laboriously cut through the wire meshing of the boot shop and then the mattress shop and the carpenters' shop and the loom shop on that daring escape of 28 January 1940, he slipped finally through the wire mesh of the brush shop to find his escape kit.

Slim had patience even in those early days, before his longest stretches in Black Peter. He took his time fixing his escape kit between the watchful patrols of workshop guards because time was all he had plenty of. He relished the planning, he found succour in the sneaky adrenaline-filled creativity of a quest for liberty. The secret making and storing of escape tools brought him joy and focus in an otherwise dreary prison world. Between the watchful stares of workshop guards, Slim had spent months fashioning an escape rope, nine metres in length, made of plaited coir, the stuff they made the mats with in the prison carpet-weaving shop, the stuff they made the mat with that Slim laid upon in the cold, damp and dark Black Peter. Every half a metre or so along this rope he double-knotted it to form footholds. Inside his escape kit was a second rope, three metres in length, and two wooden hammock sticks bound together to form a cross that he tied to the nine-metre rope.

With his escape kit in hand, he climbed to the ceiling of the brush shop and cut his way through the mesh of a fanlight ceiling window and found himself, once more, standing atop the workshop rooftop, this time in a position invisible to tower guards, the prison's Achilles heel, a perfect blind spot that Slim had deduced through patient hour after hour after hour of walking the prison yard with his head held skyward sketching rough geometry drawings in his mind between variables of the guard towers, the workshop roof and freedom.

He used his shorter rope to slip down off the workshop roof, suffering rope burns to his hands on his way down. Now back on the inner track running around the prison perimeter, he looked up at the daunting rise of Boggo Road's eight-metre brick penitentiary wall. He pulled his bound hammock cross-sticks from his escape kit. What he held in his hands was a grappling hook tied to a nine-metre rope with footholds. And he steadied himself for a throw.

Timing, planning, luck, belief. For weeks in his solitary prison cell, Slim had studied the science and technique required to lodge a grappling hook against a high wall. Along the top of the Boggo Road prison wall were corners where smaller sections of the wall met higher sections. Slim spent weeks throwing two bound matchsticks fixed into a cross and attached to string over a rough scale model of the Boggo Road penitentiary wall. He threw the hook over the wall and he worked the weighted rope along the wall top until it wedged into the corner of a small step where a smaller section of the wall met a higher section. And he told me how it felt when he pulled that rope taut into that corner and the hook stuck firm. Slim said it felt like one Christmas morning he had in the old Church of England orphanage in Carlingford when the housemaster told all those spindly orphans they were having warm plum pudding and custard for dessert at Christmas lunch. And that's what liberty tastes like, Slim said: warm plum pudding and custard. He hauled himself up that rope, his hands and feet gripping for life on the double-knotted footholds, until he sat perched high up on the prison wall, unseen in his beautiful blind spot, one side of his view from the top way up there to the blooming gardens set beyond the walls of Number 1 yard, the other side of his view the rambling brick prison that was really the only permanent home – the one and only fixed address – he had ever had in his life. He breathed that air up there deep inside him and he reversed the hook so it lodged this time into the prison side of the wall corner that would become known as 'Halliday's Leap' and he climbed on down to freedom.

*

Four floors to freedom for me. I press the button for 'Ground' in the hospital elevator. The first thing Slim did after he scrambled his way through the gardens to surrounding Annerley Road as a fugitive was to slip out of his prison clothes. Around 4.10 p.m., about when the prison wardens were calling his name at the afternoon prison muster, Slim was jumping fences through suburban Brisbane, stealing a new outfit from a series of clotheslines.

Now I'm Houdini and here's my great blink-and-you'll-miss-it illusion: slipping off my hospital gown to reveal the civilian, non-fugitive clothes I have on underneath: an old dark blue polo shirt and black jeans over my blue and grey Dunlop KT-26 running shoes. I roll the gown up into a ball of blue material I'm holding in my left hand just as the elevator stops at Level 2 of the hospital.

Two male doctors holding clipboards step into the elevator, deep in conversation.

'I said to the kid's dad, maybe if he's having this many concussions on the field you should consider a more low-impact sport, like tennis or golf,' says one doctor as I move to the back left corner of the elevator, the ball of my gown hidden behind my back.

'What did he say to that?' the other doctor asks.

'He said he couldn't take him out of the team because the finals were coming up,' the first doctor says. 'I said, "Well, Mr Newcombe, I think it comes down to what's more important to you, an under-15s premiership trophy for Brothers or your son having enough brain function to say the word 'premiership'."'

The doctors shake their heads. The first doctor turns to me. I smile.

'You lost, buddy?' he asks.

I've planned for this. Rehearsed a number of responses over the lamb roast dinner I didn't eat last night.

'No, just visiting my brother in the children's ward,' I say.

The elevator stops on the ground floor.

'Your mum and dad with you?' the doctor asks.

'Yeah, they're just having a smoke outside,' I say.

The elevator doors open and the doctors exit right and I exit towards the hospital foyer, polished concrete floors buzzing with hospital visitors and ambulance officers pushing gurneys. The first doctor spots the bandage on my right hand and stops on the spot. 'Hey, wait, kid ...'

Just keep walking. Just keep walking. Confidence. You are invisible. You believe you are invisible and you are invisible. Just keep walking. Past the water cooler. Past a family surrounding a girl with Coke-bottle glasses in a wheelchair. Past a poster of Norm, the beer-bellied dad at the centre of the 'Life. Be In It.' TV ads that make August laugh so hard.

I glance a look back over my right shoulder to see the first doctor walk to the administration desk and start talking to a woman at the desk as he points at me. Walking faster now. Faster now. Faster. You are not invisible, you idiot. You are not magic. You are a thirteen-year-old boy about to be captured by that large Pacific Islander security guard the doctor is now talking to and you are about to be sent to live with a father you do not know.

Run.

*

The Royal Brisbane Hospital is on Bowen Bridge Road. I know this area because the Brisbane Exhibition – the Ekka – is held every August a little up the road in the old showgrounds where Mum and Lyle let August and me eat all the contents of our Milky Way showbags one afternoon while we watched five large men from Tasmania furiously chop logs between their feet with axes to rousing applause. We caught the train back home to Darra from Bowen Hills train station – somewhere around here – and on the moving train I vomited the contents of my Milky Way bag into an Army Combat showbag that consisted of a plastic machine gun, a plastic hand grenade, a sling of ammunition and a jungle camouflaged headband that I'd hoped to wear on several top secret rescue missions through the streets of Darra until the headband was drowned in vomit that was two parts chocolate thickshake and one part Dagwood Dog.

A daylight moon outside the hospital. Cars zipping along Bowen Bridge Road. There's a large grey electrical box on the footpath running by the hospital. I slip behind this box and watch the Pacific Islander security guard rush out of the sliding entry doors of the hospital. He looks left, right, left again. Searching for leads, finding none. He approaches a woman in a green cardigan and fluffy slippers, having a smoke by a bus stop seat and a council bin with an ashtray.

Run now. Catch up to the crowd of people crossing the busy main road at the traffic lights. Walk into the centre of this crowd. Boy on the lam. Boy outfoxes hospital staff. Boy outsmarts world. Boy suckers universe.

I know this street. This is where we entered the Brisbane Exhibition. Lyle and Mum bought the tickets from a guy in a concrete hole in the wall. We walked through horse stables and cow shit and a hundred goats and a barn full of chickens and chicken shit. Then we walked down a hill and we came to Sideshow Alley and August and I begged Lyle to take us on the Ghost Train and then into the Maze of Mirrors where I turned and turned and turned through doors but only ever found myself. Keep walking up this street. Find someone, anyone. Like this man.

'Excuse me,' I say.

He's wearing a large army-green coat and a beanie and he's nursing a large glass bottle of Coke between his crossed legs as he leans against the concrete wall bordering the showgrounds. The Coke bottle is the kind August and I collect and return sometimes to the corner store in Oxley and the old lady who runs the store gives us twenty cents for our efforts and we spend that twenty cents on twenty one-cent caramel buds. There's a clear liquid in the man's Coke bottle and I can smell that it's methylated spirits. He looks up at me, his lips twitching, eyes adjusting to the sun over my shoulders.

'Could you point me to the train station?' I ask.

'Batman,' the man says, his head wobbling.

'Sorry?'

'Batman,' he barks.

'Batman?'

He sings the television theme tune. 'Nananananananana … Batman!' he hollers.

He's tanned from the sun and he's sweating in the large green coat.

'Yeah, Batman,' I say.

He points to his neck. The side of his neck is covered in blood. 'Fuckin' bat bit me,' he says. His head wobbles from one side to the other like the pirate-ship swings we ride on every autumn at the Brisbane Exhibition. I see now that his left eye is heavily bruised, blood-clotted.

'Are you okay?' I ask. 'Do you need some help?'

'I don't need help,' he gargles. 'I'm Batman.'

Adult men. Fucking adult men. Nutters, all of them. Can't be trusted. Fucking sickos. Freaks. Killers. What was this man's road to becoming Batman on a side street of inner-city

Brisbane? How much good was in him? How much bad? Who was his father? What did his father do? What did his father not do? In what ways did other adult men fuck his life up?

'Which way to the train station?' I ask.

'Wazzat?' he says.

'The *train station*?' I say, louder.

He points the way, an unsteady right arm and a limp forefinger pointing to an intersection left of here.

'Just keep walking, Robin,' he says.

Just keep walking.

'Thanks, Batman,' I say.

He holds out his hand.

'Shake me 'and,' he demands.

I instinctively go to shake his hand with my right but remember the dressing over my missing finger and tentatively offer my left hand instead.

'Good, good,' he says, giving a firm handshake.

'Thanks again,' I say.

Then he pulls my hand to his mouth and bites it like a rabid dog.

'Nnnngrrrrr,' he spits, his mouth slobbering over my hand. He's biting my hand but it's all skin in his mouth, jelly gums. I reef my hand away and he falls back laughing, his mouth open wide and deranged. Not a single tooth in his smile.

Run.

Sprinting now. Sprinting now like I'm Eric Grothe, powerhouse winger for the mighty Parramatta Eels, and there's a sideline beside me and a try line eighty metres in front of me. Sprint like my life depended on it. Sprint like there's jet boots on my feet and fire in my heart that never goes out. Across the intersection. My Dunlop KT-26s will guide my way. Just trust in the sleek cushioned design of the KT-26, cheapest, most effective runner in all of Kmart. Sprint like I'm the last warm-blooded boy on earth and the world is overrun by vampires. Vampire bats.

Run. Past a car dealership to my right and a hedgerow to my left. Run. Past an orange brick building to my left that takes up a whole block of land. A name fixed in fancy letters to the building. *The Courier-Mail.*

Stop.

This is where they make it. This is where they build the newspaper. Slim told me about this place. All the writers come here and they type their stories out and typesetters put their stories on metal down in the printing presses at the back of the building. Slim said he spoke to a journalist once who told him he could smell his stories being pressed in ink in the evening. There was no greater smell, the journo told Slim, than tomorrow's front page scoop being pressed in ink. I breathe deep and smell it and I swear I can smell that ink because maybe they're all on deadline and the presses are already running and I'm gonna be part of that place somehow, some day, I just know it, because why else did Batman with no teeth send me down here, down this very street where *The Courier-Mail* crime writers return to file their pieces and change the State and change the world? Batman was just a bit player, maybe, but he acted well in the grand production of *The Extraordinary and Unexpected Yet Totally Expected Life of Eli Bell.* Of course he sent me down here. Of course he did.

A police car passes through the intersection, moving across the road I'm standing on. Two officers. The officer in the passenger seat looks my way. Don't engage. Don't engage. But it's two cops in a police car and I can't resist engaging. The police officer is eyeballing me now. The police car slows, then continues across the intersection. Run.

\*

Slim had been on the run for almost two weeks before he was first reported by a civilian on 9 February 1940. A State-wide manhunt stretched to the New South Wales border and police cars lined roads leading south, where most expected Slim to go. But Slim was heading north when he pulled into a service station in Nundah, in Brisbane's suburban north, at 3 a.m., to fill up a car he'd stolen from nearby Clayfield. The service station owner, a man named Walter Wildman, was woken by the sound of petrol being pumped from a garage bowser. He promptly and justifiably sprang upon Slim with a loaded double-barrel shotgun.

'Stand still!' barked Wildman.

'You wouldn't shoot a man, would you?' Slim reasoned.

'Yes,' replied Wildman. 'I'd blow your brains out.'

This admission naturally prompted Slim to run for the driver's seat of his stolen car, which in turn prompted Walter Wildman to fire twice at Slim, attempting to blow his brains out but succeeding only in shattering the car's rear window. Slim sped off towards the Bruce Highway, heading north, as Walter Wildman phoned police to report the car's numberplate. He got as far as Caboolture, about thirty minutes out of Brisbane, before a police vehicle jumped on his tail, sparking a thrilling car chase through bush side roads and around blind corners and into and out of gullies, which ended with Slim crashing the car through a wire fence. Running into scrub on foot, Slim was quickly surrounded by some thirty detectives from Queensland Police who eventually found him hiding behind a wide tree stump. The police drove Slim back to Boggo Road and threw him back in his cell in Number 2 Division and they slammed the cell door shut and Slim sat back down on his hard prison bed. And he smiled.

'Why were you smiling?' I once asked Slim.

'I established a goal and I achieved it,' he said. 'Finally, young Eli, this good-for-nothin' orphan scumbag you're lookin' at had found something he was good at. I realised why the man upstairs made me so fuckin' tall and lanky. Good for jumpin' over prison walls.'

*

Train tracks. A train. Bowen Hills train station. The Ipswich line, platform 3. A train pulling in and a set of concrete stairs I sprint down. Maybe fifty concrete steps I'm bounding down, two at a time, one eye on the steps, one eye on the train's open doors. Then a mistimed step and my right ankle in my right Dunlop KT-26 rolls on the edge of the very last step and I dive face-first onto the rough bitumen of platform 3. My right shoulder cushions most of the impact but my right cheek and ear scrape along the surface like the back tyre of my BMX when I slam the brakes on for a long skid. But those train doors are still open so I lift myself up from the ground and stagger, winded and groggy, towards them as they start closing and I leap for my life and land inside, where three elderly women sharing a four-seat space turn to face me, gasping.

'Are you all right there?' asks an old woman holding her handbag with both hands on her lap.

I nod, sucking breath, turning to walk down the train corridor. Small bitumen gravel pebbles are lodged in my face. Air stings the open graze on my cheek. The knuckle that once controlled my missing finger screams for attention. I sit and I breathe and I pray this train stops at Darra.

*

Deserted suburbs at dusk. Maybe the world did end. Maybe it is just me and the vampires are sleeping because it's still daylight. Maybe I'm losing my mind and I shouldn't be walking like this in the sun, with the hospital painkillers wearing off, but this dream is growing real because I can smell my underarms and I can taste the sweat above my top lip. I walk past the Darra Station Road shops. Past Mama Pham's restaurant. Past an empty Burger Rings packet blowing in circles in the wind. Past the fruit and vegetable market. Past the hairdressers and the op shop and the TAB. Across Ducie Street Park with the seeds of the paspalum grass catching on the bottom of my jeans and in the white laces of my Dunlops. Almost there. Almost home.

Careful now. Sandakan Street. I scan the street from afar, hiding behind a sprawling widowmaker swaying in the afternoon breeze. No cars in front of our house. No people in the street. I move cautiously and quickly between trees, zig-zagging my way across the park towards our house. The sky is orange and deep pink above the house and night is falling. Returning to the scene of the crime. I'm tired but I'm nervous, too. Not sure this quest was such a good idea. But I'm supposed to be going places. The only way is up out of a hole. Or further down, I guess. Straight down to hell.

I scurry across the road, through the gate like I'm meant to be here because it's my house after all, or Lyle's house, I should say. Lyle's house. Lyle.

Can't go through the front. Go through the back. If the back door's locked, try Lena's window. If Lena's window is locked, try the sliding kitchen window on the old neighbour Gene Crimmins's side and maybe Mum, or was it me, forgot to put that length of metal curtain rod in the window track to lock out intruders. Intruders like me. Intruders like me with big plans.

Going places.

Back door's locked. Lena's window doesn't budge. I bring the black wheelie bin around to the kitchen window, pull myself atop the bin and reef at the window. It slides five centimetres along the window track and I'm hopeful, then it slams against the curtain rod and I'm not hopeful at all. Fuck it. Desperate times. Break a window.

I jump off the bin. It's getting dark but I can still see under the house, the dirt floor strewn with rocks, but none big enough for my needs. But this will do. A brick. Probably one of those glorious bricks from the factory up the road. A hometown brick. A Darra brick. I slip back out from under the house and I sit the brick on top of the wheelie bin and I'm pulling myself back up on top of the bin when a voice echoes over my shoulder.

'Everything all right, Eli?' asks Gene Crimmins, leaning out of his living room through an open casement window. The space between Gene's house and ours is only about three metres so he can talk softly. He's a soft talker anyway, which I've always found calming. I like Gene. Gene knows how to be discreet.

'G'day Gene,' I say, turning to him, letting go of the bin.

Gene's wearing a white singlet and blue cotton pyjama bottoms.

He registers my face.

'Bloody hell, mate, what happened to you?'

'Tripped over running down the train station stairs.'

Gene nods. 'You locked out?'

I nod.

'Your mum around?' he asks.

I shake my head.

'Lyle?'

I shake my head.

He nods.

'I saw those boys dragging him out to a car the other night,' Gene says. 'Figured they weren't all going for ice cream.'

I shake my head.

'He all right?'

'I don't know,' I say. 'But I'm hoping to find out. Just need to get inside.'

'That what the brick's for?'

I nod.

'I never saw you, all right?' he says.

'Thanks for being discreet, Gene,' I say.

'You still got those wicket keeper's hands you used to have in the backyard?' Gene asks.

'Yeah, guess so.'

'Catch,' he says.

He throws a key and I catch it with two cupped hands. The key's attached to a kangaroo bottle-opener key ring.

'That's the spare Lyle asked me to hold on to for a rainy day,' Gene says.

I nod in thanks.

'It's rainin' a bit, Gene,' I say.

'Pissin' down,' Gene says.

\*

The house is dark and silent. I keep the lights off. Our dishes from the night we had spaghetti bolognese are stacked in a dish rack beside the sink. Someone's cleaned up. Slim, I guess. I cup a hand beneath the kitchen tap and take a long drink of water. I open the fridge and find a knob of wrapped devon and a block of Coon cheese. I wonder how Slim ate on the lam. Water from creeks, robbing eggs from chook pens, maybe; stealing buns when bakers weren't looking; plucking oranges from trees. Staying fed and watered is a public activity, raising one's head is often required to make it work. There's a loaf of Tip-Top bread on the kitchen bench and I smell it in the darkness and know immediately it's green with mould. I take bites from the devon and the cheese, mixing them together in my mouth.

Not the same without bread, but filling the yawning hole in my stomach. I take the red torch from the third drawer down below the kitchen sink. Pad straight to Lena's room.

This room of true love. This room of blood. Jesus on the wall. The light from my torch lands on his sorrowful face and he looks so distant and aloof to me in the darkness.

My right hand is throbbing. My forefinger knuckle is hot and full with blood going nowhere. I need rest. I need to stop moving. I need to lie down. I slide Lena's wardrobe door across, slide Lena's old dresses along the rod they hang on. I push with my left hand against the wardrobe's rear wall and it compresses and pops back open. Lyle's secret door.

It has to be here. Why would it be anywhere else?

The light from my torch makes a small moon the size of a tennis ball bounce across the dirt ground of Lyle's secret room. I slip down and my Dunlops dig into dirt. My torchlight finds every corner of the brick-walled room. Then it circles around the middle of the room, along the walls, across the red telephone. It has to be here. It has to be here. Why would he hide it anywhere else but his secret room built for hiding things in?

But the room is empty.

I hunch down and scramble for the secret door built into the wall of the secret room. I get a grip on the door flap and stick the torch into the tunnel Lyle has dug stretching to the thunderbox beyond. The tunnel is clear of snakes and spiders. Nothing but soil and thick air.

Fuck. Heart pounding. Got to do a piss. Don't want to do this. Got to do this.

I collapse onto my belly and push myself into the hole with my kneecaps. I cradle my wounded right hand and pull myself along with my elbows scraping the dirt floor. Dirt falls into my eyes when my head bumps the tunnel ceiling. Breathe. Stay calm. Almost out. My torch shines down the tunnel and I can make something out, something resting on the floor of the thunderbox cavity. A box.

The sight of it makes me scramble quicker along the floor. I'm a crab. I'm a soldier crab. One of those little purple ones with a body like a marble. August and I would let them crawl over us in their hundreds on the shores of Bribie Island, Lyle's favourite day-trip destination, an hour north of Brisbane. Lyle would pick two or three crabs up in his hand and they'd claw at his fingers and then he'd place them casually on top of our heads. The sun would set and there'd be nobody on the beach but us boys fishing and a couple of seagulls with their hungry eyes on our pilchards.

My head emerges from the tunnel into the thunderbox and the torchlight shines over a box. A white box. One of Bich Dang's rectangular Styrofoam boxes. Of course he put it here. Of course he put it in the thunderbox.

I pull my legs up and hunch down with the torch over the box, flip the lid off with my left hand. And there is nothing in the box. The torchlight races across the box but no matter how many times I trace it back and forth, nothing appears inside. Empty. Tytus Broz got here first. Tytus Broz knows everything. Tytus Broz is one day older than the universe.

Kick the box. Kick this fucking Styrofoam box. Kick this fucking life of mine and kick fucking Lyle and fucking Tytus Broz and psychotic Iwan Krol and Mum and August and piss-ant Teddy and bullshit Slim who mustn't have ever really given that much of a shit about me if he didn't want to take me home with him in my darkest hour. Slim, of all people, who I woulda thought knew what it felt like to be rag-dolled by life and unwanted and unwished.

My right Dunlop is stomping now. Bits of Styrofoam scatter across the thunderbox floor, falling into shapes on the sawdust ground like disconnected countries on a world map. And what's this shit in my eyes, this bullshit liquid that betrays me every single time? It floods my eyes and my face and I struggle to breathe there's that much of it coming out of me. Yeah, that's it. That's how I'll go. I'll cry myself to death. I'll cry so hard I'll die of water loss right here in this shithole. A shithole end to a shithole existence. Caitlyn Spies can write my story up in the *South-West Star*.

> *The body of thirteen-year-old hospital escapee Eli Bell, who had been missing for eight weeks, was found yesterday at the bottom of a backyard shithole. He had apparently destroyed the box he'd hoped would save the life of the only man he ever really loved. His only relative available for comment, older brother August Bell, said nothing.*

Caitlyn Spies. I fall to the ground in exhaustion. I drop my bony arse into the sawdust and exhale as I rest my back on the rough wood wall of the thunderbox hole. Close your eyes. Breathe. And sleep. Sleep. I turn the torch off and rest it in my waist. It's warm in this shithole. It's cosy. Sleep now. Sleep.

I can see Caitlyn Spies. I can see her. She's walking in the sunset on Bribie Island beach. There are thousands of purple soldier crabs before her but they part for her, they map out a footpath of perfect Queensland beach sand and she paces down it slowly, acknowledging the hardworking soldier crabs with her open palms. She has dark brown hair and it blows in the sea breeze and I can see her face even though I've never seen her face. Her eyes are deep and green and knowing and she smiles because she knows me the same way she knows everything about everything. The soldier crabs at her feet and the sun falling in the sky and her top lip that curls a little when she smiles like that. Caitlyn Spies. The most beautiful girl I've never seen. She wants to tell me something. 'Come closer.

Come closer,' she says, 'and I'll whisper it.' Her lips move and her words are familiar. 'Boy swallows universe,' she says.

And she turns her head and she casts her eyes across what was once the Pacific Ocean but is now a vast galaxy of stars and planets and supernovas and a thousand astronomical events occurring in unison. Explosions of pink and purple. Combustive moments in bright orange and green and yellow and all those glittery stars against the eternal black canvas of space. We are standing at the edge of the universe and the universe stops and starts here with us. And Saturn is within arm's reach. And its rings begin to vibrate. *Buzz. Buzz.* And its vibrating rings sound like a telephone. *Ring, ring.*

'Are you going to get that?' asks Caitlyn Spies.

A telephone. I open my eyes. The sound of a telephone. *Ring, ring.* Back through the secret tunnel, back in the secret room. Lyle's secret red telephone is ringing.

I crawl back through the tunnel. Damp dirt under my bruised kneecaps and my grazed elbows. This call is so important. This call is so perfectly timed. I mean, how about them odds? Me being down here and the phone ringing while I'm down here? I reach the other end of the tunnel and clamber into the secret room and the phone is still ringing. You just wouldn't credit it. Good ol' Eli Bell, the lucky Johnny on the Spot once again, right secret place, right unknown time. I reach out to take the secret red phone handset off the secret red push button base. Wait. Think about this remarkable coincidence. Me down here just as the phone rings. Extraordinarily well timed if you don't know I'm down here. Not so extraordinary, however, if you saw me trying to climb in through the kitchen window. Not so extraordinary if Gene Crimmins has boarded the Tytus Broz gravy train and he was actually foxin' me with all that windowsill kindness. Not so extraordinary if Iwan Krol is waiting outside in a car listening to The Carpenters softly on the radio as he sharpens his Bowie knife.

*Ring, ring.* Fuck it. Sometimes when Saturn calls, you just gotta answer.

'Hello,' I say.

'Hello, Eli,' says the voice down the phone line.

That same voice from last time. The voice of a man. A real man type man. Deep and raspy, weary maybe.

'It's you, isn't it?' I ask. 'The one I spoke to when Lyle said I wasn't speaking to no one but I was.'

'That's me, I guess,' the man says.

'How'd you know I was down here?'

'I didn't,' he says.

'Then it's a hell of a fluke you got me as I was passing through,' I say.

'Not so flukey,' he says. 'I must call this number forty times a day.'

'What number do you dial?'

'I dial the number for Eli Bell,' he says.

'What number is that?'

'773 8173.'

'That's insane,' I say. 'This phone doesn't take calls.'

'Who told you that?'

'Lyle.'

'But isn't this a call?'

'Yeah.'

'So I guess it takes calls,' he says. 'Now, tell me, where are you at?'

'What do you mean?'

'At what stage of your life are you at?'

'Well, I'm thirteen years old …'

'Yes, yes,' he says, urgent. 'But be more specific. Is it close to Christmas?'

'Huh?'

'Never mind,' he says. 'What are you doing right now and why? And please don't lie because I will know if you are lying.'

'Why should I tell you anything?'

'Because I need to tell you something important about your mother, Eli,' he says, frustrated. 'But first I need you to tell me what has just happened to you and your family.'

'Lyle got taken away by some men who work for Tytus Broz,' I say. 'Then Iwan Krol chopped off my lucky finger and I passed out and woke up in hospital and Slim told me Mum got taken to the Boggo Road women's prison and Gus got taken to my father's house in Bracken Ridge and I escaped from hospital and I'm on the run like Slim in 1940 and I came here to find ... to find ...'

'The drugs,' the man says. 'You wanted to find Lyle's stash of heroin because you thought you could take that to Tytus Broz and he might exchange the drugs for Lyle but ...'

'It's gone,' I say. 'Tytus got to the drugs before me. He got the drugs and he got Lyle. He got it all.'

I yawn. I'm so tired. 'I'm tired,' I say down the phone line. 'I'm so tired. I must be dreaming this. This is just a dream.'

My eyes are closing with exhaustion.

'This is not a dream, Eli,' the man says.

'This is crazy,' I say, dizzy now, confused. A fever chill. 'How did you find me?'

'You picked up the phone, Eli.'

'I don't understand. I'm so tired.'

'You need to listen to me, Eli.'

'Okay, I'm listening,' I say.

'Are you really listening?' the man asks.

'Yes, I'm really listening.'

A long pause.

'Your mum will not survive Christmas Day,' the man says.

'What are you talking about?'

'She's on obs, Eli,' he says.

'What's obs?'

'Observation, Eli,' he says. 'Suicide watch.'

'Who are you?'

I'm feeling sick. I need to sleep. I have a fever.

'Christmas is coming, Eli,' the man says.

'You're scaring me and I need to sleep,' I say.

'Christmas is coming, Eli,' he says. 'Sleigh bells.'

'I've gotta lie down.'

'Sleigh bells, Eli,' the man says. 'Sleigh bells!'

'I gotta close my eyes.'

'Sleigh bells,' the man repeats.

What was that song she sang about sleigh bells? 'Sleigh bells ring, are you listenin'? In the lane, snow is glistenin'. Gone away is the blue bird. Here to stay is the new bird.'

'Yeah, sleigh bells,' I say to the man. 'Your end is a dead blue wren.'

And I hang up the phone and I curl up on the earth floor of Lyle's secret room and I pretend that Slim's girl Irene is sleeping down here in the hole with me. I slide into a bed with her and I spoon against her porcelain skin and I reach a comforting arm across her warm breast and she turns to kiss me goodnight with the face of Caitlyn Spies. The most beautiful face I've never seen.

# Boy Meets Girl

The office of the *South-West Star* community newspaper is in Spine Street in Sumner Park, an industrial suburb neighbouring Darra, across the Centenary Highway that takes drivers north into Brisbane's CBD or west towards the Darling Downs. The newspaper office is two doors up from the Gilbert's tyre shop where Lyle goes to get second-hand tyres. It's next door to a window tinting shop and a buy-in-bulk pet supply store called Pawsitively Pets. August and I used to ride our bikes to Spine Street to visit the army disposals store two doors up from here, where we'd look at old military bayonets and Vietnam War water bottles and try to convince the storeowner 'Bomber' Lerner – an excitable Australian patriot with a wonky left eye who loves his country and the defence of it as much as he loves Kenny Rogers – to show us the still-pinned and deadly grenade we knew he kept in a safe beneath his cash register.

The *South-West Star* office is a single-level shop space with a mirrored glass window front and a deep red banner strip of *South-West Star* adorned with four red shooting stars forming the Southern Cross. I see my reflection in the mirrored glass. I'm stronger than yesterday. More coherent. More confident in mind, body and spirit. I had a bowl of four Weet-Bix with hot water from the kitchen tap for breakfast. Showered. Dressed in a maroon T-shirt and blue jeans and the Dunlops. I put a new bandage on my finger and the rest of my hand. Found a fresh bandage in Mum's first-aid kit and re-taped the gauze pad Dr Brennan had already dressed it with. My schoolbag was still hanging over the corner post of my bed. An acid-washed blue denim backpack covered in band names – INXS, Cold Chisel, Led Zeppelin. I've never heard a single song by the Sex Pistols but that didn't stop me from scrawling their name across my backpack two years ago. Across the zipped back pocket there's a sketch of an overweight three-armed alien monster I created named Thurston Carbunkle, who sucks children whole through his nostrils and enjoys the films of Alfred Hitchcock, which is why he's always wearing a sleeveless *Psycho* T-shirt. Between these scribbles are several hard-to-read schoolyard permanent marker messages that, like my throbbing missing finger knuckle, don't age well. 'Sit on this and rotate', says one message over a sketched fist with its middle finger raised. Other messages I really should have removed in the interests of good taste, like 'Kenneth Chugg loves Amy Preston, true luv 4 eva'. Amy Preston died from leukaemia last winter. I stared at that backpack for a full minute, thinking back to simpler times. Pre-this. Pre-that. Pre–finger fucking chop. Fuck that fucking Tytus Broz. I stuffed the backpack full of clothes and food – a couple of cans of baked beans, a muesli bar from the pantry – and Slim's copy of *Papillon* that he lent me and I slipped out the back door of that Darra shithole, vowing never to return. But then I returned thirty seconds after walking out of the front gate when I realised I'd forgotten to take a piss before my long walk to Sumner Park.

I lean into the window to see if I can see through it but I can't see anything except myself up close. I pull on the handle of the mirrored glass entry door and it doesn't budge. There's an oval-shaped white speaker by the door, so I press the green button at the bottom of it.

'Can I help you?' asks a voice through the speaker.

I lean into the speaker.

'Umm, I'm here to …'

'Push the button as you speak please,' the voice says.

I push the button.

'Sorry,' I say.

'How can I help you?' the voice asks. It's a woman. A tough woman who sounds like she breaks macadamia shells in her eye sockets.

'I'm here to see Caitlyn Spies.'

'Push the button as you speak, please.'

I push the button.

'Sorry again,' I say, holding the button. 'I'm here to see Caitlyn Spies.'

'Is she expecting you?'

Well, that does it. The jig is up. Foiled at the first hurdle. Is she expecting me? Well, no. Does a rose expect to be bathed in a sun shower? Does an old-growth tree expect to be struck by lightning? Does the sea expect to ebb and flow?

'Umm, yeah … no,' I say. 'No, she's not expecting me.'

'What are you here to see her about?' the woman asks through the speaker.

'I have a story for her.'

'What's it about?'

'I'd rather not say.'

'Push the button as you speak, please.'

'Sorry, I'd rather not say.'

'Well,' the woman says, exhaling, 'then maybe you can tell me what sort of story it is so I can tell Caitlyn what the hell sort of story it is, since you're being all cagey.'

'What sort of story? I don't know what you mean?'

'News story? Feature story? Community story? Sports story? Council story? Council grievance story? What sort of story?'

I consider this for a moment. Crime story. Missing persons story. Family story. Brothers' story. Tragic story. I press the green button.

'Love story,' I say. I cough. 'It's a love story.'

'Ooooooohhhhh,' says the woman in the speaker. 'I love a good love story.' She howls with laughter.

'What's your name, Romeo?' she asks.

'Eli Bell.'

'Hold on a sec, Eli.'

I look at my reflection in the mirrored glass of the entry door. My hair's all over the place, scruffy. I should have run Lyle's curry comb through it, put a few globs of Lyle's hair gel in it. I turn and scan the street. Still on the lam. Still the wanted unwanted. Unwanted by everybody except the cops. A hulking cement truck barrels down Spine Street, followed by a courier van, a red four-wheel-drive Nissan, a yellow square-shaped Ford Falcon, its driver throwing a cigarette butt out the window.

A crackling sound comes back through the door speaker.

'Hey Romeo ...'

'Yeah.'

'Look, she's real busy right now,' she says. 'Do you want to leave a contact number and a bit of an idea about why you're here and maybe she can get back to you? These journos are always run off their feet.'

The sea will not ebb. The sea will not flow.

I press the green button.

'Tell her I know where Slim Halliday is.'

'Sorry?'

'Tell her I'm best friends with Slim Halliday. Tell her I have a story to tell her.'

190

A long pause.

'Hold on a second.'

\*

I stand for three minutes staring down at a line of black ants group-carrying plunder from a trail of pastry flakes that runs to a half-eaten sausage roll resting on the ground in the Pawsitively Pets car park. I will associate trails of ants with Caitlyn Spies and I will associate half-eaten sausage rolls with the day I tried to see Caitlyn Spies for the first time. The ants bump their heads together every now and then and I wonder if they're questioning, plotting, directing, or just apologising in those brief encounters. Slim and I watched a whole trail of ants marching back and forth along our front steps once. He was having a smoke on the steps and I asked him what he thought those ants were saying to each other as they passed, why on earth it was that they were always touching each other. He said the ants had antennae on their heads and they were talking through those antennae without really talking. Those ants were like August, they'd found their own way of communicating. They talked by feel. Little hairs on the end of the antennae, Slim said, and these hairs passed on smells and those smells told other ants where things were, where they needed to forage, where they were going, where they'd been.

'Food trail pheromones,' Slim said.

'What's a pheromone?' I asked Slim.

'It's like a smell with meaning,' Slim said. 'A chemical reaction that triggers a social response among the ants and they all get that shared meaning.'

'Smells can't have meaning,' I said.

'Sure they can,' Slim said. Slim reached his arm out from the front steps of the house and he ripped a cluster of purple flowers from a lavender bush Mum had planted in the garden. He rubbed the flowers in his closed palm and presented the roughly ground flowers to my nose and I breathed them in.

'What does that smell like?' Slim asked.

'The mother's day stalls at school,' I said.

'So maybe that means your mum,' he said. 'Or maybe now it means these ants crawling down the steps beside your mum's lavender bush. Fruitcake means Christmas. Meat pies mean Redcliffe Dolphins versus Wynnum–Manly and Sunday afternoon football. Salted beer nuts mean your uncle's tying one on. Sunlight soap means a Carlingford winter and the orphan master throwing me in a freezing cold bath to wash the dirt off my kneecaps but the dirt don't come off because he had me kneeling down in mud too long to clean off the front steps of the orphanage. Front steps just like these ones.'

I nodded.

'Trails, kid,' Slim said. 'Where we're goin'. Where we been. Just another way for the world to talk back to ya.'

\*

The speaker crackles on the *South-West Star* entry door.

'Come on in and tell your story, Romeo.'

The door unlocks and I pull it open before it locks shut again. I step into the front foyer of the *South-West Star*. It's airconditioned in here. Blue grey carpet. A water cooler with plastic white cups. A white sign-in desk, a short and stocky woman behind the desk in a crisp white security shirt with navy blue epaulettes on her shoulders. She smiles.

'Just take a seat and she'll be out soon,' the woman says, nodding me towards a two-seat couch and an armchair by the water cooler. Concern on her face.

'You okay?' she asks.

I nod.

'You don't look okay,' she says. 'Your face is all red and sweaty.'

She looks at my strapped hand.

'Who did that dressing?'

I look down at the dressing. The bandage is coming loose, creased in parts, too tight in others, like I received first aid from a blind drunk.

'My mum did it,' I say.

The woman on the desk nods, doubt across her face.

'Grab yourself a water,' she says.

I fill a plastic cup, glug it down with the cup collapsing in my left hand. Fill another and glug it down just as fast.

'How old are you?' the woman asks.

'I turn fourteen in five months,' I say.

I am changing, desk woman, inside and out. My legs are getting longer like my past. I have twenty-plus hairs growing from my right underarm.

'So you're thirteen,' she says.

I nod.

'Your parents know you're here?'

I nod.

'You been walkin' a bit, ay?' she asks.

I nod.

She casts her eyes over my backpack resting at my feet.

'You goin' some place?' she asks.

I nod.

'Where you goin'?' she asks.

'Well, I was goin' here. Then I got here. And after here I'll probably go some place else. But that depends.'

'On what?' asks the woman behind the desk.

'On Caitlyn Spies.'

The woman smiles and turns her head and what she's looking at makes me stand up.

'Well, speak of the devil.'

I stand up the way a thirteen-year-old Aztec boy might have stood up on a beach when he saw a Spanish fleet cutting across the horizon.

She walks towards me. Not towards the security woman behind the desk. Not to the water cooler. Not to the entry door. But towards me. Eli Bell. The most beautiful face I've never seen. I saw that face standing on the edge of the universe. That face spoke to me. That face has always spoken to me. Her deep brown hair is tied back and she wears thick black-rimmed spectacles and a white long-sleeve shirt that hangs loosely over light blue acid-wash jeans and the bottom of her jeans hang over brown leather boots. She carries a pen in her right hand and in that same hand she carries a small yellow Spirax notepad the size of her palm.

She stops before me.

'You know Slim Halliday?' she asks flatly.

And I freeze for two seconds and then my brain tells my mouth to open and then my brain tells my voice box to respond but nothing comes out. I try again but nothing comes out. Eli Bell. Speechless, nothing to say as he stands on the edge of the universe. My voice has temporarily left me, abandoned me like my confidence and my cool. I turn to the water cooler and pour myself another cup of water. As I drink it down my bandaged right hand begins unconsciously scribbling words in thin air. *He's my best friend*, I write on the air with my club of a bandaged hand. *He's my best friend.*

'What are you doing?' Caitlyn Spies asks. 'What is that?'

'Sorry,' I say, relieved to hear the word come out of my mouth. 'My brother, Gus, talks like that.'

'Like what?' Caitlyn Spies asks. 'You looked like you wanted to paint a house but you didn't have a paintbrush.'

I really did look like that, didn't I? She's so funny. So insightful.

'My brother, Gus, doesn't talk. He writes his words in the air.'

'Cute,' she says sharply. 'But I'm on deadline, so you want to hurry up and tell me how you know Slim Halliday?'

'He's my best friend,' I say.

She laughs.

'You're Slim Halliday's best friend? Slim Halliday hasn't been seen in the flesh in three years. Most presume he's dead already. And you're telling me he's alive and well and best friends with a ... what are you, twelve?'

'I'm thirteen,' I say. 'Slim was good friends first with ... well ... Slim was my babysitter.'

She shakes her head.

'Your parents had you babysat by a convicted killer?' she says. 'The Houdini of Boggo Road? The greatest escapee ever locked away in an Australian clink? A man who'd happily sell the kidneys of a thirteen-year-old boy if it meant a clean getaway? That's some classy parenting from your folks there.'

There's warmth in the way she says that. Humour and toughness too, but warmth mostly. Maybe I'm biased because she really looks like the girl of my dreams in a Clark Kent–style thick-rimmed specs disguise, but there's warmth in everything she says. The warmth comes through in the way her top lip kinks up gently in the corner of her mouth and there's warmth in the skin of her cheeks and the colour of her red bottom lip and the deep pools of her green eyes that look like the lilypad-fringed waters of the Enoggera Reservoir where Lyle took August and me for a swim that day we bought the Atari from that family in The Gap in Brisbane's leafy inner west. I want to dive into those green eyes and scream 'Geronimo!' and splash into the world of Caitlyn Spies and never come back up for air.

'Hey,' she says, waving a hand in my face. 'Hey, you there?'

'Yes, I'm here,' I say.

'Yeah, now you are, but just then you drifted off,' she says. 'You started staring right at me, then you went away somewhere, with this goofy look across your face like a giraffe doing a quiet fart.'

That is how I look, isn't it? She's so funny!

I turn to the two-seat couch, whispering.

'Can we sit down for a second?'

She looks at her watch.

'I've got a story for you,' I say. 'But I need to be careful how I tell it.'

She takes a deep breath, sighs on the exhale. She nods, sits down on the couch.

I sit beside her. She flips open her Spirax notepad, takes the lid off her pen.

'You gonna take notes?' I ask.

'Let's not get ahead of ourselves,' she says. 'What's the spelling of your name?'

'Why do you need to know that?'

'Because I'm knitting a cardigan with your name on it.'

I'm confused.

'It's so I can spell your name right in my story.'

'You're gonna write a story about me?'

'If this story you're about to tell me is worth writing about, yes,' she says.

'Can I give you a fake name?'

'Okay,' she says. 'Give me a fake name.'

'Theodore ... Zuckerman.'

'That's a shit fake name,' she says. 'How many Aussies you know called Zuckerman? Let's go with ... oh, I don't know... Eli Bell.'

'How do you know my name?'

She nods to the woman behind the front desk.

'You already told it to Lorraine.'

Lorraine behind the desk gives a knowing grin.

I take a breath. 'No names,' I say.

'All right, no names,' she says. 'Boy, this must be one hell of a yarn, Deep Throat.'

She crosses her legs and turns towards me then looks me in the eye. 'So,' she says.

'So what?' I wonder.

'So tell me something,' she says.

'I really enjoyed the "Queensland Remembers" story you wrote about Slim.'

'Thanks,' she says.

'I liked how you said that in the end the way he finally escaped Boggo Road was by walking out the front door as a free man,' I say.

She nods.

'That's very true,' I say. 'In the end, the greatest trick he ever pulled was surviving. That's the truth of it. People always go on about how cunning he was inside but they never talk about his patience or his will or his determination or how many times he thought about swallowing a rubber band ball filled with razor blades.'

'Nice imagery,' Caitlyn says.

'But you did leave out the most poignant part about Slim's story.'

'Do tell.'

'The fact he wanted to be good but the bad in him kept getting in the way of his plans,' I say. 'He was like any other man, he had good and bad in him, but Slim never got a chance to give the good side a long enough walk down the street. He spent most of his life inside and, when you're inside, bein' good is as good as bein' dead.'

'Aren't you a little young to be thinking about the stories of Queensland cons?' Caitlyn asks. 'Shouldn't you be playing with He–Man figures or something?'

'My brother, Gus, and I burned all our He–Man figures with a magnifying glass.'

'How old is your brother?' she asks.

'He's fourteen,' I say. 'How old are you?'

'I'm twenty-one,' she says.

That hurts. That doesn't make sense. That doesn't feel right for some reason.

'You're eight years older than me,' I say. 'By the time I'm eighteen, you're gonna be … twenty-six?'

She raises an eyebrow.

'By the time I'm twenty you're gonna be …'

She cuts me off: 'What do you care how old I'm gonna be when you're twenty?'

I look again into those green eyes.

'Because I think we're meant to be …'

What, Eli? What are we meant to be exactly? What exactly are you talking about?

The answers to the questions. Your end is a dead blue wren. Caitlyn Spies.

Boy. Swallows. Universe.

I bet August knows what we're meant to be.

'Never mind,' I say. I rub my eyes.

'Are you all right?' Caitlyn asks. 'Can I call your parents for you?'

'No, I'm all right,' I say. 'I'm just tired.'

'What happened to your hand?' she asks.

I stare at my bandaged hand. Tytus Broz. That's what you came here for. Tytus Broz. Not Caitlyn Spies.

'Listen, I'm going to tell you a story but you must be very careful about what you do with it,' I say. 'The men I'm about to tell you about are very dangerous. These men do terrible things to people.'

She looks serious now. 'Tell me what happened to your hand, Eli Bell,' she says.

'Do you know a man named Tytus Broz?' I whisper.

'Tytus Broz?' she ponders.

She starts to scribble the name in her notebook.

'Don't write it down,' I say. 'Just remember the name if you can. Tytus Broz.'

'Tytus Broz,' she says again. 'Who is Tytus Broz?'

'He's the man who took my—'

But I don't finish that sentence because a fist bashes against the office's glass shopfront, just above where we're sitting. I duck down instinctively and so does Caitlyn Spies. *Bang. Bang.* Two fists now.

'Oh shit,' says Lorraine on the front desk. 'It's Raymond Leary.'

'Call the police, Lorraine,' Caitlyn says.

\*

Raymond Leary wears a camel-coloured suit and tie with a white business shirt. Mid-fifties. His face is round and his hair is straw-coloured and scarecrow-straggly. His belly is large and his fists are fat and they bash the shopfront glass with such fury the whole glass panel rattles in place and the water cooler inside shakes a little too. Lorraine presses a button at her desk, speaks into an intercom.

'Mr Leary, please step back from the glass,' she says.

Raymond Leary screams. 'Let me in,' he barks. He puts his face against the glass. 'Let me in!'

Caitlyn moves to the front desk and I follow her. Raymond Leary bashes again on the glass. 'Stay back from the glass,' Caitlyn warns me.

'Who is he?' I ask, moving to Caitlyn's side.

'State government knocked his house down to build an exit road off Ipswich Motorway,' she says. 'Raymond got screwed in the process and then his wife got depression and she threw herself in front of a cement truck on the Ipswich Motorway, just before the new exit road was built over her house.'

'So why's he bashing on your window?' I ask.

'Because we won't tell his story,' Caitlyn says.

Raymond's clenched fists bang against the window.

'Call the police, Lorraine,' Caitlyn says again.

Lorraine nods. Picks up her desk phone.

'Why won't you tell his story?' I ask.

'Because our paper campaigned for the government to put that exit road in,' she says. 'Eighty-nine per cent of our readers wanted improvements made to that section of the motorway.'

Raymond Leary takes five methodical steps back from the glass.

'Oh fuck,' Caitlyn Spies says.

Raymond Leary runs at the glass wall. It takes a moment to actually comprehend that he does this, that this moment is real, because it's so wrong, so truly out of the norm, that it seems impossible. But it is happening. He is really running headfirst at the glass wall and his wide and fatty forehead flesh really does hit the glass wall first with all the weight of, what, a hundred and fifty kilos pushing behind it and the impact is so dramatic and hard that Caitlyn Spies and Lorraine behind the desk and me, Eli Bell – solo adventurer, hospital escapee, lam boy – draw breath sharply and brace for the inevitable shattering of all that dangerous glass but it doesn't give, it just rattles in place, and Raymond Leary's head snaps back like he's broken his neck and I see his eyes register what he's done and his eyes say he's mad, his eyes say he is now animal, his eyes say he is Taurus the Bull.

'Yes, the office of the *South-West Star*, 64 Spine Street, Sumner Park. Please hurry,' Lorraine says down the phone.

He staggers and regathers his footing and then he steps back seven paces this time and he breathes and he charges again at the glass. *Smack.* His head whips back further this time and his legs give way beneath him. Stop it, Raymond Leary. Stop it. A lump emerges in the centre of his forehead. It turns the colour and shape of the old black tennis balls August and I own that have been rubbed and handball-bashed raw from countless games in the middle of Sandakan Street. He steps back again, the rage building and exploding and building again inside him with every step back, shoulders circling in their sockets, his fists clenching. Taurus the Bull wants to die today.

Lorraine speaks urgently into her intercom. 'That's reinforced glass, Mr Leary,' she says. 'You cannot break through it.'

Challenge accepted. Raymond Leary in his frayed camel-coloured suit and his sad attack on a wall of reinforced glass. He charges again. *Whack.* And the impact knocks him down. He lands hard on his left shoulder. Spit coming from his mouth. Groggy and drunk on his own madness. He lurches to his feet, a tear in the left shoulder of his suit jacket. He's dizzy and confused. Moving from side to side. For a moment he turns his back to the glass and this is the moment I choose to rush to the front door of the office.

'Eli, what are you doing?' Caitlyn Spies barks.

I open the door.

'Eli, stop, don't go out there,' Caitlyn Spies warns. 'Eli!'

I go out there. I slip out the entry door and close it quickly behind me.

Raymond Leary wobbles on his feet, punch-drunk. He steps three times to his side and stops on the spot and turns to set his eyes on me. There's a split across his forehead and his forehead is black and swollen and the split throbs with blood and this red blood spills down his face, down the mountain of a busted nose, across the ridges of his trembling lips, along the plain of his wide and dimpled chin and onto his crisp white business shirt and tie.

'Stop it,' I say.

He stares into my eyes and he tries to understand me and I think he does because he breathes and that's what humans do. We breathe. And we think. But we get mad too. We get so sad and we get so mad.

'Please stop it, Raymond,' I say.

And he breathes again and he steps back. Confused by this moment. Confused by this boy before him. Across the road, at a hole-in-the-wall snack shop selling meat pies and chips with gravy, several men in workwear are looking over at this scene.

The street is quiet. No cars passing. This moment is frozen in time. The bull and the boy.

I can hear him breathing. He's exhausted. He's spent. Something registers in his eyes. Something human.

'They don't want to hear my story,' he says.

He turns to the glass wall and finds himself in the mirrored reflection.

'I'll hear your story,' I say.

His right hand rubs the swelling in his forehead. Blood covers his fingers and his fingers trace the blood running down his face. His right palm finds the blood now and the palm rubs the blood in circles around his forehead. He rubs it across his whole face. The colour red. He turns to me like he's just woken up from a dream. *How did I get here? Who are you?* He shakes his head in disbelief. And he drops his head and the workmen from the meat pie shop are crossing the road now and Raymond Leary seems to have stopped.

'You all right, kid?' calls one of the workmen.

And, with that, Raymond Leary raises his head and finds himself again in the glass and he runs at himself in the glass and his bloody face meets his bloody face and both versions of Raymond Leary fall unconscious to the ground.

Three workmen rush across the road, form a half-circle around Raymond Leary.

'What the fuck's his malfunction?' one of the workmen asks.

I say nothing. I just stare at Raymond Leary. He lies flat on his back with his arms outstretched and his legs outstretched like he was drawn up for scientific study by da Vinci.

Caitlyn Spies emerges cautiously from the front door, looking at Raymond Leary flat on his back.

Caitlyn's fringe hangs over her face and a light gust of wind blows it about like there's a puppet in a dress dancing across her forehead and the sun makes Caitlyn Spies beautiful because it lights up her face and makes her move outside of time, outside of life, like she's walking in slow motion along the edge of the universe.

She walks over to me. Over to me, Eli Bell. Boy on the lam. Boy in trouble.

She rests a gentle hand on my left shoulder. Her hand on me. Boy on the lam. Boy in love.

'Are you okay?' she asks.

'I'm okay,' I say. 'Is he ...?'

'I don't know,' she says. She looks closer at Raymond Leary, then steps back, shaking her head.

'You're a brave boy, Eli Bell,' she says. 'Stupid, but stupid brave.'

The sun is in me now. The sun is my heart, and all the world – the fishermen in China and the corn farmers in Mexico and the fleas on the backs of the dogs in Kathmandu – relies on the rising and falling of my full heart.

A police car pulls up on the side of the road, its front right wheel biting into the concrete guttering. Two male police officers exit the vehicle and rush to Raymond Leary on the ground. 'Step back, please,' says one officer, slipping on a pair of gloves as he kneels down to Raymond Leary. A pool of blood builds on the concrete beside Raymond's left ear.

Police.

'Goodbye, Caitlyn Spies,' I say.

I step back from the small group gathered around Raymond.

'Huh?' she says. 'Where you going?'

'I'm going to see my mum,' I say.

'But what about your story?' she asks. 'You haven't told me your story.'

'The timing's not right,' I say.

'The timing?'

'The *time*'s not right,' I say, walking backwards.

'You're a curious boy, Eli Bell,' she says.

'Will you wait?' I ask.

'Wait for what?' she asks.

Lorraine from the front desk calls out to Caitlyn from the group surrounding Raymond Leary. 'Caitlyn,' she says, 'the officers have some questions.'

Caitlyn turns her head to Lorraine and the police and the scene before the wall of glass. And I run. I sprint up Spine Street and my bony legs are quick but maybe not quicker than Christmas.

Wait for the universe, Caitlyn Spies. Wait for me.

# Boy Stirs Monster

The moon pool. All the way out here on the northern fringe of the city. The full midnight moon shines for August Bell anywhere, so why wouldn't it shine for him in Bracken Ridge, home of King Arthur and the Knights of the Round Table.

Number 5 Lancelot Street. Robert Bell's small orange brick house in the Queensland Housing Commission cluster of small orange brick homes just down the hill from Arthur Street and Gawain Road and Percivale Street and Geraint Street. Here sits Sir August the Mute, in the gutter by a black letterbox fixed to a weather-beaten stick. He has a garden hose resting on his right thigh as he fills a flat pan of Lancelot Street bitumen in precise angles to reflect a full moon so vivid that the man inside it can be seen with his lips wet whistling 'And the Band Played Waltzing Matilda'.

I watch him from behind a blue Nissan family van parked five houses further up the street. He looks up at the moon then he kinks the garden hose in his hands so the water stops and the moon pool stills, reflecting a perfect silver moon. Then he reaches for an old rusted 7-iron golf club that sits beside him and he stands and he leans over the moon pool and stares into his reflection. He flips the club upside down and, with the

205

handle end, he taps the very centre of his pool. And he sees things only he can see.

Then he looks up and sees me.

'So I guess you can talk when you want to?' I say.

He shrugs his shoulders, scribbles in the air. *Sorry Eli.*

'Say it.'

He drops his head. Considers something for a moment. Looks back up.

'Sorry,' he says.

Boy sounds soft and fragile and nervous and unsure. Boy sounds like me.

'Why, Gus?'

'Why what?'

'Why the fuck weren't you talking?'

He breathes.

'Safer that way,' he says. 'Can't hurt anyone that way.'

'What are you talking about, Gus?'

August looks down at the moon pool. He smiles.

'Can't hurt you, Eli,' he says. 'Can't hurt us. There are things I want to say, but if I said them, Eli, people would be frightened by those things.'

'What things?'

'Big things. The kinds of things that people would not understand, things that would make people misunderstand me if I said them. Then they'd misunderstand us, Eli. And then they'd take me away and who'd be left to look after you.'

'I can get by just fine on my own.'

August smiles. He nods.

A streetlight shines above us. All the lights in all the houses in the street are off, except for the living room light of our house.

He nods me over. I stand beside him and we stare into the moon pool. *Watch this*, he does not say. He taps the pool with the handle end of the 7–iron and circular ripples spread out into the pool from the central point of impact and our reflection – the two of us brothers – is fractured thirteen or fourteen times over.

August scribbles in the air. *You and me and you and me and you and me and you and me and …*

'I don't understand,' I say.

He taps the pool again and points to the ripples.

'I think I'm losing my mind, Gus,' I say. 'I think I'm going crazy. I need to sleep. I feel like I'm walking in a dream and this is the end bit that feels really real, the bit just before I wake up.'

He nods.

'Am I going crazy, Gus?'

'You're not crazy, Eli,' August says. 'But you are special. Didn't you ever have that feeling you were special?'

'I'm not special,' I say. 'I think I'm just tired.'

We both stare into the moon pool.

'So you're going to talk to people now?'

August shrugs.

'I'm still thinking about that,' he says. 'Maybe I could just talk to you?'

'Everybody's gotta start somewhere.'

'You know what I realised in all that time with my mouth shut?'

'What?'

'Most things people say don't need to be said,' he says.

He taps the moon pool.

'I've been thinking about all the things Lyle said to me,' August says. 'He said so many things, and I reckon all those things put together wouldn't say as much as he said when he'd wrap his arm around my shoulder.'

'What did Lyle tell you across the table?'

'He told me where the drugs were,' he says.

207

'Where are the drugs?' I ask.

'I'm not telling you,' he says.

'Why not?'

'Because he also told me to protect you,' he says.

'Why?'

'Lyle knew you were special too, Eli.'

I tell him about my adventure. I tell him about my quest. I tell him how I met Caitlyn Spies. I tell him how beautiful she is. How everything about her feels right. 'I feel like I know her,' I say. 'But that's impossible, right?'

August nods.

'How did you know her name that day?' I ask. 'That day you were sitting on the fence at home and you were writing her name over and over and over? Was that one of the big things? One of those things you know but can't say because it's safer that way.'

August shrugs.

'I just saw her name in the paper,' he says.

I tell him everything about her face. About her walk. About the way she speaks.

I tell him everything. About my escape from the hospital, my encounter with Batman, going back to Darra, returning to the secret room and the message from the man on the phone about Mum.

My story is interrupted by a deep howling sound coming from the living room of number 5 Lancelot Street.

'What the fuck is that?'

'That's Dad,' August says.

'Is he dying in there or something?'

'He's singing,' August says.

'Sounds like he's talking to a whale.'

'He's singing to Mum,' August says.

'Mum?'

'He does it every second night,' August says. 'He spends the first four cups of goon cursing her, calling her every name under the sun. Then he spends the next four cups singing to her.'

This strange howling wobbles and wails out through the large front sliding window built into the orange brick house. There are no words in the howling, just sorrow, a deranged vocal warbling, slobbering and woozy and guttural, like an opera singer hitting a crescendo with a mouth full of marbles.

Blue and grey flashes of television light bounce off the living room walls visible through the front window.

I scan the house for a moment.

All the houses in the street are Housing Commission houses and all these Housing Commission houses in the street are built the same: low-set three-bedroom shoeboxes with a two-step access to a porch off the left side and a concrete ramp running to the back door. My father hasn't mowed the lawn at the front of number 5 Lancelot Street. My father hasn't mowed the lawn at the back of the house either. But he must mow the front lawn more than the back because the front lawn grass reaches my kneecaps but the back lawn grass would reach my nose.

'This place is a shithole,' I say.

August nods.

'We gotta go see her, Gus,' I say. 'We gotta go see Mum. She just needs to see us and she'll be all right.'

I nod to the living room window.

'He'll take us to see her,' I say.

August tips his head to the side, a look of doubt. He says nothing.

\*

The howl singing gets stronger as we step onto the front porch. *OOOOoooowwwwwwwwwwwoooooooooooo*. The pain in it. The melodrama.

Some strange incoherent warbling along to a song about the night and fate and death.

August leads us through a thick wooden front door roughly painted a deep brown.

The floors in the living room are dark brown wood, unpolished. By the entry there's a cream-coloured cabinet from the 1960s that's mostly empty but for six or seven old mugs, a brown bowl holding a wooden banana, apple and orange, and a novelty metal faux bumper sticker: *DISLEXICS ARE TEOPLE POO*. The fibro walls of the living room are painted a peach colour and there are small and large holes and dents on every wall and these random holes and dents are interspersed with blotches of white paint where other holes have been puttied up. There's a framed print on the wall of a beautiful woman in a white dress sitting in a boat on a pond with her arms out, a look of despair on her face.

My father doesn't see us enter the house. He's somewhere in the corner haze of tobacco smoke and 1960s peyote rock music. He's kneeling on the floor half a metre from a television that has its volume down with white noise static fuzz filling the screen. My father rests an elbow unsteadily on a square white coffee table scratched in parts to reveal historical layers of multicoloured paint coatings, like the inside of a jawbreaker lolly. Beside his bare right foot is a yellow plastic cup like the ones I used to glug cordial from in primary school. Next to the cup is a silver wine cask bladder wrung to death like an old chamois.

Robert Bell's howl singing is an attempt to sing along with The Doors, coming through a stereo at full volume beside the television.

My father howls again, his voice cracking on the high notes and drowning in spit and drink on the lows. And my father can't follow the words of Jim Morrison so he puts his head back and howls and his pack of post-midnight wolves should be arriving soon. He's thin and bony with a beer belly and a salt and pepper crew cut. If Lyle is John Lennon then this man is George Harrison, gaunt and dark and haunting. A white singlet and blue Stubbies shorts. I guess he must be forty by now. Looks fifty. Tattoos look sixty, old homemade jobs like Lyle's. A python wrapped around a crucifix on his right forearm. An image of a giant ship, *Titanic* maybe, sailing across his right calf beneath the letters *S.O.S.*

A monster singing in that ghost–smoke corner of the living room, curled up and kneeling like that, howling like that. The monster looks like he belongs in some basement with Igor and his friends, Lobster Boy and Camel Girl. And my father's bloodshot right eyeball moves inside its socket beneath the tan chewing gum spread of his old and worn-in face and finds me.

'Hi, Dad,' I say.

His face wobbles as he looks at me, then his right hand fumbles for something beneath the coffee table. He finds an axe handle, a shapely hard brown wooden club without the chopping blade at the top. He grips this weapon and staggers to his feet. 'Whoooooooo ...' he snarls. 'Whhaaaa ...' His shorts are soiled with his own piss. He grits his teeth, spit coming from his mouth. Trying to say something. Trying so hard to form words. He sways as he stares at me and he finds his balance. 'UUUUUuuuuuuuu ...' he spits. He wets his lips and says it again. 'UUUUuuuuuuuuuuuuu.' Then he goes again. 'Cuuuuuuuuuuunt,' he spits, breathless, struggling to find the word. Then, quicker than I can comprehend it, he pads straight for me, raising the axe handle high, ready to swing it.

'Cuuuuuuuuuunnnnnnnnnt,' he screams.

I stand in place, my brain not presenting me with a better defence than my forearms covering my skull.

But Sir August the Mute, Sir August the Brave, stands in front of me. In one perfect motion, August's clenched right fist hooks into my father's left temple, bringing the man with the axe handle down low enough for August to grip the back of his singlet with both hands and build on his forward momentum with a heaving throw that drives his drunk head into the peach-coloured wall behind us. My father's skull puts a hole in the wall just before it drops, already unconscious, with the rest of his body to the unpolished wooden floor. We stand above him. He has his lips pressed to the floor, his eyelids closed. He still grips the axe handle.

August breathes.

'Don't worry,' he says. 'He's actually quite lovely when he's sober.'

*

August opens the old Kelvinator fridge in the kitchen. It's covered in so much rust that it leaves bronze dust on my hands when I touch it.

'Sorry, not much to eat,' August says.

There's a bottle of water in the fridge and a tub of Meadow Lea margarine and a jar of pickled onions, as well as something mouldy and black growing in the bottom crisper, an old piece of steak, maybe, or a small human.

'What have you been having for dinner?' I ask.

August opens the pantry door, points to six Home Brand packets of chicken noodles.

'Bought these a few days ago,' he says. 'I bought a bag of frozen vegetables to mix in with them. You want me to do you up some?'

'Nah, thanks. I just need to sleep.'

I follow August back past my father, splayed out unconscious in the living room, and down a hallway to the first bedroom on the left.

'This is where I sleep,' he says. The room has deep blue carpet and a single bed against the left wall, and an old wardrobe with peeling cream-coloured paint opposite the bed.

'I guess you could crash on the carpet beside me,' August says.

August points down the hallway to the bedroom at the end of it.

'Dad's room,' he says.

I point to the bedroom next to August's. Its door is closed.

'What about this one?'

'That's the library,' he says.

'The library?'

August opens the door of the bedroom and flicks on the light switch. There are no beds in this room or wardrobes or paintings on the wall. There are only books. But the books aren't stacked neatly on shelves for there are no shelves to speak of. There is only a mountain of books, paperbacks mostly, building from all four corners of the room to form a peak in the bedroom's centre that reaches the height of my eye line. Nothing in the room but a volcano-shaped pile of books in the thousands. Thrillers and westerns and romance novels and classics and action-adventure novels and thick textbooks about mathematics and biology and human movement studies and books of poetry and Australian history and war and sport and books on religion.

'Are these all his?' I ask.

August nods.

'Where does he get them all from?' I ask.

'He gets 'em from the op shops,' August says. 'I think he's read them all.'

'That's impossible,' I say.

'I don't know,' August says. 'All he does is read. And drink.'

He nods to the bedroom at the end of the hallway.

'He wakes up early in the morning, around 5 a.m., and he rolls all the smokes he's gonna smoke any given day, and that might be thirty or forty smokes, then he just reads books and smokes the smokes he's rolled.'

'Does he ever come out?'

'Yeah, he comes out when he's having a drink,' August says. 'And when he wants to watch *Sale of the Century* on the telly.'

'That's fucked up,' I say.

August nods.

'Yeah, but he blitzes *Sale of the Century.*'

'I gotta piss,' I say.

August nods, moves to the toilet and bathroom, next to my father's bedroom. He opens the toilet door and we both recoil at the smell of old urine and beer.

Above the plastic toilet top rest several torn and rough-shaped squares from *The Courier-Mail* newspaper, which August uses to wipe his arse.

The toilet's floor space is just long enough and wide enough to accommodate a porcelain toilet and an opening door and the floor is currently holding an inch-deep pool of my father's piss. A yellow fluffy toilet mat the colour of a baby chick is soaked in piss in the corner beside a toilet brush leaning against the wall. 'His aim turns to shit after the fifth cup,' August says, standing at the edge of my father's urine pool. 'You can piss from outside if you want. If you have a full tank you'll probably make it from here.'

I line up at the edge of the piss pool and unzip my fly.

\*

August takes a sheet and a towel from the hallway cupboard. In his bedroom he rolls the towel up into a pillow for my head. I lie back on his deep blue carpet and pull the sheet over me. August stands by the bedroom door. He raises his right hand to the light switch.

'You good?' he asks.

'Yeah, I'm good,' I say, spreading my legs out for a better sleeping position.

'It's good to see you, Gus,' I say.

'It's good to see you, Eli,' he says.

'It's good to talk to you,' I say.

He smiles.

'It's good to talk to you,' he says. 'Get some sleep. Everything's gonna be all right.'

'You really think so?' I ask.

He nods.

'Don't worry, Eli,' he says. 'It gets good.'

'What gets good?'

'This life of ours,' he says.

'How do you know it gets good?'

'The man on the phone told me.'

I nod. Nah, we're not crazy. We're just tired. We just need some sleep.

'Night, Gus,' I say.

'Night, Eli.'

The light goes off and darkness fills the room. August steps over me to get to his bed. I hear the springs in his bed sink down as he lies back. Silence. Eli and August Bell together again in another black bedroom. Slim says he would sometimes open his eyes in darkness like this, the darkness upon darkness underground in Black Peter, and he'd pretend the darkness wasn't darkness at all. It was just space, he says. Deep space. Deep universe.

'Gus?'

'Yes.'

'Do you think Lyle is still alive?'

Silence. A long silence.

'Gus?'

'Yes.'

'Oh,' I say, 'I was just checking you hadn't stopped talking again.'

Silence.

'Please don't stop talking to me, Gus. I like talking to you.'

'I won't stop talking to you, Eli.'

Silence. Deep universe silence.

'Do you think Lyle is still alive?' I ask.

'What do you think, Eli?'

I think about this. I think about this often.

'You remember what Lyle used to say about the Parramatta Eels when he really knew the team was gonna get beat but he didn't want to admit it?'

'Yeah,' August says.

Silence.

'Do you remember what he said?'

'Yeah, sorry,' August says. 'I just wrote it in the air.'

'Good,' I say. 'I don't want to say it.'

Just keep it in the air. That's where Lyle Orlick can stay, maybe. In the air. In my head. In my heart. In my rage. In my vengeance. In my hatred. In my time that will come. In my universe.

'You remember that day we ate all the mulberries?' August asks.

I remember. The mulberry tree that hung over the back fence of the Darra house, flopped over the fence lazily from Dot Watson's house behind us. Slim was looking after us that day but he didn't know we had eaten so many fat burgundy mulberries that day until I vomited a purple river after lunch. I ran out the back door off the laundry but I didn't make it to the grass. I chucked up the purple river all across the path that led to the clothesline. A purple stain splashed across the concrete like someone had dropped a bottle of fine red wine on it. Slim had no sympathy for my aching belly, just made me wash it up with Pine-O-Cleen and hot water. Once I'd cleaned it all up, Slim said he wanted to make a mulberry pie like the ones he had eaten in a boys' home down south.

'Remember the story he told us about the boy who had the universe in his mouth?' August asks.

We were pulling mulberries off the tree when Slim started telling us about some story he read in Boggo Road once, a story about some god, or some special guy from a religion different from the wooden cross one we knew, not one where Jesus was the hero, but one that was spoken of in the kinds of places Slim said Indiana Jones liked to visit. He said there was this special boy who was actually a special man and this special boy was running around with a bunch of other kids, older kids, playing near a sprawling fruit tree. And the older kids didn't let this special boy climb the fruit tree with them because he was too small but they let him pick up the fruits that fell from the tree as they climbed. The older kids warned the boy not to eat the fruits because they weren't clean. 'Just collect them,' said an older boy. But the boy began stuffing his mouth with the fat and juicy purple fruits that lay on the ground. He ate these fruits like he was possessed, so ravenous for them that he started picking them up with clumps of earth and shoving them in his busy mouth, fruit and soil together, shoving them in so hard that purple fruit rivers started flowing from the sides of his mouth. 'What are you doing?' the older boys asked. 'What are you doing? Explain yourself. Give us some answers. Give us all the answers.' But the boy said nothing. He did not speak. He could not speak, with his mouth so full of tainted fruit. The older kids demanded he stop but the boy kept eating, so they ran to fetch the boy's mother. 'Your boy is eating mud!' the older kids hollered. The boy's mother, mad as hell, demanded her son open his mouth to show her the evidence of his recklessness, his greed, his insanity. 'Open your mouth!' she barked. And the boy opened his mouth and the mother looked inside and saw trees and snow-capped mountains and blue sky and all the stars and all the moons and planets and suns of the universe. And the mother hugged her boy close. 'Who are you?' she whispered. 'Who are you? Who are you?'

'Who was he?' I asked Slim.

'He was the boy with all the answers,' Slim said.

*

I speak into the darkness of our bedroom.

'The boy had a whole world inside of him,' I say.

'The boy who swallowed the universe,' August says.

Silence in the dark.

'Gus,' I say.

'Yeah?' August replies.

'Who is the man on the red phone?'

'Do you really want to know?'

'Yes.'

'I don't think you're ready to know,' he says.

'I'm ready to know.'

A long pause in the universe.

'You just wrote it in the air, didn't you?' I say.

'Yes,' he says.

'Please tell me, Gus. Who's the man on the red phone?'

A long pause in the universe.

'It's me, Eli.'

# Boy Loses Balance

I will remember Mrs Birkbeck through the plastic Santa Claus dancing on a coil spring next to the phone on Mrs Birkbeck's office desk. Second week of December. Last week of school. Christmas is coming. Sleigh bells ring. Are you listening?

Poppy Birkbeck is the Nashville State High School guidance counsellor with the sunshine smile and the remarkably impervious optimism that refuses to shatter in a daily world of aborted teenage pregnancies and drug-addicted sixteen-year-olds and suburban Bracken Ridge child molesters touching up boys with wildly aggressive behavioural disorders who go home to wildly ignorant parents who go to dinner with suburban Bracken Ridge child molesters.

'Frankly, Eli,' says Mrs Birkbeck, 'I don't know why we don't just remove you from school altogether.'

Nashville High has nothing to do with Tennessee. Nashville was a suburb between Bracken Ridge and Brighton, further north towards Redcliffe, before it got squeezed out – obliterated – by time and progress. Nashville High is a thirty-minute walk from our house, through a tunnel passing under the main road that takes locals to the Sunshine Coast. I've been at the school six weeks now. On the second day a Year 10 boy named Bobby Linyette welcomed me to school by inexplicably spitting on my left shoulder as I passed by the Social Science building's water cooler. It was a golly, a real deep snort of a golly, filled with yellowy phlegm and snot and all that is wrong with Bobby Linyette, who sat laughing on the Social Science port racks amid a group of giggling zit-faced hyena buddies with mullet cuts. Bobby Linyette raised his right hand and hid his right forefinger as he waved his hand around. 'Where is pointer? Where is pointer?' he sang, a kindergarten teacher singing in the tune of 'Frère Jacques'.

I looked down at my missing forefinger. My skin was winning the war on the open wound, gradually closing around the bone, but I still had to wear a small dressing over it, all the more eye-catching to wild schoolyard lions like Bobby Linyette.

Then his pointer forefinger appeared. 'Here I am. Here I am.' He guffawed. 'Fuckin' freak,' he said.

Bobby Linyette is fifteen years old and has two chins and chest hair. In the third week of my enrolment, Bobby Linyette's friends held me down as Bobby squirted the entire contents of a tomato sauce bottle from the tuckshop into my hair and down the back of my shirt. I did not report these deeply frustrating acts to the teachers because I didn't want something as mind-numbingly predictable as school bullying upsetting my plan. August offered to stab Bobby Linyette in the ribs with Dad's fishing knife, but I asked him not to because I knew that, apart from the fact it was well past the time when August had to stop fighting my battles, this too would upset my plan. In the beginning of this sixth week of my enrolment, in the tunnel underpass as I was walking home from school last Monday, Bobby Linyette tore my canvas backpack from my shoulders and set it alight. I watched that backpack burning and the fire in my eyes told me, deep down inside, that Bobby Linyette had just upset my plan, largely because inside that backpack were my plans. A whole blue-lined school exercise book filled with all my ideas and carefully crafted strategies written in ink. I had schedules in that pad and diagrams and sketches of grappling hooks and ropes and measurements of walls. The masterpiece of these plans was sketched in pencil across the pad's central two-page opening, the product of valuable prison intel passed directly to me by the Houdini of Boggo Road. A perfect bird's-eye-view 2B-pencil blueprint of the grounds and building layout of the Boggo Road Women's Prison.

'How could you do something so ... so ... violent?' Poppy Birkbeck asks across her desk.

She dresses like one of the 1960s singers Mum loves. She dresses like Melanie Safka. Her arms are folded across her desk and from her elbows hang the fire-coloured sleeves of a loose dress, part American Indian smoking ceremony leader, part Sunshine Coast hinterland seller of sculptures carved from tree trunks.

'I mean, this is not the kind of behaviour one displays in the schoolyard,' she says.

'I know, Mrs Birkbeck,' I say sincerely, putting the plan back on track. 'It's not schoolyard behaviour. It's more like something you'd find in a prison yard.'

'It really is, Eli,' she says.

And it really was. Straight out of Boggo Road's Number 1 yard. A simple slice of porridge thuggery. All one needs is a pillowcase, something unbreakable and a breakable kneecap.

I had stolen a pillowcase from the Year 8 Home Economics class at 10 a.m. that morning. We were learning to sew. Most of us boys sewed handkerchiefs. But the real Home Economics stars like Wendy Docker sewed pillowcases adorned with stitched images of Australian fauna. I filled Wendy Docker's kookaburra pillowcase with two five-kilo weight plates I stole from the sports equipment room during our 11 a.m. Health and Physical Education class.

Shortly after the 12.15 p.m. lunch bell I found Bobby Linyette standing in line at the central quad handball courts scoffing a Chiko roll among his hyena buddies.

I approached Bobby the way my pen pal Alex Bermudez, former Rebels motorcycle gang Queensland sergeant-at-arms, said one should approach the unaware victim in a shiv attack. I knew the words of Alex's letters like I knew the words to 'Candles in the Rain' by Melanie Safka.

*You want to be coming at the victim from behind, shove the shiv in as close as you can to the kidneys. They'll drop like a bag of spuds. The key is to shove the shiv in hard enough to get your point across, but soft enough to avoid a murder charge. A fine balance indeed.*

I shuffled quick and hard at Bobby, the pillowcase twisted taut so the five-kilo weights became the head of a cotton kookaburra-embroidered mace, and I swung with force at his right kidney, just above his grey school shorts. His Chiko roll dropped to the ground as he keeled over to his right, collapsing like a crushed can of Pasito with the pain and shock of impact. He had time enough to register my face and time enough for rage blood to fill his own but not time enough to anticipate my follow-up full arm swing blow to his right kneecap. Hard enough to get my point across. Soft enough to avoid expulsion. Bobby hopped on his left foot for two steps, clutching desperately at his busted right kneecap, then he crashed down on his back on the rough skin-grazing bitumen of the handball court's King square. I stood above him with the pillowcase weights raised above his head and I knew the fury inside me was the only gift my father had given me in a decade.

222

'Cuuuuuunnnt!' I screamed down into his face. Spit was coming from my mouth. The holler was so loud and primal and frightening and mad that Bobby's friends stood back from us like they were stepping back from a bonfire with a burning can of petrol at its core.

'Stop it,' I said.

Bobby was crying now. Bobby was pale and his face was red and reeling so hard away from the pillow weights I thought his head might sink through the handball court.

'Please stop it,' I said.

*

Mrs Birkbeck's office is decorated with painted aluminium animals, a green frog clinging above a filing cabinet on the wall to my right. An eagle soaring along the wall behind her back. A koala clinging to a gum tree she's painted on the wall to my left. These decorations all serve to complement the office's real talking piece, a large framed wall print of a penguin scurrying across a vast ice desert above the words, *LIMITATIONS: Until You Spread Your Wings You'll Have No Idea How Far You Can Walk.*

On her desk beside her phone is a fundraising coin box for Shelly Huffman.

I hope Poppy Birkbeck takes that Limitations penguin poster down for Shelly.

There's a picture of Shelly smiling on the coin box in her Nashville uniform, all gappy teeth in one of those forced over-the-top smiles Artful Dodger kids like Shelly smile when some gruff photographer asks them to put a little more effort into it. Shelly is in my Year 8 class. She lives around the corner from our house in a Housing Commission place on Tor Street, which August and I walk down to get to school. Four months ago,

Shelly's parents found out that the second eldest of their four kids will live the rest of her life with muscular dystrophy. August and I like Shelly, even if she is an A-grade smartarse most days we walk past her house. She's the only friend we've made so far in Bracken Ridge. She keeps asking me to challenge her to arm wrestles on her front porch. She usually beats me because her arms are stronger boned and longer boned and she has me beat on leverage. 'Nah, hasn't come yet,' she says when she beats me. She says she'll know when the muscular dystrophy has properly arrived when I can beat her in an arm wrestle. The school is on a fundraising drive to help fit out Shelly's home with outside and inside wheelchair ramps and rails in the bathroom and Shelly's bedroom and kitchen, generally making the house what Shelly calls 'fuck-up friendly'. Then the school hopes to purchase a wheelchair-friendly family van for the Huffmans, so they can still drive Shelly to Manly on the east side of Brisbane where she likes to watch skiffs and yachts and tin rowboats sail into the Moreton Bay horizon. The school hopes to raise $70,000 to future-proof the home. The school's so far raised $6217 or what Shelly calls 'half a ramp'.

Mrs Birkbeck clears her throat and leans in close across the desk.

'I phoned your father four times and he did not answer.'

'He never answers the phone,' I say.

'Why not?'

'Because he doesn't like talking to people.'

'Can you please ask him to call me?'

'He can't.'

'Why not?'

'Our phone only takes incoming calls. The only number it can call is triple zero.'

'Can you ask him to please come in and see me? It's extremely important.'

'I can ask, but he won't.'

'Why not?'

'Because he doesn't like to leave the house. He only ever really leaves the house between the hours of 3 a.m. and 6 a.m. when nobody else is around. Or when he's pissed and he's run out of piss.'

'Watch your mouth.'

'Sorry.'

Mrs Birkbeck sighs, leans back in her chair.

'Has he taken you and August to see your mother yet?'

*

I slept in after that first night in Lancelot Street. I woke to find August's bed was empty and my neck was stiff from sleeping on a rolled bath towel. I walked out of August's room across the hall and past my father's open bedroom door on the way to the toilet. I saw him on his bed. He was reading. I opened the door of the toilet and I saw that the toilet floor was now spotlessly clean and smelling of disinfectant. I took a long piss and walked into the bathroom off the toilet. The bathroom was four white walls, a yellow bathtub, a mould-covered shower curtain, a mirror, a sink, a lonely and spent lick of yellow soap and a lime green plastic circular comb. I stared at myself in the mirror and I didn't know if I was sick from hunger or sick from the question I had to ask the man reading in the room beyond the bathroom door. I knocked on his door and he turned to me and I tried to not look like I was looking so hard at the darkness of his face and I was thankful for all the translucent blue-grey cigarette smoke filling the room that put a veil between us.

'Can we go see Mum?' I asked.

'No,' he said.

And he returned to his book.

*

Mrs Birkbeck sighs.

'I've asked him a hundred times in the past six weeks and he says the same thing,' I say.

'Why do you think he doesn't want to take you up to see her?' Mrs Birkbeck asks.

'Because he still loves Mum,' I say.

'Wouldn't that mean he'd want to see her?'

'Nah, because he hates her too.'

'Did you ever consider the possibility that your father might be shielding you from that world? Perhaps he feels you shouldn't have to see your mum in that situation.'

No, I didn't ever consider that.

'Have you spoken to your mum?'

'No.'

'Has she called the house?'

'No. I don't expect her to either. She's not well.'

'How do you know that?'

'I just know.'

Mrs Birkbeck looks at my right hand.

'Tell me again how you lost your finger?'

'August chopped it off with an axe but he didn't mean to.'

'He must have been devastated when he realised what he'd done.'

I shrug. 'He was pretty philosophical about it,' I say. 'August doesn't really do devastation.'

'How's your finger coming along?'

'It's good. Healing.'

'Are you writing okay?'

'Yeah, bit messy, but I get by.'

'You like to write, don't you?'

'Yeah.'

'What sort of things do you like to write?'

I shrug. 'I write true crime stories sometimes,' I say.

'What about?'

'Anything. I read the crime features in *The Courier-Mail* and then I write my own versions of those stories.'

'That's your goal, isn't it?'

'What?'

'To write about crime.'

'One day I'm going to write for *The Courier-Mail*'s crime pages.'

'You interested in crime?'

'I'm not interested in crime as much as the people who commit crimes.'

'What interests you about the people?'

'I'm interested in how they got to the point they got to. I'm interested in that moment when they decided to be bad instead of good.'

Mrs Birkbeck sits back in her chair. Studies my face.

'Eli, do you know what trauma is?' she asks.

Her lips are thick and she uses a lot of deep red lipstick. I will remember trauma through Poppy Birkbeck's ruby bead necklace.

'Yes,' I say.

I will remember the plan.

'And do you know that trauma can reach us in many forms, wearing many masks, Eli?' she asks.

'Yes,' I say.

'Trauma can be brief. Trauma can last a lifetime. There are no fixed ends on trauma, correct?'

'Correct.'

Stick to the plan.

'You and August have endured great trauma, haven't you?'

I shrug, nod at the fundraising coin box on her desk.

'Well, nothing like Shelly,' I say.

'Yes, but that's a different kind of trauma,' Mrs Birkbeck says. 'Nobody was responsible for her misfortune.'

'Shelly did call God an arsehole the other day,' I say.

'Watch your mouth.'

'Sorry.'

Mrs Birkbeck leans in closer across her desk, places her right hand over her left hand. There's something pious in the way she sits.

'What I'm trying to say, Eli, is that trauma and the effects of trauma can change the way people think. Sometimes it can make us believe things that are not true. Sometimes it can alter the way we look at the world. Sometimes it can make us do things we normally would not do.'

Sly Mrs Birkbeck. Woman wants to suck me dry. She wants me to throw her a bone about my missing bone.

'Yeah, trauma is pretty weird, I guess,' I say.

Mrs Birkbeck nods.

'I need you to help me, Eli,' she says. 'You see, I need to be able to explain to the heads of school exactly why we should give you another chance. It is my belief that you and your brother, August, could be genuine assets to the Nashville High community. It is my belief that you and August are very special indeed. But I need you to help me, Eli. Will you help me?'

I will remember the plan.

'Ummm ... okay,' I say.

She opens a drawer on the right of her office desk and she retrieves a rolled sheet of butcher's paper, fixed in place by a rubber band.

'This is a painting your brother created in art class two days ago,' she says.

She rolls the rubber band off the paper, the rubber snapping against the paper as she rolls it. She spreads the paper out and shows me the painting.

It's a vivid image in blues and greens and purples. August has painted the sky-blue Holden Kingswood resting on an ocean floor. Tall emerald reeds surround the car, a seahorse gallops across the underwater scene. August has painted my dream.

'Who is that, Eli?' Mrs Birkbeck asks, pointing to the painted man sitting in the front seat.

I will remember the plan.

'That's my dad, I guess,' I say.

'And who is that?' she asks, pointing to the Kingswood's back seat.

I will remember the plan.

'That's August.'

'And who is that?'

I will remember the plan.

'That's me.'

'I see,' Mrs Birkbeck says gently. 'And tell me, Eli, why are you all sleeping?'

This could really upset the plan.

# Boy Seeks Help

Five days to Christmas and I can't sleep. We have no curtains or blinds on our bedroom's single sliding window and the blue post-midnight moonlight falls on August's right arm hanging over his bed. I can't sleep because my mattress is itchy and smells like piss. Dad was given the mattress by Col Lloyd, an Aboriginal man who lives five houses up on Lancelot Street with his wife, Kylie, and their five kids, the eldest of whom, twelve-year-old Ty, slept upon this orange foam mattress before me. The smell of piss keeps me up but what woke me was the plan.

'Gus, you hear that?'

Gus says nothing.

It's a moaning sound. 'Huuuuuuuuuuuuuu.'

I think it's Dad. He's not drinking tonight because he's coming off a three-day bender. He got so spectacularly pissed on the first night of the bender that August and I were able to crawl under the gap beneath the living room lounge while he was watching *The Outlaw Josey Wales* on television and we tied the shoelaces of his Dunlop Volleys together so that when he stood up to abuse one of the many villainous Union men who foolishly killed Clint Eastwood's on-screen wife and child he would fall down heavily, crashing over the coffee table. He fell over three times before he realised his shoelaces were tied, at which point he vowed – through a largely incoherent barrage of slurred words and at least twenty-three 'cunts' – to bury us alive in the backyard beside the dead macadamia nut tree. 'As fuckin' if,' August wrote in the air with his forefinger, shrugging his shoulders as he got up to turn the TV over to *Creepshow*, which was showing on Channel Seven. On the second day of the bender, Dad put on his jeans and a button-up shirt and, with a second wind brought about by six Saturday-morning rum and Cokes and a splash of Brut cologne, he caught the 522 bus, without saying where exactly he was going. He came home that night at 10 p.m. while August and I were watching *Stripes* on Channel Nine. He walked through the back door, straight through the kitchen to the cabinet where he keeps the telephone he never answers. Beneath the telephone is the important drawer. This is the drawer where he keeps unpaid bills, paid bills, our birth certificates and his Serepax tablets. He opened the important drawer and retrieved a dog chain leash that he wrapped methodically around his right fist. He didn't even acknowledge August and me sitting on the lounge when he turned the television off followed by every light in the house. He walked to the front window and drew the old frilly cream-coloured curtains closed, peering out the crack where the two curtains met.

'What is it?' I asked, feeling sick in the stomach. 'Dad, what is it?'

He simply sat down on the lounge in darkness and tightened the dog chain around his fist. His head flopped dizzily about for a moment, then he focused on his raised left forefinger which he brought, with great concentration, to his mouth. 'Sssssssshhhhhhh,' he said. We didn't sleep that night. August and I let our imaginations run wild guessing at what dangerous entity or entities he had offended enough to warrant the dog leash fist-wrapping: some goon at the pub, some hulk on the way to the pub, some killer on the way home from the pub, every single person inside the pub, ninjas, Yakuza, Joe Frazier, Sonny and Cher, God and the Devil. August wondered what the Devil would look like standing at our door. I said he would wear light blue flip-flops and sport a mullet cut with a rat's tail and a Balmain Tigers beanie to hide his horns. August said the Devil would wear a white suit with white shoes and white hair and white teeth and white skin. August said the Devil would look like Tytus Broz and I said that name felt like something from a different world, a different time and place that we didn't belong to any more. All we belonged to was 5 Lancelot Street.

'Another Gus and Eli,' he said. 'Another universe,' he said.

Dad spent the following morning sitting on the kitchen floor by the entrance to the laundry rewinding and playing, rewinding and playing, rewinding and playing 'Ruby Tuesday' on a cassette tape until the tape jammed in the player and the reel of brown tape unspooled in his hands like a mess of curled brown hair. August and I were eating Weet-Bix at the kitchen table as we watched him hopelessly attempt to fix the tape but succeed only in pulling the tape further and further into chaotic and irreparable oblivion. This forced him to resort to his Phil Collins tapes, the only point in the whole drunken three-day domestic nightmare when August and I genuinely considered notifying the Department of Child Safety. The vivid and violent bender climaxed at 11 a.m. that morning with a spectacular blood and bile vomit over the kitchen's peach-coloured linoleum floor. He passed out so close to his own abstract gut spillage that I was able to take hold of his arm and extend his right forefinger so I could use it as a pencil to write a message he would have to see when he woke up sober. I dragged and swished his forefinger through the foul-smelling

vomit to form a capital-letters message straight from the heart:
*SEEK HELP DAD.*

*

'Huuuuuuuuuuuu.' The sound slips under the crack of our bedroom door.

Then a desperate call, frail and familiar.

'August,' Dad calls from his bedroom.

I shake August's arm. 'August,' I say.

He doesn't stir.

'August,' Dad calls. But the call is soft and weak. More a moan than a call.

I walk to his bedroom door in darkness, switch on his light, my eyes adjusting to the brightness.

He's clutching his chest with both hands. He's hyperventilating. He speaks between short, sharp breaths.

'Call ... an ... ambulance,' he says.

'What's wrong, Dad?' I bark.

He sucks for air he can't find. Gasping. His whole body trembling.

He moans. 'Huuuuuuuuuuu.'

I run down the hall, dial triple zero on the phone.

'Police or ambulance?' asks a woman on the phone.

'Ambulance.'

The phone patches through to a different voice.

'What's your emergency?'

My father is gonna die and I'll never get any answers from him.

'I think my dad's having a heart attack.'

*

Dad's next-door neighbour on the left, a sixty-five-year-old taxi driver named Pamela Waters, is drawn out to the street by the flashing lights of the arriving ambulance, her unwieldy breasts threatening to spill from her maroon nightgown. Two ambulance officers lift a gurney from the back of the ambulance and leave it by the letterbox.

'Everything all right, Eli?' asks Pamela Waters, fixing the satin belt of her gown.

'Not sure,' I say.

'Another turn,' she says knowingly.

What the fuck does that mean?

The ambulance officers, one carrying an oxygen tank and mask, rush past August and me, standing barefoot in our matching white singlets and pyjama shorts.

'He's in the room at the end of the hall,' I call.

'We know, buddy, he'll be all right,' says the oldest ambulance officer.

We go inside and stand at the living room end of the hall, listening to the ambulance officers in the bedroom.

'C'mon, Robert, breathe,' hollers the oldest officer. 'C'mon, mate, you're safe now. Nothing to worry about.'

Sucking sounds. Heavy breathing.

I turn to August.

'They've been here before?'

August nods.

'There ya go,' says the younger ambulance officer. 'That's better, isn't it?'

They carry him out of the bedroom and down the hall, an arm each under his thighs, the way the Parramatta Eels forwards carry the starry halves in grand final celebrations.

They haul him onto the gurney, Dad's face pressed to the gas mask like it was a long-lost lover.

'You all right, Dad?' I ask.

And I don't know why I care so much. Something deep inside me. Something dormant. Something pulling me towards the crazed drunk.

'I'm all right, mate,' he says.

And I know that tone in his voice. I remember that tenderness in the tone. I'm all right, Eli. I'm all right, Eli. I will remember this scene. Him on a gurney like this. I'm all right, Eli. I'm all right. The tone of it.

'I'm sorry you boys had to see this,' he says. 'I'm fucked, I know, mate. I'm fucked at this dad stuff. But I'm gonna fix meself, all right. I'm gonna fix meself.'

I nod. I want to cry. I don't want to cry. Don't cry.

'It's okay, Dad,' I say. 'It's okay.'

The ambulance officers load him into the back of their vehicle.

Dad sucks some more gas, pulls the mask away.

'There's a frozen shepherd's pie in the freezer you can have for dinner tomorrow night,' he says.

He sucks again on the mask. His eyes catch sight of Pamela gawking in her nightgown. He sucks enough air into his lungs to say something loud.

'Take a fuckin' Polaroid, Pam,' he barks, wheezing with the effort. Dad's flipping Pamela Waters the middle finger when the officers close the rear ambulance doors.

*

The next morning there is an ibis walking through our front yard. It's favouring its left leg, which is wrapped in fishing line at the base where its prehistoric black claw foot begins. The crippled ibis. August watches the ibis through the living room window. He holds his Casio calculator, taps some numbers and holds the calculator upside down: 'IBISHELL'.

I type in 5378804, turn it upside down: 'HOBBLES'.

'I'll be back before dinner,' I say. August nods, staring out to the ibis. 'Save me some pie,' I say.

Down the left side ramp, past the black wheelie bin. Dad's rusting bicycle leans against a concrete stump holding the house up beside the tan cylinder of the hot water system. Beyond the bicycle is the vast below-the-house dump of Dad's collected gallery of ancient household white goods – washing machines with engines like the ones used by QANTAS, disintegrating refrigerators filled with redback spiders and brown snakes, and discarded car doors and seats and wheels. The grass of the backyard is beyond mowing now, towering and leaning straw-coloured shoots so thick I can picture Colonel Hathi the elephant and Mowgli parting them on their way to the Big Rooster on Barrett Street. Only a machete could bring it all down now; an accidental fire, maybe. What a fuckin' shithole. 008. 'BOO'. 5514. 'HISS'.

*

The bike is a rusting black 1976 Malvern Star 'Sport Star' model, made in Japan. The seat is split and keeps pinching my arse cheeks. It goes quick but it would go quicker if Dad hadn't gone and replaced the original handlebars with handlebars from a 1968 women's Schwinn. The brakes don't work so I have to break by jamming my right Dunlop between the front wheel and front wheel brace.

It's been raining and the sky is grey and a rainbow arches over Lancelot Street, promising everybody here a beginning and an end in seven perfect colours. Red and yellow and Vivian Hipwood in 16 Lancelot Street, whose baby died of cot death and for seven days she continued to dress it and nurse it and rattle toys in front of its blue face. Pink and green and number 17, where sixty-six-year-old Albert Lewin tried to gas himself in his sealed garage but couldn't get the job done because he was only gassing himself with a rattling lawnmower because he'd sold his car two months before to pay for the vet surgery bills for his boxer dog, Jaws, who'd been put down two days before Albert pushed his green Victa into his garage. Purple and orange and black and blue: all the mums along Lancelot Street on a Saturday morning smoking Winfield Reds at the kitchen table hoping the kids don't spot the purple and orange and black and blue bruising beneath the concealer on their cheekbones. The concealer. The concealers. The concealed. Lester Crowe in 32 Lancelot Street, who stabbed his pregnant girlfriend, Zoe Penny, thirteen times in the stomach with a heroin syringe to kill his unborn daughter. The Munk brothers in 53 Lancelot Street who tied their father to a living room armchair and cut half his ear off with a tomahawk. When it's so hot in summer on this endless street and the Brisbane City Council has laid new bitumen over potholes that explode in frustration, the tar sticks to the rubber of your Dunlops like Hubba Bubba bubble gum and everybody pulls open their curtains despite all the mosquitos blowing in from the Brighton and Shorncliffe mangroves and this whole street becomes a theatre and all those living rooms are window-framed to become televisions playing a live daytime soap opera called *Thank God It's Dole Day* and a ribald comedy called *Pass the Chicken Salt* and a police procedural drama called *The Colour of a Two-Cent Piece*. Fists are thrown through these front window theatre screens and laughs are had and tears are shed. Boo fuckin' hiss. Boo fuckin' hoo.

'Hey, Eli.'

It's Shelly Huffman, leaning out her bedroom window, blowing cigarette smoke to the side of her house.

I jam my shoe in the front wheel and pull a U-turn in the middle of the street and guide Dad's rickety Malvern Star into Shelly's driveway. Her dad's car isn't in the carport.

'Hey, Shelly,' I say.

She drags on the cigarette, blows seasoned O-rings on the exhale.

'You want a drag?'

I suck two drags and blow them out.

'You by yourself?' I ask.

She nods.

'They all went to Kings Beach for Bradley's birthday,' she says.

'Didn't you want to go?'

'I did, Eli Bell, but it's this ol' bag o' bones,' Shelly says, adopting the voice of an old American grandmother from the Wild West, 'she don't walk too well across sand no more.'

'So they left you home alone?'

'My aunt's comin' soon to babysit,' she says. 'I told Mum I'd prefer the dog motel on Fletcher Street.'

'I hear they give you three meals a day,' I say.

She laughs, stubs the cigarette out on the underside of the windowsill, flicks the butt into the garden running along the neighbour's fence line.

'Heard the ambos took your old man to hospital last night,' she says.

I nod.

'What happened to him?'

'I don't know, really,' I say. 'He just started shakin'. Couldn't speak or nothin'. Couldn't catch a breath.'

'A panic attack,' she says.

'A what?'

'Panic attack,' she says casually. 'Yeah, Mum used to get 'em, few years ago. She went through a bad patch where she didn't wanna do anything, ever, because she'd start having panic attacks if she went out among too many people. She'd wake up feeling on top of the world and tell us she'd take us all to the movies at Toombul Shoppingtown, then we'd get all dolled up and she'd have a panic attack the minute she sat in the car.'

'How did she get over them?'

'I got diagnosed with MD,' she says. 'She had to get over them then.' She shrugs. 'See, that's called perspective, Eli,' she says. 'A bee sting smarts like a bitch until someone clubs you with a cricket bat. And speaking of the ol' English willow, you wanna game of Test Match? I'll let you be the West Indies.'

'Nah, can't,' I say. 'I'm gonna meet someone.'

'This part of the big secret plan?' she smiles.

'You know about the plan?'

'Gus wrote it all out for me in the air,' she says.

That pisses me off. I look up to the grey sky.

'Don't worry, I won't say a word,' she says. 'But I think you're fuckin' nuts.'

I shrug.

'Probably am,' I say. 'Mrs Birkbeck thinks I am.'

Shelly rolls her eyes. 'Mrs Birkbeck thinks we're all nuts.'

I smile.

'It is nuts, Eli ...' she says. And she looks at me with a pretty smile, all heart and sincerity. 'But it's sweet too.'

And for a moment I want to drop the plan and go inside and sit on Shelly Huffman's bed playing Test Match, and if she hit a six by her favourite batsman, the dashing South African Kepler Wessels, with the small ballbearing cricket ball cutting through the 'six' space in the left corner of the octagonal green felt cricket ground, we could celebrate with a hug and because her family is all out and because the sky is grey we could fall back on her bed and we could kiss and maybe I could drop the plan forever – drop Tytus Broz, drop Lyle, drop Slim and Dad and Mum and August – and just spend the rest of my life caring for Shelly Huffman as she fights that unfair and imbalanced arsehole God who gives Iwan Krol two strong arms to kill with and gives Shelly Huffman two legs that can't walk across the golden sand of Kings Beach, Caloundra.

'Thanks, Shelly,' I say, wheeling the Malvern Star back out her driveway.

Shelly calls from her window as I speed away. 'Stay sweet, Eli Bell.'

*

Lyle told me once they used concrete from the Queensland Cement and Lime Company in Darra to build the Hornibrook Bridge. He said it was the longest bridge built over water in the Southern Hemisphere, stretching more than two and a half kilometres from seaside Brighton to the glorious seaside peninsula of Redcliffe, home of the Bee Gees and the Redcliffe Dolphins rugby league club. The bridge has two humps on it, one at the Brighton end and one at the Redcliffe end, where boats sailing along Bramble Bay can slip underneath it.

I can smell the muddy mangroves skirting Bramble Bay on the wind that pushes the Malvern Star along the bridge, up over the first hump. Lyle called it 'Humpity Bump' bridge because of the bumps his mum and dad's car made when he was a boy crossing over the buckled and rough aggregate bitumen surface that crackles beneath my bicycle wheels today.

The bridge was closed to traffic in 1979 when they built a strong, wider, uglier bridge beside it. Now the Hornibrook is used only by a few bream and whiting and flathead fishermen and those three local kids pulling backflips off the tallowwood decking, spinning into a full and choppy green–brown tide so high the water lashes the iron safety rails that are peeling with yellow paint.

Rain on my head and I know I should have worn a raincoat but I love the rain on my head and the smell of the rain on the bitumen.

The sky gets darker the closer I get to the middle of the bridge. This is where we always meet, so this is where I find him, seated on the concrete edge of the bridge, his long legs dangling over the side. He wears a thick green raincoat with a hood over his head. His red fibreglass fishing rod with an old wooden Alvey reel rests between his right elbow and his waist as he hunches over, rolling a smoke. With his head under the hood, he can't even see me pull up in the rain, but somehow he knows it's me.

'Why didn't you wear a fuckin' raincoat,' Slim says.

'I saw a rainbow over Lancelot Street and I thought the rain was done,' I say.

'The rain's never done with us, kid,' Slim says.

I lean the bike against the yellow rails and inspect a white plastic bucket resting beside Slim. Two fat bream swim without moving forward or backwards inside the bucket. I sit beside him, my legs over the side of the bridge. The high tide water heaves and swells in peaks and valleys.

'Will the fish still bite in the rain?' I ask.

'It ain't raining down there under the water,' he says. 'The flathead come out in this. Mind you, different story fishing in a river. I've seen yellowbelly out west go bonkers in the rain.'

'How do you know when a fish is going bonkers?'

'They start preaching about the end of the world,' Slim chuckles.

The rain gets heavier. He pulls a rolled *Courier-Mail* from his fishing bag and spreads it out for me to use as a shelter.

'Thanks,' I say.

We stare at his taut line, dragged up and down by the Bramble Bay waves.

'You still want to go through with this?'

'I have to, Slim,' I say. 'She'll be all right once she sees me. I know it.'

'What if that's not enough, kid?' he asks. 'Two and a half years is a long time.'

'You said it yourself, a lag gets a little bit easier every time you wake up.'

'I didn't have two kids on the outside,' he says. 'Her two and a half years will feel like twenty of mine. That men's prison is filled with a hundred blokes who think they're bad to the bone because they've done fifteen years. But those blokes don't love nothin' and nothin' loves them back and that makes things easy for 'em. It's all those mums across the road who are true hard nuts. They wake each day knowing there's some lost little shit like you out there waiting to love them back.'

I take the newspaper off my head so the rain can hit my face and hide my wet eyes.

'But the man on the phone, Slim,' I say. 'Dad just says I'm crazy. Dad just says I made him up. But I know what I heard, Slim. I know he said what he said. And Christmas is coming and Mum loves Christmas like nobody I've ever seen love Christmas. Do you believe, Slim? Do you believe me?'

I'm crying hard now. Hard as the black sky rain is falling.

'I believe you, kid,' he says. 'But I also believe your dad is right not to take you up there. You don't need to see that world. And she don't need to see you in it. Sometimes it makes it hurt worse.'

'Did you talk to your man?' I ask.

He nods, taking a deep breath.

'What did he say?' I ask.

'He'll do it.'

'He will?'

'Yeah, he will.'

'What does he want from me in return?' I ask. 'Because I'm good for it, Slim. I'll square it, I promise.'

'Slow down, Road Runner,' he says.

He winds in his line, turning the old Alvey reel three rotations, gentle and instinctive.

'You got a bite?'

'Nibble.'

He winds in one more rotation. Silent.

'He's not doing it for you,' he says. 'I kept his brother safe through a very long porridge a very long time ago. His name's George and that's all you need to know about his name. He has a fruit wholesale business and he's been making fruit deliveries into the Boggo men's and women's for the past twelve years. The guards know George and the guards also know the things George carries inside in the false floors beneath his watermelon and rockmelon crates. But of course they're paid handsomely not to know about these things. Now, like any retail business on the outside, the Christmas season is a nice earning period for traders who care to make a few extra bucks from retail on the inside. George can usually bring in all kinds of gifts at Christmas time. He can smuggle in sex toys and Christmas cakes and jewellery and drugs and lingerie and little Rudolph lights that turn red with a tickle of his nose. He has never, however, through twelve years of successful clink trade, smuggled in a thirteen-year-old boy with a childish lust for adventure and an unshakeable hankering to see his mum on Christmas Day.'

I nod. 'I guess not,' I say.

'When you get caught, Eli – and you will get caught – you do not know George and you do not know anything about George's fruit truck. You are mute, you understand. You will take a leaf from your brother's book and shut the fuck up. There will be a total of five trucks making deliveries on Christmas Eve and Christmas morning, all with their individual illegal bonus cargo. You can guarantee the screws will try to smuggle you out as quickly and as quietly as you came in. They're the last ones who want the world knowing a thirteen-year-old boy was found running around the grounds of the Boggo Road women's prison. If they take it further up the food chain then they're more fucked than you. Press comes in, then the prison standards crowd comes in, the clink trade collapses and the wife of one of those screws don't get that special Mixmaster she's been dreaming about and that screw don't get his Sunday-morning pancakes and everything else that comes with 'em, you know what I mean?'

'Do you mean sexual intercourse?' I ask.

'Yes, Eli, I mean sexual intercourse.'

He jiggles the rod twice, studies the top of the line like he doesn't trust it.

'Another nibble?' I ask.

He nods, reeling his fishing line in a little more.

He lights a smoke with his head tucked into his chest, cups the smoke from the rain.

'So, where do I meet him?' I ask. 'How will George know who I am?'

Slim blows a drag into the rain. He slips his left hand into the top pocket of a flannelette shirt inside his raincoat. He holds a slip of paper, folded in two.

'He'll know you,' he says.

He holds the slip of paper in his hands, dwells on it.

'You asked me that day in the hospital about the good and the bad, Eli,' he says. 'I been thinkin' about that. I been thinkin' about that a good deal. I should have told you then that it's nothing but a choice. There's no past in it, there's no mums and dads and no where you came froms. It's just a choice. Good. Bad. That's all there is.'

'But you didn't always have a choice,' I say. 'When you were a kid. You had no choice then. You had to do what you had to do and then you got on a road that gave you no choice.'

'I always had a choice,' he says. 'And you got a choice today, kid. You can take this slip of paper. Or you can breathe. You can step back and breathe, ride on home and tell your old man you're looking forward to spending time with him on Christmas Day and you ain't gonna worry any more because you know you can't do your mum's time for her, and that's what you're doin', boy, you're living inside that prison with her and you're gonna be there for the next two and a half years if you don't step back for a second and breathe.'

'I can't, Slim.'

He nods, reaches his hand out with the slip of paper.

'Your choice, Eli,' he says.

The slip of paper peppered by rain. Just a slip of paper. Take the slip of paper. Take it.

'Are you gonna be angry at me if I take it?'

He shakes his head. 'No,' he says flatly.

I take the slip of paper. I tuck it in my shorts pocket without even reading what's written on it. I stare out to sea. Slim stares at me.

'You can't see me no more, Eli,' he says.

'What?'

'You can't keep spending time with an ol' crook like me, kid,' he says.

'You said you weren't gonna get angry?'

'I'm not angry,' he says. 'If you need to see your mum, all well and good, but you leave this crook bullshit behind, you hear me. No more.'

My head throbs with confusion. My eyes swell. The rain on my cheeks and on my head and in my crying eyes.

'But you're the only real friend I got.'

'Then you need to get some new ones,' he says.

I drop my head. I put my fists in my eyes, press down hard like you press down on a cut to stop it bleeding.

'What's gonna happen to me, Slim?' I ask.

'You'll live your life,' he says. 'You'll do things I only ever dreamed about. You'll see the world.'

I'm cold inside. So cold inside.

'You're cold, Slim,' I say, between the tears.

I'm so angry inside. So angry inside.

'I reckon you did kill that cabbie,' I say. 'You're a cold-blooded killer. Cold like a snake. I reckon you beat Black Peter because you don't have a heart like the rest of us.'

'Maybe you're right,' he says.

'You're a fuckin' murderer,' I scream.

He closes his eyes at the sudden noise.

'Settle down,' he says, looking up and down the bridge, seeing no one in earshot. Everybody's gone. Everybody's gotta go some time. Everybody's runnin' from the rain. Nobody runnin' to it. So cold inside.

'You deserved everything you got,' I spit.

'That's enough, Eli,' he says.

'You're full of fuckin' shit,' I scream.

Slim shouts and I've never heard him shout.

'That's enough, damn it!' he hollers. And the shouting makes him wheeze and he falls into a coughing fit. He brings his left arm to his mouth and coughs into his elbow, retching and rattling lung coughs like there's nothing inside him but old bone and the earth dust from Black Peter. He breathes deep, wheezing and spluttering, gargles and hacks up a phlegm spit that lands two metres to his right beside a couple of discarded pilchards. He calms himself.

'I done enough,' Slim says. 'And I did it to too many people. I never said I didn't deserve the time I got, Eli. I just said I didn't do that killin'. But I done enough and God knew I done enough and He wanted me to think on some other things I'd done and I did that, kid. I did my time thinkin' on those things and I thought them inside and out. And I don't need you thinkin' on them for me. You should be thinkin' 'bout girls, Eli. You should be thinkin' 'bout how you're gonna climb the mountain. How you're gonna climb outta that shithole you're livin' in there in Bracken Ridge. Stop tellin' everybody else's story and start tellin' your own for once.'

He shakes his head. Stares out to the brown-green sea.

The tip of his rod bends sharply. Once. Twice. Three times.

Slim studies the rod silently. Then he reefs on the rod with a whipping pull and it bows like the rainbow I saw over Lancelot Street.

'Gotcha,' he says.

The rain batters down and the sudden action makes Slim cough uncontrollably again. He hands me his fishing rod as he attends to a coughing fit. 'Flathead,' he says, between choking coughs. 'Monster. 'Bout ten pounds.' Three more coughs. 'Pull her in, will ya?'

'What?' I say. 'I can't ...'

'Just bloody wind it in,' he barks, standing now with his hands on his kneecaps, coughing up some vile witch's brew of tar and phlegm. And blood. There's blood in his spit and it hits the bridge's aggregate bitumen and the rain washes it away but it keeps coming. No colour as strong as the colour of Slim Halliday's red blood. I reel the line in frantically, darting my head back and forth between the sea and the blood at Slim's feet. The sea and the blood. The sea and the blood.

The flathead pulls away with the line, swimming for life. I pull harder on the Alvey, winding in long, slow rotations like I used to turn the handle on the rusty Hills Hoist in the backyard of the Darra house.

'I think it's a monster, Slim!' I scream, as suddenly awed as I am elated.

'Just stay calm,' he says between coughs. 'Give him some line when you think he's gonna snap away.'

Only when Slim's standing do I notice how thin he's become. I mean he's always been thin. He's always been Slim. Arthur Halliday needs a new nickname, but Emaciated Halliday just doesn't have the same romance.

'What are you lookin' at?' Slim wheezes, hunched over. 'Pull that monster in!'

I can feel the flathead zipping left and right through the water. Panicked. Lost. For a time he comes with me, follows the pull from the hook in his lip, like he's had some divine message that that's where he's supposed to go, that the pilchard and the hook and the Bramble Bay tide this rainy day were the ultimate goal behind all that searching for survival along the ocean bed. But then he fights. He swims away hard and the Alvey reel finger-grips punch into the heel of my hand.

'Fuck,' I shriek.

'Fight him,' Slim wheezes.

I yank on the rod and rotate the reel at once. Long, deliberate reels. Rhythmic. Purposeful. Relentless. The monster is tiring but I'm tiring too. Slim's voice from behind me.

'Keep fighting,' he says softly, coughing again.

I reel and I reel and I reel and the rain slams my face and the world seems close to me now, every piece of it, every molecule. The wind. The fish. The sea. And Slim.

The monster eases. I reel him hard and I see him approaching the top of the sea, surfacing like a Russian submarine.

'Slim, here he comes! Here he comes!' I howl, euphoric. He might be eighty centimetres long. He's closer to fifteen pounds than ten. An alien monster fish, all muscle and spine and olive green flatheaded stealth. 'Look at him, Slim!' I scream, ecstatic. I reel the Alvey so fast that I could start a fire to barbecue the monster, then wrap him in tinfoil and bake him for Slim and me by the muddy mangrove banks on the Redcliffe side of the bridge, and follow him up with some toasted marshmallows dipped in Milo. The flathead rises into the air and my rod and line are a crane hauling some priceless cargo up to a skyscraper, my monster flying through the black sky, the ocean-bed dweller feeling rain on its back for the first time, glimpsing the universe above the sea, glimpsing my gasping face, wide-eyed and joyous.

'Slim! Slim! I got him, Slim!'

But I don't hear Slim at all. The sea and the blood. The sea and the blood.

I turn from the fish back to Slim. He's lying flat on his back, his head turned to the side. Blood still on his lips. Eyes closed.

'Slim.'

The flathead whips its spiny, powerful frame in the air, snaps the fishing line cleanly.

I will remember this through the weeping. I will remember this through the way my cheek rubs against the rough bristles of his unshaved face. The way I sit so awkwardly because I don't think about sitting, I just think about him. The way I can't tell if he breathes in the rain. The blood on his lips, spilling to his chin. The smell of White Ox tobacco. The small rocks from the bridge gravel biting into my kneecaps.

'Slim,' I sob. 'Slim,' I shout. The way I bob back and forth in pitiful confusion. 'No, Slim. No, Slim. No, Slim.'

The sound of my stupid teary breathless mumbling. 'I'm sorry I said what I said. I'm sorry I said what I said. I'm sorry I said what I said.'

And the way the monster fish plunges into the brown-green sea, down deep into the high tide, having seen the universe up here.

He wanted to see it only for a second. He didn't like what he saw. He didn't like the rain.

# Boy Parts Sea

Our Christmas tree is an indoor plant named Henry Bath. Henry Bath is an Australian weeping fig. Henry Bath is five feet tall when he sits in the terracotta pot Dad keeps him in. Dad likes trees and he likes Henry Bath, with all his cluttered green leaves shaped like canoes and a grey fig trunk like a frozen carpet snake. He likes to personalise his plants because if he doesn't personalise them – picture them possessing human needs and wants in some tiny and whimsical part of a mind I am only beginning to realise operates with as much order and predictability as the insides of our lounge room vinyl beanbag – then he is less inclined to water them and the plant is more likely to succumb to the endless assault of Dad's stubbed-out rollies. He named Henry after Henry Miller and the bath he was lying back in reading *Tropic of Cancer* when he thought of naming the weeping fig.

'Why does Henry weep?' I ask Dad as we slide the tree over to the centre of the living room where the ironing board stands, 24/7, our old iron rusting away in its square metal hand.

'Because he'll never be able to read Henry Miller,' he says.

We push the pot plant in place.

'Gotta be careful where we put him,' Dad says. 'Moving Henry to a new place kinda gives 'im a shock.'

'You serious?' I ask.

He nods.

'Different kind of light shines on him, new temperature in a new place, bit of a draught maybe, change in humidity, and he thinks it must be a different season. He starts shedding his leaves.'

'So he can feel things?'

'Sure, he can feel things,' Dad says. 'Henry Bath is a sensitive son of a bitch. That's why he turns on the waterworks all the time. Like you.'

'Whaddya mean, like me?'

'You like a good cry,' he says.

'No, I don't,' I say.

He shrugs his shoulders.

'You loved to cry as a bub,' he says.

I forgot this. I forgot he knew me before I knew him.

'I'm surprised you remember,' I say.

'Of course I remember,' he says. 'Happiest days of my life.'

He stands back and assesses the new location of Henry Bath. 'Whaddya reckon?' Dad asks.

I nod. August holds two pieces of Christmas tinsel in his hands, one twinkling red and one twinkling green, both of them losing their tinsel fibres over time, like Henry Bath slowly loses leaves and Dad might be slowly losing fibres of his mind.

August lays the tinsel carefully over Henry Bath and we stand around the weeping fig, marvelling at the saddest Christmas tree in Lancelot Street and possibly the Southern Hemisphere.

Dad turns to us both.

'I got a Christmas box coming from St Vinnies later this afternoon,' he says. 'Got some good gear in 'em. Can of ham, pineapple juice, some liquorice squares. I thought we could have a bit of a day of it tomorrow. Give each other gifts 'n' shit.'

'What, you got us gifts?' I ask, dubious.

August smiles, encouraging. Dad scratches his chin.

'Well, no,' he says. 'But I had an idea.'

August nods. *Great, Dad*, he writes in the air, urging Dad on.

'I had this thought that we could each choose a book from the book room and we could wrap it up and put it under the tree,' Dad says.

Dad knows how much August and I have been enjoying his bedroom book mountain.

'But not just any ol' book,' he says. 'Maybe something we've been reading or something that's really important to us or something we think someone else might enjoy.'

August claps his hands, smiling. Gives a thumbs-up to Dad. I'm rolling my eyes as if my eye sockets were filled with two loose Kool Mint lollies from a St Vincent de Paul Christmas charity box.

'Then, you know, we can eat some liquorice squares and read our books for Christmas,' Dad says.

'And how is this any different from any other day for you?' I ask.

He nods. 'Yeah, well, we can all read in the living room,' he says. 'You know, we can read together.'

August punches me in the shoulder. *Stop being a dick. He's trying. Let him try, Eli.*

I nod. 'Sounds great,' I say.

Dad goes to the kitchen table and tears a TAB betting ticket into three pieces, scribbles a name on each piece with the pencil he uses to circle horses in the form guide. He screws the pieces up and holds them in his hand.

'You get first pick, August,' Dad says.

August picks a piece of ticket, opens it with a glint of Christmas spirit in his eye.

He shows us the name: *Dad.*

'All right,' Dad says. 'August picks a book for me. I pick a book for Eli and Eli picks a book for August.'

Dad nods. August nods. Dad looks at me.

'You will stick around for it, won't ya, Eli?' Dad asks.

August looks at me. *You're an arsehole. Really.*

'Yeah, I'll stick around,' I say.

*

I don't stick around. At 4 a.m., Christmas morning, I place a copy of *Papillon* for August beneath the Christmas tree, wrapped in the sports pages of *The Courier-Mail*. Dad's wrapped his book for me in *The Courier*'s Classifieds pages. August has wrapped his book for Dad in the up-front news pages.

I walk to the train station in the nearby seaside suburb of Sandgate – famed for its fish and chips and nursing homes – taking the shortcut crossing over the motorway to the Sunshine Coast, normally a frantic exercise of Evel Knievel–level insanity requiring Bracken Ridge kids to leap a steel guardrail, dodge four lanes of speeding traffic, leap another steel guardrail and slip through a hole the size of a dinner plate in a council wire fence, while going undetected by police or, worse, concerned parents who have been pressuring the local council to build a footbridge across the highway for years. But this morning the motorway is empty. I take my time slipping over the guardrails, whistling 'God Rest Ye Merry Gentlemen' as I go.

Beyond the motorway is Racecourse Road, edging the Deagon Racecourse where, this early Christmas morning, in the half-light of a slow-waking sun, a young female rider does trackwork on a plucky mahogany thoroughbred. An old man in a beanie watches her ride, leaning against the racecourse fence. He looks a bit like Slim, but it can't be Slim because Slim's in hospital. Houdini Halliday is trying to escape from

253

fate. Houdini Halliday is hiding in the bushes, ducking down as the skeleton in the cloak with the sharpened sickle snoops around him.

'Merry Christmas,' says the old man.

'Merry Christmas,' I nod, quickening my pace.

Only four trains running today and the 5.45 a.m. train to Central stops at Bindha Station, beside the iron pipes and the exposed factory conveyor belts of the foul-smelling Golden Circle Cannery, not so foul-smelling today because the cannery is closed. There was a Golden Circle one-litre can of orange and mango fruit juice in our St Vincent de Paul Christmas charity box that was dropped off yesterday afternoon by a warm-faced woman with ginger hair and red polished fingernails. There was a can of Golden Circle pineapple slices also, canned and shipped by the good folks of the Golden Circle Cannery beside Bindha train station.

The old red truck is waiting where Slim's note said it would be waiting. It splutters in neutral on the corner of Chapel Street and St Vincents Road. The front of the truck is all fat curves and rust, like something Tom Joad would've driven on the road to California. The back of the truck is four iron walls forming a rectangular box with a blue canvas top, the size of Dad's kitchen. I grip the shoulder straps on the backpack I'm carrying and approach the driver's side door.

A man sits at the wheel smoking a cigarette, right elbow resting out his window.

'George?' I ask.

He's Greek, maybe. Italian. I don't know. About Slim's age, bald head and chubby arms. He opens his door and slips out of the truck, stubs his cigarette out beneath a pair of worn running shoes that he wears with thick grey socks that bunch at his ankles. He's short and stocky but quick in his movements. A man on the move.

'Thanks for doing this,' I say.

He doesn't say anything. He opens the back of the truck, swings the metal back door wide and latches it to the side of the truck. He nods me up. I climb into the truck and he climbs up behind me.

'I won't say a word, I promise,' I say.

George says nothing.

The truck is filled with crates of fruit and vegetables. A box of pumpkins. A box of rockmelons. A box of potatoes. A pallet jack by the left wall. By the rear door is a large empty square crate sitting on a forklift pallet. George leans over into the crate and pulls out a false wood bottom two-thirds of the way down into the box. He nods his head right two times. I've read enough silent nods from August to know that what he means is, 'Get in the box.' I drop the backpack in the box and lift my legs over the side and lie down in the box.

'Will I be able to breathe in here?'

He points to drilled air holes on each wall of the crate. It's an impossibly tight fit, only achieved by lying on my left side with my legs pulled up hard to my belly. I cushion my head under my backpack.

George assesses my fit and, satisfied, lifts the sheet of wood that forms the crate's false bottom and places it over my crowbarred body.

'Wait,' I say. 'Do you have any instructions for what I should do at the other end?'

He shakes his head.

'Thank you,' I say. 'It's a good thing you're doing. You're helping me help my mum.'

George nods. 'I'm not talking, boy, because you don't exist, you understand?' he says.

'I understand,' I say.

'You stay quiet and you wait,' he says.

I nod three times. The false wood bottom comes down over my body.

'Merry Christmas,' George says.

Then the darkness.

*

The engine rattles into life and my head bangs against the crate floor. Breathe. Short, calm breaths. No time for one of those nasty panic attacks of Dad's. This is living. This is what Slim used to call living life at the coalface. All those other saps standing back from the coalface worried about the rock wall caving in, but here I am, Eli Bell, scraping the walls of life, finding my seam, finding my source.

There's Irene in the darkness. A silk slip. Her exposed calf muscle, perfect skin and a freckle on her ankle. The truck speeds along the road. I can feel George's gear changes, I can feel every bump in the road. There's Caitlyn Spies on the beach now. And she's wearing Irene's silk slip and she's calling me. She beams and she turns her head to see the eternal universe.

The truck slows, comes to a stop and I hear an indicator and the truck turns left into the bump of a driveway. The truck moves forward then reverses and I hear the sound of the reversing beep. The truck stops. The rear door opens and I hear George sliding an iron ramp from inside the truck and slamming it down on concrete. Then the sound of a machine, forklift probably, moving up the ramp. The smell of engine oil and petrol. The machine close to the crate. The crate shakes and rocks as two metal forks stab through the pallet beneath me and suddenly I'm elevated inside the box. I'm moving, my head banging against the crate as the forklift moves down the iron ramp and is dropped heavily onto concrete. The forklift teeth slide out of the pallet and the machine moves back and forth, so close I can smell the rubber in its moving wheels. *Beep, beep.* Zip, zip. Left, right. Then the sound of the forklift teeth raising another box in the air, then something heavy raining on the false bottom above me. *Bang, bang, bang, bang. Buddddddderrduddderrrr.* The weight of the crate's new cargo flexes the false floor and my heart races. There's fruit above me. I can smell it. Watermelons. Then I'm floating again, elevated by the forklift, dropped back into the truck. And we're moving again.

*

I close my eyes and I look for the beach but all I see is Slim and he's lying on his side like he was on the bridge, old blood on his lips. And I see footprints in the sand and I follow these footsteps and I see that the footsteps belong to a man and that man is Iwan Krol and he's dragging a man behind him along the beach and the man he is dragging is Lyle, wearing the same shirt and shorts he was wearing on the night we saw him last, the night he was dragged out of the house in Darra. I can't see Lyle's head because it's hanging down as he's being dragged but I know the truth. I've known the truth ever since he disappeared. Of course I can't see his head. Of course I can't see his head.

*

The truck brakes hard, takes a long turn right. Then a hard left, up a sloping driveway with what feels like speed bumps. The truck stops.

'Season's greetings, Georgie Porgie,' calls a man outside the truck.

George and the man talk but I can't hear what they're saying. They laugh. I catch words. Wife. Kids. Swimming pool. On the piss.

'Bring her in,' the man says.

The sound of a large mechanical door or a gate opening. The truck moves forward, motors up a gentle slope and stops again. Two men talking to George now.

'Merry Christmas, Georgie,' one says.

'We'll make it quick, mate,' says another man. 'Tina making the cassata this year?'

George says something back to the men to make them laugh.

The door opens on the back of the truck. I hear the footsteps of two men climbing into the truck. They're inspecting the crates beside mine.

'Look at this shit,' says one of the men. 'These bitches eat better than us. Fresh cherries. Grapes. Plums. Rockmelon. What? No chocolate-coated strawberries? No toffee apples?'

They don't even touch the box I'm in.

They step back out of the truck. Close the rear door.

The sound of a rattling roller door rising.

'In ya go, Georgie,' calls one of the men.

The truck moves forward slowly, takes several turns left and right, then stops. And again the rear door opens and the iron ramp slams down on the concrete.

And again I'm elevated and I'm moving, on the forks of George's pallet jack this time, no engine, just rusting metal levers rattling. Down the ramp and onto a concrete floor. George brings down six more crates and drops them beside me. I hear him slide the iron ramp back up into the truck. I hear him close the rear door and then I hear his sneakers squeak as he walks towards my crate of watermelons with the false floor from some suburban Queensland spy book that nobody bothered to write. He whispers into an air hole.

'Good luck, Eli Bell,' he says. He taps the box twice and shuffles away.

The truck's engine roars to life, echoing loud in this room I'm in, and fumes from the exhaust fill my cramped and increasingly claustrophobic spy space.

Then silence.

\*

I make this time go fast with my fear. My fear makes me think. My thinking manipulates time. Where is she? Is she okay? Will she want to see me? What am I doing here? The man on the red phone. The man on the red phone.

What was that thing Mrs Birkbeck, guidance counsellor to the lost and restless, said about kids and trauma? What was that thing about believing things that never happened? Is this really happening right now? Could I really be here, trapped at the bottom of a box of watermelons on Christmas Day? Sublime to the ridiculous and the ridiculous to the bottom of a box of fruit.

How long have I been here now? One hour, two hours? If I'm this hungry it must be lunchtime. Must be three hours. I'm so fuckin' hungry. August and Dad are probably having that canned ham as I speak. Reading their Christmas books and sucking on Golden Circle pineapple slices. August's probably telling Dad how rugged and legendary prison escapee Henri Charrière was nicknamed 'Papillon' on account of the butterfly tattoo inked into his tanned and hairy chest. That's what I'm gonna do if I get out of here. I'm gonna go down to Travis Mancini's house on Percivale Street in Bracken Ridge and ask him to do one of his homemade Indian ink tattoos: a bright blue butterfly spreading its wings from the centre of my chest. And when other kids see me swimming down at the Sandgate swimming pool they will come up and ask me why I have a blue butterfly tattooed across my chest and I can say it's my tribute to the will of Papillon, to the enduring power of the human spirit. I can say that I got that tattoo after I smuggled myself into the Boggo Road women's prison to save my mother's life and I got the butterfly tattoo because I was a cocoon that day, I was a boy larva trapped in a pupal casing of watermelons, but I survived, I busted out of those watermelons renewed, metamorphosed.

Boy swallows past. Boy swallows himself. Boy swallows universe.

A door opening and closing. Footsteps. Rubber soles squeaking on polished concrete. Someone standing by the crate. Hands on the watermelons. The watermelons being removed from the crate. I feel the weight shifting on the false bottom. Relaxing. Light floods my eyes as the false bottom is removed. My pupils fight the light and focus on the face of a woman leaning over the crate, looking down on me. An Aboriginal woman. Big-boned and imposing, maybe sixty years old. Grey roots in her black hair.

'Oh, look at you,' she says warmly. She smiles and her smile is earth and sunshine and a blue butterfly flapping its wings. 'Merry Christmas, Eli,' she says.

'Merry Christmas,' I say, still crushed like a stomped Pasito can inside the box.

'You wanna get outta there?' the woman asks.

'Yeah.'

She offers me her right hand and helps me up. There's a tattoo of a Dreamtime rainbow serpent twisting colourfully up the inside of her right arm. We learned about the rainbow serpent in Year 5 Social Studies at school: giver of life, wondrous and majestic but not to be fucked with, not least because he might have regurgitated half of Australia into being.

'I'm Bernie,' she says. 'Slim told me you'd be dropping by for Christmas.'

'You know Slim?'

'Who doesn't know the Houdini of Boggo Road?' she replies. A grave look on her face. 'How is he?'

'I don't know,' I say. 'He's still in hospital.'

She nods, stares warmly into my eyes. 'I should warn you you've become the talk of the whole joint,' she says. She brushes a soft hand across my right cheek. 'Oh, Eli,' she says. 'Every woman here who ever had a cup o' milk in her tit is gonna wanna hold you.'

I scan the room we're standing in, stretching, clicking my aching neck back into a functioning place. We're in a kitchen, part practical cooking space with sweeping metal benches and sinks and drying racks, industrial ovens and stovetops. The entry door to the kitchen is closed and steel roller doors have been pulled down over a service bain-marie with twelve compartments. We're standing in a kind of storage room space flowing off the kitchen; there's a roller door on the rear wall of the kitchen which I must have come through.

'This is your kitchen?' I ask.

'No, it's not my kitchen,' Bernie says, feigning offence. 'This is my restaurant, Eli. I call it "Jailbirds". Well, sometimes I call it "Cell Block Ate", that's A-T-E, and sometimes I call it "Bernie's Bars and Grill", but mostly I call it "Jailbirds". Best beef burgundy you'll find south of the Brisbane River. Shit location for a restaurant, of course, but the staff are friendly and we get a steady stream of about a hundred and fifteen loyal guests every breakfast, lunch and dinner.'

I chuckle at this. She laughs, raising a finger to her mouth. 'Sssshhh, you gotta stay quiet as a mouse, you hear me?'

I nod.

'Do you know where my mum is?'

She nods.

'How is she?'

Bernie stares at me. There's a tattooed star formation on her left temple.

'Oh, sweet Eli,' she says, her hands cupping my chin. 'Your mum has told us about you. She told us how special you and your brother are. And we all heard how you wuz tryin' to get here to see your mum but your old man wasn't havin' it.'

I shake my head. My eyes catch a box of red apples on the kitchen bench.

'You hungry?' Bernie asks.

I nod.

She steps to the apple box, wipes one on her prison pants the way Dennis Lillee shines a cricket ball, throws me the apple.

'You want me to fix you a sandwich or somethin'?' she asks.

I shake my head.

'We got Corn Flakes in here. I think Tanya Foley down in D Block has a box of Froot Loops she had smuggled in. I could rustle up a bowl of Froot Loops for ya.'

I bite into the apple, juicy and crisp. 'The apple's great, thanks,' I say. 'Can I go see her?'

She sighs, pulls herself up onto the steel kitchen workbench, neatens out her prison shirt.

'No, Eli, you can't just go see her,' she says. 'You can't just go see her because, and I don't know if you've worked this out just yet, this is a fuckin' women's prison, matey, and it's not some fuckin' summer holiday resort where you can just wander on across to B Block and ask the concierge to page your fuckin' mum. Now, get this straight, you've only come this far because Slim begged me to let you come this far and you better start telling me why I should let this crackpot adventure of yours go any further.'

The sound of a choir echoes outside the kitchen.

'What is that?' I ask.

A beautiful choir. Angel voices. A Christmas song.

'That's the Salvos,' Bernie says. 'They're singin' up a storm next door in the rec room.'

'They come every Christmas?'

'If we've been good little elves,' she says.

The song gets louder, three-part harmonies squeezing through the crack beneath the door to Bernie's Jailbirds restaurant.

'What's that song they're singing?'

'You can't hear it?'

Bernie starts to sing. '*Sleigh bells ring, are you listening, In the lane, snow is glistening. A beautiful sight, we're happy tonight. Walking in a winter wonderland.*' That song. That fucking song. She slides off the bench, moves closer to me, a dumb look on her face. She sways to me, smiling. Something about her smile is unsettling. There's madness in Bernie. She's looking at me but she's looking through me too. '*Gone away is the blue bird,*' she sings. '*Here to stay is the new bird ...*'

There's a knock on the closed kitchen door.

'Come in,' Bernie calls.

A woman in her twenties enters the kitchen. She has blonde tufts of hair at the front of her scalp and blonde tufts of hair at the base of her scalp and the rest of the hair in between has been shaved in a crewcut. Her arms and legs are bone with no meat and her beaming smile to me when she enters the kitchen is the greatest gift I've received so far this increasingly unusual Christmas Day. Then her smile fades when she turns to Bernie.

'She's not coming out,' the woman says. 'She's fuckin' vacant, Bern. She's just staring at the wall, like she's dead to the world inside her head. She's not there at all.'

The woman looks at me. 'Sorry,' she says.

'Did you tell her he's standing right here in the kitchen?' Bernie asks.

'Nah, I couldn't,' she says. 'Lord Brian's letting her keep the door closed. He's worried she'll 'ave another spac attack.'

Bernie drops her head, thinking. She raises her arm at the woman, her head still down. 'Eli, this is Debbie,' she says.

Debbie smiles at me again.

'Merry Christmas, Eli,' Debbie says.

'Merry Christmas, Debbie,' I say.

Bernie lifts her head, turns to me.

'Look, kid, you want it straight or you want it with the chocolate sauce and the cherry on top?' Bernie asks.

'Straight,' I say.

She sighs.

'She doesn't look good, Eli,' she says. 'She hasn't been eatin' nothin'. She won't come out of her cell. I can't remember the last time she went outside for 3 p.m. rec. She was doin' cooking classes with me here for a bit but she stopped doin' that. She's in a dark place, Eli.'

'I know she is,' I say. 'That's why I asked Slim to get me in here.'

'But she doesn't want you seeing her that way, you understand me?' she says.

'I know she doesn't want to see me,' I say. 'I know that. But the thing is, Bernie, she does want to see me even though she doesn't want to see me and I need to go down there and tell her everything is gonna be all right because when I tell her that everything will be all right – that's what always happens. It always turns out all right when I tell her it's going to.'

'So, let me get this straight, you just go out there and tell your mum it's all gonna be peachy for her inside this shithole and,' Bernie clicks her fingers, 'voilà, everything is all right for Frankie Bell?'

I nod.

'Just like that?' she asks.

I nod.

'Like magic?'

I nod.

'You some kinda magic man, Eli?' she asks.

I shake my head.

'Nah, come on, little cuz, maybe you're the new Houdini of Boggo Road?' she says mockingly. 'Maybe Slim sent us all the new Houdini to magically bust us all outta here. Can you do that, Eli? Maybe you could wave your wand and you could magic me right out to Dutton Park train station and I could go see one of my kids. I got five of 'em out there somewhere. I'd be happy to see just one of 'em. Me youngest maybe. Kim. How old would Kim be now, ya reckon, Deb?'

Debbie shakes her head.

'C'mon, Bern,' she says. 'Poor kid's come this far. Let's just take him to see his mum. It's Christmas, for fuck's sake.'

Bernie turns to me.

'She just needs to see me for a minute,' I say.

'I'm just looking out for your mum, kid,' she says. 'No mother in the world wants her kid to see her like she is right now. Why should I let you go down there and hurt her even more than she's already hurtin', you know, just to make your Christmas Day a little merrier?'

And I stare so deep and serious into her eyes I can see her steely soul. 'Because I don't know magic, Bernie,' I say. 'Because I don't know anything about anything. But I know what my mum told you about my brother and me was right.'

'What's that?' Bernie asks.

'We're special.'

*

The prisoners of B Block are performing a musical this Christmas Day on a makeshift stage in the recreation room, and the ladies from blocks C, D, E and the F Block temporary huts, where spillover newcomers go when the main cells are full, have all gathered for a joyous and well received post-lunch Christmas concert. The B Block Christmas performance is a fusion of the Nativity story and the musical *Grease*. The play features two female cons playing Mary and Joseph in the guise of John Travolta and Olivia Newton-John. The three wise men are all members of the Pink Ladies gang. Baby Jesus is a doll dressed in leathers, and instead of spending a night in a manger the future lord and saviour rests up in the boot of a cardboard Greased Lightning. The musical is called *When a Child is Born to Hand Jive*.

The play's climactic showstopper, Mary singing 'You're the One That I Want For Christmas', brings the house down and a thunderous cheer echoes through B Block. Even the screws, three heavyset men in green-brown uniforms standing at triangular points around the knee-slapping audience, find themselves immersed in the riotous cabaret stylings of the woman playing Mary in stick-on black leggings.

'All right, let's go,' whispers Bernie, making the most of the play's magnetic and colourful all-eyes-on-stage distraction.

I'm tucked inside a large black wheelie bin and Bernie is pulling me along, the bin's lid closed above me. My feet squash down paper plates cleared from the prison dining tables at Christmas lunch. I'm up to my ankles in leftovers of canned ham and tinned peas and corn. She wheels me out of the prison kitchen area, past the dining room, crosses an open floor space behind the rec room, scurries past the audience with its head turned to Mary. She turns the bin on a sharp right and my body is mashed against the greasy and foul-smelling inside walls. She scurries thirty or forty paces along and sits the bin upright again, opens the lid, pops her head inside.

'What's my name?' she asks.

'I don't know,' I say.

'How the fuck did you get inside this place?'

'I attached myself to the bottom of one of the delivery trucks.'

'Which truck?'

'I don't know,' I say. 'The white one.'

Bernie nods.

'Outcha get,' she whispers.

I stand up out of the bin. We're in a cell block corridor lit only by the light of a frosted glass floor-to-ceiling window at the end of the corridor, some eight prison cells along. Each cell has a rectangular hard-glass window panel the size of Dad's letterbox built into the centre of it.

I slip out of the bin, my backpack still over my shoulders. Bernie nods to the cell two doors along the corridor.

'It's that one,' she says. She closes the lid on the bin and scurries away.

'You're on your own now, Houdini,' she whispers. 'Merry Christmas.'

'Thanks Bernie,' I whisper.

I approach Mum's cell. The door's window is too high up for me to see into, even on the tips of my toes. But there's a recess in the thick door and I can grip my fingers on it and pull myself up, using my knees to help push me up higher. My right hand slips because it only has four fingers to hold on with, but I go again, clutching hard at the window space. And I see her. She wears a white shirt underneath what looks like a light blue painter's smock. Her prison uniform makes her look so young, smaller and more fragile than I've ever seen her. She looks like a little girl who should be milking dairy cows in rolling Swiss hills. On the right wall of the cell is a desk and in the right rear corner are a chrome toilet and wash basin. There are two bunks bolted to the left wall of the cell and she sits on the edge of the lower bunk, her hands cupped together and being squeezed between her kneecaps. Her hair is everywhere, hanging over her face and over her ears. She wears the same blue rubber sandals Bernie was wearing. My arms can't hold my weight and I slip off the door. I climb again, gripping harder to the recess in the door. A longer look inside this time. I see the truth of it all. The skeletal shinbones of her legs. The elbows like the balls of a hammer, arms like the sticks I'd use to spark the fire that would burn to the ground this long-life-lightbulb jailhouse home for mums on Christmas Day. Her cheekbones have moved higher on her face and her cheek flesh has disappeared, turned to a claypan of thin skin, and her face doesn't look like it was grown by life but drawn, shaded by a humourless and macabre colourist in pencil that could be rubbed away by a drop of spit and a swiftly moving forefinger. But it's not the legs or the arms or the cheekbones that trouble me; it's the eyes, staring ahead at the wall opposite her. Blank staring. So lost in that wall it looks like her brain's been removed. She looks like Jack Nicholson after the lobotomy in *One Flew Over the Cuckoo's Nest*, and the setting fits. I can't make out what she's staring at on that wall but then I can. It's me. It's me and August, arm in arm. A photograph stuck to the cell wall. We have our shirts off, playing in the backyard of the Darra house, and August is forcing his belly right out with his right-hand fingers making alien gestures in his tiresome 'ET phone home' routine. I'm playing his extended belly like a bongo drum.

I tap my knuckle gently on the glass panel. She doesn't hear. I knock, hard and quick. She doesn't hear me. I slip off the door and I jump back on again. 'Mummmmmm,' I whisper. I knock again, knock twice then three times, the last one too loud, too hard. I look right, up along the corridor. Laughter and applause still echo around the corner of B Block as the stars of *When a Child Is Born to Hand Jive* make their triumphant end-show bows. 'Mummmm!' I strain in a whisper. I knock louder. Two heavy bangs and she turns her head to me. Finds me looking frantically at her through the window. 'Mum,' I whisper. I smile. And she lights up for a flicker, a light switches on inside her and switches off just as fast. 'Merry Christmas, Mum.' And I'm crying now. Of course I'm crying now. I didn't know how much I needed to cry for her until now, hanging by my fingers to the door of cell 24 in the Boggo Road women's clink. 'Merry Christmas, Mum.'

I beam at her. See, Mum. See. After all this, after all these mad moments, after Lyle, after Slim, after you getting put away, it's still the same old me. Nothing changes, Mum. Nothing changes me. Nothing changes you. I love you more, Mum. You think I love you less but I love you more because of it all. I love you. See. See that on my face.

'Open the door, Mum,' I whisper. 'Open the door.'

I slip off and I climb back up and a nail splits hard on my right hand middle finger and blood runs down the top of my hand. 'Open the door, Mum.' And I can't hold on now and I wipe my eyes and the tears make my fingers slippery but I cling on again just long enough to see her staring blankly at me, shaking her head. *No, Eli.* I read that. I read it like I spent a decade reading my brother's silent gestures. *No, Eli. Not here. Not like this. No.* 'Open the door, Mum,' I spill. 'Open the door, Mum,' I beg. She shakes her head. She's crying now too. *No, Eli. I'm sorry, Eli. No. No. No.*

My fingers slip off the door and I fall to the hard polished-concrete floor of the prison corridor. I struggle to find my breath in my tears and I lean back against the door. I bang my head twice, hard, against the door, which is harder than my head.

And I breathe. I breathe deep. And I see the red telephone in Lyle's secret room. And I see the sky-blue walls of Lena Orlik's bedroom. I see the picture frame of Jesus who was born today. And I see Mum in that room. And I sing.

Because she needs her song. I don't have a record player to play her song, so I sing her song instead. The one she played so much. Side one, third thick line from the edge. That song about a girl who never said where she came from.

And I turn and sing into the cracks in the door. I sing into the light of a crack one centimetre wide. I lay down on my belly and sing into the crack in the bottom of the door.

Ruby Tuesday and her pain and her longing and her leaving and my cracking Christmas Day voice. I sing it. I sing it. Over and over. I sing it.

And I stop. And there is silence. I bang my forehead against the door. And I don't care any more. I'll let her go. I'll let them all go. Lyle. Slim. August. Dad. And my mum. And I'll go find Caitlyn Spies and I'll tell her I'm letting her go too. And I'll be dumb. And I won't dream. And I will crawl into a hole and read about dreamers like my dad does and I'll read and read and drink and drink and smoke and smoke and die. Goodbye Ruby Tuesday. Goodbye Emerald Wednesday. Goodbye Sapphire Sunday. Goodbye.

But the cell door opens. I can smell the cell immediately and it smells like sweat and damp and body odour. Mum's rubber sandals squish on the floor by my side. She falls to the floor, crying. She puts a hand on my shoulder, weeping. She falls on me in the doorway of her cell.

'Group hug,' she says.

I sit up and wrap my arms around her and I squeeze her so tight I worry I'm going to break one of the weak bones in her ribcage. I drop my head onto her shoulder and I didn't know I missed that smell, that smell of Mum's hair, that feeling of her.

'Everything's gonna be all right, Mum,' I say. 'Everything's gonna be all right.'

'I know, baby,' she says. 'I know.'

'It gets good, Mum,' I say.

She hugs me tighter.

'It all gets good after this,' I say. 'August told me, Mum. August told me. He says you just have to get through this little bit, just this little bit.'

Mum weeps into my shoulder. 'Sssssshhhhhh,' she says, patting my back. 'Ssssssssshhhhhhhh.'

'Just get through this bit and it all goes up from here. August knows it, Mum. This is the hardest bit, right here. It doesn't get any worse.'

Mum weeps harder. 'Sssssssshhhhhh,' Mum says. 'Just hold me, sweetie. Just hold me.'

'Do you believe me, Mum?' I ask. 'If you believe me then you'll believe it will get better and if you believe it then it will.'

Mum nods.

'I'm gonna make it better, Mum, I promise,' I say. 'I'm gonna get us a place where you can go when you come out and it will be good and it will be safe and we can be happy and you can be free there, Mum. This is just time. And you can do what you want with time, Mum.'

Mum nods.

'Do you believe me, Mum?'

Mum nods.

'Say it.'

'I believe you, Eli,' she says.

Then a female voice echoes down the corridor.

'What thaaaaa faaaaarrrrk is this shit?' barks a red-haired woman with a large belly and a backward lean, standing in her prison clothes, holding a plastic dessert bowl filled with wobbly red jelly, staring at Mum and me in the doorway of cell 24. She turns her head to the recreation area, hollering, 'What sort of crèche you screws runnin' here?'

She slams her dessert on the ground, furious. 'How the fuck does Princess Frankie deserve a contact today?' she barks.

Mum holds me tighter.

'I gotta go, Mum,' I say, pulling out of the embrace. 'I gotta go, Mum.'

She clings to me hard and I have to pull myself away from her. She drops her head, crying, as I stand up. 'We'll get through this little bit, Mum,' I say. 'It's only time. You're stronger than time, Mum. You're stronger than it.'

I turn and run down the corridor as a tall and broad-shouldered prison screw rounds the corner into Mum's cell wing, following the gaze of the red-haired woman. 'What the fu—' he says, stunned by the sight of me. I grip the arm straps of my backpack and sprint up the corridor. The screw has his hand on the top of the baton fixed into his belt. I see Brett Kenny in my mind's eye – glorious five-eighth for the Parramatta Eels. I see all those backyard afternoons August and I spent practising Kenny's blinding weave runs, his devastating right step.

'Stop right there,' the screw demands. But I sprint harder, weaving left and right up the corridor, making the most of a four-metre-wide space, snaking up it like Brett Kenny would snake through a Canterbury Bulldogs defensive line. I fade hard to the right side of the corridor and the lumbering screw with his big lumbering legs and his tractor-tyre belly fades with me into my line of movement. I'm within two metres of his reach when he props on both legs and puts his arms out wide to swallow me up, to net me like a slippery Bramble Bay flathead – a slippery eel – and it's then that I step hard and quick off my bouncing right foot and zip like a shot bullet to the far left of the corridor, ducking under his ambitious and useless flailing right arm as I go. Brett Kenny finds the gap and the sea of blue and yellow Eels supporters in the western stands of the Sydney Cricket Ground rise to their feet. I turn left into B Block's open recreation and dining hall area and the space is filled with forty prison women, standing and sitting around dining tables and card tables and chess tables and knitting tables. Another prison screw – a short man, but muscular and fast – spots me from across the hall and gives chase. I run through the dining hall, searching for an exit door, and the women laugh and holler and clap their hands. Another screw joins the chase from the left side of the dining room. 'Stop!' the screw barks. But I don't stop. I sprint through the middle aisle of the hall as Mum's fellow prisoners bash their hands in delight on their food tables, making afternoon-tea bowls of Christmas pudding, jelly and custard bounce between their fists. I find no exit door and the screws are circling in on me from either side so I turn back around and take a diagonal run across the hall's steel dining tables. The screw I sidestepped in the corridor now enters the dining hall, angrily pushing through a sea of prisoners who have rushed from their seats before the Nativity-meets-*Grease* stage spectacular to see the surreal scene of the boy bouncing across Boggo Road tables and chairs like the hero of a Looney Tunes sketch. The screws angrily and clumsily hop onto the tables in chase and rush through aisles to head me off, barking threats I can't quite hear beneath the roar of the SCG crowd. *Kenny! Brett Kenny! Into space. The master, Eli Bell, heading for the try line. Certain to score. Certain to etch his name into rugby league legend.*

I leap between tables like a Russian ballerina, evading the swiping arms of the hapless screws the way Errol Flynn evaded the blades of cinematic pirates, and the prisoners are inside a rock 'n' roll show now, pumping their fists at the exploits of the dashing Eels five-eighth with the jets in the rubber soles of his Dunlop KT-26s. I leap off one table onto the polished concrete floor at the entrance to the dining hall where the women prisoners stand back – a parting of the sea of female cons – to form a loose guard of honour I can run through. And these women know my name somehow.

'Go, Eli!' they scream.

'Run, Eli!' they scream.

So I run and I run until I can see an exit door beyond the common area joining the kitchen and the cells and the dining hall. It's a door that opens out to a lawn outside. Freedom. *Kenny! Brett Kenny for the try line!* Sprinting, sprinting. The screws on my tail and another screw, a fourth screw, coming at me from my right to block my access to the exit door. It's the fullback for the Canterbury Bulldogs. The fullback screw. Every team's last line of defence, the best technical defender in the team, agile and strong, always making arcing and streaking cover tackle runs across the field to end the grand final dreams of gods like Brett Kenny. Mum used to run as a girl, was a fine sprinter. Won sprint races at athletics carnivals. She once told me the way to get an extra kick, the extra edge, was to get lower to the ground, picture yourself as a plough and your legs are digging up the earth and you're digging into the earth for the first fifty of a hundred-metre dash and digging yourself out again for the last fifty, leaning your head back and your chest out across the finish line. So I'm the plough now as the fourth screw arcs across the prison floor but I'm not a strong enough plough and his trajectory is certain to meet up with mine before I can meet up with the back door to the freedom lawn. But then a Christmas miracle, a holy apparition in prison clothes. It's Bernie, slowly walking her wheelie bin, absent-mindedly but not absent-mindedly at all, crossing into the path of the raging fourth screw. 'Outta the way, Bernie!' the screw hollers, weaving around her.

'What?' Bernie says, turning around blind like a slapstick silent movie star, making a clumsy show of moving the bin backwards now, apparently unwittingly, into the screw's line of chase. The screw tries to jump the slanted bin but clips a foot on the top of it and crashes spectacularly, belly first, into the polished prison floor.

I burst out of the rear B Block door and run out to a well-kept grass lawn rolling down to a fenced tennis court. I run and I run. *Brett Kenny, man of the match for the third straight week in a row, running well past the dead ball line now, running right into history.* Eli Bell. The elusive Eli Bell. Call me Merlin. The Wizard of the Boggo Road women's prison. The only boy to ever escape that B Block shithole. The only boy to ever escape Boggo Road. I can smell the grass. There is white clover in the grass and bees buzzing in the clover. The kinds of bees that make my ankles swell when they sting me. But get over it, Eli. There are worse things in this world than bees. The lawn slopes down to the tennis court and I look behind me as I run. Four screws in frantic chase, barking things I cannot understand. I slip my right arm out of an arm strap on my backpack as I run. I unzip the backpack and reach an arm in and grip a rope. It's time, Eli. The moment of truth.

*

I started with matches first, like Slim did in his cell. Matches and a line of string. Matches tied by a twisted rubber band in the centre to form a cross-shaped grappling hook. Timing, planning, luck, belief. I believe. I believe, Slim. Hour after hour I spent in my bedroom studying the science and technique of lodging a grappling hook against a high orange-brown brick wall. When I was ready, I fixed my own real-life roped grappling hook out of a fifteen-metre length of thick rope, knotted at fifty-centimetre intervals for grip points, and two roped pieces of cylindrical wood I cut up from an old rake handle Dad had lying under the house. I took the grappling hook down to the Bracken Ridge Scouts Centre on Saturday afternoons where they had a makeshift high wall that they ask young boy scout groups to scale in team-building exercises. Throw after throw after throw, I finessed my grappling hook wall-lodging technique. An uptight scoutmaster caught me carrying out these curious prison break rehearsals one afternoon. 'What exactly do you think you're doing, young man?' the scoutmaster asked.

'Escaping,' I said.

'Excuse me,' the scoutmaster asked.

'I'm pretending to be Batman,' I said.

\*

I take a sharp left turn at the tennis court, sprint into a small path leading between the prison's C Block cells to my left and a sewing workshop shed to my right. Losing breath. Tiring now. Gotta find the wall. Gotta find the wall. I pass the F Block temporary demountable cells. I turn behind me. I can't see the screws. I rush to the top prison wall. It's an old brown brick wall, high and imposing. I'm not sure my rope is long enough for the wall I stand before so I rush along the perimeter, searching, searching, searching, for a space in the brown brick fortress where a higher stretch of wall meets a lower stretch. Bingo. I quickly unravel my grappling hook rope and leave a two-metre stretch of rope which will be my throwing segment. I look up at the wall corner where high meets low and I twirl the rope twice like a cowboy with a lasso, with the weight of the rake handle cut-offs acting as a guiding projectile readying for launch. I'll only get one shot. Help me, Slim. Help me, Brett Kenny. Help me, God. Help me Obi-Wan, you're my only hope. Help me, Mum. Help me, Lyle. Help me, August.

A Hail Mary toss. An act of pure faith and ambition and belief. I believe, Slim. I believe. The hook sails up into the air and over the high wall fence. I step two paces to my right, holding the rope taut, positioned so the hook can do nothing else but lodge into the high–low wall corner when I pull down on it.

'Oi!' calls a screw. I turn to see him, maybe fifty metres away running beside the fence wall, another screw not far behind him. 'Stop that, you little prick,' the screw calls.

I grip a rope knot and pull myself with both hands up the wall, planting my gripping and reliable and blessed Dunlop KT-26s against the wall face, my back parallel with the grass lawn below me. I am Batman. I'm Adam West in those old *Batman* TV shows, scaling a Gotham City office tower. This is working. This is actually fucking working.

The lighter a person is, the easier this is. Slim was Slim when he made his climb up a wall like this one but I'm the boy, the boy who climbed the walls, the boy who fooled the screws, the boy who escaped from Boggo Road. Merlin the Magnificent. The Wizard o' the Women's.

Only sky from this angle. Blue sky and cloud. And flashes of the top wall. Six metres up now. Seven metres. Eight maybe. Nine metres. This must be ten metres all the way up here with my head in the clouds.

The rope is taut and burning my hands. The middle finger on my right hand aches with the stress of working overtime in the absence of his forefinger co-worker.

Two screws rush to stand below me, looking up at me. They sound like Lyle when he used to get angry with me.

'Are you fucked in the head, kid?' one calls. 'Where do ya think yer gonna go?'

'Come on down from there,' says the other screw.

But I keep crawling up the wall. Scaling and scaling. Like one of those SAS soldiers in Britain who rescue all those people from terrorist hostage scenarios.

'Yer gonna kill yourself, you idiot,' the second screw says. 'That rope ain't strong enough to hold you.'

Of course this rope is strong enough. I've tested it seventeen times down at the scouts' centre. Dad's old rope I found beneath the house, sitting in his rusted wheelbarrow, caked in dust and dirt. Up and up I go. Oh, the air up here. Was this what it felt like for you, Slim? The thrill of it all? The sight of the top? The thought of what waited beyond these walls? The story of the unknown.

'Come on down now and you won't get in any more trouble,' says the first screw. 'Come on down, mate. Christ Almighty, it's fuckin' Christmas Day. Yer mum don't wanna see you dead on Christmas Day.'

I'm a metre from the top of the wall when I pause to catch my breath, one last air suck before I make my triumphant crawl over the top, before I achieve the impossible, before Merlin pulls his last stunned rabbit from his hat. I take three deep breaths, my legs stiff against the wall. I pull myself higher, so high I can see the hook segments from Dad's rake pressing against the wall. Straining against the weight but holding fast. The summit. Everest's lonely tip. I turn my head briefly and look down for a moment at the screws.

'See you on the flipside, boys,' I say grandly, a stroke of roguish pluck striking me all this way up here in the thinner air of the wall top. 'You go tell those fat cats on George Street there ain't no wall in Australia high enough to hold the Wizard of Boggo Ro—'

A single segment of Dad's rake handle snaps and I fall backwards through the air. The blue sky and the white cloud reel away from me. My arms flail and my legs kick at nothing and my whole life flashes before my eyes. The universe. The fish swimming through my dreams. Bubble gum. Frisbees. Elephants. The life and works of Joe Cocker. Macaroni. War. Waterslides. Curried egg sandwiches. All the answers. The answers to the questions. And a word I don't expect spills from my terrified lips.

'Dad.'

# Boy Steals Ocean

The memorial plaque reads: *Audrey Bogut, 1912–1983, loving wife of Tom, mother of Therese and David. A life like theirs has left a record sweet for memory to dwell upon.*

Seventy-one years for Audrey Bogut to pass.

The memorial plaque next to that one reads: *Shona Todd, 1906–1981, beloved daughter of Martin and Mary Todd, sister to Bernice and Phillip. The cup of life with her lips she prest, a taste so sweet she gulped the rest.*

Seventy-five years for Shona Todd to pass.

'C'mon, it's about to start,' I say to August.

We walk into a small brick chapel in the centre of the Albany Creek Crematorium. Winter, 1987. Nine months into my great time lapse experiment.

Slim's right. It's all just time. Thirty-nine minutes to drive from our house in Bracken Ridge to the Albany Creek Crematorium. Twenty seconds to tighten my shoelace. Three seconds for August to tuck his shirt in. Almost twenty-one months until Mum comes out. I am fast becoming a master manipulator of time. I will make twenty-one months feel like twenty-one weeks. The man in the wood coffin taught me that.

Seventy-seven years it took for Slim to die. He spent the past six months in and out of hospital, cancer creeping in to too many corners of that tall frame of his. I tried to visit him when I could. Between school. Between homework and afternoon TV. Between my growing up and his getting out. His last great escape.

'CRIME ERA CLOSES' read the headline in *The Telegraph* Dad handed me yesterday. 'A gripping chapter in the Queensland crime annals closed this week with the death in Redcliffe Hospital of Arthur Ernest "Slim" Halliday, 77.'

Time stops in this chapel. No noise from the few mourners around the coffin, a couple of men in suits, nobody in here that knows anybody else.

My hand reaches into my pants pocket and I feel for the last words Slim ever wrote to me. It was a message he wrote at the end of the instructions he gave me for meeting mysterious George and his prison smuggler fruit truck.

*Do your time,* he wrote, *before it does you. Your friend always, Slim.*

Do your time, Eli Bell, before it does you.

A crematorium official says something about life and time but I miss it all because I'm thinking about life and time. And then Slim's coffin is taken away.

It's over quick. Quick time. Good time.

An old man in a black suit and tie approaches August and me as we walk back out the chapel doors. He says he's an old bookmaker friend of Slim's. He says Slim did some work for him after prison.

'How did you boys know, Slim?' he asks. His face is warm and friendly, a smile like Mickey Rooney's.

'He was our babysitter,' I say.

The man nods, puzzled.

'How did you know Slim?' I ask the man in the black suit.

'He lived with me and my family for a time,' the old man says.

And I realise in this moment that there were other lives Slim led. There were other vantage points. Other friends. Other family.

'It's nice of you to come and pay your respects,' the old man says.

'He was my best friend,' I say.

He chuckles.

'Mine, too,' the old man says.

'Really?' I ask.

'Yeah, really,' the old man says. 'Don't worry,' he whispers. 'A man can have many best friends and none any more or less best than the other.'

We walk along the crematorium lawn, rows of grey gravestones forming grim and uniform lanes in a cemetery beyond the chapel.

'Do you think he killed that cabbie?' I ask.

The old man shrugs.

'I never asked him,' the old man says.

'But you would know, wouldn't you?' I ask. 'I reckon you'd get a feeling on that. Your instinct or somethin' would tell you if he did it.'

'Whaddya mean, "instinct"?' the old man asks.

'I was around a guy once who killed many people and my instinct told me he killed many people,' I say. 'There was a chill down my spine that told me he killed many people.'

The old man stops on the spot.

'I never asked him about it, purely out of respect,' the old man says. 'I respected the man. If he didn't do that killin', then I respect him more still and God rest his soul. I never got no chill down my spine around Slim Halliday. And if he did do that killin', then he was one hell of a tribute to rehabilitation.'

That's a nice way of putting it. Thanks, mysterious old man. I nod.

The old man puts his hands in his pockets and walks off down a row of the cemetery. I watch him walk down that row of gravestones like he possesses the most carefree soul to ever inhabit a body.

August is hunched over inspecting another wall of gold plaques dedicated to the departed.

'I need to get a job,' I say.

August gives a sharp look over his shoulder. *Why?*

'We gotta get a place for Mum when she gets out.'

August looks deeper into a plaque.

'C'mon, Gus!' I urge, walking away. 'No time to waste.'

*

I landed flush into the arms of the screws that day I fell from the wall of the Boggo Road women's prison. To their great credit the screws seemed more concerned for my mental health than furious with my misadventures.

'Ya think he's mental?' pondered the youngest screw, who had a ginger beard and freckles across his forearms. 'What'll we do with him?' ginger asked his fellow screw.

'Let Muzza make the call,' the second screw said.

The two screws walked me in a pressure hold, each man gripping an arm, back up the lawn to the other two screws, the older and more experienced ones with not enough in the tank to chase a teenage boy through a prison yard.

What took place inside the office of the prison administration building was a strategy meeting between prison screws, which, for me, was akin to being witness to four early Neanderthals working out the rules of Twister.

'He could fuck up a lot for us, Muz,' said the largest screw.

'We gotta call the warden?' asked ginger.

'We're not calling the warden,' said the man they called Muzza, Muz and, the least preferred, Murray. 'He'll hear about it in good time. He loses just as much from this shit getting out as we do. He doesn't need to hear about it when he's home eating Christmas ham with Louise.'

Muzza thought about things for a moment. He bent down to my eye level.

'You love your mum very much, don't you, Eli?' he asked.

I nodded.

'And you're a bright boy aren't you, Eli?' he asked.

'Not bright enough, it seems,' I said.

Muz chuckled. 'Yes, true shit,' he said. 'But you're bright enough to know what can happen in a place like this when people make our lives difficult. You know that, right?'

I nodded.

'All sorts of things can happen in the night in here, Eli,' he said. 'Real horrible things. Things you wouldn't believe.'

I nodded.

'So tell me how you spent your Christmas?'

'I spent it eating canned pineapple from St Vinnies with me brother and me dad,' I said.

Muz nodded.

'Merry fuckin' Christmas, Eli Bell,' he said.

The ginger screw, whose name turned out to be Brandon, drove me home in his car, a purple 1982 Commodore. He played a cassette tape of Van Halen's *1984* all the way home. I tried to pump my fists to the sonic thump of 'Panama' but my freedom of expression was hampered somewhat by my left hand being handcuffed to Brandon's rear left armrest.

'Rock on, Eli,' Brandon said, uncuffing me and letting me out, as per my request, three doors down from our house on Lancelot Street.

I scurried light-footed into the house to find August asleep on the living room couch, *Papillon* resting open on his chest. I saw cigarette smoke down the hallway in Dad's room. Beneath the saddest Christmas tree ever decorated was a present wrapped in newspaper, a large rectangular book, a felt pen *Eli* scrawled across it. I tore the paper away to find the gift inside. It was no book. It was a block of paper, maybe 500 blank pages of A4. On the first page was a brief message.

*To burn this house down or set the world on fire. Up to you, Eli. Merry Christmas. Dad.*

\*

He gave me another block of paper for my fourteenth birthday, along with a copy of *The Sound and the Fury* because he noticed that my shoulders were broadening and he said any young man needs broad shoulders to read Faulkner.

It's on one of those pieces of A4 paper that I write my list of possible occupations within bike-riding distance that would provide enough money for August and me to save for a deposit on a house in The Gap, in Brisbane's lush western suburbs, which Mum can move into upon her release:

- Chip fryer at the Big Rooster takeaway restaurant on Barrett Street.
- Shelf stacker at the Foodstore grocery shop on Barrett Street, with the frozen food section August and I hang out in on the hottest summer days, debating which ice block is more bite for your buck out of a Hava Heart, a Bubble O' Bill and, the unchallengeable masterpiece, the banana Paddle Pop.
- Paperboy for the mad Russians who own the Barrett Street newsagency.

- Bakery assistant for the bakery next door to the newsagency.
- Cleaning out Ol' Bill Ogden's pigeon loft on Playford Street (last resort).

I give this some more thought, tapping my blue Kilometrico pen on the paper. And I scribble one more potential occupation, drawing on my limited skill set:

- Drug dealer.

\*

A knock on the front door. This never happens. The last time someone knocked on the front door was three months ago when a young police officer came to chase up Dad about a drink-driving incident three years ago in which several local mothers said he knocked over a stop sign outside the childcare centre on Denham Street.

'Mr Bell?' the young officer said.

'Who?' Dad said.

'I'm looking for Robert Bell?' the officer said.

'Robert Bell?' Dad pondered. 'Nahhhh, never heard of 'im.'

'What's your name, sir?' the policeman asked.

'Me?' Dad said. 'I'm Tom.'

The officer took out a notepad.

'Do you mind if I ask your surname, Tom?' the policeman asked.

'Joad,' Dad said.

'How do I spell that?' the policeman asked.

'Joad like toad,' Dad said.

'So ... J-O-D-E?' the officer said.

Dad shuddered.

A knock on the door always means something dramatic in this house.

August drops his *Papillon* – he's read it twice already – on the living room couch and rushes to the front door. I follow close behind.

It's Mrs Birkbeck. School guidance counsellor. Red lipstick. Red bead necklace. She holds a manila folder filled with papers.

'Hi, August,' she says tenderly. 'Is your father there?'

I shake my head. She's come to save the world. She's come to cause trouble because she's too fucking earnest and self-inflated to know the difference between caring and carelessness is exactly the size of a five-centimetre thorn lodged in your arsehole.

'He's sleeping,' I say.

'Can you wake him for me, Eli?' she asks.

I shake my head again, turn from the door and pace slowly down the hall to Dad's bedroom.

He's reading Patrick White in a blue singlet and shorts, rolled cigarette in his mouth.

'Mrs Birkbeck's at the door,' I say.

'Who the fuck is Mrs Birkbeck?' he spits.

'She's the school guidance counsellor,' I say.

He rolls his eyes. He hops up from his bed, stubs his cigarette out. He hacks up a chesty tobacco spit to clear his throat, spits it into the ashtray on his bed.

'You like her?' he asks.

'She means well,' I say.

He walks up the hall to the front door.

'Hi,' he says. 'Robert Bell.'

He smiles and there's sweetness in his smile, a softness I've not really seen. He offers his hand for shaking and I don't think I've seen him do that either, shake another person's hand like that. I thought it was just August and me he knew how to interact with on a human level, and we usually just communicate in nods and grunts.

'Poppy Birkbeck, Mr Bell,' she says. 'I'm the boys' guidance counsellor at school.'

'Yeah, Eli's been telling me about all the wonderful guidance you've been giving to my boys,' he says.

The lying bastard.

Mrs Birkbeck looks quietly and briefly moved. 'They have?' she replies, looking at me, her cheeks glowing red. 'Well, Mr Bell, I believe your boys are very special. I believe they have great potential and I guess I consider it my job to inspire them enough to turn potential into reality.'

Dad nods his head, smiling. Reality. You know, midnight anxiety fits. Suicidal depressive episodes. Three-day benders. Fist-split eyebrows. Bile vomit. Runny shit. Brown piss. Reality.

'Educating the mind without educating the heart is no education at all,' Dad offers.

'Yes!' Mrs Birkbeck says, taken aback.

'Aristotle,' Dad says earnestly.

'Yes!' Mrs Birkbeck says. 'I live my life by that quote.'

'Then you keep on livin', Poppy Birkbeck, and you keep on inspirin' those kids,' Dad says sincerely.

Who the fuck is this guy?

'I will,' she smiles. 'I promise.' Then she refocuses. 'Look, Robert, can I call you Robert?'

Dad nods.

'Ummm ... the boys weren't at school again today and ... umm ...'

'I'm sorry about that,' Dad interjects. 'I took the boys to a funeral of an old friend of theirs. It's been a tough couple of days for 'em.'

She looks at August and me.

'A tough couple of years, I understand,' she says.

We all nod, Dad, August and me, like we're starring in some sick midday movie.

'Can I talk to you for a minute, Robert?' she asks. 'Maybe just the two of us?'

Dad takes a deep breath. Nods.

'You two make yourselves scarce, will ya?' he says.

August and I pad down the ramp at the side of the house, down past the hot water system and a couple of Dad's old rusting engines. Then we duck under the house, weave through Dad's store of unwanted and unworking washing machines and refrigerators. The space beneath the house narrows as the earth floor climbs up towards the living room and kitchen areas of the house. We crawl up to the top left corner of the under-house area, damp brown dirt caking our kneecaps, and sit right beneath the wooden floor of the kitchen where Dad and Mrs Birkbeck talk about August and me at the octagonal table Dad usually passes out on at midnight on sole-parent pension day. We can hear every word through the cracks between the floorboards.

'In all honesty, the work August produces is brilliant,' Mrs Birkbeck says. 'His artistic control and originality and innate skill represent a genuine artistic talent, but he … he …'

She stops.

'Go on,' Dad says.

'He troubles me,' she says. 'Both the boys trouble me.'

I never should have told her a word. She had rat written all over her.

'Can I show you something?' echoes Mrs Birkbeck's voice through the cracks.

August is lying down with his back on the dirt. He's listening but he's not caring about what he's hearing. With his hands tucked behind his head like that, he might as well be daydreaming by the Mississippi River with a straw of grass in his mouth.

But I care.

'This is a painting August did in art class last year,' she says.

There's a long pause.

'And these ...' We hear the sound of paper in her hands. '... these were done early this year and these were done just last week.'

Another long pause.

'As you can see, Mr Bell ... ummm ... Robert ... August appears obsessed with this particular scene. Now, somewhat of an issue has formed between August and his art teacher, Miss Prodger, because while Miss Prodger believes August is one of her most outstanding and committed students, he simply refuses to paint any other image but this one. Last month the students were asked to paint a still life, and August painted this scene. The month before that they were asked to paint a Surrealist image, and August painted this. Last week August was asked to paint an Australian landscape; August painted that same scene again.'

August stares straight up at the floorboards, unmoved.

Dad remains silent.

'I would never normally betray the confidence of a student,' she says. 'I consider my office a sacred space for sharing and healing and educating. I sometimes call it the Vault and only myself and my students know the password to the Vault and the password is "Respect".'

August rolls his eyes.

'But when I feel the safety of individuals within our school community might be at risk, then I feel I must say something,' she says.

'If you think August is gonna hurt someone then you're sniffin' the wrong rabbit hole, I'm afraid,' Dad says. 'That boy don't hurt no one who don't deserve it. He doesn't do anything on a whim. He doesn't carry out a single action that he hasn't first thought through a hundred times over.'

'That's interesting you say that,' she says.

'Say what?' Dad replies.

'A hundred times over,' she says.

'Well, he's a deep thinker,' Dad says.

Another long pause.

'It's not the other students I'm concerned about, Robert,' she says. 'I truly believe August – and those thoughts he keeps running over in that extraordinary mind of his – is of risk to no one but himself.'

A chair slides briefly across the wooden floor of the kitchen.

'Do you recognise that scene?' she asks.

'Yeah, I know what he's paintin',' Dad says.

'Eli called it "the moon pool",' she says. 'Have you ever heard him call it that, "the moon pool"?'

'No,' Dad says.

August looks at me. *What did you tell her, Eli, you fuckin' rat?*

I whisper: 'I had to give her somethin'. She was gonna kick me outta school.'

August looks at me. *You told that crazy witch about the moon pool?*

'When Principal Gardner told me of the recent traumas in their lives I thought it was natural that the effects of these events would manifest themselves in the boys' behaviours in some way,' Mrs Birkbeck says above the floorboards. 'I believe they are both suffering from some kind of post-traumatic stress disorder.'

'What, like shellshock or something?' Dad asks. 'You reckon they been in a war, Mrs Birkbeck? You reckon those boys just got back from the Somme, Mrs Birkbeck?'

Dad's starting to lose his patience.

'Well, of a kind,' she says. 'Not a war of bullets and bombs. But a war of words and memories and moments, just as damaging to a growing boy's brain, one could say, as anything on the Western Front.'

'You sayin' they're loopy?' Dad asks.

'I'm not saying that,' she says.

'Sounds like you're sayin' they're nuts,' he says.

'What I'm saying is some of the things running through their heads are ... unusual,' she says.

'What things?'

August looks at me. *Why do you think I never told anyone but you, Eli?*

'Things that could potentially be harmful to both boys,' Mrs Birkbeck says. 'Things that I feel I am obligated to tell the Department of Child Safety.'

'Child Safety?' Dad echoes. The words are acid on his tongue.

August looks at me. *You fucked it all up, Eli. See what you've done. You couldn't keep your mouth shut, could you? You couldn't be discreet.*

'I feel those two boys are planning something,' Mrs Birkbeck says. 'It feels like they're heading towards some destination that maybe none of us will know about until it's too late.'

'Destination?' Dad asks. 'Please tell me where they're going, Mrs Birkbeck? London, Paris, the Birdsville Races?'

'I don't mean a physical place, necessarily,' she says. 'I mean they're heading to certain destinations in their minds that are not safe for teenaged boys to go to.'

Dad laughs.

'You get all that from August's little watercolours?' Dad asks.

'Have your boys ever engaged in any suicidal behaviours, Robert?' Mrs Birkbeck asks.

August shakes his head, rolls his eyes. I place an imaginary pistol below my chin, giggling, blow my imaginary brains out.

August chuckles, hangs himself, tongue out, on an imaginary noose.

'Eli said August was painting his dreams,' Mrs Birkbeck says. 'The moon pool was from Eli's dreams, he said. But he said he associated deep feelings of fear, feelings of darkness, with the moon pool. He said he could recall this dream in vivid detail, Robert. Has Eli ever spoken to you about his recurring dreams?'

August has a twig in his hand that he breaks into small bits. He throws a bit of stick at my head.

'No,' Dad says.

'He can recall his dreams with remarkable clarity,' she says. 'There is great violence in these dreams, Robert. When he tells me about some of these dreams he can describe the sound of his mother's voice, the way drops of blood look on the wooden floors of a house, he can tell me the smells of things. But I told him that dreams do not come accompanied with smells. Dreams do not come with sound. And I asked Eli to start calling these dreams what they are.'

A long pause.

'What are they?' Dad asks.

'Memories,' Mrs Birkbeck says.

August writes in the air. *Child Safety takes August Bell to hell.*

August writes in the air. *Child Safety teaches Eli Bell to never tell.*

'Eli said the car went into the moon pool two days before Frances left you,' Mrs Birkbeck says.

'Why do you want to dredge all this shit up?' Dad asks. 'Those boys are doin' all right. They're movin' on. They can't move on when bleeding hearts like you keep dredgin' up shit and twistin' things around in their heads and replacin' things that happened in their heads with things that happened in your head.'

'Eli said you drove them into the moon pool, Robert.'

And the dream feels so different when she says it like that. You drove them into the moon pool. He did drive us into the moon pool. Nobody else did. It had to be him. We were in the back seat and we were playing corners, rolling against each other in the back seat with the weight of a turn squashing one of us into the side door.

'I like your sons, Robert,' Mrs Birkbeck says. 'I've come here today in the hope, for their sake, that you can convince me I should not inform the department that August and Eli Bell live in fear of their only guardian.'

I remember the dream. I remember the memory. It was night and the car turned sharply off the road and the car bounced along gravel and between tall gum trees that passed by my window like God was shuffling through images on a life slideshow.

'It was a panic attack,' Dad says. 'I have panic attacks. I get 'em all the time. Had 'em even when I was a kid.'

'I think Eli believes you did it on purpose,' Mrs Birkbeck says. 'I think he believes you intentionally swerved off the road that night.'

'So did his mother,' Dad says. 'Why do you think she fucked off?'

A long pause.

'It was a panic attack,' Dad says. 'Go ask the cops in Samford if you don't believe me.'

Samford. Yes. Samford. It was rural. Had to be Samford. All the trees and hills. The wheels bounced hard on dips and ditches in the rolling land beneath us. I had enough time to look across at Dad in the front seat. 'Close your eyes,' he said.

'I was takin' 'em out to Cedar Creek Falls,' Dad says.

'Why would you go to Cedar Creek Falls at night-time?' Mrs Birkbeck asks.

'You doin' the cop work now?' Dad asks. 'You love this, don't you?'

'What?'

'Having me over a barrel', he says.

'How exactly do I have you over a barrel?'

"Cause you can take those boys away from me with the tick of a box,' Dad says.

'It's my job to ask difficult questions if those difficult questions ensure the safety of my students,' Mrs Birkbeck says.

'You think you're serving your profession so nobly, so compassionately,' Dad says. 'You'll take those boys from me and you'll split 'em up and you'll strip 'em bare of the only thing that keeps 'em going, each other, and you'll tell your friends over a bottle of chardonnay from Margaret River how you saved two boys from their monster dad who nearly killed them once and they'll bounce from foster home to foster home until they find each other again at the gate of your house with a can of petrol and they'll thank you for sticking your nose into our business as they're burning your house down.'

Close your eyes. I close my eyes. And I see the dream. I see the memory. The car hits the lip of a dam edge – the backyard dam of someone's farm in rural Samford, in the fertile hills of Brisbane's western fringe – and we're flying.

'The boys were left unconscious,' Mrs Birkbeck says.

I can't hear Dad respond.

'It was a miracle anyone survived,' she says. 'The boys were unconscious but you pulled them out somehow?'

The magic car. The flying sky-blue Holden Kingswood.

Dad sighs. We can hear the sigh through the cracks.

'We were going camping,' Dad says. He leaves big gaps between his sentences. To think and drag on his smoke. 'August loved camping under the stars. He loved looking up at the moon when he slept. Me and their mum had been going through some … issues.'

'She ran away from you?'

Silence.

'Yeah, I guess you could say that.'

Silence.

'I guess I was thinking too much about it all,' Dad says. 'I should never have been drivin'. Got the big shakes just before a blind lip in Cedar Creek Road and that blind lip led to a blind corner. Wasn't easy to see on the road. My brain turned to mush.'

Long silence.

'I got lucky,' Dad says. 'Them boys had their windows down. August always had his window down to look out at the moon.'

August is still.

And the moonlight shines on the black dam water in my mind. The full moon reflected in the dam. The dam pool. That damn moon pool.

'Bloke who owned the little cottage near the dam came racing out,' Dad says above us through the floorboards. 'He helped me drag the boys out.'

'They were unconscious?'

'I thought I'd lost 'em.' Dad's voice wavers. 'They were gone.'

'They weren't breathing?'

'Well, that's the tricky thing of it, Mrs Birkbeck,' Dad says.

August gives a half-smile. He's enjoying this story. Nodding his head knowingly, as if he's heard it before but I know he hasn't. I know he can't have heard it.

'I woulda sworn they weren't breathing,' Dad says. 'I tried resuscitating them, shook 'em like crazy to wake 'em up. And I couldn't wake 'em. Then I start screaming to the sky like a lunatic and I look back down again at their faces and they're awake.'

Dad clicks his fingers.

'Just like that,' he says, 'they come back.'

He drags on his smoke. Exhales.

'I asked the ambos about it when they lobbed up and they said the boys mighta been in shock. Said it mighta been hard for me to find a pulse or check their breathing because their bodies were so cold and numb.'

'What do you think about that?' Mrs Birkbeck asks.

'I don't think anything about that, Mrs Birkbeck,' Dad says, frustrated. 'It was a panic attack. I fucked up. And not an hour has passed in my life since that night that I haven't wished I could turn that car back onto Cedar Creek Road.'

A long pause.

'I don't think August has stopped thinking about that night,' Mrs Birkbeck says.

'How do you mean?' Dad asks.

'I think that night left a deep psychological imprint on August,' Mrs Birkbeck says.

'August has seen every psychologist in south-east Queensland, Mrs Birkbeck,' Dad says. 'He's been analysed and tested and probed and prodded by people like you for years and none of 'em have ever said he was anything more than a normal kid who don't like talkin'.'

'He's a bright boy, Robert. He's bright enough not to tell those psychologists any of the things he tells his brother.'

'Such as?'

I look at August. He shakes his head. *Eli. Eli. Eli.* I look up at the floorboards, covered in messages and sketches August and I have scribbled under here in permanent marker. Bigfoot riding a skateboard. Mr T driving the DeLorean DMC-12 from *Back to the Future*. A poor sketch of Jane Seymour nude with breasts that look more like metal garbage can lids. A scribbled collection of dumb one-liners: *I was wondering why the ball was getting bigger and bigger, and then it hit me. The banker wanted to check my balance so she pushed me over. I didn't want to believe Dad was stealing from the road works, but all the signs were there.*

'Why did he stop talking?' Mrs Birkbeck asks.

'Not sure,' Dad says. 'He hasn't told me yet.'

'He told Eli he doesn't talk because he's afraid he'll let his secret slip out,' she says.

'Secret?' Dad spits.

'Have the boys ever mentioned a red telephone to you?' she asks.

August boots my right shin. *Fuckwit.*

A long pause.

'No,' Dad says.

'Robert, I'm sorry to be the one to tell you, but August has been telling Eli a number of troubling things,' Mrs Birkbeck says. 'Traumatic things that are, I believe, themselves borne of trauma. Potentially harmful thoughts from a bright boy with an imagination too wild for his own good.'

'All older brothers tell their younger brothers all kinds of bullshit,' Dad says.

'But Eli believes it all, Robert. Eli believes it because August believes it.'

'Believes what?' Dad asks, frustrated.

Her voice turns to a whisper we can hear only faintly through the floorboard cracks.

'It would appear August has become convinced that he … ummm … I don't know how to say this … ummm … he believes he died that night in the moon pool,' she says. 'He believes he died and came back. And I think he believes he's died before and come back before. And maybe he believes he's died like that and come back like that several times.'

A long pause in the kitchen. The sound of Dad lighting a smoke.

'And it seems he told Eli that ... well ... he believes there are now other Augusts in other ... *places.*'

'Places?' Dad echoes.

'Yes,' Mrs Birkbeck says.

'What sort of places?'

'Well, places beyond our understanding. Places that are found at the other end of the red telephone the boys talk about.'

'What fuckin' ... Sorry ... what red telephone?' Dad barks, losing patience.

'The boys say they hear voices. A man at the end of a red telephone.'

'I have no fuckin' idea what you're on about.'

Mrs Birkbeck speaks now like she's disciplining a six-year-old. 'The red telephone that sits in the secret room beneath the house their mother shared with her partner, Lyle, who has inexplicably disappeared off the face of the earth.'

Dad takes a long drag. A long silence.

'August hasn't spoken since that night of the moon pool because he doesn't want to risk letting slip the truth behind his great secret,' Mrs Birkbeck says. 'And Eli is adamant the magic red phone is true because he's spoken to a man on the other end of the phone who knows things about him he couldn't possibly know.'

Another long pause. And Dad laughs. He howls, in fact.

'Oh, that's fuckin' priceless,' he says. 'That's fuckin' spectacular.'

I hear him slapping his knees.

'I'm glad you can see the funny side,' Mrs Birkbeck says.

'And you believe that my boys truly believe all of this?' Dad asks.

'I believe both of their minds, quite some time ago perhaps, developed a complex and mixed belief system of real and imagined explanations for compounding moments of great trauma,' she says. 'I believe they are either deeply psychologically damaged or ... or ...'

She pauses.

'Or what?' Dad asks.

'Or ... it couldn't hurt to consider the other explanation for it all,' she says.

'What's that?' Dad asks.

'That they are more special than you and I could possibly understand,' Mrs Birkbeck says. 'Maybe they do hear things that are beyond their own understanding as well and this red phone they're talking about is the only way they know how to make sense of the impossible.'

'That's fuckin' ridiculous,' Dad says.

'Maybe so,' Mrs Birkbeck says. 'Whatever the case – however fantastical these theories are – my point is that I truly fear these beliefs, even if they were formed in the imagination, might one day cause great harm to August and Eli. What if August's belief in what he calls "coming back" transfers itself to some mistaken sense of ... invincibility.'

Dad chuckles.

'I worry these thoughts have placed your boys on a path of recklessness, Robert.'

Dad dwells on this for a moment. The flint of his lighter striking. An exhalation of smoke.

'Well, you don't need to worry yourself about my boys, Mrs Birkbeck,' Dad says.

'I don't?'

'Nah,' Dad says. 'Because that's all a pile of horseshit.'

'How so?' asks Mrs Birkbeck.

'I mean August is nuts and bolts,' Dad says.

'Sorry, nuts and bolts?'

'He's straight up and down,' Dad says. 'I mean it sounds like Eli's taking the piss. He's spinnin' you a fantastical bullshit yarn to pull himself outta some shit he got himself in. It's a win–win. You believe it and you think he's special. You don't believe it and you think he's fucked in the head but you still think he's special. Look, he's a storyteller. And I hate to tell you, Mrs Birkbeck, but Eli was born with the two qualities of any good storyteller – the ability to string a sentence together and the ability to bullshit.'

I look at August. He nods his head in agreement. The legs of one of the kitchen chairs slides across the kitchen floorboards. Mrs Birkbeck sighs.

August sits up and moves into a crawl position, crab-walking back out from beneath the house. At the back of the under-house area, where there's enough room between the dirt ground and the house's floorboards for August to stand, he stops at one of Dad's abandoned washing machines. It's a top loader. He opens the lid of the washing machine and looks inside, closes the lid again. He waves me over. *Open the lid, Eli. Open the lid.*

I open the lid and inside the washing machine is a black garbage bag. *Look inside the bag, Eli. Look inside the bag.*

I look inside the bag and inside it there are ten rectangular blocks of heroin wrapped in brown greaseproof paper and wrapped again in clear plastic. The blocks are the size of the bricks they make at the Darra brickworks.

August says nothing. He closes the lid to the washing machine and marches up the side of the house, back up the ramp, and into the kitchen. Mrs Birkbeck turns in her chair and immediately sees the intensity on August's face.

'What is it, August?' she asks.

He licks his lips.

'I'm not gonna kill myself,' he says. He points at Dad. 'And we love him very much, which is only half as much as he loves us.'

# Boy Masters Time

Do your time before it does you. Before it does the roses on Khanh Bui's prize-winning garden on Harrington Street. Before it peels the paint off Bi Van Tran's yellow Volkswagen van, still parked like it always is on Stratheden Street.

Time is the answer to everything, of course. The answer to our prayers and murders and losses and ups and downs and loves and deaths.

Time for the brothers Bell to grow up and for Lyle's stash of heroin to grow in value along the way. Time puts hairs on my chin and my underarms and takes its time putting hairs on my balls. Time puts August in his final year at school, with me not far behind him.

Time makes Dad a half-decent cook. He makes us meals most nights he's not drinking. Chops and frozen vegetables. Sausages and frozen vegetables. A good spaghetti bolognese. He roasts mutton that we eat for a week. Some mornings, while the rest of the world is sleeping, he's waist-deep in the mangroves of Cabbage Tree Creek, in seaside Shorncliffe, catching us mud crabs with claws that bulge like Viv Richards' biceps. Some afternoons he walks halfway down to the Foodstore supermarket to get the groceries and he comes back with nothing and we don't ask why because we know he got the panics, because we know his nerves now, how they ruin him, how they eat him alive from the inside where his arteries and his veins carry all that memory and tension and thought and drama and death.

Some days I join him on the bus because he asks me to watch over him as he travels. He needs me to be his shadow. He asks me to talk to him. He asks me to tell him stories because they calm his nerves. So I tell him all the stories Slim told me. All those yarns about all those crims from Boggo Road. I tell him about my old pen pal, Alex Bermudez, and how those men inside wait for only two things in life, death and *Days of Our Lives*. When the nerves get too much, he gives me the nod and I press the bell for the bus to stop and Dad takes his breath by a bus stop and I tell him everything is going to be all right and we wait for the next bus back home. Small steps in our Dunlops. He gets a little further each trip out of the house. Bracken Ridge to Chermside. Chermside to Kedron. Kedron to Bowen Hills.

Time makes Dad cut down on his drinking. Mid-strength beer comes to Queensland and Dad stops flooding the toilet with piss. They'll never measure these things but I know more cartons of mid-strength beer in Bracken Ridge mean less Bracken Ridge mums presenting before Dr Benson in the Barrett Street Medical Centre with split eye sockets.

Time puts Dad in a job. He soups up on enough Serepax to get him outside the front door and onto a bus that takes him into a job interview at the G. James Glass and Aluminium factory on Kingsford Smith Drive, Hamilton, not far from the Brisbane CBD. For three weeks he works on a factory line cutting lengths of aluminium into various shapes and sizes, earning enough to buy a small bronze-coloured 1979 Toyota Corona for $1000 from his loose Bracken Ridge Tavern mate, Jim 'Snapper' Norton, on a payment basis of $100 every payday for ten weeks. He smiles when he opens his wallet on Friday afternoon and shows me three grey-blue money notes, the ones we never see, the ones with Douglas Mawson on them standing in a snow jumper, the Antarctic cold freezing the many hairs on his iceberg-sized balls. I've never seen Dad more proud and he's so proud this night he actually laughs more than he cries on the piss. But in the fourth week of this wondrous paid work, his foreman berates him for something he didn't do – someone plugged in the wrong numbers on a line of metal sheeting and $5000 worth of metal came up five centimetres short – and Dad can't absorb the injustice so he calls the foreman 'obtuse' and the young foreman doesn't know what that means so Dad tells him. 'It means you're a freckle-faced cunt,' he says. And on his way home he stops into the Hamilton Hotel, off Kingsford Smith Drive, to toast what he might have made of that wondrous paid work with eight pots of full-strength XXXX. And pulling out of the Hamilton Hotel driveway he's stopped by police who send him to a judge for drink-driving and the judge takes away his driver's licence and sentences Dad to a further six weeks' community service and August and I have very little to say when Dad informs us that his court-ordered community service will be carried out assisting the aged and ailing groundsman, Bob Chandler, at our very own Nashville State High School. I have even less to say when I look out my classroom window in Maths A class to find Dad beaming proudly up at me, standing beside the giant *ELI!* he's mowed into the manicured grass lawn that fronts the Mathematics and Science block.

Time makes the phone ring.

'Yeah,' Dad says. 'Okay. Yeah, I understand. What's the address? Okay. Yep. Yep. Bye.' He puts the phone down. August and I are watching *Family Ties* and eating sandwiches with devon and tomato sauce.

'Yer mum's gettin' out a month early,' he says. And he opens the drawer beneath the telephone, pops two Serepax, and walks on down the hallway to his bedroom, sucking those nerve lollies down like Tic Tacs.

*

Time makes the soft red roses on Khanh Bui's prize-winning garden turn hard, makes them grow into themselves like Dad did after that brief and colourful moment in the spring sun of the G. James Glass and Aluminium factory line.

I walk past Khanh Bui's house on the way to Arcadia Street in Darra. I remember what Khanh Bui's front garden looked like when it won first prize in a neighbourhood garden competition as part of a Darra State School fete celebration five years ago. It was like a lolly shop of colour then, a mix of ornamental and native plants that Khanh Bui would hose every morning we walked to school, standing in his blue and white pyjamas. Some mornings his wrinkly old dick would be sticking unassumingly out of the fly in his pyjamas but Mr Bui would never notice because his garden was so damn enchanting. But it's all gone dry and dead now, straw-coloured and bristly like the grass oval in Ducie Street Park.

As I turn into Arcadia Street I stop on the spot.

Two Vietnamese men are sitting in white plastic garden chairs at the top of Darren Dang's driveway. They wear black sunglasses and they sit in the sun in Adidas nylon tracksuits with white sneakers. The tracksuits are navy blue with three yellow stripes running down each side of their jackets and pants. I approach the front driveway slowly. One of the men holds his hands up to me. I stop. Both men stand from their chairs and reach for something out of view behind Darren's large and secure front fence.

They are now holding large and sharp-looking machetes when they approach me.

'Who are you?' asks one of the men.

'I'm Eli Bell,' I say. 'I'm an old friend of Darren's from school.'

'What's in bag?' the same man spits with a thick Vietnamese accent.

I look up and down the street, look up into the living room windows of the two-storey houses surrounding us, hoping nobody nosy is sticking their nose into this smelly business down here.

'Well, it's kinda sensitive,' I whisper.

'What da fuc' uuu doin' here?' asks the man, impatient, his default facial expression being a snarl.

'I've got a business proposal for Darren,' I say.

'You mean Mr Dang?' the man snaps.

'Yes, Mr Dang,' I clarify.

My heart is racing. My fingers grip the straps of my black backpack.

'Business proposal?' the man asks.

I look around again, take a step closer.

'I have some ... ummm ... merchandise ... I think he might be interested in,' I say.

'Merchandise?' the man suggests. 'You BTK?'

'Pardon me?'

'You BTK we cut your fuckin' tongue out,' the man says, his wide eyes suggesting he might enjoy said cut.

'No, I'm not BTK,' I say.

'You Mormon?'

I laugh. 'No,' I say.

'You Jehovah's Witness?' the man spits. 'You trying to sell fucking hot water system again?'

'No,' I say.

I briefly ponder what kind of strange parallel universe Darra I've walked back into. BTK? *Mister* Darren Dang?

'I have no idea what you're talking about,' I say. 'Look, I just came to say g'day to Darren ...'

The Vietnamese men move closer, their hands working over the wooden handles of their machetes.

'Pass me your bag,' he says.

I step back. The man raises his machete.

'Bag,' he says.

I pass over the bag. He hands it to his offsider who looks inside. He speaks in Vietnamese to the man who appears to be his superior.

'Where you get this merchandise?' the superior asks.

'Darren's Mum sold it to my mum's boyfriend a long time ago,' I say. 'I've come to sell it back.'

The man looks at me silently. I can't see his eyes through his black sunglasses.

He pulls a black two-way radio transceiver from his pocket.

'What's your name again?' he asks.

'Eli Bell,' I say.

He talks into the transceiver in Vietnamese. The only words I catch are 'Eli Bell'.

He puts the transceiver back into his pocket, beckons me closer.

'Come,' he says. 'Arms up.'

I raise my hands and the two Vietnamese men frisk my legs and arms and hips.

'Gee, security's really picked up around here,' I say.

The superior's right hand fidgets around my balls. 'Gentle,' I say as I squirm.

'Follow me,' he says.

We don't go up into the house where Lyle once made his deals with the exotic 'Back Off' Bich Dang. We pass Darren's large yellow brick house down the left side. It's only now that I realise the house's high wood fence is lined with barbed wire.

This is less a backyard than a fortress. We walk to a granny flat behind the main house that is more like a council toilet block made of white painted concrete blocks, a good place for drug dealers, or Hitler, to strategise. The gate man knocks once on the peach-coloured door of the bunker and says a single word in Vietnamese.

The door opens and the gate man leads me into a hallway lined with framed black and white photographs of Darren Dang's family members back home: wedding photographs, family functions, one shot of a man crooning into a microphone, another shot of an old lady holding a giant prawn by a brown river.

The hallway leads to a living room where a dozen or so Vietnamese men stand in navy blue nylon Adidas tracksuits with yellow stripes down the sides of their arms and legs. They all wear black sunglasses like the men on the gate. These men in blue tracksuits stand around one man who sits in a red nylon Adidas tracksuit with white stripes running down his arms and legs. He sits at a sprawling timber office desk, running his eyes over several documents on the table. He does not wear black sunglasses. He wears mirrored aviator sunglasses with gold frames.

'Darren?' I say.

The man in the red tracksuit looks up and I see a scar running from the left edge of his mouth. He takes his sunglasses off and his eyes adjust to my face. Eyes squinting.

'Who the fuck are you?' he asks.

'Darren, it's me,' I say. 'It's Eli.'

He puts his sunglasses down on the table, reaches into a drawer beneath the desk. He pulls out a flick-knife and the blade snaps into view as he rounds the desk and approaches me. He rubs the bottom of his nose, sniffs sharply two times. His eyeballs are pulsing like lightbulbs losing power. He stands before me and runs the blade along my right cheek.

'Eli who?' he whispers.

'Eli Bell,' I say. 'From school. Fuck me, Darren. It's me, mate. I used to live just down the road.'

He puts the blade up to my eyeball.

'Darren? Darren? It's me.'

Then he freezes. A smile explodes across his face.

'Haaaaaaaaaaaaaaa!' he hollers. 'You see your face, bitch!' he screams. His friends in navy blue tracksuits howl at my expense. He adopts a thick Australian outback accent. 'You hear this bitch?' he says to his audience. '"It's me, maaaate. It's meeeeeeeeeeeee, Eeeeloiiii."'

He slaps his thighs then wraps his arms around me, blade still fixed inside his right fist. 'Come here, Bell End!' he laughs. 'What the fuck's up with you? You don't call, you don't write. I had big plans for us, Tink.'

'It all went to shit,' I say.

Darren nods in agreement. 'Yeah, a whole bunch of runny ol' Eli Bell shit,' he says. He grips my right hand, lifts it into view, runs his finger across the pale white nub of my missing finger.

'You miss it?' Darren asks.

'Only when I'm writing,' I say.

'No, I mean, Darra, dumb arse, you miss Darra?'

'I do,' I say.

Darren walks back to his desk.

'Can I get you anything?' he asks. 'Got a fridge full of soft drink in the room there.'

'You got any Pasito?'

'Nah,' Darren says. 'Got Coke, Solo, Fanta and Creaming Soda.'

'I'm good,' I say.

He leans back in his desk chair and shakes his head.

'Eli Bell is back in town!' he says. 'It's good to see you, Tink.'

His smile goes flat. 'That was fucked what happened to Lyle,' he says.

'Was it Bich?' I ask.

'Was it Bich, what?' he replies.

'Was it Bich who ratted on Lyle?'

'You think it was Mum?' he asks, perplexed.

'No, I don't think so,' I say. 'But was it?'

'She considered Lyle a client, just like Tytus Broz,' he says. 'Aside from the fact rattin' is bad business, she had no reason to rat about any side business she had goin' on because she was just doing business, Tink. If Lyle was dumb enough to start tradin' with her behind his boss's back, that was his business, not hers. His cash had the same numbers printed on it as anybody else's. Nah, man, you know exactly who ratted his arse out.'

No. No, I really don't know. Not exactly. Not at all.

Darren looks at me, mouth open, dumbstruck.

'You really are one sweet kid, Eli,' Darren says. 'Don't you know the biggest rats are always closest to the cheese?'

'Teddy?' I say.

'I'd tell you, Tink, but I don't eat no cheese,' he says. Darren's friends nod.

Piss-weak fucksack so-called friend Tadeusz 'Teddy' Kallas. The fuckin' cheese eater.

'Where is your mum?' I ask.

'She's up in the house resting,' he says. 'She got the Big C about a year ago.'

'Cancer?'

'Nah, cataracts,' he says. 'Poor Bich can't see no more.'

The gate man drops my backpack on his desk. Darren looks inside.

'You still importing for Tytus Broz?' I ask.

'Nah, that pussy has gone to Dustin Vang and BTK,' he says.

'That incident with your precious Lyle didn't help relations between Mum and Tytus.'

Darren sticks his knife in the bag, pulls it back out with its tip holding grains of Lyle's high-grade heroin.

'What's BTK?' I ask.

Darren inspects the gear on his knife like a jeweller inspecting the clarity of diamonds.

'Born To Kill,' Darren says. 'It's the new world, Tink. Everybody's gotta be gang-affiliated now. BTK. 5T. Canal Boys. The exporters back home have all these rules around shit now. Everything goes through abracadabra Cabramatta down south and all the heads in Cab were forced to split into sides when all the heads back in Saigon split into sides. That punk bitch Dustin Vang went BTK and my mum went 5T.'

'What's 5T?'

Darren looks around at his friends. They smile. They all chant something in Vietnamese. He stands and unzips his red nylon Adidas jacket, pulls down a white singlet to reveal a tattoo on his chest, a large numeral '5' with a 'T' in the shape of a dagger, stabbing into a throbbing black heart emblazoned with five Vietnamese words: *Tình*, *Tiền*, *Tù*, *Tội* and *Thu*.

The 5T gang chant in unison. 'Love, Money, Prison, Sin, Revenge'.

Darren nods. 'Fuck yeah,' he says approvingly.

There's a knock on the door of the bunker. A young Vietnamese boy, maybe nine years old, dressed in his own navy nylon Adidas tracksuit, enters the office area. He's sweating. He hollers something at Darren in Vietnamese.

'BTK?' replies Darren.

The boy nods. Darren nods his head at a senior gang member to his right, who nods in turn at three other members who rush out of the bunker.

'What is it?' I ask.

'Fuckin' BTK crew walking down Grant Street,' Darren says. 'They're not supposed to be walkin' on fuckin' Grant Street.'

Darren is frustrated, impatient. He looks down at my bag again.

'How much?' he asks.

'Sorry?' I say.

'How much?' he repeats. 'What are you asking?'

'For the gear?' I clarify.

'No, Tink, for you to blow my Charlie dick. Yes, how much you askin' for the gear?'

'That's the gear your mum sold Lyle almost four years ago,' I say.

'You don't say,' he says, dry and sarcastic. 'I thought you might have started up your own import business out at bumfuck Bracken Ridge.'

I make my sales pitch. I rehearsed it six times in our bedroom yesterday, but there weren't fourteen intimidating Vietnamese men in sunglasses staring at me in my bedroom.

'I figure with the focus Queensland Police have put on the heroin trade of late that prices for gear of that integrity ...'

'Ha!' laughs Darren. 'Integrity? I like that, Tink, sounds like your sellin' me an English butler or something. *Integrity.*' The gang members laugh.

I soldier on.

'... gear of that quality, I figure, would be tough to come by and so I'm thinking, for the amount we have in that bag there, a fair price would be ...'

I look into Darren's eyes. He's done this before. I've never done this. Five hours ago I was drawing my stick portrait as a knight holding Excalibur in the heat mist on Dad's bathroom shower door. Now I'm making a heroin deal with the sixteen-year-old leader of the 5T gang. 'Ummmm ...' Damn it, don't say 'ummmm'. Confidence. 'Er ... $80,000?'

Darren smiles. 'I like your style, Eli,' he says.

He turns to another gang member. Talks in Vietnamese. The gang member rushes into another room.

'What's he doing?' I ask.

'He's grabbing you your $50,000,' Darren says.

'Fifty thousand?' I echo. 'I said $80,000. What about inflation?'

'Tink, the only inflation I can see right now is the hot air blowing up your arse.' Darren smiles. 'Yes, it's probably worth at least $100,000, but as much as I love you, Eli, you are you and I am me and the problem with being you right now, aside from the fact you can't bowl a cricket ball to save yourself, is the fact you would not have the faintest clue where to take that gear anywhere beyond that door behind you.'

I turn around and look at the door behind me. Fair point well made.

Darren laughs. 'Aaaaah, I've missed you, Eli Bell,' he says.

Three gang members burst back into the office barking frantic words at Darren.

'Fuckin' gook cunts,' Darren barks.

He barks at his gang members in thick Vietnamese. The gang members all rush to an adjoining room and re-emerge just as fast carrying machetes. Another gang member emerges from a separate room holding my $50,000 in three brick-shaped blocks of $50 notes. The men with machetes file down the hallway with military diligence, clanging their machetes excitedly against the hallway walls as they exit the bunker.

'What the fuck's going on?' I ask.

'Fuckin' BTK have broken the peace agreement,' Darren says, opening a long drawer in his desk. 'They're about two minutes from my fuckin' house. I'm gonna cut their fuckin' BTK heads off like the catfish cunts they are.'

He brings out a gleaming gold-coloured custom-made machete emblazoned with the 5T logo.

'What about me?' I ask.

'Oh, yeah,' he says.

He leans back down to his drawer and pulls out another machete, tosses it to me.

I fumble for the handle and the blade nearly lodges into my foot on its way to the ground. I quickly pick up the weapon.

'No,' I say. 'I mean, we need to finish the deal.'

'Tink, the deal's fuckin' done,' he says.

His helper hands me my backpack. The drugs have disappeared from the bag and been replaced with blocks of cash.

'Let's go,' Darren says.

Darren rushes down the hallway, a warrior's bloodlust across his face.

'I think I'll just wait in here till you guys are all done,' I say.

''Fraid not, Tink,' he says. 'We got enough money in this bunker to feed Big Rooster to the people of Vietnam for six months. We gotta lock this joint up.'

'I'll just slip out over the back fence,' I say.

'We got barbed wire walls on all sides. Ain't no way outta here but through that front gate,' he says. 'What's wrong with you anyway? These BTK fuckers wanna take over our crib. They want all the Darra territories. You gonna let these fuckers take over our hometown? This is our turf, Tink. We gotta defend it.'

*

The battle starts much like any other throughout history. The heads of each opposing clan exchange words.

'I'm gonna cut your nose off, Tran, and stick a key ring through your nostril,' Darren calls from the front of his house on the cul-de-sac of Arcadia Street, standing in the centre of a group of 5T members that has now swelled to about thirty.

At the entrance to the street stands the man who I guess is named Tran, before his gang of fidgety BTK barbarians who do indeed appear to have been placed on this earth for the sole purpose of ending the lives of others. Tran holds a machete in his right hand and a hammer in his left, leading a group that outnumbers Darren's by at least ten.

'I'm gonna cut your ears off, Darren, and sing the Marching Song into them every night before supper,' Tran says.

Then the clanging starts. Gang members on both sides clanging the metal weapon of the man next to them. A rhythmic clanging that escalates in intensity. A call to war. A song of doom.

And something inside me, my own lust for life, my own quest for peace perhaps, or maybe just my innate fear of having a machete lodged into my scalp, makes me push through the huddle of 5T members from my position behind them.

'I'm sorry,' I say. 'I'm sorry.' I walk into the centre of Arcadia Street, the very centre of the divide between these two bloodthirsty groups. 'I'm sorry to interrupt,' I call. And the clanging of machetes halts. Silence fills the street and my shaky voice echoes across Darra.

'I know there's no reason why you should listen to me,' I call. 'I'm just some idiot who dropped in to see his mate. But I really feel an outsider's perspective might help you guys resolve any grievances you may have against each other.'

I turn to each side. A look of profound befuddlement can be seen on the faces of Darren and Tran.

'Sons of Darra,' I say. 'Sons of Vietnam. Was it not war that forced your families from their homelands? Was it not hate and division and miscommunication that brought you to this beautiful suburb in the first place? There's a strange land out past the borders of Darra and that place is called Australia. And that place isn't always nice to newcomers. That place isn't always welcoming to outsiders. You guys will face enough fights out there, out there beyond this sanctuary of home. You need to fight together out there, not against each other in here.'

I point to my own head.

'Maybe it's time we all started using a bit more of this,' I say.

And I raise my machete.

'And a bit less of this.'

I slowly and symbolically place my machete flat on the bitumen of a motionless Arcadia Street. Darren looks at his men. Tran lowers his arms for a moment and looks across at his soldiers. Then he looks back at me. Then he raises his weapons once more.

'Tan coooooong!' he screams. And the BTK army charges forth, machetes and hammers and crowbars raised to the Brisbane sky.

'Kill 'em all!' screams Darren, as the merciless 5T army sprints forward, rubber shoes rushing on the street and metal clanging in anticipation. I turn and sprint to the side of the street just as the two rabid armies meet in an explosion of flesh on flesh and blade on blade. I leap over a knee-high fence and into the front garden of a small cottage home, four doors up from Darren's house. I fall to my belly and crawl across the cottage home's front lawn, praying a BTK member hasn't spotted my escape. I crawl to the side of the house and find shelter behind a white rosebush from where I take one last look at the Great Machete Battle of Arcadia Street. Blades whistling through air, fists and elbows finding foreheads and noses. Legs kicking into stomachs. Knees meeting eyeballs. Darren Dang leaps briefly and triumphantly out of the melee on an arcing flight towards some unsuspecting rival warrior. My hand reaches to the bottom of my backpack to feel for the fifty grand still sitting in there. And I thank the gods of war for remembering the sixth 'T'. Turn and run.

# Boy Sees Vision

Can't wait to tell her. Can't wait to see her. In my vision she's wearing a white dress. Her hair is long, falling over her shoulders. She kneels and sweeps me into her arms. I hand her the money we made for her and she weeps. That night we drive out to The Gap and we lay that money down on the desk of a bank in The Gap Village shopping centre and she tells a handsome banker that the money is her deposit on a small cottage home with a white rosebush out the front.

Our bus stops on Buckland Road, in the suburb of Nundah, in Brisbane's north. A big autumn sun warms the top of my head, burns my ears and neck. We amble past the Corpus Christi Church, a mighty brown brick cathedral with a green dome on top like the tops of all those important London buildings I see in the set of *Encyclopaedia Britannica* scattered through the book hill inside Dad's library room.

I might just miss that shoebox shithole Dad calls home. I'm gonna miss those holes in the wall. I'm gonna miss all those books. I'm gonna miss Dad on the sober nights when he's playing *Sale of the Century* with us and he's laughing at Tony Barber's jokes and he's thrashing every last person the show calls a carry-over champion. I'm gonna miss Henry Bath. I'm

316

gonna miss walking to the shops to buy sober Dad's smokes. I'm gonna miss sober Dad.

We turn off Buckland Road into Bage Street. I stop.

'This is it,' I say. 'Sixty-one.'

August and I stand before a sprawling timber Queenslander home, raised high on tall and spindly stump legs, a house with so much aged and rickety character it feels like it's leaning on a walking stick cracking a joke about the Irish famine.

A tall staircase covered in peeling blue paint takes us up to old French doors, weathered and rotting, splintery to touch. I knock twice with my left hand that has five fingers.

'Coming,' sings a woman's high-pitched voice.

The home's front door opens and a nun stands before us. She's old and wears a white dress with short sleeves. A blue and white habit covering her hair and bordering a gentle and beaming face. A large silver cross swaying on a necklace.

'Now you must be August and Eli,' she says.

'I'm Eli,' I say. 'He's August.' August smiles and nods.

'I'm Sister Patricia,' she says. 'I've been looking after your mum for a few days, helping her find her feet a wee little bit.'

She looks deep into our eyes. 'I've heard all about you two,' she says. She nods at me. 'Eli, the talker and the storyteller.' She nods at August. 'And August, our dear wise and quiet man. Ohhhh, what rare fire and ice we have here, hey.'

Fire and ice. Yin and Yang. Sonny and Cher. It all works.

'Come on in,' she says.

We walk through the doors and stand respectfully in the sunroom of the sprawling house. A large framed image of Jesus hangs above the hallway entry. It's not too different from the image in Lena's bedroom. Sad young Jesus. Handsome young Jesus. Keeper of my greatest sins. Knower. Forgiver. The man who gives me a break on all that hateful thinking I've been doing lately. All that dark hoping. That the men who put my mother here will burn. That these men we once knew will bleed for the things they did. Let them drown. Give them hell, give them disease and wrath and pestilence and pain and eternal fire and ice. Amen.

'Eli?' says Sister Patricia. 'You there, Eli?'

'Yes, sorry,' I say.

'Well, what are you waiting for?' she says. 'You need me to hold your hand?'

We walk on through the hallway.

'Second room on the right,' calls Sister Patricia.

August walks ahead of me. The hallway is carpeted. A sideboard carries framed prayer messages and trays of rosary beads and a vase of purple flowers. The whole house smells of lavender. I will remember Mum through lavender. I will remember Mum through rosary beads and vertical joint wood walls painted aqua. We pass the first bedroom on the right and there's a woman sitting at a desk in the bedroom, reading. She smiles at us and we smile back and walk on down the hallway.

August stops for a brief moment before the door of the second bedroom on the right. He looks over his shoulder at me. I place my hand on his right shoulder. We talk without talking. *I know, mate. I know.* He walks into the bedroom and I follow my older brother and I watch her sweep him into her arms. She was crying before he entered. She's not wearing white, she's wearing a light blue summer dress, but her hair is long like the vision and her face is warm and whole and here.

'Group hug,' she whispers.

We're taller here than we were in the vision. I forgot about time. The vision lagged, spoke of things that weren't and not things that would be. She sits on a single bed and I remember how she sat on that bed in Boggo Road. And those two women could not be more different. The worst of her in my head and the best of her here.

And this is the her that will be.

*

Mum closes the door of the bedroom and we don't come back out for three straight hours. We fill in the gaps of all that time missed. The girls we like at school, the sports we play, the books we read, the trouble we make. We play Monopoly and Uno and we listen to music on a small clock radio near Mum's bed. Fleetwood Mac. Duran Duran. Cold Chisel, 'When the War is Over'.

We go out to a common room for dinner and Mum introduces us to two women who were with her inside and who are also finding their feet for a wee little bit in this rickety old house of Sister Patricia's. The women are named Shan and Linda and I reckon Slim would have liked them both. They both wear singlets and they don't wear bras and they both have raspy smoker laughs and when they laugh their boobs bounce in their singlets. They tell dry yarns about the miseries of life inside but they tell them with almost enough sprinkles of sunshine to make August and me believe it wasn't so bad for Mum in there. There were friendships and loyalty and care and love. They joke about the meat that was so hard it broke their teeth. There were practical jokes and pranks on screws. There were ambitious escape attempts, like the Russian former child athlete who built a pole vault in a calamitous attempt to vault the prison walls. And of course there was no greater day than when the crazy boy from Bracken Ridge broke into Boggo to see his mum at Christmas.

Mum smiles at that story but it makes her cry too.

*

We set up a thick doona as a bed in Mum's bedroom. We use cushions from the living room couch as our pillows. Before we sleep Mum says she has something to tell us. We sit either side of her on the bed. I reach for my backpack. There is $50,000 inside it.

'I've got something to tell you too, Mum,' I say. I can't keep it in me. Can't wait to tell her. Can't wait to tell her our dreams will come true. We're free. We're finally free.

'What is it?' she asks.

'You go first,' I say.

She brushes my fringe out of my face, smiles.

She drops her head. Thinks some more.

'Go on, Mum, you go first,' I urge.

'I don't know how to say it,' she says.

I push her gently on the shoulder. 'Just say it,' I chuckle.

She breathes deep. Smiles. Smiles so wide it makes us smile with her.

'I'm moving in with Teddy,' she says.

And time is up. Time is undoing. Time is undone.

# Boy Bites Spider

There's a redback spider plague in Bracken Ridge. Some confluence of heat and humidity is causing redback spiders across Lancelot Street to crawl beneath plastic toilet seat lids. On my last day of Year 11, our next-door neighbour, Pamela Waters, is bitten on the arse while doing one of her boisterous number twos that bubble and squeak across the fence sometimes from her dunny. August and I aren't sure who to feel more sorry for, Mrs Waters or the unsuspecting redback who bit a chunk out of her arse flesh for supper.

I found a book on spiders in Dad's library room and I've been reading about redbacks. The book says the female redbacks are sexual cannibals who eat their male partners while simultaneously mating with them, which is similar to the mating and eating rituals of some of the girls at my school. The cute little spiderling sons and daughters of these killer lovers are sibling cannibals who spend up to a week on the maternal web before floating away on the wind.

One week. That's how long Mum wants August and me to stay at Teddy's house over the summer holidays. One week with Teddy the rat. I'd prefer to stay here in Bracken Ridge with Dad and the sexual cannibal redbacks.

*

'Which planet has the most moons?' asks Tony Barber inside our fuzzy television, posing questions to three contestants on the pastel pink and aquamarine set of *Sale of the Century*.

Dad has thirty-six beers and three cups of Fruity Lexia under his belt and he still beats all three contestants to the answer.

'Jupiter!' he barks.

'What's the capital of Romania?' Barber asks.

'A knot is the collective noun for which amphibian?' Barber asks.

'How the fuck in her right mind did Frankie Bell trust that pissant Teddy Kallas?' Barber asks. I sit up in my seat, finally interested in Dad's favourite show.

'And for a pick of the fame board, who am I?' asks Barber. He asks the question straight down the tube. He asks me directly. 'I was born to a couple that never was. The youngest of two boys, my older brother stopped speaking when his father drove him into a dam at the age of six. When I was thirteen years old the man I believed I was going to grow up with was dragged away to unseen oblivion by the enforcer of a suburban drug dealer masquerading as a small business seller of artificial limbs. Just when I thought things were getting better, my mother moved in with the man I believe brought about the death of the man I loved most in life. A rolling tumbleweed of confusion and despair, I am Eli who?'

*

August is in our room, painting. Oil on canvas. He says he might become a painter.

'Just like your old man,' Dad says whenever this subject comes up, making his usual link between August's often startling, occasionally unsettling oil paintings and Dad's first job as an apprentice for the End of the Rainbow House Painting company in Woolloongabba.

A collection of canvases lies around the room, on the walls, beneath his sagging bed. He's prolific. He's been working on a series where he paints insignificant suburban scenes from the streets of Bracken Ridge against impossibly grand backdrops of outer space. In one painting he placed our local Big Rooster restaurant floating in front of the spiral galaxy Andromeda, 2.5 million light years from earth. In another, he placed a scene of two kids from McKeering Street playing backyard cricket with their wheelie bin for stumps, backgrounded by a red starburst galaxy that looked like stomach blood reacting to a shotgun shell. Yet another shows a Foodstore supermarket trolley floating 100,000 light years away on the edge of the Milky Way. He did a painting of Dad in a blue singlet, lying on his side on the couch, smoking a rollie and circling the form guide, before a backdrop of a vast and colourful celestial gas cloud at the very edge of the known universe where, Gus said, all universal matter smells like Dad's farts.

'Who's that?' I ask from the bedroom door.

'It's you.'

August's paintbrush dabs at a Black & Gold choc chip ice cream lid that he's using as a paint palette. It's me on the canvas. It's me from my Nashville High School photo. I need a haircut. I look like I play bass in the Partridge Family. Late-teen pimples, big dumb late-teen ears, greasy late-teen nose. I'm sitting at a brown school classroom desk looking out the classroom window, a worried look on my face, and through that classroom window is outer space.

'What is that?'

Some intergalactic phenomenon, a luminous green blob forming among the stars.

'It's you looking out the window in Maths and you've seen a light that's taken 12 billion years to reach you,' August says.

'What's it mean?' I ask.

'I don't know,' he says. 'I think it's just about you seeing the light.'

'What are you gonna call it?'

*'Eli Sees the Light in Maths Class.'*

I watch August add a deeper shade to my oil-paint Adam's apple.

'I don't want to go to Teddy's house,' I say.

Brush and dab. Brush and dab.

'I don't either,' he says.

Brush and dab. Brush and dab.

'But we're still gonna go, aren't we?' I say.

Brush and dab. Brush and dab.

August nods. *Yes, Eli, we have to go.*

\*

Teddy's eyes have sunk inwards since I last saw him and his stomach has pushed outwards. He stands in the doorway of a two-storey Queenslander house in Wacol, one suburb south-west of Darra, which he inherited from his parents who now live in a nursing home in Ipswich, twenty more minutes' drive along Brisbane Road.

August and I are standing at the top of a rickety staircase with iron rails so old and flimsy the staircase feels like a rope bridge Indiana Jones and his loyal sidekick, Short Round, might traverse over a pool of crocodiles.

'Long time no see, ay boys,' Teddy says, his fat arm around Mum like she's a keg of beer.

I see you in my head almost every day, Teddy.

'Long time,' I say.

August is behind me, leaning his hand over the staircase rail to grip what looks like a wild yellow apricot from a tree hanging over the house's front stairs.

'Good to see you, Gus,' Teddy says.

August looks at Teddy, gives a half-smile, tugs a fruit from the tree.

'That's Mum's loquat tree,' he says. 'Been here more than fifty years that tree.'

August smells the fruit.

'Go ahead, have a bite,' he says. 'Tastes like a pear and pineapple all in one.'

August bites, chews a chunk of loquat. Smiles.

'You want one, Eli?' Teddy asks.

I want nothing from you, Teddy Kallas, except your head on a spike.

'No, thanks, Teddy.'

'You boys wanna see somethin' cool?'

We say nothing.

Mum gives me a sharp eye.

'Eli,' Mum says, not having to say any more.

'Sure, Teddy,' I say with all the personality of a loquat.

It's a truck. A hulking orange 1980 Kenworth K100 Cabover parked down the side of his sprawling yard beneath a monstrous mango tree that drops its flying-fox-sucked green fruit on the truck's engine bonnet.

Teddy says he drives this truck for Woolworths, hauling fruit up and down Australia's east coast. We climb into the truck with him and he turns the ignition and the rattling food-hauling beast wakes.

'You want to honk the horn, Eli?'

I'm not fuckin' eight years old any more, Teddy.

'That's okay, Teddy,' I say.

He honks it himself and gives a thrilled chuckle, the way a pea-brained fairytale giant might chuckle at a thieving farmboy bouncing on a pogo stick.

He takes his CB radio and fiddles with some frequency knobs in search of some close mates he says are somewhere out there in trucker land. These trucker mates all slowly check in, sweary blokes called Marlon and Fitz and some Australian trucking legend wanker known as 'The Log' on account of his dick size.

I liked Teddy Kallas when I first met him. I liked how Teddy and Lyle got along like the best friends they were. Teddy seemed to see in Lyle what I saw in him. I thought Teddy looked a bit like GI Blues–era Elvis Presley, the way he combed his hair back with gel, something about the curl of his puffy lips. But now every part of him is puffy, so he looks like Vegas Elvis. Deep-fried peanut butter sandwiches Elvis. He ratted on Lyle. He told Tytus Broz he was running a drug business on the side. He had Lyle dragged away and quartered and he thought it would get him the girl and get him in the good books with Tytus Broz. But Tytus cast him out because Tytus knew rats couldn't be trusted. Rats have to go get real jobs driving Woolworths food trucks up and down the east coast of Australia. He started visiting Mum inside and I guess she wanted to believe he didn't rat because I guess she wanted the visits. I wasn't going up there to Boggo. August wasn't going up. Nobody allowed us to go up there without Dad. But Mum had to talk to someone on the outside, if only to be reminded that the outside still existed. So she talked to the rat. He'd visit every Thursday morning, Mum says. He was funny, she says. He was kind, she says. He was there, she says.

'I like driving trucks,' Teddy says. 'I get out on the highway and I just get into this zone. I can't explain it.'

Please don't then, Teddy.

'You know what I do sometimes on the road?'

You, Marlon, Fitz and The Log masturbate in a kind of CB radio circle jerk?

'What?' I bite.

'I talk to Lyle,' he says.

He shakes his head. We say nothing.

'You know what I say to him?'

Sorry? Please forgive me? Please release me from the 24/7 soul-binding agony of my guilt and my betrayal and my greed?

'I talk to him about the milk truck.'

Teddy and Lyle stole a milk truck when they were boys, he says. It happened in Darra. They drove off in the milk truck while the milko was chatting on the doorstep to Lyle's mum, Lena. They took a reckless joyride in the truck, maybe the happiest six minutes of both their lives. Lyle let Teddy out at a corner store before he returned the milk truck, wearing the consequences on his own. Because Lyle Orlik was a good and decent boy who happened to grow up into a suburban skag pusher.

'I miss him,' he says.

And his thoughts are interrupted by two large German shepherds barking at the driver's door of the truck.

'Hey boys!' he beams out the truck window. 'Come meet my boys,' he urges us.

He slips out of the truck and play wrestles with his dogs in his backyard.

'This bloke is Beau,' he says, vigorously rubbing the head of one dog, his left hand reaching out to tickle the belly of the other dog. 'And this feller is Arrow.'

He looks lovingly into their eyes.

'These boys are the only family I got now,' Teddy says.

August and I say something to each other we do not say. *What a fuckin' loser.*

'Come see their house,' he says, giddy.

Beau and Arrow's kennel beneath the house. Less a dog house than a two-level dog retreat set on a concrete slab. Hardwood palings with flourishes of shaped plywood for windows and doors resembling the kind found on a cottage Hansel and Gretel might stumble across wandering lost in the woods. The whole thing is built on stumps and Beau and Arrow have a ramp with foot notches to access their blanketed and cushioned dream home.

'Built it meself,' Teddy says.

August and I say something to each other we do not say. *What a prize fuckin' loser.*

*

It's all peachy perfect here at Teddy's house for the first three days of our stay. Loquat perfect. Teddy smiles at Mum to show us he cares and he buys us Paddle Pops to win us over and tells us trucker jokes, almost all of which are deeply racist and end with an Aboriginal/Irishman/Chinaman/woman being found in the front bullbar of an eighteen-wheeler. Then Dustin Hoffman makes everything go south on the fourth night of our stay.

We're driving home from the Eldorado cinema in Indooroopilly when something about Dustin Hoffman's performance in the movie we just saw, *Rain Man*, reminds Teddy of August.

'Can you do that sorta stuff, Gus?' Teddy asks, looking through the rearview mirror at August in the back seat.

August says nothing.

'You know,' Teddy pushes, 'can you count up a pile of toothpicks in a single look? You got any special powers like that?'

August rolls his eyes.

'He's not autistic, Teddy,' I say. 'He's just fuckin' quiet.'

'Eli!' Mum snaps back at me.

The car is silent for a full five minutes. Nobody talks. I watch the yellow glowing of roadside lights. The glowing is the fire inside me, forging a question out of flame. I ask it flat, not a hint of emotion.

'Teddy, why did you rat on your best friend?'

And he says nothing. He just stares at me in the rearview mirror and he doesn't look like Elvis from any kind of era or

328

time or place or context any more because Elvis never went to hell. Elvis never had a devil phase.

*

He says nothing for two more days. He wakes late in the morning and trudges heavily past Mum and August and me at the breakfast table eating Corn Flakes and Mum says, 'Good morning', and he doesn't even look up as he silently walks out of the house.

Dad does this sometimes to August and me after we've had a big blow-up in the lounge room during one of his benders. He's the one who picks a fight with us, he's the one who keeps slapping us across the backs of our heads when we're trying to watch *21 Jump Street*, he's the one who always pushes August too far and he's the one August punches in the eye just to get a moment's respite. And yet it's us who get the cold shoulder. Most of the time Dad wakes up the next morning, assesses the bruising on his face and apologises. But sometimes he gives us the silent treatment. Like we're the arseholes. Like we're the dicks in all this. Fuckin' adults.

Teddy's acting like we're not in his house, like we're ghosts, spectres in his living room playing games of Pictionary and The Game of Life while he plays the wrongfully persecuted mute inside his bedroom.

Then I feel shit for making Mum feel shit and when she asks August and me to help her cook some lamb shanks for dinner August gives me one of those looks that says, *You'll help her cook these lamb shanks because it means something to her and you'll enjoy it and if you don't I'm gonna cave your skull in.*

We make the lamb shanks, slow-cook them for a day just like little iddy widdy Teddy likes them.

Teddy leaves the house at midday, marches through the kitchen.

'Where you going?' Mum asks.

He says nothing.

'Can you be back for dinner at six?' she says.

Nothing.

'We're making you lamb shanks,' she says.

Say something, you fuck.

'With the red wine sauce, just how you like 'em,' Mum says. Mum's smile. Look at that smile, Teddy. Look at that sun inside her. Teddy? Teddy?

Nothing. He walks out of the kitchen, down the back stairs. Down, down, down, the devil going down and the devil's sunshine girl doing her best to laugh it off.

We slow-cook the lamb shanks in a steel pot that once belonged to Teddy's grandmother, big enough to take a bubble bath in. We cook them for half a day and then some, turn them every hour in a sauce made of red wine, garlic, thyme, four bay leaves, chopped onions, carrots and celery sticks. By the time it comes to taste testing, pieces of lamb are falling off those shanks like chocolate in the hands of that ethereal lady in white from the Flake ad who August has a crush on.

*

Teddy doesn't make it back by 6 p.m. We've already started eating at the dining room table when he pads in two hours later.

'Yours is in the oven,' Mum says.

He stares at us. Assesses us. August and I can smell the piss on him the minute he sits down at the table. And something else inside him. Speed, maybe. The trucker's little helper on a long-haul drive up to Cairns. His eyes can't fix on us and he's breathing loud and he keeps opening and closing his mouth like he's thirsty, thick white balls of saliva pooling in the corners of his lips. Mum goes to the kitchen to serve his meal and he stares at August across the table.

'How was your day, Teddy?' I ask.

But he does not answer, he just keeps staring at August, who has his head down in his plate, dragging flakes of lamb through red wine sauce and mashed potato.

'What's that?' Teddy says, staring at August. 'I'm sorry. I didn't hear you.'

'He didn't say anything, Teddy,' I say.

He leans in closer to August, heaving his fat stomach onto the table so far that his Winfield Reds fall out of the pocket of his blue denim work shirt.

'Can you repeat that for me? Maybe a little louder this time.'

He turns his left ear theatrically to August.

'No, no, I understand, mate,' Teddy shrugs. 'I'd be lost for words too, if my old man did that to me.'

My brother looks up at the betrayer and smiles. Teddy rests back in his dining chair and Mum places his meal in front of him.

'We're glad you made it,' Mum says.

He forks some mash like a child. Bites into a shank like a shark. He looks across at August again.

'You know what his problem is, don't you?' he says.

'Let's just eat our dinner, hey, Teddy,' Mum says.

'You indulged this vow-of-silence bullshit,' Teddy says. 'You made these boys as crazy as their fuck-up father.'

'All right, Teddy, that's enough,' Mum says.

August looks up again at Teddy. August is not smiling this time. He's just studying Teddy.

'I gotta hand it to you, boys,' Teddy says. 'It sure is brave of ya to sleep under the same roof as the bloke who tried to drive you into a fuckin' dam.'

'That's enough, Teddy, damn it!' Mum screams.

Teddy howls. 'Yep, exactly.' He laughs. 'Dam it, hey boys? Dammmmmmmm it.'

Then he screams, too. Louder than Mum. 'Nup, nup,' he barks. 'This was my dad's dinner table. My dad built this fuckin' table and now it's my fuckin' table and my dad was a good fuckin' man and he raised me right and I'll say what the fuck I want at my fuckin' table.' He bites another lamb shank like he's biting the flesh from my left forearm.

'Nup, nup,' he shouts. 'You can all fuck off.'

He stands. 'You don't deserve to sit at this table. Get away from my table. You're not worthy of this table, you fuckin' crazies.'

Mum stands now. 'Boys, we can finish our meals in the kitchen,' she says, her hands lifting up her dinner plate. Then Teddy's hand smacks the plate loudly back down on the table, cracking the plate into three pieces, splitting it like a peace sign. 'Leave your fuckin' plates here,' Teddy snarls.

August and I are already standing, moving away from our chairs, moving towards Mum.

'Nup, nup,' Teddy says. 'Only family eat at this table.'

He makes a loud farmyard whistle and his beloved German shepherd dogs run up the back stairs, in through the kitchen and into the dining room. Teddy pats his hands in front of my table place, pats August's too. 'Up 'ere boys.' Beau dutifully bounds up onto my chair and Arrow loyally leaps onto August's. Teddy nods his head. 'Eat up, boys,' he says. 'These lamb shanks are restaurant quality.'

The dogs sink their heads into our plates, their tails wagging with euphoria.

I look across at Mum.

'Let's go, Mum,' I say.

She stands staring at the growling dogs eating up the day she spent cooking. She turns and paces silently, robotically, into the kitchen. There's an old canary yellow kitchen cabinet lining the wall near the oven where our lamb shanks pot sits, filled with four more lamb shanks we're saving for lunch tomorrow.

Mum stands silently in the kitchen, just thinking, for maybe a full minute. Thinking.

'Mum, let's go,' I say. 'Let's just leave.'

Then she turns to face the kitchen cabinet and she drives her right fist into a row of eight old country-style dinner plates that once belonged to Teddy's grandmother, standing upright along the cabinet behind a flexible white band. She punches them like she's programmed to punch them, like something mechanical inside her is operating her arms. She's not even realising how much the broken ceramics are cutting up her knuckles, spreading dark red blood across the pieces still standing behind the band. And August and I are so stunned we can't move. I can't get a word out of my mouth, so frozen and perplexed am I by her actions. Blood and fists. Punch after punch. Her fists then smash the sliding glass door that fronts the cup section of the cabinet. She reaches in and clutches an FM 104 radio station mug and she grabs a World Expo '88 mug and she grabs a pink Mr Perfect Mr Men cup and she walks back into the dining room and whip-throws all these mugs hard at Teddy's head, the third mug, Mr Perfect, colliding with his right temple.

And he rushes at her with a blind amphetamine rage. August and I throw ourselves instinctively between him and Mum, ducking our heads for protection, but he knees us in our thin-skulled heads with his fat kneecaps that are the size of cricket helmets and he barges his way, brute fury and power, to Mum whose hair he clutches from behind and he drags her out of the kitchen. He drags her along the linoleum kitchen floor, so hard that clumps of her hair are falling out in the pulling. He drags her down – the devil drags her down, down, down – the back wooden stairs. He drags her behind him, holding her by her head like he's dragging a heavy rug or a cut tree branch, her backside and heels bouncing hard against the steps. And I wonder something in this moment, a clear thought reaches me in this perfectly terrifying moment, as the monster drags my mum to hell. Why is Mum not screaming? Why is Mum not crying? She is silent in this moment and I realise now, as the time in this moment stretches out flat and looped and infinite, that she's not screaming because of her boys. She doesn't want us to know how scared she is. A rage-filled, speed-buzzing psychopath is dragging her by the hair down a wooden staircase and she is only thinking of us. I look at her face and her face looks at me. The details. The unspoken. Don't be scared, Eli, her face tries to say as the monster reefs her head. Don't be scared, Eli, because I've got this under control. I've lived through worse, matey, and I've got this. So don't cry, Eli. Look at me, am I crying?

At the bottom of the staircase, he drags Mum to the entry ramp of Beau and Arrow's downstairs dog kennel. He grips the back of Mum's neck forcefully and he presses her face into Beau and Arrow's dog bowl. She gags as her face sinks into a mushy brown mess of old meat chunks and jelly.

'You fuckin' animal,' I scream, driving my right shoulder as hard as I can into Teddy's ribs but I can't move his fat and vast frame.

'I made you dinner, Frankie,' Teddy screams, eyes wide and electric. 'Dog food. Food for a dog. Food for a dog. Food for a dog.'

I push and punch at his face from below but the punches have no impact. He can't feel in this moment so he can't be moved. But then a large silver object flashes past my eyes and I see this silver object connect with Teddy's head. Something warm that feels like blood and flesh splatters across my back. But it doesn't smell like blood. It smells like lamb. It's the pot we slow-cooked the lamb shanks in. Teddy falls to his knees, stunned, and August swings the pot again, straight at his face this time and this swing knocks him out, lays him flat on the miserable concrete beneath this miserable house of inheritance.

'Go out to the street,' Mum instructs us calmly. She wipes her face with her shirt and she suddenly looks like a warrior in this moment, not a victim, an ancient survivor wiping the blood of the fallen off her cheeks and nose and chin. She runs back up the stairs and into the house and meets us out on the street five minutes later with our bags and a backpack for herself.

\*

We catch the train from Wacol to Nundah one hour later. It's 10 p.m. when we knock on the door of Sister Patricia's house on Bage Street. She takes us in immediately and she doesn't ask why we're here.

We sleep on spare mattresses in Sister Patricia's sunroom.

We wake at 6 a.m. and join Sister Patricia and four transitioning ex-prison women for breakfast in the dining room. We eat Vegemite on toast and sip apple juice from the Golden Circle Cannery. We sit at the end of a long brown table big enough to fit eighteen or twenty people. Mum is quiet. August says nothing.

'Soooooooo,' I whisper.

Mum sips a black coffee.

'So what, matey?' Mum says gently.

'So what now?' I ask. 'Now that you've left Teddy, what are you gonna do now?'

Mum bites into her toast, wipes crumbs from the corners of her mouth with a napkin. My head is bursting with plans. The future. Our future. Our family.

'I reckon tonight you come spend the night with us,' I say. I say things as fast as I think them. 'I reckon you should just turn up on Dad's doorstep with us. Dad will be shocked to see you but I know he'll be good to you. He's got a good heart, Mum, he won't be able to turn you away. He won't have it in him.'

'Eli, I don't think ...' Mum says.

'Where would you like to move to?' I ask.

'What?'

'If you could choose anywhere to live, and money wasn't an obstacle, where would you want to go?' I ask.

'Pluto,' Mum says.

'Okay, anywhere in south-east Queensland,' I say. 'Just name the place, Mum, and Gus and me, we're gonna make it happen for you.'

'And how do you boys suppose you'll do that?'

August looks up from his breakfast plate. *No, Eli.*

I think for a moment. Measure my thoughts.

'What if I told you I could get us a place in ... I don't know ... The Gap?' I say.

'The Gap?' Mum echoes, puzzled. 'Why The Gap?'

'It's nice there. Lots of cul-de-sacs. Remember when Lyle took us to buy the Atari?'

'Eli ...' Mum says.

'You'll love it in The Gap, Mum,' I say, excited. 'It's beautiful and green and right at the end of the suburb is this big reservoir surrounded by bushland and the water in it is so crystal clear ...'

Mum slaps the table.

'Eli!' she snaps.

She drops her head. She cries.

'Eli,' she says, 'I never said I was leaving Teddy.'

# Boy Tightens Noose

The capital of Romania is Bucharest. The collective noun for a group of toads is a knot. The collective noun for a group of Eli Bells is a prism. A cage. A hole. A prison.

Saturday night, 7.15 p.m., and Dad is sleeping by the side of the toilet. He passed out directly after vomiting into the porcelain bowl and he sleeps soundly now beneath the toilet roll holder, and when he breathes out, air from his nostrils blows three hanging sheets of one-ply like a white flag of surrender blowing in the wind.

I give up. I want to be just like him.

But Sir August the Unmoved does not share my enthusiasm tonight for using Lyle's hard-earned drug money to drink and eat ourselves to death.

My initial plan is to spend five hundred bucks on a takeaway food frenzy at the Barrett Street shops. We can start with Big Rooster – a whole chicken, two large chips, two Cokes, two corn cobs – then move along the shops to the fish and chip shop, the Chinese shop, then the deli for large dim sims and choc-chip ice cream. After that we can slip down to the Bracken Ridge Tavern and we can go into the public bar and ask one of

Dad's old barfly acquaintances, Gunther, if he'll buy us a bottle of Bundaberg Rum for a pineapple.

*You're being a fuckwit*, August does not say. So I drink alone tonight. I ride to the Shorncliffe Pier with a bottle of rum and the pockets of my jeans filled with four hundred bucks in cash. My legs dangle over the pier beneath a flickering pier light. Beside me is the severed head of a mullet. I sip the rum straight and think of Slim and realise how warm the rum makes me feel and how it won't feel so bad spending the next year of my life spending the remaining $49,500 of Lyle's drug money on rum and chicken Twisties. I drink until I pass out on the edge of the pier.

*

The sun wakes me and my head throbs and I stare into the lips of the dried mullet head. I drink from a green council water fountain for two straight minutes. I strip to my underpants and swim in the lice-filled waters by the pier. I ride home and find August sitting on the lounge room couch exactly where I left him last night. He's smiling.

'What?' I ask.

*Nothing.*

We watch television. It's lunch in a test match between Australia and Pakistan.

'How we goin'?'

August writes in the air. *Dean Jones on 82.*

I'm tired. My bones are stiff. I lean my head back and close my eyes on the couch.

But August clicks his fingers. I open my eyes again to see him pointing at the TV screen. He points at a Channel Nine local midday news bulletin.

'Christmas has come early for one very special family in Bracken Ridge in Brisbane's northern suburbs,' says the newsreader, a woman with big black hair-sprayed hair. Then there's a shot of Shelly Huffman in her wheelchair with her parents outside their house on Tor Street.

'That's Shelly!' I say.

August laughs. Nods his head, claps his hands.

The newsreader's voice rolls over a series of images of Shelly and her parents weeping and hugging each other.

'For the past three years, parents of four Tess and Craig Huffman have been trying to raise the $70,000 they need to transform their home into a disability-friendly space for their seventeen-year-old daughter, Shelly, who is living with muscular dystrophy. As of yesterday, they had raised $34,540 through school and community fundraising drives. Then, this morning, Tess Huffman opened her front door.'

In the bulletin, Shelly's Mum, Tess, wipes a tear from her eye and talks to a reporter in her front yard. She's holding a box wrapped in Christmas wrapping.

'I was going down to the bakery to get some scones because Shelly's grandma was due to come around,' she says. 'I open the front door and there's this box on the doormat wrapped in this nice wrapping paper.'

The wrapping paper is a series of intersecting rows of candy canes and Christmas trees. 'I tear it open and look inside and there's all this cash,' Tess says, sobbing. 'It's a miracle.'

The footage cuts to a police officer standing in Shelly's front yard.

'We're looking at a total of $49,500 in cash,' says the straight-faced police officer. 'We're still making some investigations into the origins of the money, but from early assessments it would appear the money was donated by a genuine good Samaritan with a big heart.'

I turn to August. He's beaming, slapping his knees.

The on-the-ground reporter can be heard off camera asking Shelly a question.

'What do you want to say to that good person out there who left this money on your doorstep, Shelly?'

Shelly's squinting, looking into the sun.

'I just wanna say … I just wanna say … whoever you are … I love you.'

August stands in celebration, nodding his head in triumph.

I stand and take two long steps before diving at his pelvis and driving him into the sliding window over the front porch. The window almost shatters on the impact of August's rear skull. I throw a flurry of uppercut punches at his stomach and chin.

'You fuckin' idiot!' I scream. Then he lifts me up from the waist and throws me with a sweeping hurl on top of the television. The newsreader tips over off Dad's brown TV stand. The peach-coloured ceramic lamp sitting on top of the TV breaks into eight jagged pieces on the wooden floor. Dad marches out of his bedroom. 'What the fuck is going on 'ere!' he barks.

I charge at August again and he drives his left then right fists into my face, and I throw a round of formless punches back as Dad comes between us.

'Eli,' he screams. 'Give it a rest.'

Dad pushes me back and I take a breath.

'What have you done?' I scream. 'You've lost your mind, Gus. You're fuckin' crazy.'

He scribbles in the air. *I'm sorry, Eli. I had to.*

'You're not special, Gus,' I say. 'You're just fuckin' nuts. You didn't get brought back. There's no more universes than this one and it's a fuckin' hole. There's no more Augusts out there. There's only one and he's fucking deranged.'

August smiles. He scribbles in the air.

*You were gonna get caught with that money, Eli.*

'Just talk, fuckhead,' I scream. 'I'm sick of your fuckin' scribbles.'

We all catch our breath. The newsreader is still talking out of the television lying face up behind Dad's TV stand: 'Well, if that story doesn't warm your heart I don't know what will,' she says.

August and I stare at each other. August talking more than I can in silence. *I had to do it, Eli.*

The phone rings.

*It was no good in our hands, Eli, all that money. No good. Shelly needs it more than us.*

'Mrs Birkbeck was right about you, Gus,' I say. 'I reckon you had to make up all that bullshit about the people on the phones because you were damaged. You were so fucked up by reality you ran away into fantasy.'

*But you heard them, Eli. You heard them on the phone, too.*

'I was playing along, Gus,' I say. 'I bought into the bullshit because I felt sorry for you being such a nutter.'

*I'm sorry, Gus. I'm sorry.*

'Well, here's the reality, Gus,' I say. I point at Dad. 'He's so fuckin' crazy he tried to drive us into a dam. And you're just as crazy as him and maybe I'm just as crazy as you.'

I turn to Dad. I don't know why I say it but I say it. It's all I want to say. It's all I want to know.

'Did you mean to do it?'

'What?' he says softly.

He's lost for words. He's mute.

'Everybody mute,' I scream. 'Whole world gone mute. Let me rephrase that, because maybe it's too hard to understand and I understand that because I sure as shit can't understand why you'd mean to do it, but did you mean to drive us into the dam?'

The phone rings. Dad is momentarily stunned by the question.

'Teddy says you tried to fuckin' kill us,' I shout. 'Teddy says it wasn't some panic attack bullshit. Teddy says you're fuckin' crazy.'

The phone rings. Dad shakes his head, furious.

'For fuck's sake, Eli, you gonna answer the phone?' Dad asks.

'Why don't you answer it?' I reply.

'It's your mum,' Dad says.

'Mum?'

'She called this morning,' Dad says.

'You spoke to her?' I ask.

He spoke to her. Dad spoke to Mum. That's a phenomenon I'm not familiar with.

'Yeah, I spoke to her. Some people in this house know how to communicate using their voice box,' he says.

The phone rings.

'What did she want?'

'She didn't say.'

The phone rings. I pick it up.

'Mum.'

'Hey, sweetheart.'

'Hey.'

Long silence.

'How are you?' she asks.

Terrible. Never been worse. Heart like a brick. Hurricane for a head. I woke up hungover from the rum last night and now I'm hungover and missing $49,500.

'Good,' I lie, sucking in breaths.

'You don't sound too good?'

'I'm all right, how are you?'

'Good,' she says. 'Be better if you and August dropped round soon.'

Long silence.

'What do you think?'

'What do I think about what?'

'Do you think you might want to come around and see me again?'

'Not while he's there, Mum.'

'He wants to see you boys, Eli,' she says. 'He wants to say sorry in person for what he did.'

This again. Mum believing another suburban Queensland male leopard is gonna change his spots.

'Mum, crazy fuckin' coward abusers don't change their crazy fuckin' coward spots.'

Long silence.

'He really is sorry about all that,' she says.

'He say sorry to you?' I ask.

'Yes.'

'What did he say?'

'I don't want to go into specifics but ...'

'Could you ... please?'

'What?'

'Could you please go into specifics? I'm sick of fragments. All you people ever do is talk in fragments and I don't ever get any specifics. You always say you'll tell me when I'm older but I get older and the stories only get more vague. Nothing fits. It's all cracked glass bullshit. You don't tell stories. You tell beginnings and middles and ends but you don't tell stories. You and Dad have never told me a single complete story.'

Long silence. Long silence and tears.

'I'm sorry,' she says.

'What did Iwan Krol do to Lyle?'

Tears.

'Don't do this, Eli.'

'He cut him up, didn't he? Darren told me what he does. If he's nice he chops the head off first ...'

'Stop it, Eli.'

'But if he's feelin' real sadistic, maybe if he hasn't had his lunch yet, or maybe if he woke up on the wrong side of his coffin, he chops off the ankles first and he keeps them muzzled but he keeps them alive. Then he chops the wrists and then a leg and then an arm, maybe. Back and forth he goes ...'

'Eli, I'm worried about you.'

'Not as worried as I am.'

Long silence.

'I called to tell you something,' Mum says.

'You cut off Teddy's head?'

Long silence. Stop it, Eli. You're losing your mind. Find it, Eli. Find your lost mind.

'Are you done?' Mum asks.

'Yeah,' I say.

'I've been doing some study,' she says.

That's great.

'That's great.'

'Thanks. Are you being sarcastic?'

'No. It's really great, Mum. What are you studying?'

'Social work. I started reading the books inside. The government kicks in a bit for my tuition and all I have to do is read up a storm. I think I've read more textbooks on the subject than some of my tutors.'

'That's really great, Mum.'

'You proud of me?'

'I'm always proud of you.'

'What for?'

'Bein' here.'

'Bein' where?'

'Just bein'.'

'Yeah,' she says. 'Look, I'm calling because a woman in my Communications lecture says her nephew is a young journalist at *The Courier-Mail*. I told her that's where my boy, Eli, dreams of working. I told her he's going to be a great police rounder ...'

'Roundsman.'

'Yeah, a great police roundsman, and she says I should tell my boy that the paper is always hiring youngsters for cadetships.

You just got to go knock on the door and ask if you could apply for one.'

'I don't think it's that simple, Mum.'

'Sure it is. I looked up the name of the big editor-in-chief on the newspaper. His name is Brian Robertson. You go in and ask for him to come down from his office and see you for two minutes – just two minutes – because that's all it will take for him to see it.'

'See what?'

'The spark,' she says. 'He'll see it. He'll see how special you are.'

'I'm not special, Mum.'

'Yes, you are,' she says. 'You just don't believe it yet.'

'I'm sorry, Mum, I gotta go. I'm not feeling well.'

'Are you sick? What's wrong?'

'I'm okay, I'm just not up for talking so much. You wanna talk to August?'

'Yeah,' she says. 'You go ask that editor for one of those cadetships, Eli. You do it. Two minutes. That's all you need.'

'I love you, Mum.'

'I love you, Eli.'

I pass the phone to August.

'Can you stay out of the room for a bit?' I say.

He nods. August never talks down the phone to Mum. He just listens. I never know what she says to him. I guess she just says.

*

I close the door on our bedroom and lift a thin slab of A4 paper up onto my bed. Paper. For burning this house down or setting the world on fire. With my spark. There's a chewed blue Kilometrico ballpoint pen on my bedhead. I write on the paper but the ink won't come through the ballpoint. I roll the pen furiously between my palms to heat it up and the ink runs enough for me to write and underline the title of my story.

## A Noose of Eli Bells

*In the event I die in a suburban Bracken Ridge inferno or in the event that I am splattered on the Sandgate Station platform 1 railway line by the 4.30 a.m. train to Central after I've greased the rails with Vaseline like Ben Yates did two years ago when Shannon Dennis told him under no circumstances – not even if he completed his butcher's apprenticeship – was she going to have his child, I feel it is important for me to at least lay down some of the specifics surrounding the disappearance of Lyle Orlik. The facts of the matter are, first and foremost, Teddy Kallas had Lyle Orlik killed because he was in love with my mum. My mum does not love Teddy Kallas but she did love Lyle Orlik, a good and decent man who just happened to be a peddler of smack. It took me some time to come to terms with the realities of Lyle's fate but I now accept he was most likely severed limb from limb by a man named Iwan Krol, the psychopathic muscle of Tytus Broz, whose artificial limb factory in Moorooka, south Brisbane, is a front for a vast heroin trafficking empire spread across south-east Queensland.*

*In the event I am found splattered across the Sandgate Station railway line, please direct all subsequent questions as to why, as well as all bills for any clean-up costs, to Teddy Kallas of Wacol, south-west Brisbane.*

*For the record, I am not, nor ever was, special. I thought for a while there that August and I really were special. I thought for a while there I really was hearing those voices down the line on Lyle's mysterious red phone. But I realise now we are not special. I realise Mrs Birkbeck is right. The human mind will convince us of anything in the name of survival. Trauma wears many masks. I have worn mine. But no more. Teddy Kallas is right. My brother and I were never special. We were just fuckin' crazy.*

A knuckle knocks on my bedroom door.

'Go away, August,' I say. 'I'm on a roll here.'

I wait for the door to open despite my request. It doesn't. But a copy of today's *Courier-Mail* slides into the room beneath the door.

The paper is open at a 'Special Investigation' in the middle feature pages of the paper: 'SUBURBAN WARFARE – ASIAN HEROIN GANG WARS ERUPT IN THE STREETS OF BRISBANE'.

It's a sweeping investigation into the violence between Darra's 5T and BTK gangs and the widespread trafficking of Golden Triangle heroin across south-east Queensland. It's a well-researched and well-written piece speaking of suspected anonymous Brisbane drug kingpins and Vietnamese drug families posing as humble and hardworking restaurateurs while expanding million-dollar drug networks north from Melbourne and Sydney. The journalist has quoted an ex-drug enforcement police officer who has complained of corrupt politicians and police heads 'turning a blind eye for too long' to the spread of heroin out of the outer western Brisbane suburbs. The police informant speaks of widespread suspicions among officers that several prominent Brisbane businessmen have made their fortunes 'secretly riding the golden dragon of the illicit Asian drug scene'.

'They're out there walking among us,' the informant says. 'So-called upstanding members of Brisbane society getting away with murder.'

I search for the journalist's byline. I lie back on my bed and I write the journalist's name in the air with my middle finger that sits beside the lucky finger with the lucky freckle I lost to an upstanding member of Brisbane society currently getting away with murder. Her name looks beautiful up there in the invisible air.

Caitlyn Spies.

# Boy Digs Deep

I first see the man in the yellow two-door Ford Mustang when I'm sitting on the seats outside the Sandgate train station eating a sausage roll with sauce for lunch. He pulls up in the space in the car park reserved for buses and he stares out his window at me. Mid-forties, maybe. He looks big from here, tall and muscular in the cramped car seat. He has black hair and a black moustache. Black eyes watching me. We make eye contact but I turn away awkwardly just when I think he might have nodded at me. He pulls away from the bus stop and parks his car in the station's car park. He hops out of his car. My train to Central arrives and I dump the last bite of sausage roll in the bin and pace quickly up to the top end of the station platform.

I disembark at Bowen Hills train station, skip down a side street to the large red brick building with the fancy letters spelling *The Courier-Mail* on a sign attached to its front wall. It took me three months to summon up the plums to come here. This is where the paper is put together. This is where Caitlyn Spies works. She made it. She made it all the way from the *South-West Star* to where she belongs. Part of the paper's crime-writing team, probably the team's brightest shining star.

'I'm here to see the editor-in-chief, Brian Robertson,' I say with an air of confidence to the woman at the front desk. She's short with short black hair and bright orange hoop earrings.

'Is he expecting you?' the woman on the desk asks.

I fix my tie. It's strangling my neck. Dad tied it too tight. It's Dad's tie. He picked it up at St Vinnies for fifty cents. The tie is covered in the letters of the alphabet, with the letters *W, O, R, D* and *S* highlighted in bright yellow. Dad said it would convey my love of words to the editor-in-chief, Brian Robertson.

'Yes,' I say, nodding my head. 'But only in the sense that he should expect the most promising young budding journalists in Brisbane to enter the door of this building expecting to see him.'

'So he's not expecting you?' she replies.

'No.'

'What were you hoping to see him about?' the woman asks.

'I would like to apply for a cadetship on his fine and influential newspaper.'

'Sorry,' the woman with the orange hoop earrings says, returning her eyes to a logbook filled with names and dates and signatures. 'Cadet applications closed two months ago. We're not taking any more juniors on until November next year.'

'But, but ...' But what, Eli?

'But what?' the woman asks.

'But I'm special.'

'What?' the woman howls. 'Come again?'

You dickhead, Eli Bell. Breathe. Rephrase.

'Well, I feel like I could do some great things for his newspaper,' I say.

'Because you're special?'

No, I'm not special. I'm just fucking crazy.

'Well, I'm not really special,' I say. 'Just keen. And different. I'm different.'

'How sweet,' the woman says sarcastically. She looks at a glass security door between the building's foyer and the wider bowels of the editorial floor from where I can almost smell the ink on the thumbs of sub-editors and the cigarettes in the ashtrays of the racing writers and the Scotch in the glasses of the political journalists and I can hear the sound of history being typed by men and women who don't know how to touch-type because they have no sense of touch, they only have a sense of smell, a sense for sniffing out a yarn. 'But different won't get you through that security door, I'm afraid,' she says.

'What will get me through that door?'

'Patience and time,' the woman says.

'But I've done my time.'

'You have?' the woman laughs. 'What are you, sixteen? Seventeen?'

'I'm almost seventeen.'

'Old-timer, then,' she says. 'You still in school?'

'Yeah, but my soul graduated years ago.'

I lean in to the long counter she stands behind.

'Look, truth is, I've got a story for him,' I say. 'And once he hears this story he'll know I'm different from all the other applicants and he'll want to give me a shot.'

The woman with the orange hoop earrings rolls her eyes and smiles, puts her pen down on her logbook.

'What's your name, kid?' she asks.

'Eli Bell.'

'Look, Eli Bell, you're not gettin' through that door today,' she says. She looks up at the glass entry door to this foyer, leans in to the counter to whisper to me. 'But I can't stop you from sitting out near that hedge over there at around 8 p.m. tonight,' she says.

'What happens at 8 p.m.?' I ask.

'Jesus, mate, you are special,' she says, shaking her head. 'It's when the boss goes home, ya goose.'

'Riiiiiiight!' I whisper. 'Thank you. Just one more thing, what does the boss look like?'

She doesn't take her eyes off me.

'See those three framed photographs of the three serious and sour-lookin' men on the wall behind my left shoulder?'

'Yeah.'

'He's the bloke in the middle.'

\*

Brian Robertson exits the building at 9.16 p.m. He looks younger in the photo above the counter in the foyer. His hair is greying on the sides of his scalp and these greys rise to thinning ash-coloured curls on top of his head. His reading glasses hang from a cord around his neck. A navy blue wool vest over a white business shirt. He carries a brown leather briefcase in his right hand, three broadsheet newspapers tucked under his left arm. There's a toughness in his face, a hardness. He looks like one of the old rugby league players from the early 1900s that I saw in some of Dad's old Australian rugby league books, a face from the days when men juggled representative football commitments with battles on the Western Front. He pads down the three small steps from the building's entry and I emerge from the darkened hedge where I've sat and meandered around like a stalker for the past six hours.

'Mr Robertson?'

He stops.

'Yes?'

'I'm sorry to bother you, but I wanted to introduce myself.'

He scans me up and down.

'How long have you been sitting out here for?' he grumbles.

'Six hours, sir.'

'That was foolish.'

He turns and walks on towards the building's car park.

I skip two paces to catch up with him.

'I've read your newspaper since I was eight years old,' I say.

'So since last year?' he replies, eyes ahead.

'Ha!' I laugh, pacing sideways to capture his gaze. 'That's funny. Umm, I wanted to see if you would ...'

'Where did you get that tie from?' he asks, eyes still ahead.

He looked at me for maybe half a second and he caught the detail of my tie. The guy sees details. Journalists see details.

'My Dad got it from St Vinnies.'

He nods.

'You ever hear about the Narela Street Massacre?' he asks.

I shake my head. He walks hard as he tells his story.

'Cannon Hill, eastern Brisbane, 1957, bloke named Marian Majka, Polish immigrant, mid-thirties, kills his wife and his five-year-old daughter with a knife and a hammer. He sets fire to his house then walks on over to the house opposite his. Kills the mum in that house too, along with her two daughters. Then he starts piling all the dead bodies up because he's gonna set them all alight and this little girl from the neighbourhood – ten-year-old girl named Lynette Karger – knocks on the door. She's come to pick up her friends to go to school like she does every other day. And Majka kills her too and adds her body to the pile and sets it alight. He then shoots himself and the cops arrive to see the horror show. Little Lynette still had her school lunch money clutched in her hand.'

'Jesus,' I gasp.

'I turned up to the house that morning to report on it all,' he says. 'I saw that whole sick mess up close.'

'You did?'

'Yep,' he says, walking hard. 'And still I haven't seen anything more disturbing than that tie you're wearing.'

He walks on.

'It's all the letters of the alphabet,' I say. 'I was hoping it would appeal to your love of words.'

'Love of words?' he echoes. He stops on the spot. 'What makes you think I love words? I hate words. I despise them. Words are all I ever see. Words haunt me in my sleep. Words get beneath my skin and they creep into my mind when I'm having a warm bath and they infest my nervous system when I'm at my granddaughter's christening when I should be thinking about her precious face but I'm thinking about the fucking words in tomorrow's page-one headline.'

He's clenching his fist and he doesn't realise it until he walks on further to the car park. I lay my cards down.

'I was hoping you would consider me for one of your cadetships?'

'Not possible,' he barks, cutting me off. 'We've picked our cadets for the foreseeable future.'

'I know, but I think I have something to offer you that others can't.'

'Oh, yeah, such as?'

'A page-one story,' I say.

He stops.

'A page-one story?' he smiles. 'Okay, let's hear it.'

'Well, it's complicated,' I say.

He walks away immediately.

'Too bad,' he says.

I catch up with him again.

'Well, it's a little hard to explain it all to you right here as you're walking to your car.'

'Bullshit,' he says. 'Cook Finds Australia. Hitler Invades Poland. Oswald Kills Kennedy. Man Conquers Moon. They were complicated stories too. You've already wasted too many of your beloved words kissing my arse so I'll let you have just three more. Tell me your story in three words.'

Think Eli. Three words. Think. But my mind is blank. I see only his sour face and nothing else in my mind. My story in three words. Just three words.

Nothing. Nothing. Nothing.

'I can't,' I say.

'That's two,' he says.

'But ...'

'That's three,' he says. 'Sorry, kid. You're welcome to apply next year.'

And he walks away, up the driveway into a shed filled with expensive automobiles.

*

I will remember this sinking feeling through the colour of the moon tonight. It's orange, a crescent sliver up there like a wedge of rockmelon. I will remember these failures and letdowns and hopeless cases through the graffiti on the concrete wall opposite platform 4 of Bowen Hills train station. Someone has spray-painted an image of a large throbbing penis but the penis's knob end is an impressive image of earth spinning beneath the words: *Don't fuck the world!* On a long maroon platform seat I loosen my strangling tie and study the letters of the alphabet, trying to find three words to tell my story. Eli Misses Opportunity. Eli Fucks Up. Eli Fucks World. I'm lost in the letters of this horrific tie.

Then a voice from the other end of my platform seat.

'Eli Bell.'

I follow the voice and I find her. We're the only two people on the platform. We're the only two people on earth.

'Caitlyn Spies,' I say.

She laughs.

'It's you,' I say.

There's something too strong and wonder-filled in my stupid, open-mouthed, jaw-dropped gasping.

'Yeah,' she says. 'It's me.'

She wears a long black coat and her long brown hair falls over her shoulders. Dr Martens boots. The cool air seems to make her pale face glow. Caitlyn Spies glows. Maybe that's how she draws all those prized story sources to her. Maybe that's how she gets them to open up and spill their inner psychological beans. She mesmerises them in her glow. In her fire.

'You remember me?' I say.

She nods.

'I do,' she smiles. 'And I don't know why. I always forget a face.'

A loud train rattles in to platform 4 in front of us.

'I see your face every day,' I say.

She can't hear that over the train noise.

'Sorry? What was that?'

'Never mind.'

Caitlyn stands, gripping the strap of a brown leather satchel over her right shoulder.

'You on this one?' she asks.

'Where's it going?'

'Caboolture.'

'I'm ... ummm ... yeah. This is my train.'

Caitlyn smiles, studies my face. She yanks on the silver handle of a middle carriage door and steps into the train. It's empty. Only us two on the train. Only us two in the universe.

She sits in a four-seat bay, two empty seats facing two empty seats.

'May I sit here with you?' I ask.

'You may,' she says, adopting a regal voice, laughing.

The train pulls away from Bowen Hills station.

'What are you doing in Bowen Hills?' she asks.

'I was meeting your boss, Brian Robertson, about a cadetship,' I say.

'Seriously?' she replies.

'Seriously.'

'You had a meeting with Brian?'

'Well, not a meeting exactly,' I say. 'I hid behind a hedge for six hours and approached him when he was exiting the building at 9.16 p.m.'

She rolls her head back, laughing.

'And how did that go for you?' she asks.

'Not so great.'

She nods sympathetically.

'I remember thinking there might be a teddy bear heart beneath that monster exterior when I first met Brian,' Caitlyn says. 'There's not. It's just another monster inside biting the head off a teddy bear. But he really is the best newspaper editor in the country.'

I nod, stare out the window as the train passes the old Albion flour mill.

'You want to be a journalist?' she asks.

'I want to do what you do, write about crime and what makes criminals tick.'

'That's right,' she says. 'You knew Slim Halliday.'

I nod.

'You gave me a name,' she says. 'I looked him up. The limbs guy.'

'Tytus Broz.'

'Tytus Broz, yes,' she says. 'I remember you were telling me a story about him and then you rushed off. Why'd you take off so fast that day?'

'I had to go see my mum urgently.'

'Was she all right?'

'Not really,' I say. 'But she was all right once I saw her. That's nice of you.'

'What?'

'Asking that little question about my mum like that, that's nice. I guess you learn that as a journalist after a while.'

'Learn what?'

'Asking the nice little questions in between the big important questions. I reckon that would make people feel better when they're talking to you.'

'I guess so,' she says. 'You know, I ended up doing some digging on your limbs guy, Tytus Broz.'

'You find anything?'

'I phoned a few people. Everybody said he was the kindest bloke in the south-west suburbs. Honest as they come, everybody said. Generous. Gives to charity. He's an advocate for the disabled. I called a few cops I knew back then in Moorooka. They said he was a pillar of the community.'

'Of course they said that,' I say. 'The cops are the greatest beneficiaries of his charitable soul.'

I look up at that orange crescent moon.

'Tytus Broz is a bad man doing very bad things,' I say. 'That artificial limb business is a front for one of the biggest heroin importation syndicates in south-east Queensland.'

'You got any proof of this, Eli Bell?'

'My story is my proof.'

And a missing lucky fucking finger if I can ever fucking find it.

'You told anyone your story yet?'

'No, I was going to tell your boss but he insisted I tell him the whole story in three words.'

She laughs.

'He does that,' she says. 'He put me on the spot with that in my job interview. He asked me to encapsulate my whole life up to that point and everything I believe in into a three-word headline.'

Caitlyn Is Beauty. Caitlyn Is Truth. Caitlyn Is Here.

'What did you say?' I ask.

'It was dumb, just the first stupid thing that came to my head.'

'What was that?'

She cringes.

'Spies Digs Deep.'

And for the next eight stops along the Caboolture line she tells me why that headline works for her life story. She tells me how she wasn't supposed to survive her birth because she was born not much bigger than a can of Pasito. But her mum died giving birth to her instead and she always felt that was some divine deal her mum made, life for life, and the knowledge of that trade-off plagued her from the start. She could never be lazy. She could never switch off. She could never give up, even in her teens when she went through a Goth phase and she hated her life and she wanted to fuck the world like that hilarious earth knob graffiti she sees every night she takes the train home from Bowen Hills train station. Because her mum didn't die for her daughter to give a half-arsed effort. So Spies dug deep. Always. In sports carnivals at high school. In social netball games where she's way too competitive and the umpire is always barking 'CONTACT!' at her when she elbows her rival wing attack. Spies Digs Deep. And she tells herself that when she's working the phones on her stories. She says those three words now like a stupid self-help book mantra. Spies Digs Deep. Spies Digs Deep. And she's said it so many times now it's become her blessing and her curse. She digs too deep with people. Looks for their faults instead of their virtues. She never really had the right boyfriend at university or any other time and she doesn't see herself finding anyone really right for her in the future because Spies Digs Deep.

'Oh fuck, see,' she says. 'I'm going way too deep now.'

'That's okay,' I say. 'What do you think you're actually digging for?'

She thinks on this for a moment, playing with the cuff on her coat.

'That's a nice little in-between question there, Eli,' she smiles. 'I don't know. Probably just why? Why am I here and she's not? Why is she not here when all those rapists and murderers and thieves and frauds I write about every day get to live and breathe in perfect health?'

She shakes her head, snaps out of her line of thinking.

'C'mon,' she says, 'gimme three words for the life story of Eli Bell?'

Boy Sees Future. Boy Sees Her. Boy Digs Deep.

'I can't think of anything,' I say.

Her eyelids close in, probing. 'Why don't I believe you, Eli Bell?' she replies. 'I wouldn't be surprised at all if your greatest problem is actually thinking too many things.'

The train slows. She looks out the window. There's nobody out there. Not a soul on earth. Just the night.

'This next stop is mine,' she says.

I nod. She studies my face.

'This wasn't your train, was it?' she says.

I shake my head. 'No, this wasn't my train,' I say.

'So why'd you get on this train?' she asks.

'I wanted to keep talking with you.'

'Well, I hope the conversation was worth the long trip home for you.'

'It was,' I say. 'You want to know the truth?'

'Always.'

'I woulda hopped on a train to Perth just to hear you talk for thirty minutes.'

She smiles. Drops her head, shaking it.

'You're a ham, Eli Bell,' she says.

'Huh? A ham? What does that mean?'

'You're over the top.'

'What's that got to do with ham?'

'I'm not sure,' she says. 'Don't worry, you're a sweet ham.'

'Honey leg ham?'

'Yeah,' she says. 'Something like that.'

She stares into my eyes. I'm lost in the fire of her.

'Where did you come from, Eli Bell?' she ponders mystically.

'Bracken Ridge.'

'Mmmmmmm,' she continues to ponder.

The train slows.

'You want to hop off here with me?'

I shake my head. This seat feels good right now. The world feels good right now.

'Nah, I'm just gonna sit here for a bit.'

She nods, smiling.

'Listen,' she says, 'I'm gonna look back into Tytus Broz.'

'Spies digs deep,' I say.

She raises her eyebrows, sighs. 'Yeah, Spies digs deep.'

She walks to the doors of the carriage as the train comes to a stop.

'And, by the way, Eli, if you want to write for the paper, just start writing for the paper,' she says. 'Write Brian a story so good he'd be mad not to run it.'

I nod.

'Thanks.'

I will remember devotion through this lump in my chest. I will remember love through a wedge of rockmelon. The lump is an engine inside me that makes me move. She walks off the

360

train and my heart thumps into first, second, third, fourth gear. Move. I rush to the carriage doors and call out to her.

'I know my three words,' I say.

She stops and turns around.

'Oh yeah?'

I nod. And I say these three words loud.

'Caitlyn and Eli.'

The carriage doors close and the train pulls away from the station but I can still see her face through the door windows. She's shaking her head. She's smiling. Then she's not smiling. She's just looking at me. Digging her eyes into me.

Spies digs deep.

# Boy Takes Flight

The ibis has lost its left leg. It stands on its right foot, its black left leg a stump cut off at the joint where the missing clawed foot might have once bent to take flight. The fishing line cut right through its leg. The bird must have been in agony for months as the fishing line cut off circulation to the foot. But now it's free. Hobbled but free. It just let the foot go. It just wore the pain and then let it go. I see it hop now in my front yard from the living room window. It hops into the air and flaps its working wings to take a brief flight four metres over to an empty chip packet that's blown over to our letterbox. The bird sticks its long black beak into the chip packet and finds nothing and I feel sorry for it and I throw him a chunk of my silverside and pickles sandwich.

'Don't feed the birds, Eli,' Dad says, smoking a cigarette with his feet resting on the coffee table, watching Brisbane's relatively new and promising rugby league outfit, the Brisbane Broncos, playing Mal Meninga's near-invincible Canberra Raiders. Dad's been spending more time out in the living room watching television with August and me. He's drinking less but I don't know why. Tired of the black eyes, maybe. Tired of cleaning up pools of vomit and piss, I guess. I think August and me being here has been good for him and sometimes I wonder if us not being here was the hill from which the spirit wagon of his life rolled down out of control. Sometimes he makes jokes and we all laugh and I feel a warmth I thought only American television sitcom families experienced: my beloved Keatons of *Family Ties* and the Cosbys and the really kinda weird eager beaver Seavers of *Growing Pains*. The dads in those shows spend a great deal of their time talking to their kids in their living rooms. Steven Keaton – the dad of my dreams – seems to do nothing but sit on his couch or at his kitchen table talking to his children about their myriad teenage calamities. He listens and listens and listens to his kids and he pours glasses of orange juice and hands them to his kids as he listens some more. He tells his kids he loves them by telling his kids he loves them.

Dad tells me he loves me when he forms a pistol out of his forefinger and thumb and points it at me as he farts. I nearly cried the first time he did that. He tells us he loves us by showing us the tattoo we never knew he had on the inside of his bottom lip: *Fuck you*. Sometimes when he's drinking, he gets all weepy and he'll ask me to come closer to him and he'll ask me to hug him and it feels strange to hold him close to me but it feels good too, with his face hair rubbing like sandpaper against my softer cheeks and it's strange and sad the feeling of sorrow I feel because I know he might not have actually been physically touched, except by accident, by another human for about fifteen years.

'I'm sorry,' he dribbles in these embraces. 'I'm sorry.'

And I just assume he means, *I'm sorry for driving you into that dam that crazy night all those dark years ago because I'm such a fuckin' mixed up nut but I'm tryin', Eli, I'm tryin' real, real hard*, and I hug him tighter because I have a forgiveness weakness in me that I hate because it means I'd probably forgive the man who removed my heart with a blunt knife if he said he needed it more than me or if he said his period of bloody heart removal came at a complicated time in his life. Ultimately, in these embraces, to my surprise, hugging Dad back feels like the good thing to do and my hope is to grow into a good man, so I do it.

A good man like August.

August is at the living room coffee table counting money. That grateful, wide-eyed smile of Shelly Huffman's from the midday news bulletin that day stayed with my brother, August, sentimental mute that he is. It lit something inside him. Giving, he came to realise, might be the thing that has been missing from the lives of the brothers Bell, August and Eli. *Maybe that's why I got brought back*, he did not say not so long ago.

'You didn't get brought back, August,' I said. 'Because you didn't fuckin' go anywhere.'

He didn't listen. He was too inspired. Giving, he realised, was the thing missing from most lives of Australian suburban family units who have, for better or worse, indulged in a spot of small-time crime. Crime, he reasoned, is by nature a selfish pursuit; all robbing and hustling and swindling and stealing and dealing and taking and no giving. So, for the past three weeks August has been door-knocking streets with a donation bucket fundraising on behalf of the South-East Queensland Muscular Dystrophy Association across Bracken Ridge and its neighbouring suburbs of Brighton, Sandgate and Boondall. He's regimented and obsessive about it. He draws up maps and timetables of his door-knocking routes and commitments. He did research in the Bracken Ridge library, using demography statistics to find wealthier pockets of Brisbane to door-knock, then he caught the train out to these areas this week: Ascot, Clayfield, the old money of New Farm and, across the river, to sleepy Bulimba where, Slim once told us, the old widowed grandmothers keep thick rolls of cash in their bedpans because they know no self-respecting burglar or, worse, sticky-fingered family member is ever gonna scrutinise an old lady's piss pot. I thought his whole not-talking trip might hamper August's ability to fundraise but it's proven somewhat of a secret weapon. He simply holds up his fundraising bucket, emblazoned with a South-East Queensland Muscular Dystrophy Association sticker and makes a gesture with his hands that suggests he does not talk and most kind-hearted people – and when you doorknock enough homes you start to realise the human heart's default state is actually kindness – take this gesture as meaning he's deaf and dumb somehow because he himself – the warm-faced young man with the bucket – is living with muscular dystrophy. Maybe we'd all be much more effective communicators if we all shut up more.

*

'Why can't I feed the birds?'

'It's selfish,' Dad says.

'How is it selfish when I'm giving the bird my sandwich?'

Dad joins me at the front window, looks at the one-legged ibis in our yard.

'Because ibis don't eat silverside and pickles sandwiches,' Dad says. 'You're only giving it the sandwich chunks because you want to feel good about yourself. That's a selfish mindset. You start feeding that bird from this window every day then it'll start dropping by every afternoon like we're fuckin' Big Rooster and it brings its friends and then none of those birds get the strength and exercise they usually get from finding food the hard way so you drastically alter their metabolisms, not to mention cause widespread civil war among the Bracken Ridge ibis community as they battle to be the first to chomp into your silverside and pickles treat. Moreover, you suddenly get an unnaturally high level of birds in one place, which affects the ecological balance of the whole Bracken Ridge area. I know I don't always practise this but, basically, you know, the whole point of life is doing things that are right over things that are easy. Because you want to feel good about yourself, suddenly the ibis are spending less time in the wetlands on a tree and more time on the ground in a fuckin' car park rubbing shoulders with the pigeons, and then we start getting inter-species contact and weaker immune systems in the birds and higher stress hormones and from that little petri dish of dynamite springs salmonella.'

Dad nods his head next door at Pamela Waters, in her gardening gear on her hands and knees, pulling weeds from a row of orange gerberas.

'Then Pam goes down the Barrett Street deli and buys three slices of leg ham but Max has left his deli cabinet window open for the past two hours and all those slices of delicious leg ham have been tainted with salmonella and Pam kicks the bucket two weeks later and doctors can't work out whodunit but it was the ham and salad roll whodunit, in the sunroom with the baguette.'

'So my silverside sandwich chunks could one day kill Mrs Waters?'

'Yeah, on second thoughts, feed the fuckin' birds.'

We reel back laughing. We watch the ibis for a long moment.

'Dad.'

'Yeah?'

'Can I ask you something?'

'Yeah.'

'Are you a good man?'

He looks out to the amputee ibis, trying to chew and swallow a chunk of white Tip Top bread.

'Nah, probably not, I'd say,' he says.

We stare out the window in silence.

'Is that why Mum ran away from you?'

He shrugs. Nods his head. Maybe no. Probably yes.

'I gave her plenty of reasons to run,' he says.

We watch the ibis some more, bobbing about and studying the yard.

'I don't think you're a bad man,' I say.

'Why, thanks Eli,' he says. 'I'll remember to put that hearty endorsement on my next job application.'

'Slim was a bad man once,' I say. 'But he came good.'

Dad laughs. 'I do appreciate it when you compare me to your murderer friends.'

Then the yellow Ford Mustang passes our house. That same man driving it. Big guy. Black hair, black moustache, black eyes, staring at us as he passes the house. Dad stares back at him. He drives on down the street.

'What's his fuckin' problem?' Dad says.

'I saw him last week,' I say. 'I was sitting on the seats outside Sandgate train station and he was staring at me from his car.'

'Who do you think he is?'

'Fucked if I know.'

'Try not to fuckin' swear so much, will ya.'

\*

The phone rings in the afternoon. It's Mum. She's calling from the phone box at Sandgate train station. She's scared. She's crying. She can't go to Sister Patricia's house because he'll find her there. Teddy knows Sister Patricia's house.

I'm gonna fuckin' kill him. I'm gonna stab him in the kidney with a small knife.

I place the phone down.

Dad is on the lounge watching a Malcolm Douglas adventure documentary. I sit down one lounge cushion away from him.

'She needs us, Dad,' I say.

'What?'

'She needs you.'

He knows what I'm thinking.

'She's got nowhere else to go.'

'No, Eli,' he says.

On television, outback adventurer Malcolm Douglas has his right hand inside a mangrove mud hole.

'I'll clean out the book room. She can help around the house. Just a few months.'

'No, Eli.'

'Have I ever asked for anything from you?'

'Don't do this,' he says. 'I can't.'

'Have I ever asked for a single thing from you?'

Malcolm Douglas pulls a raging Far North Queensland mud crab from the mud hole.

I stand and walk to the front window. He knows it's the right thing to do. The ibis with one leg hops and hops and flies over the houses of Lancelot Street. The ibis knows it's the right thing to do.

'You know what a good man once said to me, Dad,' I say.

'What?'

'The whole point of life is doing what's right, not what's easy.'

*

Her summer dress is frayed and stretched. She stands barefoot by the train station phone box. August and I wait for her smile because her smile is the sun and the sky and it makes us warm. We smile at her as we rush closer to the phone booth. She has nothing. No bags. No shoes. No purse. But she will still have her smile, that brief celestial event, when her lips open from right to left and she curls her upper lip and she tells us in that smile that we're not crazy, we are correct about everything, and it's just the universe that is wrong. And she sees us and she beams that smile and it turns out the universe is right and it's the smile that is wrong because Mum is missing her two front teeth.

Nobody talks on the drive home from the station. Dad is driving and Mum sits in the front passenger seat. I sit behind her and August sits beside me, reaching his left hand over to regularly rub Mum's right shoulder reassuringly. I can see Mum's face in the reflection of the car's side mirror. That upper lip can't curl right because it's fat. Her left eye is black and there is blood pooled in the white of her eyeball. I'm gonna stab his fuckin' eyes out. *I'm gonna stab his fuckin' eyes out.*

It's only when Dad pulls into our driveway that a word is spoken. They are the first words I've ever witnessed Mum say to Dad.

'Thank you, Robert,' she says.

*

August and I set about removing the mountain of books from Dad's book depository. We don't have enough boxes to box them all. There must be ten thousand paperbacks and, in turn, some fifty thousand silverfish swimming through their pages.

Augusts writes in the air. *Book sale.*

'You're a genius, Gus.'

We drag out an old table Dad has lying under the house. The book stall is erected on the footpath, just near our letterbox. We make a sign out of one of Dad's XXXX beer cartons, scribble on the blank brown inside of the cardboard: *BRACKEN RIDGE BOOK BONANZA – ALL BOOKS 50 CENTS.*

If we sell ten thousand books, we make $5000. That's enough for Mum to get a bond on a rental place. That's enough for Mum to buy some shoes.

August and I are carting stacks of paperbacks between the book room and the stall outside while Mum and Dad are drinking Home Brand black teas and talking about what I believe are the old times. They have a shorthand these two. Then I realise they were lovers once.

'But you don't even like steak,' Dad says.

'I know,' Mum says. 'And this stuff they served was so tough you could use it to prop up a wonky table. But a couple of the girls showed me how to carve a circle of meat close to the bone on any old road kill and make it look like eye fillet.'

They cared for each other in the time before they hated each other. There is something alive in Dad's eyes that I've not seen before. He's so attentive to her. Not in his fake way that he usually is when he needs to charm someone. He laughs at things she says and what she says is funny. Black comedy bits Mum says about prison food and the wild adventure of the past fifteen or so years of her life.

I see something. I see the past. I see the future. I see my mum and dad fucking their way to my existence and I want to vomit but I want to smile too, because it's nice to think they might have started out with high hopes for our so-called family. Before the bad days. Before they got swallowed up by the universe.

The phone rings.

I rush to the phone.

'Eli, wait,' Mum says. I stop. 'It might be him,' she says.

'I hope it is,' I say.

I raise the handset to my right ear.

'Hello.'

Silence.

'Hello.'

A voice. His voice.

'Put your mum on the phone.'

'You gutless fuck,' I say down the phone.

Dad shakes his head.

'Tell him we've called the cops,' Dad whispers.

'Mum called the cops, Teddy,' I say. 'The boys in blue are coming for you, Teddy.'

'She didn't call the cops,' Teddy says. 'I know Frankie. She didn't call the cops. Tell your mum I'm coming to get her.'

'You better stay the fuck away from her or—'

'Or what, little Eli?' he barks down the phone.

'Or I'm gonna stab your fuckin' eyes out, Teddy, that's what.'

'Oh yeah?'

I look at Dad. I'll need some back-up on this.

'Yeah, Teddy. And my dad is gonna break your coward fuckin' face in two like he breaks coconuts with his bare hands.'

Dad's face fills with surprise. 'Put the fuckin' phone down, Eli,' Dad says.

'Tell your mum I'm coming to get her,' Teddy barks.

'We'll be waiting right here, you gutless cunt,' I say. It's the rage that does it to me. It makes me different. I feel something inside me building. All my gathered rage squashed down into my ribs in my youth. I scream, '*We'll be waiting right here, Teddy.*'

The phone goes dead. I put the handset down. I look at Dad and Mum. August is on the couch, shaking his head. They all stare at me like I'm deranged, which I might well be.

'What?' I say.

Dad shakes his head. He stands and opens the pantry door. He uncaps a bottle of Captain Morgan. He slugs half a cup of cheap rum.

'August, go get the axe handle, will ya?'

\*

Slim once told me the greatest flaw of time is that it doesn't really exist.

It's not a physical thing, like Teddy's neck, for example, that I can reach out and strangle. It can't be controlled or planned around or manipulated because it's not really there. The universe didn't put the numbers on our calendars and the Roman numerals on our clocks, we put them there. If it did exist and I could reach out and strangle it in two hands, I would. I would grab time in my hands and bring it under my arms in a headlock where it couldn't move and time would be frozen under my armpit for eight years and I could catch up in age with Caitlyn Spies and she might consider kissing the lips of a grown man her age. I'd have a beard because hair would have finally started growing on my face by then. I'd have a deep voice that would talk to her about politics and homewares and what sort of dog we should get that might suit our small backyard in The Gap. If we didn't put those numbers on the clock then Caitlyn Spies wouldn't age, Caitlyn Spies would just be, and I could be with her. I've only known bad timing. I've only ever felt out of step with time. But not this day. Not this moment by the front living room window of 5 Lancelot Street, Bracken Ridge. High noon. Where's the rolling tumbleweed and the old granny closing the shutters on the town saloon?

Dad standing nervously with his axe handle in his right hand. August standing here with a thin metal bar we normally use as a lock chock on the kitchen window. Me standing with my Gray-Nicolls single scoop – the Excalibur-in-the-stone of cricket bats – that I bought from the Sandgate pawnbrokers for $15. Feeble, potbellied warriors in singlets, thongs and shorts before battle. We'd all die for our queen, locked safely in the book room down the hall that we're slowly emptying of books. Even Dad would die for her, I reckon. Maybe he can prove his love to her. Maybe this is his road to redemption, a few steps into his front yard and an axe handle into Teddy's temple, and Mum falls gratefully into his thin arms and tattooed Ned Kelly on his right shoulder gives a hearty thumbs-up to true love.

'Why the fuck did you say I would break his face?' Dad asks.

'I thought it would scare him off,' I say.

'You know I can't fight for shit, don't ya?' he says.

'I thought that was just when you were pissed.'

'I fight better when I'm pissed.'

We're fucked. Such is life.

\*

Then the yellow Ford Mustang pulls into the street and – lump in my throat, wobble in my knees – pulls into our driveway.

'It's him,' I gasp.

Black hair, black eyes.

'That Teddy?' Dad asks.

'No, it's the guy I saw outside the train station.'

He cuts the ignition and hops out of the car. He wears a grey coat and slacks, black shirt under the coat. He looks too formally dressed for someone visiting Bracken Ridge. In his left hand he carries a small boxed gift wrapped in red cellophane.

He walks across the front yard towards the living room window where the three of us – the Bell boys – stand with our dumb ogre weapons locked in our sweaty palms.

'If you're one of Teddy's mates you better stop right there, mate,' Dad says.

The man stops.

'Who?' the man replies.

Then a second car pulls up at the kerb by the letterbox. A large blue Nissan van. Teddy climbs out of the passenger seat. The driver of the van climbs out too, and a third man slides the van's rear passenger door along and slams it shut behind him.

All three are as large and lumbering as each other. They look like the Tasmanian woodchoppers who always win first place at the Ekka. They have the unmistakeable knuckle-dragging, plus-plus-sized-arse gait of the Queensland long-haul truck driver. Teddy probably called them on his CB radio, called for back-up like a seven-year-old boy playing with his cops and robbers play set. What a fuckin' haemorrhoid. Maybe one of them is The Log, the big dickhead with the big dick. I'll be sure to kick him in the balls. I would laugh out loud at these buffoons if they weren't all carrying aluminium baseball bats.

Teddy marches to the middle of our front yard and calls through the window, oblivious to the man in the grey coat standing beneath us holding a wrapped gift in his left hand.

'Get the fuck out 'ere now, Frankie!' Teddy hollers.

He's got the bluster of drugs in him again. The mania of long-haul speed.

The man in the grey coat steps casually and calmly to the side of the scene, watches Teddy with a puzzled look on his face, something like a panther, I realise just now, making way for a donkey.

Mum appears behind me at the window.

'Go back to the room, Fran,' Dad says quietly.

'Fran?' Teddy shouts. 'Fran? Is that what he used to call ya, Frankie? You think you might shack back up with this loon?'

The man in the grey coat has now moved to the two steps that lead to our small front concrete porch. He sits down and studies the scene, a thoughtful forefinger over his lips.

Mum squeezes between me and August and leans out the window.

'We're done, Teddy,' Mum says. 'No more. I'm not coming back again. Never again, Teddy. We're done.'

'Nup, nup, nup,' Teddy says. 'We're not done till I say we're fuckin' done.'

I grip my Gray-Nicolls harder. 'She said fuck off, Teddy Bear, are you deaf?'

Teddy smiles. 'Eli Bell, bein' the big man for his mummy,' he says. 'But I know your knees are shaking, you little cunt. I know you'll piss your pants if you have to stand at that window any longer.'

I have to hand it to him, his insights are spot on. I've never wanted to piss so bad and I've never wanted more to be wrapped up in a warm blanket slurping Mum's chicken soup while watching *Family Ties.*

'You come near her I'll stab your fuckin' eyes out,' I say through clenched teeth.

Teddy looks at his goons. They nod at him.

'All right, Frankie,' he says. 'You don't want to come out, I guess we better come get ya.' Teddy and his thug friends march towards the steps of the front porch.

That's when the man in the grey coat stands. That's when I realise how broad the man in the grey coat's shoulders are, how much the grey coat hugs the muscular arms of the man in the grey coat. His gift stays sitting on the first step to the porch.

'The lady said you're done,' says the man in the grey coat. 'And the boy said fuck off.'

'Who the fuck are you?' Teddy spits.

The man in the grey coat shrugs.

'If you don't know me then you don't want to know me,' the man says.

I'm starting to love this man like I love Clint Eastwood in *Pale Rider.*

The two men stare at each other.

'Go home, mate,' the man in the grey coat reasons. 'The lady said you're done.'

Teddy shakes his head, laughing, turns back to his two goons, who are gripping their baseball bats, spoiling for action, speed-thirsting for water and blood. As Teddy turns back he sucker swings his aluminium baseball bat hard and fast at the head of the stranger on our porch steps and the stranger ducks like a boxer, not taking his eyes off the threat, and he drives his clenched left fist hard into Teddy's fatty right ribcage and he pushes up from his feet beneath Teddy, transferring the power in his calves and his thighs and his pelvis into the fury of his right fist that uppercuts the bottom of Teddy's chin. Teddy wobbles on his feet in a bash haze and he finds his focus just in time to see the stranger's forehead butting into the tip of his nose, making his nose bones snap, crackle and pop in an abstract splatter painting of human blood. I know this man now for what he is. A prison animal. A freed prison animal. The panther. The lion. I cry tears of madman happiness when I see Teddy's mangled face lying unconscious on the ground and a name reaches my dry lips.

'Alex,' I whisper.

Teddy's goons reluctantly move closer but they're stopped immediately in their tracks by the black handgun the stranger whips from behind his waist belt.

'Back up,' the stranger says. He points his gun at the head of the closest goon.

'You,' he says. 'Driver. I got your licence plate number so I got you now, do you understand?'

The van driver nods, dumbstruck and frightened.

'You drag this fat piece of shit back to the hole he crawled out of,' the stranger says. 'When he wakes up you be sure to tell him Alexander Bermudez and two hundred and thirty-five Queensland chapter members of the Rebels say he's done with Frankie Bell. You follow?'

The van driver nods. 'I'm sorry, Mr Bermudez,' he stutters. 'I'm so sorry.'

Alex looks across at Mum, watching the surreal scene from the window.

'You still got some things of yours at his place that you need?' he asks Mum.

Mum nods. Alex nods knowingly, looks back at the driver as he belts his gun back behind his waist. 'Driver, before sundown tomorrow you will have the lady's belongings sitting on this porch by the front door, you follow?'

'Yes, yes, of course,' the van driver says, already dragging Teddy along the grass of the front yard. The two goons heave Teddy inside the blue van and start off up Lancelot Street. The driver nods respectfully at Alex one last time and Alex nods back. He turns to us at the window. 'I always told my mum that's the worst part about this country,' he says, shaking his head. 'All the fuckin' bullies.'

*

Alex sips a tea at the kitchen table.

'That's a nice cuppa, Mr Bell,' he says.

'Call me Rob,' Dad says.

Alex smiles at Mum. 'You raised two fine boys Mrs Bell,' he says.

'Call me Frankie,' she says. 'Yeah, ummm, they're all right, Alex.'

Alex turns to me.

'I had some dark periods inside,' he says. 'Everybody just assumes the head of an organisation like mine would be flooded with letters from friends on the outside. But the reality is, in fact, the complete opposite. No bastard writes to ya because they think every other bastard is writin' to ya. But no man is an island, ya know, not the Prime Minister of Australia, not fuckin' Michael Jackson, and not the Queensland sergeant-at-arms of the Rebels outlaw motorcycle gang.'

He looks back at Mum.

'Young Eli's letters were probably the best thing about my lag,' he says. 'This bloke made me happy. He taught me a bit about what's important in bein' human, ya know. He didn't judge. He didn't know me from a bar of soap but he gave a shit.'

He looks at Mum and Dad.

'I guess you guys taught him that?' he says.

Mum and Dad shrug their shoulders awkwardly. I fill the silent space.

'I'm sorry I suddenly stopped writing,' I say. 'I've been in a bit of a hole myself.'

'I know,' he says. 'I'm sorry about Slim. You get to say goodbye?'

'Sort of.'

He pushes the gift he's been carrying across the table.

'That's for you,' he says. 'Sorry about the wrapping. Us bikies aren't known for our gift-wrapping skills.'

I pull back the roughly taped and folded red cellophane at each end, slide the box out. It's an ExecTalk Dictaphone, colour black.

'It's for your journalising,' he says.

And I cry. I cry like a seventeen-year-old baby in front of the formerly imprisoned, highly influential senior member of the Rebels outlaw motorcycle gang.

'What's wrong, mate?' he asks.

I don't know. It's my loose knee-jerk tear ducts. I've no control over them.

'Nothing,' I say. 'It's perfect, Alex. Thanks.'

I take the dictaphone out of its box.

'You're still gonna be a journalist, aren't ya?' he asks.

I shrug my shoulders.

'Maybe,' I say.

'What, but that's your dream, isn't it?' he asks.

'Yeah, it is,' I say, suddenly glum. It's the faith he has in me. I liked it more when nobody believed in me. It was easier that way. Having nothing expected of you. Having no bar set to reach or fail to reach.

'So what's the problem, Scoop?' he asks, chipper.

There are batteries in the box. I slip the batteries in the dictaphone. I test the buttons.

'Breaking into journalism hasn't been as easy as I thought it would be,' I say.

Alex nods.

'Can I help?' he asks. 'I know a thing or two about breaking into things.'

Dad laughs nervously.

'What's so hard about it?' Alex asks.

'I don't know,' I say. 'You gotta find a way to stand out from everybody else.'

'Well, whaddya need to stand out from everybody else?'

I ponder this for a moment.

'A page-one story.'

Alex laughs. He leans over the kitchen table and hits the red record button on my new ExecTalk Dictaphone. 'Well,' he says, 'what about an exclusive sit-down with the Queensland sergeant-at-arms of the Rebels outlaw motorcycle gang? Gotta be a yarn in that.'

Such is life.

# Boy Drowns Sea

Can you see us, Slim? August smiling like this. Mum smiling like this. Me slowing time like this in my nineteenth year on earth. Pull it up, thanks, Slim. Let me stay here in this year. Let me stay in this moment by Dad's couch, with August's eyes bright and wondrous as we stand around him reading a typed letter from the Office of the Premier of Queensland.

I know, Slim. I know I haven't asked Dad about the moon pool. I know this happiness depends on me and August and Mum forgetting the bad old days. We lie to ourselves, I know, but isn't there a little white lie in all acts of forgiveness?

Maybe he didn't mean to drive us into that dam that night. But maybe he did. Maybe you didn't kill that taxi driver. But maybe you did.

You did your time for it. You did your time and then some. Maybe Dad has too.

Maybe Mum needed him to do his time and then she could come back to him. Maybe she might give him a second chance. She's good for him, Slim. She's made him human. They're not lovers or nothin', but they're friends and that's good because he chased all his other friends away with all the drink and all the damage.

Maybe all men are bad sometimes and all men are good sometimes. It's just a matter of timing. You were right about August. He did have all the answers. He keeps telling me he told me so. He keeps telling me he saw this coming because he's been here before. He keeps telling me he's come back from somewhere. We both have. And he means the moon pool. We've come back from the moon pool.

He keeps scribbling his finger in the air. *I told you, Eli. I told you, Eli.*

*It gets better*, he said. *It gets real good.*

*Dear Mr August Bell,*
*On 6 June the people of Queensland will unite as one and rejoice in 'Queensland Day', an unprecedented celebration of our great State's official separation from New South Wales on 6 June 1859. As part of our celebrations, we are recognising five hundred 'Queensland Champions' who have contributed to the State through outstanding endeavour. We are delighted to invite you to attend the inaugural Queensland Champions ceremony on 7 June 1991 in Brisbane City Hall where you will be recognised in the COMMUNITY CHAMPIONS section for your tireless efforts to raise funds for the SOUTH-EAST QUEENSLAND MUSCULAR DYSTROPHY ASSOCIATION.*

\*

Alex Bermudez spent four hours in our kitchen telling me his life story. When we finished he turned to August.

'What about you, Gus?' he asked.

*What?*, August scribbled in the air.

'He says, "What?",' I translated.

'Is there anything I can help you with?' Alex asked.

It was in this moment, as August scratched his chin on the couch with *Neighbours* playing on the television, that he was struck with the idea for Criminal Enterprises, Australia's first underground charity organisation funded by a network of leading south-east Queensland crime figures. He asked Alex for a donation to his muscular dystrophy bucket. Alex dropped $200 into the bucket and then August went one step further. With me laboriously translating his air scribbles, August pitched Alex an idea he had for an ongoing charity commitment from the Rebels outlaw motorcycle gang and, moreover, any other wealthy criminals in Alex's friendship circle who had perhaps always wanted to give back to the communities they so readily plundered and destroyed. The State of Queensland's vast criminal underworld, August said, represented an untapped charity resource just begging to be capitalised on. Even in a festering and dark underworld populated by murderous thugs and men who'd stab their own grandmothers for an in-ground swimming pool in summer could be found a few big-hearted men who wanted to give back to those less fortunate than themselves. August saw a whole range of special needs and education services that might be better serviced by the goodwill of local crooks. They might, for example, support young women and men from the wrong sides of the tracks through university medicine courses. They might, for example, care to fund a scholarship program for the children of retired or down-at-heel criminals with special needs. There was a Robin Hood element to it, August said. What the crims lost in the pocket they would gain in their souls; it would give them some small ribbon of meaning to wave at the great judge in the sky when they rang the doorbell at the pearly gates.

I saw where August was going and I put my own existential spin on his point.

'I think what Gus is tryin' to say is, don't you ever wonder what it's all for, Alex?' I said. 'Imagine when it comes time to hang up your pistol and your knuckle-duster and on your last day of work you look back on all that crooked business and all you have to show for it is a mountain of cash and a collection of tombstones.'

Alex smiled. 'Lemme sleep on it,' he said.

One week later an Australia Post courier van dropped off a box parcel at our house, addressed to August. The box was filled with $10,000 in random twenties, tens, fives, twos and ones. The box's sender details read: *R. Hood, 24 Montague Road, West End.*

\*

Can you see us, Slim? Mum messing up August's hair.

'I'm so proud of you, August,' Mum says.

August smiling. Mum crying.

'What is it, Mum?' I ask.

She wipes her eyes.

'My boy's a Queensland Champion,' she sobs. 'They're gonna ask my boy to get up on stage in that hall and they're gonna thank him for bein' ... for bein' ... for bein' him.'

Mum takes a breath. She gives stern instructions.

'We're all gonna go, all right,' she says.

I nod. Dad squirms.

'We're all gonna get dressed up,' Mum says. 'I'm gonna buy a nice dress for it. I'm gonna get my hair done.' She's nodding. 'We're gonna look great for you, Gus.'

August nods, beaming. Dad squirms.

'Fran, I ... ahhh ... I probably don't need to go,' he mutters.

'Bullshit, Robert, you're going.'

\*

Can you see my desk, Slim? Can you see my fingers tapping words on the typewriter at my desk, Slim? I'm writing a piece on race 8 at Doomben. You're looking at *The Courier-Mail*'s back-up of the back-up of the back-up turf writer. The chief back-up turf writer, Jim Cheswick, complimented me on a piece I wrote last week on the McCarthys, three generations – grandfather, father, son – of trotting drivers – they're called drivers in the trots, not jockeys, Jim says – racing in the same event at the Albion trots. Grandfather won by two lengths.

Brian Robertson is kinder than people give him credit for. He gave me a job and he even let me finish school before I took it up. My job on the newspaper is essentially a free-wheeling shit-kicker grunt role that I am grasping tight with both hands and nine fingers. If something big happens in State or Federal parliament I get sent out to shopping centres to ask random people questions set for me by our grizzly chief-of-staff, Lloyd Stokes.

'Is the State of Queensland going down the toilet?'

'Does Bob Hawke care about Queensland going down the toilet?'

'How will Queensland pull itself out of the toilet?'

I write about weekend sporting results in local community competitions. I write about tide times and every Friday morning I phone an old fisherman named Simon King for a weekly column called 'Simon Says', where we give readers Simon King's predicted fishing hot spots along the Queensland coastline. You'd like Simon, Slim, he knows that fishing's not about the catchin' at all and it's all about the sittin'. All about the dreaming.

I write about homes in the property pages. I write three-hundred-word stories – the property editor, Regan Stark, calls them 'advertorials' – about expensive homes being pushed by the real estate companies who pay the most advertising dollars to fill our pages. Regan says my writing is too enthusiastic. She says there is no room for simile in three-hundred-word property advertorials and she's always showing me how to shave my sentences down from something like, 'The sweeping outdoor entertainment deck cradles the north and east sides of the home like a mother wallaby curling around a newborn joey', to something more like, 'House has L-shaped verandah'. But Regan says I shouldn't stop being enthusiastic because – more than even pen and paper – enthusiasm is a journalist's greatest tool outside of Gilbey's Gin. But I'm just doing like you, Slim. I'm just keeping busy. I'm just doin' my time. Every day is one day closer to Caitlyn Spies. We share the same room at work, Slim. It's just that the room – the main newsroom in the building – is about a hundred and fifty metres long and she sits at the front of the room on the crime desk by the office of the editor-in-chief, Brian Robertson, and I sit at the far back of the room by a loud photocopier and Amos Webster, the seventy-eight-year-old man who edits the crosswords, whom I prod on the shoulder several times a day to ensure he's not dead. I love it here, Slim. The smell of the place. The sound of the presses in the brick buildings beneath us when we write. The smell of cigarette smoke and the way the old men swear about older politicians they knew in the 1960s and younger women they screwed in the 1970s.

It was you who got me the job, Slim. It was you who changed my life. I want to say thanks, Slim. If you can see me. Thanks. It was you who told me to write to Alex. It was Alex who gave me his story. It was that story that got my story onto the front page of *The Courier-Mail*. 'REBEL WITHOUT A PAUSE' the headline read on my 2500-word exclusive on the life and times of the recently released Rebels leader, Alex Bermudez. I didn't get a byline for the yarn but that's all right. The piece was changed dramatically by the editor, Brian

Robertson, on account of me filling it with what Brian called 'flowery bullshit'.

'How did you possibly jag a sit-down interview with Alex Bermudez?' Brian asked at his desk, reading my printed draft that I had mailed him with a cover letter describing, again, my desire to write for *The Courier-Mail*'s esteemed crime-writing team.

'I wrote him letters in prison that cheered him up on the days he was down,' I said.

'How long were you writing him letters?'

'From about the age of ten until I was thirteen.'

'Why did you start writing letters to Alex Bermudez?'

'My babysitter told me it might mean a lot to someone like him because he didn't have any family or friends writing to him.'

'He didn't have any family or friends writing to him because he's a highly dangerous, possibly sociopathic convicted criminal,' Brian said. 'I take it your babysitter wasn't the Mary Poppins type?'

'No,' I said, 'he wasn't.'

'How do I know this isn't a load of bullshit fantasy from a bullshit kid who wants to come work for me?'

Alex knew he would say that. I passed Brian a phone number for Alex.

I watched him across the desk as he spoke to Alex Bermudez on the phone, confirming the details and quotes in the story.

'I see,' he said. 'I see ... Yeah, I think we can run it.'

He nodded, staring at me blankly. 'Well, no, Mr Bermudez, I'm afraid it won't be "word for word" because the kid writes like he wants to be fuckin' Leo Tolstoy and he buried the lead down in the nineteenth paragraph. And, furthermore, no newspaper of mine will ever open a page-one story with a quote from a fuckin' poem!'

Alex had suggested opening with this quote from *The Rubáiyát of Omar Khayyám*, the poem I sent him in the prison mail:

*Oh, come with old Khayyám, and leave the Wise*
*To talk; one thing is certain, that Life flies;*
*One thing is certain, and the Rest is Lies;*
*The Flower that once has blown forever dies.*

He said he had learned that poem by heart. He said he had leaned on that poem through his lag. He said it brought him wisdom and comfort. He said it brought him out of the hole, like it brought Slim out of the hole, four decades before him. That quote was a thematic emotional thread through my piece because it spoke of Alex's regrets for the things he'd done to others which were threaded to the things he'd had done to him as a boy.

'Do you like it?' I asked Brian.

'No,' Brian said flatly. 'It's a fawning fuckin' sob story about a fuckin' crim cryin' into his bucket over his life of A-grade professional scumbaggery.'

He cast his eyes back over my story draft.

'But it has its moments,' he said. 'How much you lookin' for?'

'What do you mean?'

'Payment?' he said. 'How much per word?'

'I don't want any money for it,' I said.

He placed the draft on his desk. Sighed.

'I want to write for your crime team,' I said.

He dropped his head, rubbed his eyes.

'You're not a crime writer, kid,' Brian said.

'But I just wrote you 2500 exclusive words on one of Queensland's most notorious criminals?'

'Yeah, and five hundred of those words were about the colour of Alex's eyes and the intensity of his gaze and the way he fuckin' dressed and the fuckin' boat dreams he had in the slammer.'

'That was a metaphor for him drowning inside and longing for freedom.'

'Well, it made me long for a fuckin' bucket, mate. I'll give it to ya straight so ya don't waste any more time on it: the truth is, kid, crime reporters are born, not made, and you weren't born a crime reporter. You'll never be a crime reporter and you'll probably never be a news reporter for that matter, because you have too many thoughts swimming around in too small a head. A good news reporter has only one thing on their mind.'

'The unvarnished truth?' I said.

'Well, yeah ... but he's thinking about something else even before that.'

'Justice and accountability?'

'Yeah ... but ...'

'Being an objective servant of the people in the industry of information?'

'No, mate, all he has on his mind is the fuckin' scoop.'

Of course, I thought. The scoop. The all-powerful scoop. Brian Robertson shook his head, loosened the tie around his neck.

'You, son, I'm afraid, were not born a crime reporter,' he said. 'You were, however, born a colour writer.'

'A colour writer?'

'Yeah, a fuckin' colour writer,' he said. 'The sky was blue. The blood was burgundy. Alex Bermudez's bike that he rode away from home on was fuckin' yellow. You like all the little details. You don't write news. You paint pretty pictures.'

I dropped my head. Maybe he was right. I've always written like that. Remember, Slim? Vantage points. Stretching a moment in time to the infinite. Details, Slim.

I stood up out of the chair opposite Brian's desk. I knew I'd never be a crime reporter.

'Thanks for your time,' I said, glum and defeated.

I walked forlornly to his office door. Then the editor's voice stopped me on the spot. 'So when can you start?' he asked.

'Huh?' I said, puzzled by his question.

'I could use a back-up of the back-up of the back-up turf writer,' Brian said. He almost smiled. 'Plenty of pretty pictures to be painted down at the track.'

*

Details, Slim. She has two creases running from the right corner of her mouth when she smiles. She eats chopped-up carrots for lunch on Mondays and Wednesdays and Fridays. On Tuesdays and Thursdays she eats celery sticks.

She wore a Replacements T-shirt to work two days ago and at lunchtime I took the train into the city and bought a Replacements cassette tape. It was called *Pleased To Meet Me*. I listened to that tape sixteen times in one night and then I went to her desk the next morning to tell her that the last song on side two of the tape, 'Can't Hardly Wait', was the perfect marriage of lead singer Paul Westerberg's raw garage punk rock early days with his burgeoning love of celebratory love pop more reminiscent of B.J. Thomas's 'Hooked on a Feeling'. I didn't tell her that the song is, in fact, the perfect marriage of my heart and my mind which can't stop beating and thinking for her; that it's the sonic embodiment of the urgency in my adoration for her, the embodiment of the impatience she has put in me, how she makes me will time to quicken, hurry up, hurry up, so she can walk through the door, so she can blink like she does, so she can laugh with the other crime writers in her pod, so she can look over here – over here, Caitlyn Spies –

389

some one hundred and fifty metres all the way over to nobody me and the dead guy in the crossword pod.

'Really?' she said. 'I hate that song.'

Then she opened a drawer beneath her desk. She handed me a cassette tape.

The Replacements' *Let it Be*. The band's third album. 'Track nine,' she said, '"Gary's Got a Boner".' She said the word 'boner' like she might have said the word 'lavender'. She does that, Slim. She is magic, Slim. Every word she says comes out as the words 'lavender' and 'luminescence' and 'longing' and … and … and what's that other L word, Slim? You know the one they're always talking about. You know that word, Slim?

*

Brian Robertson's self-combustive hollering echoes across the newsroom.

'So where have the fuckin' pens gone?' he screams.

I stand up from my chair to assess the cyclone of movement happening far away at the serious end of the newsroom, human shrapnel and debris spreading outwards from the nuclear bomb of my editor standing with his fist furiously gripping a copy of our Sunday sister newspaper, the *Sunday Mail*.

My elderly pod friend and crossword king Amos Webster rushes back to his desk and sits down, all but burying himself beneath a tower of dictionaries and thesauruses.

'I'd sit down if I were you,' he says. 'The boss is on the warpath.'

'What's wrong?' I ask, still standing, watching Caitlyn Spies nod her head at her word processor, absorbing Brian Robertson's blitzkrieg of directions and unvarnished journalistic truths about how newspapers live and die on being first.

Brian Robertson explodes again, flame and shrapnel bursting from his lips. Seasoned journalists run for their lives.

'Who wants to tell me where the fuckin' pens have gone?' he screams.

I whisper to Amos.

'Why doesn't someone just give him a bloody pen?' I say.

'He's not looking for a pen, you primate,' Amos says. 'The Penns. He wants to know what happened to the Penns, that family that disappeared in Oxley.'

'Oxley?'

Neighbouring suburb to Darra. Home of the Oxley pub. Home of the Oxley laundromat. Home of the Oxley overpass.

'No fuckin' prizes on my fuckin' newspaper for comin' fuckin' second!' Brian screams across the newsroom, before marching to his office and slamming his office door so hard it wobbles like the brown boards Rolf Harris flexes on telly through 'Tie Me Kangaroo Down Sport'.

'Veronica Holt scooped us again,' Amos whispers.

Veronica Holt. The *Sunday Mail*'s chief crime reporter. She's thirty years old and she only drinks Scotch whisky on ice and she freezes the ice cubes for her drinks by staring at them. She wears skirt suits in charcoal black and onyx black and jet black and soot black. Her news sense is as sharp as the points on her ink-black heels. The Commissioner of Police once demanded Veronica Holt issue a 'public withdrawal' of a story she wrote about Queensland Police frequenting brothels across suburban Brisbane. On talkback radio the following morning Veronica Holt responded directly to the commissioner: 'I'll withdraw my story, Mr Commissioner, when your men withdraw their weapons from Brisbane's illegal brothel houses.'

I scurry to a row of newspapers from across Australia, a reference shelf for staff, found near the water cooler and the newsroom stationery cabinet. A stack of yesterday's *Sunday Mail* newspapers rests on the shelf, tied with white twine. I cut the twine with a pair of scissors from the stationery cabinet and read the front page of yesterday's *Sunday Mail*.

'Brisbane Family Vanishes as ...' These words on the *Sunday Mail*'s front page are the set-up words to the cover's banner headline: 'DRUG WAR EXPLODES'.

A Veronica Holt power-slam page one about the mysterious and inexplicable vanishing of three members of a three-member Oxley family, the Penns, set indelicately against the backdrop of what Queensland Police are calling 'escalating frictions between rival factions of clandestine illegal narcotic networks stretching across Queensland and Australia's east coast'.

Through anonymous sources – largely her uncle, Dave Holt, a retired senior sergeant for Queensland Police – Veronica Holt has stitched together a thrilling crime yarn that doesn't explicitly say the Penn family, prior to their puzzling disappearance, were long entrenched in Brisbane's criminal underworld but gives just enough suggestive backstory to show Veronica's loyal and often salivating readers how the Penns were as crooked as Dad's toilet piss aim on single-parent pension night.

The father, Glenn Penn, was recently released from Woodford Prison, north of Brisbane, after serving two years for small-time heroin dealing. Mother Regina Penn was a Sunshine Coast surfer girl who waited tables for a time in a notorious Maroochydore bloodhouse hotel, Smokin' Joe's, known to be frequented by big-time criminals like Alex Bermudez – he's mentioned in the story – and small-time criminals like Glenn Penn who want to be like Alex Bermudez. Glenn and Regina's eight-year-old son, Bevan Penn, is the boy in the family picture on page one with his face obscured. He's wearing a black Teenage Mutant Ninja Turtles shirt. The clean skin. The poor and innocent eight-year-old boy swept up in the undertow of his mum and dad's poor thinking. The Penn family's Oxley neighbour, a widowed grandmother named Gladys Riordan, is quoted in Veronica's splash piece: 'I heard screams coming from the house around midnight about a fortnight ago. But that lot was always screaming late at night. Then, not a peep. Nothing at all for two straight weeks. I thought they might have gone away. Then the police came around and told me they had been reported as missing persons.'

Gone. Vanished. Disappeared off the face of the earth.

I wonder for a moment if Bevan Penn has a mute brother who's not in the photograph. Maybe the Penns have a gardener who is known as one of Queensland's greatest prison escapologists. Maybe the Penns didn't disappear at all, they're just holed up in the secret room Glenn Penn built beneath the family's single-level home in suburban Oxley where the boy is taking tips from nameless grown men on the other end of a red telephone.

Cycles, Slim. Things coming back around again, Slim. The more things change, the more they stay fucked.

I know Brian Robertson told me not to sniff around the crime desk but I can't help it. It calls me. It draws me. Whenever I'm walking over to Caitlyn Spies I lose track of time. That is, I arrive at her desk and I never know exactly how I arrived there. That is, I know instinctively that I passed the Sports desk and the Classifieds room to my left and the beer fridge beside the Motoring writer, Carl Corby, and the framed Queensland State of Origin rugby league jersey signed by the courageous Wally Lewis, but I don't recall passing these things because I am only ever locked inside the vision tunnel of Caitlyn Spies. I always die on the way through this tunnel and she is the life-preserving light at the end of it.

She's talking on the old black rotary-dial phone at her desk.

'Buzz off, Bell.'

That's Dave Cullen, the paper's hotshot police roundsman. Solid reporter. Solid ego. He's a decade older than me and has the facial hair to prove it. Dave Cullen runs triathlons in his spare time. Lifts weights. Rescues children from burning buildings. Glows.

'She needs to concentrate,' Dave says, head down in his word processor, fingers tapping furiously.

'What did the cops tell you about the Penn family?' I ask.

'What's it to you, Bellbottoms?'

Dave Cullen calls me Bellbottoms. Bellbottoms is not a crime reporter. Bellbottoms is a fairy who writes colour.

'They find any clues in the house?'

'Any clues?' Dave laughs. 'Yeah, Bellbottoms, they found a candlestick in the conservatory.'

'I grew up out that way,' I say. 'I know that street well. Logan Avenue. It runs down to Oxley Creek. Gets flooded all the time.'

'Awww, shit, thanks, Eli, I'll mention that in my intro.'

He taps furiously into his word processor as he speaks. '"Shocking revelations have emerged in the case of the missing Penn family from Oxley with sources not at all close to the family saying they lived on a street that often flooded in heavy rain events."'

Dave Cullen leans back in his chair proudly. 'Fuck, mate, this is gonna put the cat among the pigeons. Thanks for the tip.'

But the joke is on the great triathlete weight-lifting smartarse Dave Cullen because as he's enacting this posturing sideshow of malicious sarcasm my eyes are searching for details across his work desk. A Batman coffee cup with the Caped Crusader's fist causing the word 'Kapow' to explode from the cheek of the Joker. A large orange in a state of decay. A small photograph of the Queensland swimming champion Lisa Curry pinned to his desk divider. A Birdsville Hotel stubby cooler holding six blue ballpoint pens. And a lined Spirax notepad open beside his desk phone. On this notepad are several scribbled lines in shorthand from which I can identify several key words. These words are

*Glenn Penn, Regina, Bevan, heroin, Golden Triangle, Cabramatta, king, reprisal.*

But there are two words I find more compelling than any others. Dave Cullen has placed a question mark beside these two words and he has underlined them. These two words make me shiver. Absurd words that make no sense on their own but make some sense if you have spent a bizarre childhood being raised by drug dealers in the outer western suburb of Darra.

*Llama hair?*

The name falls out of me. It erupts from me. The hot molten lava of his name.

'Iwan Krol.'

I say it too loud and Caitlyn Spies spins around immediately on her chair. She recognises the name. She stares at me. Spies digs deep. Spies digs right.

Dave Cullen is puzzled.

'What?' he says.

Brian Robertson's door opens and Dave Cullen sits up in his seat.

'Bell!' the editor barks.

It's a thunderous holler that makes me jump as I turn towards the monster standing in his office doorway.

'What did I tell you about sniffin' round the fuckin' crime desk?' Brian shouts.

'You said, "Stop sniffin' round the fuckin' crime desk,"' I say, displaying my uncanny journalistic recollection of the facts.

'Get in here now!' Brian screams, walking back to his office desk.

I take one last look at Caitlyn Spies. She's still on the phone but she's looking at me, giving me an encouraging smile now, nodding knowingly, giving the kind of smile fair maidens give to knights who are about to be eaten alive by mythological dragons.

I enter Brian's office.

'I'm sorry, Brian, I was just trying to give Dave some—'

He cuts me off.

'Sit down, Bell,' he says. 'I've got a project I need you to turn around quick.'

I sit in one of two empty swivel chairs sitting across from his single brown leather desk chair that does not swivel for anyone.

'You heard of the Queensland Champions awards?' he asks.

'Queensland Champions?' I gasp.

'It's a load of back-slapping bullshit the government's organised for Queensland Day,' he says.

'I know it,' I say. 'My brother, Gus, has been nominated for an award in the Community Champions category. This Friday night my mum and dad and I are going to City Hall to watch Gus accept his award.'

'What's he gettin' his award for?'

'He walks around the streets of Brisbane with a bucket asking people to give money to help Queenslanders with muscular dystrophy.'

'A man's gotta do,' Brian says. He lifts a booklet of papers and drops them over on my side of the desk. A list of names and phone numbers. 'We've come on board as a sponsor for the night and we're gonna give a bit of coverage to ten Queenslanders who'll get awards.'

He nods at the sheets in front of me.

'There's a bunch of names and contact numbers the government has given us,' he says. 'I want you to go interview them. Gimme twenty centimetres on each of 'em and I need it to the subs by 4 p.m. Friday. We'll run them Saturday after the awards night. Can you do it?'

My own project. My first big project for the great Brian Robertson.

'I can do it,' I say.

'Now I want you to go flowery on this one,' he says. 'You have my blessing to go full florist on this one.'

'Full florist, got it.'

Boy writes flowery. Boy writes violets. Boy writes roses.

I scan the list of names on the paper. It's a predictable mix of popular Queensland Champions from the worlds of sport and art and politics and sport.

A gold medal–winning Olympic cyclist. A famous golfer. A powerful voice for Indigenous rights. A gold medal–winning Olympic swimmer. There's a lovable yet cantankerous TV chef whose cooking show, *Tummy Grumbles*, is a fixture of daytime television in Queensland. A powerful voice for women's rights. A bronze medal–winning Olympic rower with loads of charm. There's a half-blind man named Johannes Wolf who climbed to the top of Mt Everest and buried his glass eye beneath the snow at the summit. There's a mother of six who ran around Ayers Rock 1788 times in 1988 to celebrate Australia's bicentenary and raise money for Queensland Girl Guides.

I take a moment to process the last name on the list of Queensland Champions. The winner of the Senior Champion award. Below his name is a supporting statement that runs for about nine centimetres in journalist copy length, about as long as my right forefinger would be now if it was still attached to my right hand.

'An unsung hero of Queensland philanthropy,' the award statement reads. 'A man who began his life in Queensland as a Polish refugee, who lived with his family of eight inside the Wacol East Dependants Holding Camp for Displaced Persons. A man who has transformed the lives of thousands of Queenslanders living with disabilities. A truly deserving Senior Champion.'

The Lord of Limbs. Ahab. The man who made Lyle disappear. The man who makes everybody disappear. I read the name three times to make sure it's real.

Tytus Broz. Tytus Broz. Tytus Broz.

'Bell?' Brian says.

I don't respond.

'Bell?' Brian says.

I don't respond.

'Eli,' he barks. 'You there, kid?'

Only then do I realise my right fist is scrunching the papers with the names that my editor just handed me.

'You all right?' he asks.

'Yeah,' I say, smoothing out the papers between my hands.

'You went all pale just then,' he says.

'I did?'

'Yeah, your face went all white, like you'd seen a ghost.'

A ghost. The ghost. The man in white. White hair. White suit. Whites of his eyes. Whites of his bones.

'I'll be damned,' Brian says. He's leaning across the desk. He's looking at my hands. I place my right hand in my pocket.

'You're missing a finger?' he asks.

I nod.

'How long you worked here now?'

'Four months.'

'And I never noticed you're missing your right forefinger.'

I shrug my shoulders.

'You must be good at keeping it hidden.'

I hide it from myself.

'I guess I am.'

'How'd you lose it?'

A ghost walked into my house and took it. When I was a boy.

# Boy Conquers Moon

Wake. The springs in my bed have snapped and my mattress is so thin that a sprung spring is stabbing through the mattress into my coccyx. I'm leaving here. I must go. Bed is too small. House is too small. World is too big.

Can't keep sharing a room with my brother, no matter how low cadet wages are at the paper.

After midnight. Moon through the open window. August sleeping in his bed. The rest of the house in darkness. Mum's bedroom door is open. She sleeps in the library room now there are no more books in it. August got rid of them all in the Bracken Ridge Book Bonanza, which ended up running for six consecutive Saturdays, with August making a disappointing $550 from the whole endeavour. He shifted almost 10,000 books through Bracken Ridge's Housing Commission sector, but, amid disappointing sales, eventually reached the philosophical plateau that suggested giving the majority of books away for free. It wouldn't help Mum get back on her feet any quicker but it would increase the chances of Bracken Ridge teens being exposed to Hermann Hesse, John le Carré and *The Three Reproductive Phases of Silverfish*. Because of my brother, August, there are men down at the Bracken Ridge Tavern on

Saturday afternoons now drinking beers over Superforms and betting cards while they discuss the psychological resonance of *Heart of Darkness* by Joseph Conrad.

I walk down the hall, still in my boxer shorts and an old black Adidas T-shirt that I've been wearing to bed, thin and comfortable and full of holes eaten away by what I believe might be silverfish, who survive on diets of Adidas T-shirts and books by Joseph Conrad.

I pull the fading cream curtain back on our wide front living room window. Open the window right up. Lean out and breathe the night air in deep. Look up at that full moon. Look out at the empty street. I see Lyle back in Darra. He's standing in that suburban night in his roo-shooting coat smoking a Winfield Red. I miss him. I gave up on him because I was scared. Because I was gutless. Because I was angry at him. Fuck him, right. His fault for hopping in bed with Tytus Broz. Not my fault. Cut him out of my mind along with the Lord of Limbs. Cut them off like the ibis cut its own leg off because the fishing line was killing it.

It's the moon that pulls my legs outside. My legs are moving and my mind follows. Then my mind follows my hands to the green garden hose looped around the tap fixed to the front of the house. I turn the hose on and kink the hose in my right hand so the water won't spill through the orange nozzle. I drag the hose to the gutter by the letterbox. I sit and stare up at the moon. The full moon and me and the geometry between us. I release the kink and the water rushes onto the bitumen, pooling quickly in a flat pan in the street. The water runs and the silver moon wobbles in the forming puddle.

'Can't sleep?'

I forgot how much he sounds like me. It's like he's me and I'm standing behind myself. I look behind me to see August. His face lit by the moon, rubbing his eyes.

'Yeah,' I say.

We look into the moon pool.

'I think I've got Dad's worry gene,' I say.

'You don't have his worry gene,' he says.

'I'm going to have to live my life as a recluse,' I say. 'I'm never gonna go outside. I'm gonna rent a Housing Commission home just like this one and fill two of the rooms with tinned Black and Gold spaghetti and I'll eat spaghetti and read books until I die choking in my sleep on a ball of lint from my belly button.'

'What is for you will not pass you by,' August says.

I smile at him.

'You know, I think you might have a baritone in that voice you never use,' I say.

He laughs.

'You should try singing some time,' I say.

'I think talking's enough for now,' he says.

'I like talking to you, Gus.'

'I like talking to you, Eli.'

He sits down in the gutter beside me, studies the hose water rushing into the moon pool.

'What are you worrying about?' he asks.

'Everything,' I say. 'Everything that's been and everything that's about to be.'

'Don't worry,' he says. 'It all gets—'

I cut him off. 'Yeah, it all gets good, Gus, I know. Thanks for reminding me,' I say.

Our reflections morph and disfigure like monsters in the moon pool.

'Why do I have this feeling that tomorrow is going to be the most significant day of my life?' I ponder.

'Your feelings are well founded,' August says. 'It is going to be the most significant day of your life. Every day of your life has been leading up to tomorrow. But of course every day of your life led up to today.'

I look deeper into the moon pool, leaning over my hairy and thin legs.

'I feel like I have no say in things any more,' I say. 'Like nothing I do can change what is and what is going to be. I'm in that car in the dream and we're crashing through the trees towards that dam and there's nothing I can do to change our fate. I can't get out of the car, I can't stop the car, I just go up and then I go down into the pool. And then all that water comes in.'

August nods at the moon pool.

'Is that what you see in there?' August asks.

I shake my head.

'I don't see nothin'.'

August looks deeper, too, into the growing moon pool.

'What do you see?' I ask.

He stands in his pyjamas. Woolworths cotton ones for summer. White with red stripes, like the nightwear for a member of a barber shop quartet.

'I can see tomorrow,' he says.

'What do you see tomorrow?' I ask.

'Everything,' he says.

'You care to be a little more specific?' I say.

He looks at me, puzzled.

'I mean, it's awfully convenient for you to maintain your sense of idiotic mystery with all these general comments relating to your bullshit conversations with your multiple selves from multiple dimensions,' I say. 'How come they never told you anything useful, these red phone selves of yours? Like, who's gonna win the Melbourne Cup next year? Gold Lotto numbers next week, maybe? Or, oh, I don't know, whether or not Tytus Broz is gonna fuckin' recognise me tomorrow?'

'Did you speak to the police?'

'I called them,' I say. 'I asked a constable to put me onto the lead investigator. He wouldn't do that without me giving my name first.'

'You didn't give him your name, did you?'

'No,' I say. 'I told the constable they need to investigate a man named Iwan Krol in relation to the Penn family. I asked the constable to write that name down. I said, "Are you writing this down?", and he said he wasn't because he first wanted to know who I was and why I didn't want to give him my name and I said I didn't want to give my name because Iwan Krol is dangerous and so is his boss. And the constable asked who Iwan Krol's boss is and I said his boss is Tytus Broz and the constable said, "What, the charity guy?", and I said, "Yeah, the fuckin' charity guy." And he said I was crazy and I said I'm not fuckin' crazy, it's this fuckin' State of Queensland that's fuckin' crazy and you're fuckin' crazy if you don't listen to me when I tell you that the llama hair the forensic science unit found in the Penns' house belongs to Iwan Krol who has been running a llama farm on the outskirts of Dayboro for the past two decades.'

'Then the constable wanted to know how you knew about the llama hair?'

I nod.

'So I hung up.'

'No skin off their nose,' August says.

'Huh?'

'What do they care if the criminals of Queensland are slowly picking themselves off?'

'I think they have to care when one of the people who has gone missing is an eight-year-old boy.'

August shrugs, looks deeper into the moon pool.

'Bevan Penn,' I say. 'They pixelated his face in all the photos but, I swear, Gus, he's us. He's you and me.'

'What do you mean, he's you and me?'

'I mean, that coulda been us. I mean, his mum and dad look like Mum and Lyle looked when I was eight years old, you know. And I been thinkin' how Slim used to talk about cycles and time and things always coming back around again.'

'They do,' August says.

'Yeah,' I say, 'maybe they do.'

'Just like we come back,' he says.

'I don't mean like that.'

I stand up.

'Stop it, Gus,' I say.

'Stop what?'

'Stop that bullshit about coming back. I'm sick of hearing it.'

'But you came back, Eli,' he says. 'You always come back.'

'I didn't come back, Gus,' I say. 'I don't come back. I'm just fuckin' here in the one dimension. And those voices you heard on the end of the phone were the voices in your head.'

He shakes his head.

'You heard them,' he says. 'You heard them.'

'Yeah, I heard the voices in my head too,' I say. 'The batshit crazy voices in the heads of the Bell brothers. Yeah, Gus, I heard 'em.'

He stares into the moon pool.

'Do you see her?' he asks.

'See who?'

He nods at the water.

'Caitlyn Spies,' August says.

'What about Caitlyn?' I ask, looking into the moon pool, following his gaze, finding nothing.

'You should tell Caitlyn Spies.'

'Tell her what?'

He looks into the pool. He taps the puddle of water with his bare right foot and the moon pool ripples into ten separate stories.

'Tell her everything,' he says.

Mum's voice from the front window of the house. She's trying to scream and whisper at the same time.

'What the hell are you two doing out there with that hose?' she hollers. 'Get back in bed.' Her stern warning voice now. 'If you're tired for tomorrow ...'

Mum's stern warnings are always open-ended, always leaving the possible consequences of waking up tired for tomorrow as intimidatingly infinite.

If you're tired for tomorrow ... I'll beat your backsides so red you'll put Rudolph out of work. If you're tired for tomorrow ... the stars will disappear from the night skies over Bracken Ridge. If you're tired for tomorrow ... the moon will crack like a gobstopper between your teeth and the colours inside the moon will blind humanity. Sleep, Eli. Tomorrow is coming. Everything is coming. All of your life is leading up to tomorrow.

\*

Dad reads *The Courier-Mail* at the kitchen table at breakfast. He's smoking a roll-your-own and reading the World Affairs pages. I can read the paper's front page over my Weet-Bix bowl. It's an enlarged picture of Glenn Penn's prison photograph. He's got a menacing and hard face. Blond hair in a crew cut, bent and misshapen teeth like a row of old garage doors opening halfway. Acne scars. Pale blue eyes. He gives a half-dumb half-smile in the photograph as though that prison photo was a rite of passage to be ticked off his list of dreams, like making it all the way with a pretty girl and making it all the way to Turkey with ten condoms full of heroin in his stomach and up his arse.

The picture's accompanying story is a co-byline piece by Dave Cullen and Caitlyn Spies about Glenn Penn's neglected and misspent youth. The usual story: Dad whips Mum with the cord from an electric fry pan; Mum spreads rat poison through Dad's toasted ham, cheese and tomato sandwich; eight-year-old Glenn Penn burns his local post office down. Dave Cullen holds the top byline but I know Caitlyn wrote this. I know this because there's a compassion in the piece and it doesn't feature Dave Cullen's regular go-to impact phrases 'shocking revelation', 'murderous intent' and 'digitally penetrated'. Caitlyn's interviewed several teachers and parents at Bevan Penn's primary school. They all say he's a good kid. A good boy. Quiet. Never hurt a fly. Reads a lot. A library geek. She's telling the full story about the boy in the Teenage Mutant Ninja Turtles shirt with the face made of pixels.

'What are you wearing tonight, Eli?' Mum asks from the living room.

Mum's ironing clothes with Dad's old, faulty Sunbeam iron that sends electric shocks through the user on the 'linen' setting and leaves black tar marks on my work shirts if I turn it up any higher than the 'synthetic' setting.

It's 8 a.m. – almost ten hours before August is due to accept his award in the Brisbane City Hall Queensland Champions ceremony – and Mum's already buzzing around the living room the way Mr Bojangles buzzed around a drunk tank.

'I'm just wearing this,' I say, nodding down to my untucked plaid deep purple and white work shirt and blue jeans.

Mum is mortified.

'Your big brother is going to be named a Queensland Champion and you're gonna front up looking like a child molesterer.'

'Molester, Mum.'

'Huh?' she says.

'Child molester. Not child *molesterer*. And what exactly is it about what I'm wearing that makes me look like a child molester?'

She studies me for a moment.

'It's the shirt,' she says. 'The jeans, the shoes. The whole thing just screams, "Run, Joey."'

I shake my head, dumbfounded, swallow my last spoonful of Weet-Bix.

'Do you have time to come home and change before we go in?' she asks.

'Mum, I've got an important interview at 3 p.m. in Bellbowrie and a story I've gotta file by 6 p.m. back in Bowen Hills,' I say. 'I don't have time to come home and change into a tuxedo for Gus's big glory night.'

'Don't you dare be cynical about this moment,' Mum says. 'Don't you dare, Eli.'

Mum's pointing at me with a pair of her slacks under her arms ready for ironing. 'This is the best day ... of ...' Her eyes fill with tears. She drops her head. 'This is a ... great ... fucking ... day,' she sobs.

Something deep in that face. Something primal. Dad puts the paper down on the table. He looks confused, lost for comfort solutions to the unexpected display of that unsettling womanly eye wetness known in more human circles as tears. I move to her. I hug her. 'I'm gonna wear a nice jacket, Mum, all right,' I say.

'You don't own a nice jacket,' Mum says.

'I'll grab one of the work ones they have on the emergency rack.'

The shared emergency rack of hanging black coats for parliament and the magistrates court that all smell like whisky and cigarettes.

'You're gonna be there, right, Eli?' Mum says. 'You're gonna be there tonight?'

'I'm gonna be there, Mum,' I say. 'And I won't be cynical, Mum.'

'You promise?'

'Yeah, I promise.'

I hug her tight.

'This is a great day, Mum. I know it is.'

This is a great fucking day.

*

Judith Campese is the public relations woman from Queensland Champions. She's been helping me all week with the feature spread I'm writing for tomorrow's newspaper about ten winners from tonight's glittery gathering in Brisbane City Hall.

She phones me at my work desk at 2.15 p.m.

'Why are you still at your desk?' she asks.

'I'm just filing Bree Dower,' I say. Bree Dower is the mother of six who ran around Ayers Rock 1788 times in 1988 to celebrate Australia's bicentenary and raise money for the Queensland Girl Guides. Not the greatest twenty centimetres I'll ever write. My story begins with the ham-fisted introductory line, 'Bree Dower's life was going around in circles' and I stretch the long bow of this entry point about how she quit her dead-end job as a real estate agency secretary all the way to how she found her purpose in life going around in circles at Uluru.

'You better get a hurry on,' Judith Campese says. She has a royal British undercurrent to her voice, sort of Princess Diana if Princess Diana managed a Fosseys fashion store.

'Thanks for the advice,' I say.

'Just a quickie,' she says. 'Can you give me an idea of the questions you plan on asking Mr Broz?'

'It's not really policy for us to flag questions before interviews.'

'Just ballpark?' she sighs.

Well, I figure I'll open with the gentle ice-breaker, 'What did you do with Lyle, you twisted old cunt?', then move seamlessly to, 'Where's my fucking finger, you animal?'

'Ballpark?' I say. 'Who are you? What do you do? Where? When?'

'Why?' she says.

'How'd you guess?'

'Oh, that's good,' she says. 'He really has a lot to say about why he does the things he does. It's kinda inspirational.'

'Well, Judith, I look forward to hearing about why he does the things he does.'

Across the newsroom, I can see Brian Robertson marching my way, staring at me as he approaches, so filled with steam his head needs a blast pipe.

'I gotta go, Judith,' I say, hanging up the phone and returning to the Bree Dower piece.

'Bell,' Brian barks from thirty metres away. 'Where's the Tytus Broz copy?'

'I'm just going out there now.'

'Don't fuck it up, all right,' he says. 'The ad reps say he might come on board with some serious ad money. Why are you still at your desk?'

'I'm filing the Bree Dower story.'

'She the Uluru nutter?'

I nod. He reads the piece over my shoulder and my heart stops momentarily.

'Ha!' he smiles. I realise I've never seen his teeth before this moment. '"Bree Dower's life was going around in circles."' He pats me on the back with his thick, heavy left hand. 'Rolled gold, Bell. Rolled gold.'

'Brian?' I say.

'Yeah?' he says.

'There's a real big story on Tytus Broz I think I can write for you.'

'Great, kid!' he says, enthusiastic.

'But it's not an easy story for me to—'

I'm cut off by Dave Cullen calling across the room from the crime desk.

'Boss, just got a quote from the Commissioner ...' Cullen hollers.

Brian rushes off. 'We'll talk when you're back, Bell,' he says, distracted. 'File Broz a-sap.'

\*

Waiting for a taxi to Bellbowrie. It's forty minutes away in the outer western suburbs. I've got to be there in thirty minutes. I stare at my reflection in the glass entrance to our building. Me standing here in the floppy oversized black coat I yanked from the newsroom's spare coat rack. Hands in deep coat pockets. Do I look that different as an eighteen-year-old from how I looked at thirteen? Longer hair. That's about it. Same skinny arms and legs. Same nervous smile. He's going to recognise me instantly. He's going to spot my missing finger and he's going to whistle a secret whistle that only dogs and Iwan Krol are attuned to and Iwan Krol will drag me out to a work shed behind Tytus Broz's Bellbowrie mansion and there he will slice off my head with his knife and my head will still function severed from my body and I will be able to answer him when he scratches his chin and asks me, 'Why, Eli Bell, why?' And I will answer like I'm Kurt Vonnegut. 'Tiger got to hunt, Iwan Krol. Bird got to fly. Eli Bell got to sit and wonder why, why, why?'

A small red Ford Meteor sedan screeches to a loud stop in front of me.

Caitlyn Spies pushes open the passenger-side door.

'Get in,' she barks.

'Why?' I ask.

'Just get in the car, Eli Bell!' she says.

I slip into the passenger seat. Close the door. She slams on the accelerator and I fall back in the seat as we speed into traffic.

'Iwan Krol,' she says, her right hand on the steering wheel, her left hand passing me a manila folder holding a slab of photocopied papers sitting beneath a police mugshot of Iwan Krol.

She turns to me and the sun lights up her hair and her face through the driver's-side window and her perfect green eyes dig deep into my own.

'Tell me everything.'

\*

The Ford Meteor speeds down a Bellbowrie back road that snakes through cluttered bushland growth of old widowmaker eucalypts and suffocating lantana bushes that have knitted together across kilometres of scrub.

A street sign ahead.

'Cork Lane,' I say. 'This is it.'

Cork Lane is a dirt road with large wheel divots and rocks the size of tennis balls that cause Caitlyn's ill-suited car to bounce us up and down in our seats.

I had twenty-seven minutes to tell Caitlyn everything. She has saved her questions to the end.

'So Lyle gets dragged away and just vanishes off the face of the earth?' she says, her hands working hard on the steering wheel, struggling to keep the car moving straight.

I nod.

'That fits the file,' Caitlyn says, nodding at the folder in my hands. 'I heard you talkin' to Dave. I wrote down that name you said. Iwan Krol. There are only four registered llama farmers or llama pet owners currently living in the greater south-east Queensland region, your man Iwan Krol being one of them. So I called the other three and asked 'em straight up to tell me where they were on 16 May, right, the day the cops suspect the Penn family went missing. They all had perfectly believable and boring accounts of where they were. So then I go down to Fortitude Valley police station and I ask an old school friend of mine, Tim Cotton, who's now a constable in the Valley, to dig me up anything they have on file on Iwan Krol and he passes me a brick of papers and I go to photocopy them and as I'm photocopying all these papers I'm reading all these statements from police where they've gone to Iwan Krol's property in Dayboro on five separate occasions – five bloody times – across the past twenty years on cases of missing persons known or connected to Iwan Krol. And five times nothing sticks. Then, last night, I drop the file back to Tim Cotton and I'm buying him a meatball pizza down at Lucky's in the Valley to thank him for his help and he pauses for a moment between trying to get in my pants and you know what he says?'

'What?'

She shakes her head.

'He says, "You might want to let this one go to the keeper, Caitlyn."'

She slaps the steering wheel hard.

'I mean, he actually fucking voices that shit, a fucking police officer, Eli? An eight-year-old kid's gone missing and he says, "Let this one go to the keeper." This is exactly why I fucking hate cricket!'

The car stops at an imposing white iron security gate built into a tall clay-coloured concrete security wall. Caitlyn winds her window down then reaches her arm out to a red intercom buzzer.

'Hello,' says a gentle voice.

'Hi, *Courier-Mail* here for the interview with Mr Broz,' Caitlyn says.

'Welcome,' says the gentle voice.

The gate slides open with a clunk.

Tytus Broz's house is white like his suits and his hair and his hands. It's a sprawling white concrete mansion with towering columns and Juliet balconies and a white wood double-door entry big enough to fit a white yacht through at full white mast. It's more New Orleans bayou plantation mansion than Bellbowrie millionaire's hideaway.

Dappled sunlight twinkles through the leaves of eight flourishing elm trees that line the long and twisting driveway that splits a vast manicured lawn and eventually ends at a wide set of white polished marble steps.

Caitlyn parks the car at a yellow gravel visitor's bay left of the marble steps, slips out of the car and pops the car boot.

The sound of birds in the elm trees, a light wind. Nothing else.

'How am I gonna explain who you are?' I whisper.

Caitlyn reaches into the boot and presents an old black Canon camera, a long hard grey lens, like one of the cameras our sports photographers use in Lang Park on game days.

'I'm the snapper,' she smiles, closing one eye to gaze through the lens.

'You're not a photographer.'

'Puh!' she sniggers. 'Point and click.'

'Where'd you get that camera?'

'Snuck it out of the repairs cabinet.'

She walks to the towering entry door.

'C'mon,' she says. 'You're late for your interview.'

\*

Ring the doorbell. The doorbell rings in three places within the sprawling house, one ring echoing into another like a small music piece. Heart full of hope. Heart in my throat. Caitlyn grips her camera like it's a war hammer and she's leading a group of drunk Scots into battle. No more sound but the birds in the elm trees.

So far from anything here. So far from life and the world. I realise now how much the house doesn't fit the setting. The white towering columns don't fit with the native landscape surrounding us. There's something wrong, something off about this place.

One half of the wide double-door entry swings open. As it swings open I remember to slip my right hand with its missing forefinger inside my deep right coat pocket, slip it out of view.

A short woman in a formal grey work dress, a maid's uniform I guess. Filipino maybe. Big smile. She opens the door wider to reveal a frail and thin woman in a white dress. Flesh so thin on her face it looks like her cheeks have been painted in oils across her pronounced cheekbones. A warm smile. A face I know.

'Good afternoon,' she says, elegantly bowing her head briefly. 'You folks from the paper?'

Her hair is grey now. It used to be blonde–white. It still hangs straight and long over her shoulders.

'I'm Hanna Broz,' she says, placing her right hand to her chest. But the hand is not a hand at all. It's a plastic fake but like none I've ever seen. It looks like one of Mum's hands, like it's been tanned and weathered by the sun. It sticks out of the white sleeve of a cardigan she wears over her dress. I look at her left hand by her side and it's the same. There are freckles on this one. It's stiff but it looks real, made of some kind of moulded silicone. All for show and not for function.

'I'm Eli,' I say. Don't say your last name. 'This is my photographer, Caitlyn.'

'I might just grab a quick headshot if you don't mind?' Caitlyn says.

Hanna nods. 'That should be fine,' she says, turning away from the door. 'Come. Dad is in the reading room out back.'

Maybe Hanna Broz is fifty now. Or forty and tired. Or sixty and grateful. What did she do with the past six or so years since I last saw her? She doesn't recognise me but I recognise her. That was her father's eightieth birthday party. Mama Pham's restaurant in Darra. A different time. A different Eli Bell.

\*

The house is a museum of collected antiques and gaudy oil paintings the size of the floor space in my bedroom. A medieval suit of armour holding a jousting stick. An African tribal mask fixed to a wall. Sweeping polished wood floors. A set of Papua New Guinean tribal warrior spears in a corner here. A painting of a lion tearing apart a gazelle over there. A long living room with a fireplace and a television wider than my bed is long.

Caitlyn cranes her neck to a bronze chandelier that looks like a steel huntsman spider weaving a web of lightbulbs.

'Nice place,' she says.

'Thank you,' Hanna says. 'We didn't always live like this. My father came to Australia with nothing. His first home in Queensland was a room shared with six other men in the Wacol immigration camp.'

Hanna stops on the spot. She stares at my face.

'Do you know it?' she asks.

'Know what?'

'The Wacol East Dependants Holding Camp for Displaced Persons?'

I shake my head.

'Did you grow up in the outer west?' she asks. 'I feel like I know you.'

Smile. Shake my head.

'Nah, I'm north side,' I say. 'Grew up in Bracken Ridge.'

She nods. Staring into my eyes. Hanna Broz digs deep. She turns, scurries on down the hall.

A Napoleon bust. A bust of Captain Cook near a replica *Endeavour*. A painting of a lion tearing apart a grown man this time. The lion is tearing the man's limbs off, has two legs and an arm piled beneath his feet, sinking its teeth into the man's remaining arm.

'You might have to be patient with Dad,' Hanna says, pacing through a long dining room to the back of the mansion. 'He's not as ... how should I say ... robust ... as he once was. You might have to repeat your questions a couple of times and remember to speak loudly and concisely. He can drift off sometimes like he's on another planet. He's had some ill health of late but he's excited about these awards tonight. In fact, he has a surprise planned for all the guests and he wants to give you two a sneak preview.'

She opens two red wood doors to a vast reading room. It feels like the reading room of a royal. Two floor-to-ceiling walls of bookshelves, left side and right. Hundreds of hardback books with old bindings and gold lettering. Burgundy carpet. Blood-coloured carpet. The room smells like books and old cigar smoke. A dark green velvet reading lounge and two dark green velvet armchairs. There is a large mahogany writing desk at the end of the room and this is where Tytus Broz sits, eyes down, reading a thick hardback book. Behind him is a vast rear wall of glass so clean and pure you could squint your eyes and be convinced there wasn't a glass wall there at all. The only clue to the door that's been built into the centre of the glass wall are two sets of polished silver hinges that allow the door to open out to the magical and rambling lawn that runs seemingly for a kilometre or so, past concrete water fountains and perfectly angular hedges and flowerbeds tended by bees and perfect sunlight, down to what looks like a small vineyard, but that view must be a trick of the light because such things can't be found in the lantana outskirts of Bellbowrie, Brisbane. Resting on his desk is a rectangular box about twenty-five centimetres tall and twenty centimetres wide, draped in a red silk covering cloth.

'Dad,' Hanna says.

He doesn't look up from his reading. White suit. White hair. White spine in my back tingling to tell me to run. Run away now, Eli. Pull back. It's a trap.

'Excuse me, Dad,' Hanna says, louder.

He flips his head up from his book.

'The people from the paper are here to talk to you,' Hanna says.

'Who?' he spits.

'This is Eli and his photographer, Caitlyn,' Hanna says. 'They've come to talk to you about the award you are going to receive tonight.'

Some new sun of remembrance dawns in his mind.

'Yes!' he says, pulling the reading glasses from his eyes. He excitedly taps the box covered in the red silk. 'Come. Sit. Sit.'

We move forward slowly, sit in the two elegant black visitor chairs at his desk. He's so much older. The Lord of Limbs doesn't seem as frightening as he seemed to a thirteen-year-old. Time, Slim. Changes faces. Changes stories. Changes points of view.

I could jump right over that desk and strangle his near-dead neck, stab my thumbs into his near-dead zombie eyes. The fountain pen. The fountain pen resting upright in the stand beside his desk phone. I could stab that fountain pen into his chest. His cold white chest. Stab my name into his heart. His cold white heart.

'Thank you for your time, Mr Broz,' I say.

He smiles and his lips tremble. His lips are wet with saliva.

'Yes, yes,' he says impatiently. 'What would you like to know?'

I place my ExecTalk Dictaphone on the desk with my left hand, my unseen right hand and its missing digit gripping a pen to take notes on my lap beneath the desk top.

'Do you mind if I record this?' I ask.

He shakes his head.

Hanna steps back from us softly and takes a watchful owl position from the dark green reading lounge behind us.

'You are being honoured at tonight's Queensland Champions ceremony for your lifelong commitment to enhancing the lives of Queenslanders living with physical disabilities,' I say. He nods, following my ego-massaging opening set-up closely. 'What started you on this extraordinary journey in the first place?'

He smiles, points over my shoulder to Hanna, sitting attentively upright on the reading lounge. She smiles, self-consciously smooths her hair behind her right ear.

'More than half a century ago, that beautiful woman sitting over there was born with a transverse deficiency, what is known as "amelia",' he says. 'She was born with two congenital amputations at the upper arm. A fibrous band within the membrane of the developing foetus that was our Hanna grew constricted.'

He speaks matter-of-factly, like he's reading from a pancakes recipe. Blood clots forming in the foetus. Stir in four cracked eggs. Rest in fridge for thirty minutes.

'A tragically complicated birth followed and we lost Hanna's beloved mother ...' He pauses a moment. 'But ...'

'What was her name?' I ask.

'Excuse me?' Tytus says, bristling at the interruption.

'I'm sorry,' I say. 'Do you mind if I get the spelling of your late wife's name?'

'Her name was Hanna Broz, like her daughter,' he says.

'Sorry, please go on.'

'Well … where was I?' Tytus says.

I look at my notepad.

'You said, "A tragically complicated birth followed and we lost Hanna's beloved mother" and then you paused and then you said, "But".'

'Yes … but …' he says. 'But the world and I were gifted an angel that I vowed, there and then, would lead a life filled with all the riches and wonders available to any other Australian baby born that day.'

He nods at Hanna.

'I kept my vow,' he says.

I'm going to be sick. The question pops from my lips but I don't ask it. Someone else inside of me asks it. Some other being. Someone braver. Someone who doesn't cry so easily.

'Are you a good man, Tytus Broz?' I ask.

Caitlyn whips her head towards me.

'Excuse me?' Tytus asks, shocked. Confused.

I stare into his eyes for a long moment. Snap back to my normal piss–weak self.

'I mean, what's your advice to other Queenslanders on how they, too, can do so much good for this great State?'

He rests back in his chair, studying my face. His chair swivels and he turns to his side and he looks out through that grand pure and clean all–glass wall and he ponders his answer as the bees tend his pink and purple and red and yellow flowers.

'Don't ask for permission to change the world,' he says. 'Just go ahead and change it.'

He cups his hands, rests his chin on his fingers contemplatively.

'I guess, in all honesty, it was the realisation that nobody was going to change the world for me,' he says, gazing out to a cloudless blue sky. 'Nobody was going to do the work for me. I had to turn up for all those other kids out there like my Hanna.'

He turns back to his desk.

'Which brings me to my surprise,' he says. 'I have prepared a little treat for tonight's guests.'

His lips are wet. His voice is raspy and weak. He gives a serpent smile to Caitlyn.

'Would you like to see it?'

Caitlyn nods, yes.

'Go on then,' Tytus says, not moving from his chair.

Caitlyn warily leans forward, removes the red silk cloth.

It's a rectangular glass box. Pure and clean glass like the glass wall in front of us. Perfect edges, like the whole box was shaped somehow from one sheet of glass. Inside the glass box, fixed to a hidden and small metal stand, is an artificial limb. A right human forearm and hand, propped on the stand as though it was floating.

'This is my gift to Queensland,' Tytus says.

It might as well be my hand in there. Caitlyn's hand. So real it looks. From the skin colour and texture to the natural sun blemishes and discolourations on the forearm to the milky moons rising in the fingernails. The milky moons that make me remember the day I learned to drive with Slim. The freckles on this artificial limb that make me remember my lucky freckle on my lucky finger. There is something dark in the making of this perfect limb. I know this in my soul and in the nub of bone on my missing finger.

'Human to the touch, human in its movement,' Tytus says. 'For the past twenty-five years I have employed and engaged the world's finest engineers and human movement scientists with a single vision, to transform the lives of limb-deficient kids like my Hanna.'

He fawns over the box like it was a newborn baby.

'Underline this word in your notebook,' he says. 'Electromyography.'

I scribble the word in my notepad. I don't underline it because I'm too busy underlining the words, 'Smack empire funds science?' Four-word story. Can tell it in three words. Drugs fund research. Drugs buy ...

'Breakthrough!' Tytus says. 'This is only a prototype. High definition anatomically shaped silicone-based exterior. Revolutionary. Transformative. Conspicuously inconspicuous. A genuinely discreet exterior harmoniously integrated into a mechanical interior using electromyography – EMG – signals from existing contracted muscles within the amputee's residual limbs to control the movement of the artificial limb. Electrodes attached to the skin's surface record the EMG signals and these beautiful and informative human signals are amplified and processed by motors we have built into several points along our limb. Real movement. Real life. That's how we change the world.'

The room is silent for a moment.

'It's remarkable,' I say. 'I imagine there are no limits to where you could take this.'

He beams and laughs, looking over at Hanna behind us.

'Life without limbs, Hanna?' he says.

'Life without limits,' she says back.

He bangs his fist triumphantly on the table.

'Life without limits, exactly!' he says.

He turns around again to that vast cloudless blue sky hanging over his endless green lawn.

'I have seen the future,' he says.

TRENT DALTON

'You have?' I say.

'I have.'

Beyond the glass wall of the reading room there is a lone bird in the sky over Tytus Broz's manicured gardens. Against the backdrop of the eternal blue sky, this small bird zips and whirls and whips through air and the bird's frantic and electric flight show captures Tytus's gaze.

'It's a world without limits,' he says. 'It's a world where kids born the way Hanna was born can control their prosthetic limbs directly through the brain. Real-life limbs controlled by neural feedback that can reach out and shake your hand or pat a dog in the park or throw a frisbee or bowl a cricket ball or wrap their arms around their mum and dad.' He breathes deep. 'That's a beautiful world.'

The bird outside his glass wall windows dips like a Spitfire fighter plane and then darts unexpectedly upward like a rollercoaster and makes a full loop before changing its flight path dramatically and speeding, unexpectedly, towards us. The bird is flying straight to us, to us three here around this office desk, to me and the girl of my dreams, and the man of my nightmares. I know it can't see the glass wall. I know it only sees itself. I know it sees a friend. I see the colour of the bird as it nears the glass. Flashes of vivid and electrifying blue on its forehead and tail. Like the blue in the storm lightning I see from the front window of Lancelot Street. Like the blue in my eyes. That kind of blue. Not just azure blue. Magic blue. Alchemy blue.

And the blue bird slams headfirst and hard into the glass wall.

'Oh my,' says Tytus, shifting back in his seat.

The bird hovers, stunned by the impact against the glass, flaps its wings and flutters its tail furiously, then flies back from whence it came in a darting left turn that zigs into a right turn

422

that zags into a left and whips into a right again and the bird is bouncing on air like a split atom and it knows not where it's going until it finds its purpose and that purpose is itself, the other bird it sees in the glass wall, and it flies hard and fast to meet itself once more, zooming into itself, the Spitfire plane, the kamikaze bomber descending from the blue sky. The flashes of an unprecedented blue again on its forehead and tail. And it slams once more into itself. Into the impenetrable glass wall. It hovers, stunned, and flies away again, determined to find itself once more and it does. It zooms around in an arching left turn that seems to never end until it does because the bird rights itself and zips into an air stream that sharpens its blinding velocity.

Caitlyn Spies cares for it, of course, because her heart can accommodate the sky and everything flying therein.

'Stop it, little birdy,' she whispers. 'Stop it.'

But the bird can't stop. Faster than ever now. *Slam.* And from that horrid impact, this time it does not hover stunned. It simply drops to the ground. Falls with a soft thud on the gravel outside Tytus Broz's glass reading room door.

I stand from my chair and Tytus Broz is surprised when he watches me pass his desk and open the glass door out to the vast lawn. The smell of the lawn. The smell of the flowers. Yellow gravel dust and pebbles cracking and scratching beneath the soles of my Dunlops when I kneel down gently beside the fallen bird.

I carefully pick it up with the four fingers of my right hand and I can feel its fragile twig bones beneath that perfect blue as I cup it in the palms of both my hands. It's warm and soft and the size of a mouse when its wings are tucked up like this. Caitlyn has followed me out here.

'Is it dead?' she asks, standing over me.

'I think it is,' I say.

The blue on its forehead. More flashes of blue over its little ears and more on its wings, like it flew through some magic blue dust cloud. I study the bird in my hands. This lifeless flyer. It has bewitched me momentarily with its beauty.

'What sort of bird is that?' Caitlyn asks.

A blue bird. Are you listening, Eli?

'Oh, what do you call them again?' Caitlyn ponders. 'My grandma gets them in her backyard ... They're her favourite bird. It's so beautiful.'

Caitlyn kneels down, leans over the dead bird, rubs a pinkie finger over its exposed belly.

'What are you gonna do with it?' she asks softly.

'I don't know,' I say.

Tytus Broz is now standing in the glass doorway.

'Is it dead?' he asks.

'Yeah, it's dead,' I say.

'Stupid bird seemed so determined to kill itself,' he says.

Caitlyn slaps her hands.

'Wren!' she says. 'I remember now! That's a wren.'

And, with that, the dead blue wren comes back. Like it was just waiting for Caitlyn Spies to recognise it, because, like all living things – like me, me, me – it lives and dies on her breath and her attention. Back. Its peppercorn eyes open first and then I feel its feet gently scratch the skin on my palms. Its head moves, a brief rock. Groggy and stunned. The bird's eyes turn to me and in a flash something is transferred that is beyond my understanding, beyond the universe of here, something tender, but then it's gone and it's replaced by the bird's realisation that it rests in a human hand and some electromyographical signal inside its perfect construction tells its weakened wings to flap. Flap. Flap. And fly away. And we three, Eli Bell and the girl of his dreams and the man of his nightmares, watch the blue bird dart left then right as it finds its strength then loops once again because it likes to be alive. But it does not fly far. It merely flies to the far right side of this grand manicured lawn nursed by a groundsman paid in drug money. It flies over a green wood shed, some kind of tool shed maybe. The shed is open with a green John Deere tractor parked inside it. Then the bird flies further to a concrete structure I have not yet noticed. I missed it. It's a kind of square concrete bunker hidden in a huddle of elms and covered in jasmine vines and other wild plants lining the lawn's far right fence. A concrete box with a single white door built into its front and the jasmine vines spill over its roof and connect to the lawn so it looks like the structure has grown up from the earth. The blue bird lands on a vine hanging just above the box's door. And there it stays, darting its small storm-blue head left and right like it's as puzzled as much as anyone by the past five minutes of its curious existence.

Curiouser and curiouser. Curious concrete structure. I'm looking at it strangely and Tytus is looking at it strangely and then he knows I'm looking at it strangely.

I forget my right hand is hanging down with its four fingers. Conspicuously conspicuous. Tytus's old and unreliable eyes zero in on this hand.

I stand quickly, slipping my hands into my pockets. 'Well, I think I've got enough, Mr Broz,' I say. 'I better get back and file this thing for tomorrow's paper.'

He has a puzzled look on his face. Off on another planet. Or maybe just off to five years ago on this planet when he instructed his Polish standover psycho mate, Iwan, to cut off my real-life forefinger from my real-life hand.

He eyeballs me suspiciously.

'Yes,' he says, ponderously. 'Yes. Very well.'

Caitlyn raises her camera.

'Do you mind if I take a quick snap, Mr Broz?' Caitlyn asks.

'Where do you want me?' he replies.

'Just back at the desk inside is fine,' she says.

He sits back at his desk.

'Big smile,' Caitlyn says through the lens.

Caitlyn clicks a shot and the camera pops with a blinding flash that hurts all our eyes. Too bright. Stuns us all in the room.

'Dear God,' Tytus cries, rubbing his eyes. 'Turn that flash off.'

'Sorry, Mr Broz,' Caitlyn says. 'This camera must be faulty. Someone should toss it in the repairs cabinet.'

She aims her lens once more.

'Just one more,' Caitlyn says, like she's talking to a three-year-old.

Tytus forces a smile. Fake smile. Artificial smile. Silicone-based.

*

In the Ford Meteor, Caitlyn tosses the camera by my feet in the front passenger seat. 'Well, that was weird,' she says.

She turns the ignition. Drives too fast out of Tytus Broz's driveway.

I'm silent. She does the talking.

'Okay, gut impressions first,' she says, talking to herself as much as to her junior reporter. 'I mean, correct me if I'm wrong, but there is something rotten in the State of Queensland,' she says, pressing hard on the accelerator as the car splits through Bellbowrie scrub on the black bitumen road back to Bowen Hills. 'To pee or not to pee, that is the question? You ever seen anyone so creepy? You see his old bag of bones body rattling in that suit? He kept licking his lips like he was licking the sticky bit on an envelope.'

She's rambling dot points, fast and loud. Sometimes she takes her eyes off the road to see my face. 'I mean, what's with his daughter and him? What about all that crazy stuff in his house? Okay, where do you want to start?'

I'm looking out the window. I'm thinking of Lyle in the front yard of the Darra house. I'm seeing him standing in his work clothes showered in a rainbow spray from my hose.

'Let's start at the end, huh, and work our way forward to the beginning,' she says.

Forward to the beginning. I like that. That's all I've ever been doing. Moving forward to the start.

'I don't know about you but my crazy-meter was tingling all over,' she says. 'There's something wrong with all this, Eli. Something very, very wrong with all this.'

She's rambling nervously. Filling the silence. She looks across at me. I turn my head to the road in front, repeated broken white bitumen lines lost under the car.

I know what I have to do.

'I've gotta go back,' I say. I say it louder than I intended. I say it with feeling.

'Back?' Caitlyn says. 'Why do you want to go back?'

'I can't say,' I say. 'I have to be mute on this. There are things people can't say. I know that now. There are things too impossible to say out loud so they're best left unsaid.'

Caitlyn hits the brakes hard and turns the car sharply to a dirt bank on the side of the road. The front wheels lose traction momentarily and she reefs on the steering wheel to keep the vehicle from crashing into a rocky slope on my passenger side. She skids to a stop. Switches off the car.

'Tell me why we should go back, Eli.'

'I can't, you'll think I'm nuts.'

'Don't worry about me thinking you're nuts because I've felt exactly that since the moment I met you,' she says.

'You have?' I reply.

'Sure,' she says. 'You're a loon, but I mean that in the best possible way. Like a Bowie-type loon, Iggy Pop–type loon, Van Gogh–type loon.'

'Astrid-type loon,' I say.

'Who?'

'She was a friend of my mum's when I was a kid,' I say. 'I thought she was nuts. But good nuts. Lovable nuts. She told us she heard voices and we all thought she was crazy. She said she heard a voice telling her my brother, August, was special.'

'He sounds special, from what you've told me about him,' Caitlyn says.

I breathe.

'I've gotta go back,' I say.

'Why?' she asks.

I breathe. Forward to the start. Backwards to the end.

'The bird,' I say.

'What about the bird?'

'A dead blue wren.'

'Yeah, the wren?'

'One day when I was a kid …' And so ends my vow of silence. It lasted a staggering forty-three seconds. '… I was sitting in Slim's car and he was teaching me how to drive a manual and I was distracted like I always am and I was staring out the window and I was watching Gus who was sitting on the front fence writing the same sentence in the air with his finger because that was his way of talking. And I could tell what he was writing because I knew how to read his invisible words in the air.'

I pause for a long moment. There's a semicircle of dust on Caitlyn's windscreen.

Her windscreen wipers have smeared a rainbow of old dirt over to my passenger side. That rainbow of dirt reminds me of the milky moons in my thumbnails. Those milky moons remind me of that day in the car with Slim. The small details that remind me of him.

'What was he writing?' she asks.

The sun is falling. I have to file my story for tomorrow. Brian Robertson will be steaming already. Mum and Dad and Gus are probably travelling into Brisbane City Hall now. Gus's big night. A confluence of events. A convergence. Detail upon detail.

'He wrote, "Your end is a dead blue wren."'

'What was that supposed to mean?'

'I don't know,' I say. 'I don't even think Gus knew what it meant or why he was saying it, but he said it. And one year later, they were the first words I ever heard come out of his mouth. The night they took Lyle away. He looked into Tytus Broz's eyes and he said, "Your end is a dead blue wren." It means that dead blue wren represents some kind of end for Tytus Broz.'

'But that bird in your hand wasn't dead, it flew away, and I'm not even sure if it was a wren,' she says.

'It felt like it was dead to me,' I say. 'But it came back. And that's what Gus is always saying. We come back. I don't know. Old souls, like Astrid used to say. Everybody's got an old soul but only the special ones like Gus get to know that. Everything that happens has happened. Everything that is going to happen has happened. Or somethin' like that. I got up and went out to that bird and I picked it up because I felt like I had to. And then it went and landed on that concrete bunker thing at the side of the lawn.'

'That bunker did give me the creeps,' Caitlyn says.

She looks ahead down the winding road back home. The setting orange sun lighting her deep brown hair. Her fingers tap the steering wheel.

'I never believed Gus was special,' I say. 'I didn't believe Astrid could hear voices from spirits. I didn't believe a word of it. But ...'

I stop. She looks across at me.

'But what?'

'But then I met you and I started believing in all kinds of things.'

She gives a half-smile. 'Eli,' she says, dropping her head, 'I think it's real sweet how you feel for me.'

I shake my head, shift in my seat.

'I see you when you look at me,' she says.

'I'm sorry.'

'Don't be sorry. I think it's beautiful. I don't think anyone's ever looked at me like you look at me.'

'You don't have to say it,' I say.

'Say what?'

'What you're gonna say about the timing,' I say. 'How I'm still a boy. Or maybe only just a man. You're gonna say the universe fucked it up. It put me near you but the timing was off. Nice try but about a decade out. You don't have to say it.'

She nods. Curls up her lips.

'Wow,' she gasps. 'Is that what I was gonna say? Damn, how about that? Here I was thinking I was gonna tell you all about a strange feeling I had when I first met you.'

Caitlyn starts the car, slams the accelerator and spins the tyres as she pulls a sharp U-turn back in the direction of Tytus Broz's mansion.

'What did you feel?' I ask.

'Sorry, Eli Bell,' she says. 'Not enough time. I think I just worked out what's in that bunker.'

'What's in there?'

'Well, it's pretty obvious, isn't it?'

'What?'

'The end is in there, Eli,' she says, leaning hard on the steering wheel as the tyres howl on the bitumen road. 'The end.'

*

In a soft twilight we're parked in dark shadow under a sprawling purple jacaranda tree that rises up to the top of Tytus Broz's fence, some fifty metres from the security gate. A small white Daihatsu Charade pulls out of the gate, turns left onto the road into the city.

'That them?' I ask.

'No,' Caitlyn says. 'Car's too small, too cheap. That was the help.'

She nods to the glove box.

'Look inside the glove box will you, there should be a little flashlight,' she says.

I pop the glove box open, sift through six or seven scrunched tissues, two small notepads, eight or so chewed pens, a pair of yellow-rimmed sunglasses, a cassette tape of *Disintegration* by The Cure and, about the size of a lipstick, a small green flashlight with a black push-button on one end and a small bulb the size of a human iris.

I switch it on and the light flashes a pitiful beam of artificial light big enough to illuminate a night-time barbecue held by a family of green ants.

'What sort of torch is this?' I ask.

'I use it when I can't get my key in the door at home late at night.'

Caitlyn snatches the flashlight from my hand and sharpens her gaze ahead.

'Here they come,' she says.

A silver Mercedes Benz pulls out of the driveway. Chauffeur-driven. Tytus and his daughter Hanna Broz in the back seat. The Mercedes turns left out of the driveway, motors on towards the city. Caitlyn reaches into the footwell on my side, grabs her camera from the faulty camera cabinet and slings the black strap over her left shoulder.

'Let's go,' Caitlyn says.

She slips out of the car, lifts her left Dr Martens boot up to the joint of the jacaranda tree where three main branches of the trunk split off in separate directions. A rip in the left knee of her black jeans stretches further as she hauls herself up. She then monkey crawls up one thick branch that rises up to the top of the clay-coloured fence. She doesn't think. She only acts. Caitlyn Spies. A doer. I get lost for a moment just watching her move. The natural courage in her. Not even blinking before she crawls up a branch high enough to break her neck if her trusty British boots slipped off it.

'What are you waiting for?' she asks.

I lift my left leg up to the tree's central trunk joint, my rear thigh muscle threatening to tear. She stands on the branch and walks it like a gymnast on a balance beam before lying down, hugging the branch momentarily and reaching her legs down ambitiously towards the clay-coloured wall the branch has grown above. Next, she stands on the wall, crouches down, then drops her legs over the side while pressing her belly hard against the top. She pays her potential landing only half-a-second of attention then releases her grip and vanishes.

I crawl up the branch, less graceful. Darkness now. I jump to the wall, dangle my legs over the side. I pray the landing is soft. Drop. My feet find earth and the impact knocks me off them. I stagger backwards and land hard on my arse bones.

A yard in darkness. I can see the lights on in Tytus's mansion ahead but I can't see Caitlyn in the dark of the lawn. 'Caitlyn?' I whisper. '*Caitlyn.*'

Her hand on my shoulder.

'Minus ten for the dismount,' she says. 'C'mon.'

She scurries low and quick across the lawn, skirting the left side of the grand house we walked through with Hanna only hours ago. We're like special ops soldiers. Chuck Norris in *The Octagon.* Low and hard. Round the corner of the house, onto the rear lawn. Stone fountains. Hedge mazes. Floral garden beds. We split through these, sprinting on towards the white door of the bunker being swallowed whole by vines and shrubbery and weed. Caitlyn stops at the door. We both keel forward, sucking in air, hands on thighs. Journalism and sprinting are chalk and cheese, oil and water, Hawke and Keating.

Caitlyn turns the silver knob on the door.

'Locked,' she says.

I suck in more air.

'Maybe you should go back to the car,' I say.

'Why?'

'Sentencing ladder,' I say.

'What?'

'The sentencing ladder,' I say. 'Right now we're probably on the bottom rung of the sentencing ladder. Trespassing onto property. I'm about to go up a rung.'

'To what?'

I walk to the small tool shed neighbouring the bunker.

'Breaking and entering,' I say.

The smell of oil and petrol in the tool shed. I pad down the side of the parked John Deere tractor. A row of gardening and lawn tools leaning against the back of the tool shed. A hoe. A pick. A shovel. A rusty-bladed axe. An axe big enough to chop off Darth Vader's melon.

I pad back to the bunker door, holding the axe in both hands.

The answer, Slim. Boy finds question. Boy finds answer.

I raise the axe high above my shoulder, its heavy rusted blade aligned on a rough trajectory towards the five centimetres of door space between the doorknob and the door edge.

'I feel like I've gotta do this,' I say. 'But you don't have to, Caitlyn. You should go back to the car.'

She stares into my eyes. The moon above us. She shakes her head.

I loosen my shoulder to swing. I go to swing.

'Eli, wait,' Caitlyn says.

I stop.

'What is it?'

'I just had a thought,' she says.

'Yeah?'

'Your end is a dead blue wren?' she says.

'Yeah.'

'What if it's not even about Tytus Broz's end? What if "your end" means *your* end? The end for you, not for him.'

This notion makes me shiver. It's suddenly cold here by this dark bunker. We look at each other for a long moment and I'm grateful for this moment with her, even if I'm terrified and even if I know somewhere deep inside me that she is right about the possibility that 'your end' means my end and my end means our end. The end of Caitlyn and Eli.

And I bring the blade down on the door and the axe bites hard and violently into a door that is already weather-beaten. Wood fragments pop and split and I bring the blade back up and I plunge it into the door again, much like, if I'm honest with myself, the blade I see in my mind's eye plunging into Tytus Broz's geriatric skull. The bunker door flies open, revealing a concrete staircase descending sharply, deep into the earth. Only moonlight illuminates the staircase to the sixth step and the rest is darkness.

Caitlyn stands at my shoulder, looking down into the staircase.

'What the hell is this, Eli?' she says gravely.

I shake my head, walk down the staircase.

'I don't know.'

I count the steps going down. Six, seven, eight … twelve, thirteen, fourteen. Then the ground. Concrete ground beneath my feet.

'You smell that?' Caitlyn asks.

The smell of disinfectant. Bleach. Cleaning products.

'It smells like a hospital,' Caitlyn says.

I rub my hands along the walls in the darkness. Concrete besser block walls on both sides of a hall – a walkway, a tunnel – maybe two metres wide.

'Your flashlight,' I say.

'Right,' Caitlyn says.

She reaches into her pocket. Her thumb clicks the torch and a small orb of white light illuminates about a foot of space in front of us. Enough to see the white door built into the left side of the concrete hall. Enough to see the white door on the right side directly facing the door on the left.

'Oohhhhhh shit,' Caitlyn murmurs. 'Shit, shit, shit, shit, shit, shit.'

'You wanna get outta here?' I ask.

'Not yet,' she says.

I walk further into the darkness. Caitlyn turns the knobs on both doors.

'Locked,' she says.

The polished concrete floor. The claustrophobic hall. Rough concrete walls. Dead air and disinfectant. Caitlyn's shaky light bounces along the walls. Five metres into darkness. Ten metres into the darkness. Then the pitiful flashlight lands on two more white doors built into the hall. Caitlyn turns the door handles.

'Locked,' she says.

We walk on. Another six metres, seven metres into darkness. And the hallway ends. The underground tunnel ends on one more white door.

Caitlyn reaches for the knob.

'Locked,' she says. 'What now?'

Forward to the beginning. Backwards to the end.

I rush back down the hall to the first door we passed.

I drive the axe into the door latch. Once, twice, three times. The door flies open in a splintery mess of door chips and cracks and splinters.

Caitlyn shines the flashlight into the room. The room is the size of a standard home garage. She enters the room, waves the light around furiously, nothing steady in her movements, so all that we see comes in brief flashes. Workbenches line the walls and on these workbenches are cutting tools and power saws and moulding instruments interspersed with artificial limbs in various stages of creation. A plastic arm falling over at the elbow, unfinished. A metal shin and foot, like something from science fiction. A foot made of carbon. Hands made of silicone and metal. It's a mini artificial limb lab. But there's nothing professional about it. It's the laboratory of a madman. Too busy to be the work of someone qualified. Too rabid.

I cross the hallway to the second room. Dig the axe five times into the space between the doorknob and the door edge. Something primal driving me, something vicious and animal. Fear. The answers, maybe. The end. Your end is a dead blue wren. The door cracks and I kick the rest in with my shoe, stomping and stomping and stomping. The door opens and Caitlyn's light falls upon another work room, this one with three benches surrounding a medical operating table and what rests upon this operating table makes us reel back in horror because it looks like a headless human body but it is not. It is an artificial body, a fake plastic body comprised of artificial limbs; a silicone-based torso roughly connected to a monstrous mix of limbs with uneven skin tones. A morbid hybrid horror of hack-test-dummy artificial-limb experimentation.

I run to the next door on the left, further up this horror movie hall, this spook hall like something from a fairground sideshow alley; a man missing his two front teeth is going to appear soon in a ticket booth, selling popcorn and another ticket to Tytus Broz's Bunker of Doom. I drive the axe into the door, this time with more force because I've got a run-up. Hack. Hack. *Crack.* Shrieks of splintered wood as the door pops open. I kick it further ajar and pad breathlessly into this next room, my heart bracing for the impact of what we'll find. Caitlyn's light bounces erratically across the room. Concrete walls. Flash. Shelving. Flash. Glass specimen jars. Rectangular glass boxes, perfectly blown from one piece of perfect glass. Something inside the glass boxes. Something hard to see in the darkness, in such poor light from Caitlyn's flashlight. Scientific specimens, my brain tells me, replacing grim fact with something I can understand. The stonefish my old high-school teacher, Bill Cadbury, kept above his desk in a jar of preservation fluid. Those specimen jars I saw in the old Queensland Museum on school excursions, jars holding organic matter. Preserved starfish. Preserved eels. Preserved platypus. That makes sense. That's something I understand. Caitlyn's orb of light finds another medical table in the centre of this room and upon this table is another artificial body of connected limbs. Another body built from artificial feet, legs, arms; four limbs and a woman's silicone-sleeved torso. I understand this. This is within my knowing. Science. Experimentation. Engineering. Research.

But, wait. Wait, Slim. The breasts on this artificial adult female body are pale white and saggy and ... and ... and ...

'Oh my God,' Caitlyn gasps. She unslings her faulty camera from her left shoulder and, in a kind of trance, snaps several photographs of the room.

'It's real,' she says. 'They're fucking real, Eli.'

*Snap.* The camera's flash pops, too bright for such a dark room. It stuns my eyes but it lights up the room too. *Snap*, she goes again. And this time my eyes adjust enough to take the whole room in. Not platypus. Not eel. The glass boxes are filled with human limbs. Ten, fifteen glass boxes across the shelves lining the walls. A human hand floating in a gold-copper-coloured formaldehyde solution. A human foot floating in glass. A forearm with no hand attached to it. A calf sawn neatly at the ankle so it looks like a leg of butcher-cut ham. *Snap.* The faulty and too-bright camera flash illuminates the medical table and Caitlyn vomits where she stands because the body on the table is a composite of uneven limbs, all frozen in time. Plastinates. Impregnated with a plastic solvent. Bathed in a liquid polymer. Cured and hardened in this room that smells like a hospital.

'What the fuck is going on here, Eli?' Caitlyn shudders.

I take her flashlight from her hand and run it over the body on the medical table. Epoxy resin covers the limbs so they shine in light, resemble the body parts of a waxwork. Each limb is disconnected from the other. Feet placed against shins and thighs but not fully attached. Arms placed beside shoulder joints but not connected. It's like we've walked into some macabre problem-solving game tasking children to fashion a full human body from a toy box of plastinates. The flashlight runs along the body. Legs. Belly. Breasts. And the head of a woman who was smiling beside fake flowers in a shopping mall family portrait on page 3 of today's *Courier-Mail*. It's the plastinate head of Regina Penn.

By the medical table is a metal tray on rollers holding a large white plastic tub filled with a toxic-smelling liquid, another kind of clear preservation fluid. I take two cautious steps to this bucket and peer inside to find the head of Regina's husband, Glenn, staring up at me.

I hand Caitlyn the flashlight and I run out the door of this fever room, raising the axe that I plunge hard into the locked white door on the other side of the hall.

'Eli, slow down!' Caitlyn screams.

But I can't slow down. I can't, Slim. My arms are heavy and tired and I'm exhausted, slowed by fatigue but energised at the same time by shock and dread and curiosity.

I swing the axe again and it shatters the door at its lock. Kick, stomp, bash, stomp. Open.

I stand panting in the room's entryway. Caitlyn brushes my right shoulder as she enters the room and runs the small flashlight across this space in a one-eighty-degree arc. The room smells of harsh and cooked plastics. The room smells of work and disinfectant and formaldehyde. No medical table in the centre of the room. But more workbenches and more shelves lining the walls. Caitlyn's light falls upon the workbenches and there is a collection of tools spread across the benches: cutting tools, scraping tools, moulding tools, hammers and saws, dark hardware for dark work. More tools spill from an old black leather bag, resting on its side, like a bookie's tote bag. Beside the black bag is a collection of smaller specimen jars. These jars are the size of Vegemite jars or peanut butter jars. I approach these small jars.

'Can I use the flashlight?' I ask.

I bring the light close, I lift a random jar from the group of ten or so all filled with preservation fluid. There is a label made from torn masking tape fixed to the yellow lid of the jar. I run the light across the label, written in a rough cursive: *Male, 24, L ear.* I hold the jar into the light to inspect a twenty-four-year-old man's left ear floating in fluid.

I hold a second jar up.

*Male, 41, R thumb.*

I run the flashlight over the masking tape labels on the jars.

*Male, 37, R hallux.*

I raise the glass up to my eyes to see a floating severed big toe.

*Male, 34, R ring finger.*

I scan six more jars and settle the flashlight on one last jar.

*Male, 13, R index.*

I hold this jar up. The light of Caitlyn's torch makes the preservation fluid shine like a golden sea. And inside this golden sea is a pale right forefinger that reminds me of home because there is a freckle on the middle knuckle of it that reminds me of the freckle Slim's girl, Irene, had high up on her inner left thigh, that freckle of hers that became something sacred in Slim's mind way down in the hole. Sounds crazy, Slim, I said, but I have a freckle here on the middle knuckle of my right forefinger and I have this feeling inside me that this freckle brings me luck. My lucky freckle, Slim. My silly sacred freckle.

'What is it?' Caitlyn asks.

'It's my ...' I can't finish the sentence. I can't say it aloud because I'm not sure this is real. 'It's ... mine.'

'This is insane, Eli,' Caitlyn says. 'We have to get outta here.'

I shine the flashlight to the shelves above me. I'm steeled now because I'm whole and because this is a dream. I'm dreaming this. This nightmare is fantasy.

So, of course, there are human heads lining the shelves. Faces of small-time criminals. Plastinates. The grotesque plastinated heads of small-time and big-time criminals. Trophies, maybe. Research tools, more likely. Black hair and brown hair and blond. A man with a moustache. A Pacific Islander man. Men with puffy lips and damaged faces where they've been beaten, tortured. I'm dizzied by these faces. Sickened and frenzied.

'Eli, let's go,' Caitlyn says.

But one head keeps me still. One face keeps me frozen. The flashlight finds it at the end of a shelf above me. And I know immediately I am standing inside a moment of trauma. The trauma is in me and the trauma that will happen has already happened. But the face makes me move. This face I love.

I reach for the black bag on the bench, tip it upside down and the tools inside it clatter against the concrete floor.

'What are you doing?' Caitlyn asks.

I reach my right arm high up on the shelf above me.

'We're gonna need this one,' I say.

'What for?' she asks, turning her eyes away from me, outwardly repulsed.

'For the end of Tytus Broz.'

*

Axe in my hand. Black leather tote bag over my shoulder. I'm shuffling behind Caitlyn as we scurry back down the hall. Hope in our hearts. Hearts in our throats.

'Wait,' I say. I stop on the spot. 'What about the door at the end?'

'Let the cops open that one,' Caitlyn says. 'We've seen enough.'

I shake my head.

'Bevan,' I say.

I turn and run back towards the last locked door at the end of the corridor, heaving the axe over my shoulder. This is what a good man does, Slim. Good men are brash and brave and fly by the seat of their pants that are held up by suspenders made of choice. This is my choice, Slim. Do what is right, not what is easy. *Crack.* The axe drives into the final door. Do what is human. August would do this. *Crack.* Lyle would have done this. *Crack.* Dad would do this. *Crack.*

The good-bad men in my life helping me swing this rusty axe. The doorknob falls off and the splintered door pops open.

I push it wider, stand in the doorway as it swings to a right angle. Caitlyn's feeble light is waving behind me, beaming over my right shoulder to settle on a pair of blue eyes. An eight-year-old boy named Bevan Penn. Short dusty brown hair. Dirt over his face. Caitlyn steadies her light on the boy and the scene becomes clearer. The boy stands in an empty room with a concrete floor and concrete walls like the other rooms. But there are no workbenches or shelves in this room. There is only a cushioned stool. And upon this stool is a red telephone and the boy holds the red telephone's handset to his ear. Confusion over his face. Fear, too. But also something else. Knowing.

He holds the handset out to me. He wants me to take it. I shake my head.

'Bevan, we're gonna get you outta here,' I say.

The boy nods. He drops his head and weeps. He's lost his mind down here. He holds the handset up to me again. I walk closer to him, grip the handset tentatively. I bring the handset to my right ear.

'Hello.'

'Hello, Eli,' says the voice down the phone line.

That same voice from last time. The voice of a man. A real man type man. Deep and raspy, weary maybe.

'Hi.'

Caitlyn watches me, stunned. I turn away from her. Turn my eyes to the boy, Bevan Penn, watching me, expressionless.

'It's me, Eli,' the man says. 'It's Gus.'

'How'd you find me down here?'

'I dialled the number for Eli Bell,' he says. 'I dialled 77—'

'I know the number,' I say, cutting him off. '773 8173.'

'That's right, Eli.'

'I know this isn't real,' I say.

'Sssshhhhh,' the man says. 'She already thinks you're crazy enough.'

'I know you're just the voice in my head,' I say. 'You're a figment of my imagination. I use you to escape from moments of great trauma.'

'Escape?' the man echoes. 'What, like Slim over the Boggo Road walls? Escape from yourself, Eli, do ya, like the Houdini of your own mind?'

'773 8173,' I say. 'That's just the number we'd tap into the calculator when we were kids. That's just "Eli Bell" upside down and back to front.'

'Brilliant!' the man says. 'Upside down and back to front, like the universe, hey Eli? You still got the axe?'

'Yes.'

'Good,' the man says. 'He's coming, Eli.'

'Who?'

'He's already here, Eli.'

And then a fluorescent bar light fixed to the ceiling above us shimmers twice and flicks on. I drop the handset, let it hang from the cord. The whole underground hall is lit up now, ceiling lights buzzing to life from one main power source.

'Oh fuck,' whispers Caitlyn. 'Who's that?'

'That's Iwan Krol,' I whisper.

*

It's the flip-flops we hear first, the rubber thongs of a menacing Queenslander descending the concrete steps to this man-made hell bunker. *Flip. Flop. Flip. Flop.* Rubber on concrete. Walking down the hall now. The sound of busted doors swinging open. First door on the left. First on the right. *Flip. Flop. Flip. Flop.* The second door on the left swinging open, kicked at twice. A long silence. The sound of the second door on the right swinging open. A long creaking swing, the hinges busted. Another long silence. *Flip. Flop. Flip. Flop.* Rubber on concrete.

Close now. Too close. My weak bones stiffen. My amateur heart frozen. My amateur mongrel lost to me now.

Iwan Krol reaches the door to this room. The red telephone room. He stands in the entryway. Blue thongs. Light blue short-sleeved button-up shirt tucked into dark blue shorts. He's an elderly man now. But he's still tall and muscular and sun-damaged. There is strength in those arms. A man who works a farm when he's not sawing the limbs off small-time Queensland criminals who made the fatal mistake of meeting Tytus Broz. The silver hair that was once only creeping from his scalp into a ponytail has fully evacuated, along with his ponytail. His dark eyes. His twisted crazy eye smile that says he likes having three innocents cornered like this in a room beneath the earth.

'Only one way out,' he smiles.

We're standing in the farthest corner of the concrete room, Caitlyn and I forming a protective wedge around Bevan Penn, who huddles behind us. I'm not holding the axe any more because Bevan's holding it, hiding it behind my back, as per my dubious plan to get us the fuck out of this nightmare.

'We're journalists from *The Courier-Mail*,' Caitlyn says.

We're moving back, moving back, deeper into the corner until there's no more corner left to move back into.

'Our editor is fully aware of our whereabouts.'

Iwan Krol nods. Weighs up the possibility of this. Stares into Caitlyn's eyes.

'What you meant to say was, "You *were* journalists from *The Courier-Mail*,"' he says. 'And if, by chance, your editor is indeed at that swanky do in town with my employer and he is indeed thinking about you down here beneath my employer's lawn, then …' – he shrugs, pulling a shining and long Bowie knife out from behind his pants – 'I guess I better make this quick.'

He marches forward like a heavyweight boxer leaving a blue corner at the sound of a bell. Predatory.

I let him come closer. Closer. Closer. Three metres away. Two metres away.

Half a metre from us.

'Now,' I say.

And Caitlyn points her faulty camera at Iwan Krol's face and clicks a blinding flash. The predator turns his head, momentarily stunned, still recalibrating his eyesight as the axe that is now in my hands takes an achingly long arcing journey towards his body. I'm aiming for his torso but the camera flash is so bright it stuns me too, and my aim is skewed. The rusty axe blade misses his chest and his belly and his waist completely but it finds flesh at the end of its journey, lodges into the mid-dorsal area of his left foot. The axe blade cuts clean through the foot and his stupid fucking blue flip-flop and digs into concrete. He looks down at his foot, transfixed by the scene. We're transfixed by it too. Curiously, he doesn't howl in agony. He studies his foot the way a brontosaurus might have studied fire. He raises his left leg and the ankle end of his foot raises in the air with it but all five toes stay planted to the concrete. Five grubby toes resting on a cut cake of rubber flip-flop.

His eyes and my eyes move at once from his foot to meet on the same eye line. Rage fills his face. Red death. The predator. The reaper.

'Run!' I scream.

Iwan Krol swings his Bowie knife swiftly at my neck but I'm swift too. I'm Parramatta Eels halfback Peter Sterling, ducking and weaving under a swinging arm from a Canterbury Bulldogs prop. The heavy black leather tool bag tucked under my left shoulder is now my old leather football. I duck and step left as Caitlyn and Bevan Penn run right and we meet at the door of this dark and evil place.

'Go!' I scream.

Bevan runs in front, then Caitlyn, then me.

'Don't stop,' I scream.

Sprinting. Sprinting. Past the open doors to these sick rooms, these Frankenstein rooms with the real and fake body parts, these underground dens of design where madness and mongrel take hold because in the ground we're that much closer to hell. Sprinting. Sprinting. To the stairs that go up to life. To the stairs that go up to a future with me in it. First step, second step, third step. I turn around as I climb the stairs and the last I see of Tytus Broz's secret underground play space is a Polish-Queensland psychopath named Iwan Krol limping down the concrete hall painting a trail of blood with his axe-cut left foot. The blood is burgundy.

*

The tyres on the Ford Meteor screech around the corner from Countess Street into Roma Street. Caitlyn shifts gears with her left hand and turns the wheel in sharp, deliberate jolts, slams the accelerator into and out of bends. Something deep in her eyes. Trauma, maybe. The magnitude of the scoop, maybe. Which reminds me of work. Which reminds me of Brian Robertson.

The face on the clock on the Brisbane City Hall clock tower is the same silver colour as the full moon. The face on the clock says it's 7.35 p.m. and I've missed my deadline for tomorrow's paper. I see visions of Brian Robertson in his office bending bars of steel in anger as he curses my name for not filing twenty measly centimetres of fawning colour about the glories of a Queensland Champion named Tytus Broz.

I find Bevan Penn in the reflection in the rearview mirror. He sits in the back seat. He stares out his window, stares up at that full moon. He hasn't said a word since our car tyres left a cloud of gravel dust to blow on that sprawling jacaranda in Bellbowrie. Maybe he never will say a word again. Some things can't be put into words.

'Nowhere to park,' Caitlyn says. 'Nowhere to fucking park.'

The central CBD gutters of Adelaide Street are lined with cars.

'Fuck it,' Caitlyn says.

She yanks on the steering wheel hard. The Ford cuts across Adelaide Street and bounces hard up a kerb into King George Square, the central meeting point of the city of Brisbane, a paved square of manicured lawns and military statues and a rectangular fountain kids piss in when they've drunk too much lemonade at the annual Christmas tree lighting ceremony.

Caitlyn slams on the brakes directly outside the Brisbane City Hall entry doors.

A young male City Hall security guard rushes to the car. Caitlyn winds her window down in expectation.

'You can't park here,' the security guard says, dumbstruck, clearly disturbed by this unexpected threat to the hall's security.

'I know,' she says. 'Call the police. Tell them Bevan Penn is in my car. I won't be moving until they get here.'

Caitlyn winds up her window and the security guard fumbles for the two-way radio on his belt.

I nod at Caitlyn.

'I'll be back,' I say.

She gives a half-smile.

'I'll keep this guy distracted,' she says. 'Good luck, Eli Bell.'

The security guard barks into his transceiver. I slip out of the car and scurry in the opposite direction from City Hall, past the water fountain and across King George Square, then I double back, taking a wide and clandestine angle to the hall's grand entry door, behind the security guard who is busy shouting at Caitlyn through her closed car window. There's a welcome desk inside the hall. A bright, beaming Indian woman on the desk.

'I'm here for the awards,' I say.

'Your name, sir?'

'Eli Bell.'

She scans a wad of papers with printed names. I have the black tote bag over my left shoulder. I slip it off my shoulder, down behind the desk, out of her view.

'Have they announced the community awards yet?'

'I believe they're announcing them now,' she says.

She finds my name, ticks it with her pen. She tears a ticket from a pad, hands it to me.

'You're in row M, sir,' she says. 'Seat seven.'

I scurry to the doors of the auditorium. A vast and round room built for fine music. Maybe five hundred red chairs and important people in black suits and nice dresses, divided into two main groups split by a central aisle. Polished wood floors running to a polished wood stage with five levels of choir staging before a backdrop of imposing brass and silver acoustic pipes.

The MC tonight is the woman who reads the news for Channel Seven, Samantha Bruce. She comes on every afternoon, straight after *Wheel of Fortune*. Dad calls Samantha Bruce a 'quinella'. A double win. Easy on the eye but bright too. He recently confessed this adoration for the newsreader when I asked him if he would ever entertain marrying another woman and he came back with his quinella theory and how his dream date would be a night with Samantha Bruce in Kookas restaurant at the Bracken Ridge Tavern, during which Samantha Bruce would stare longingly across the table at him, whispering the same word over and over: 'Perestroika'. I then asked Dad what the womanly equivalent of a trifecta would be.

'Shuang Chen,' he said.

'Who's Shuang Chen?' I asked.

'She's a Shanghai dental nurse I read about.'

'What makes her the trifecta?'

'She was born with three tits.'

Samantha Bruce leans into a lectern microphone.

'Now we move to our Community Champions,' the newsreader MC says. 'These are the unsung Queensland heroes who are always putting themselves last. Well, ladies and gentlemen, tonight we put them first and foremost in our collective heart.'

The packed house applauds. I walk through the central aisle, looking at row numbers on the edge of seats. Row W for why. Row T for the time has come for Tytus Broz. Row M for my mum and my dad. Sitting together seven seats along row M. My parents. Two spare chairs beside them. Mum sparkles in a black dress that shimmers in some form of light that shines down on her and I look up to find where that light comes from and it's the ceiling of the auditorium. The whole ceiling is a domed silver-white moon that takes on the colours of the greens and reds and purples that flash on stage. The full moon inside this theatre.

Dad wears a grey vinyl jacket that he obviously bought for $1.50 at the Sandgate St Vinnies. Aquamarine slacks. The fashion sense of a twenty-year agoraphobe who never sees enough humans to follow fashion. But he made it here and the fact he made it here and is still sitting here makes me all wet-eyed. Cheesy fuck I am. Even after everything. All that warped madness beneath the earth. The blinky tears again.

An usher taps me on the shoulder.

'Are you lost?' the usher asks.

'No, I'm not lost,' I say.

Mum spots me out of the corner of her eye. She smiles and hurries me to her with a wave.

The newsreader starts reading names into the lectern microphone.

'Magdalena Godfrey, Coopers Plains,' she says.

Magdalena Godfrey proudly walks on stage from its left wing. She beams as she receives a gold medal on a Queensland maroon ribbon and a certificate from a man on stage in a suit. The man in the suit puts his arm around Magdalena and ushers her towards a photographer front-of-stage who snaps three quick shots of Magdalena giving a goofy smile over her certificate. On the third shot, Magdalena bites into her gold medal for laughs.

'Sourav Goldy, Stretton,' Samantha Bruce says.

Sourav Goldy takes the stage and bows, takes a certificate and his gold medal.

I squeeze past six people pulling their knees back courteously in their seats. My black tote bag bumps their heads and their shoulders as I pass.

'Where the hell have you been?' Mum whispers.

'I was working on a story.'

'What the hell do you have in that bag?'

Dad leans over.

'Sssshhhh,' he says. 'Gus is up.'

'August Bell, Bracken Ridge.'

August pads onto the stage. His black jacket doesn't fit him well, his tie's too loose and his cream-coloured chinos are ten centimetres too long and his hair is scruffy, but he's happy and so is my mum, who drops the evening's booklet program on the ground in a hurry so she has two free hands to clap her brilliant selfless weirdo mute son.

Dad puts a forefinger and thumb in his mouth, blowing a sharp and inappropriate whistle like he's calling an outback cattle dog home at sunset.

Prompted by Mum's applause, a vigorous clapping spreads through the auditorium and this makes my mum so proud she has to stand to keep from exploding.

August shakes hands with the man in the suit, gratefully accepts his medal and certificate. He smiles proudly for his photograph; he waves into the crowd and Mum waves back desperately, despite the fact August's wave was more general, in a queen's drive-by kind of way. Mum's going through the six stages of motherly loving: pride, elation, regret, gratitude, hope and pride again. Each of these stages is navigated through tears. August then walks off the right side of the stage.

I stand and begin squeezing past the knees of the people sitting beside me to my right.

'I'm sorry,' I say. 'Excuse me. My apologies. Sorry about this.'

'Eli,' Mum whisper-screams. 'Where are you going?'

I turn and offer a wave that I hope conveys my hope to be back at my seat in a brief moment. I rush up the central aisle to the back of the auditorium and make for a side door that opens to a walkway where backstage staffers in black shirts and black pants are buzzing about with coffee urns and teacups and silver platters of scones and biscuits. I run forward a few steps, then go back to a walk when an official- and important-looking woman gives me a quizzical eye. I smile casually like I'm meant to be there. Confidence, Slim. Moving in magic. She doesn't know a thing because I move in magic. I turn through a door that looks like it's heading to the toilets and the official-looking woman with the evil eye continues up the side-of-hall walkway. I go back out the doorway I just came through and slip casually and efficiently behind a black curtain at the side of the stage.

August. He walks towards me. A big curling smile on his face with his gold medal bouncing on his chest as he springs along the polished wooden floors of the stage wing. But his smile fades when he sees my smile fade.

'What is it, Eli?'

'I found him, Gus.'

'Who?'

I open the black tote bag and August looks inside. He stares down into the bag. August says nothing.

He nods his head to the side. *Follow me.*

He hurries to the door of a green room running off the side-of-stage area, opens it swiftly. A carpeted room. Tables and chairs. Hard black instrument cases. Speaker equipment. A fruit platter of orange and rockmelon skins, watermelon pieces half eaten. August shuffles to a chrome tool tray on wheels. On the tray sits a box covered in a red silk cloth. A name card sits beside it. *Tytus Broz*. August lifts one corner of the silk cloth to reveal Tytus Broz's glass box holding his prototype-silicone-arm life's work. His big reveal. His great gift to the State of Queensland.

August doesn't say something. What he doesn't say is, *Pass me the bag, Eli.*

*

We slip back out the side of the black curtain into the hall's side thoroughfare. Moving quickly now. The brothers Bell. The survivors, Eli and August, the Queensland Champion. The gold medallist and his younger brother who worships him. Walking hard. Then the official who gave me the evil eye before gives me that same evil eye again as she passes back down the walkway and time slows in this moment because that woman is ushering a man to the backstage area. An old man dressed in white. White suit. White hair. White shoes. White bones. The old man catches sight of my face late and my face registers in his mind only after I've passed by his shoulder. Time and perspective. Time doesn't exist and from any perspective this scene would always see Tytus Broz stop and scratch his head as he wonders about the young man he passed carrying the black tote bag just like the one he keeps in his bunker of very bad things. But from any perspective he would be puzzled because when time resumed at normal speed we would always be gone. Escaped. Gone to see our mum and dad.

\*

'And at last we come to our final award for the evening, ladies and gentlemen,' says the newsreader MC. 'One single award winner truly deserving of our inaugural Queensland Senior Champion Award.'

I'm squeezing past the knees of the long-suffering six people sitting next to us in Row M. August waits in the central aisle.

I'm gesturing to Mum that we need to go. Throwing thumbs over my shoulder, pointing at August. I reach my seat.

'We need to go, guys,' I say.

'Don't be so rude, Eli,' Mum says. 'We'll stay for the last award.'

I put a hand on Mum's shoulder. Serious face. Never more serious face.

'Please, Mum,' I say. 'You don't want to see this one.'

And the Channel Seven newsreader joyfully calls the inaugural Queensland Senior Champion to the stage.

'Tytus Broz,' she sings.

Mum's eyes turn from me to the stage and it takes a moment to connect the name with the figure in the white suit moving slowly onto the stage to accept his award.

She stands. She says nothing. She moves.

\*

'What's the bloody rush?' Dad asks as we reach the grand entry doors of Brisbane City Hall.

But his train of thought is derailed by the flashing lights of two police cars on the paved King George Square, the cars parked in a V-shape blocking in Caitlyn's Ford Meteor.

Maybe ten sky-blue-uniformed police officers walking towards us. Two more police officers carefully assisting Bevan Penn to the back of a police car. Bevan's gaze finds me in the chaos. He nods. Appreciation in that nod. Confusion. Survival. Silence.

'What the fuck's goin' on 'ere?' Dad ponders aloud.

Caitlyn Spies walks among the police officers. She leads them, in fact. Spies digs deep. She enters the hall foyer and points through the doors of the auditorium.

'He's already up there,' she says. 'That's him in the white.'

The police officers file into the auditorium.

'What's going on, Eli?' Mum asks.

Our eyes follow the police officers as they assume positions throughout the auditorium waiting for Tytus Broz to finish a long and self-inflating speech about the past four decades he has dedicated to Queensland's disabled community.

'It's the end of Tytus Broz, Mum,' I say.

Caitlyn walks over to me.

'You okay?' she asks.

'Yeah,' I say. 'You okay?'

'Yeah, they've sent three police cars to the Bellbowrie house.'

Caitlyn turns her eyes to Mum and Dad; they're watching this scene like it was a moon landing.

'Hi,' Caitlyn says.

'This is my mum, Frances,' I say. 'My dad, Robert. My brother, Gus.'

'I'm Caitlyn,' she says.

Mum shakes Caitlyn's hand. Dad and Gus smile.

'So you're the one he's always talking about?' Mum says.

'Mum,' I say, short and sharp.

Mum's looking at Caitlyn, smiling.

'Eli says you're a very special woman,' she says.

I roll my eyes.

'Well,' Caitlyn replies, 'I think I'm only just starting to realise how special your boys are, Mrs Bell.'

Mrs Bell. I don't hear that much. Mum likes it as much as I do.

Caitlyn turns her eyes to the auditorium. Tytus Broz is still talking on stage. He's talking about selflessness and making the most of the time we have on earth. We can't see his face from here because there are too many people gathered in the foyer before the auditorium doors.

'Keep pushing,' Tytus says. 'Never give up. Whatever you want to achieve. Keep going. Never waste a single opportunity to transform your wildest dreams into your favourite memories.'

He coughs. Clears his throat.

'I have a surprise for you all tonight,' Tytus Broz announces grandly. 'The sum of my life's work. A vision for the future. A future where young Australians who are not blessed with all the gifts of our glorious God are, instead, blessed by the gift of human ingenuity.'

He pauses.

'Samantha, if you will be so kind.'

Perspective, Slim. Infinite angles on a single moment. Maybe there are five hundred people in this auditorium and each person views this moment from their own individual perspective. I view it in my mind because my eyes can only see Caitlyn. We can't see the stage from where we stand but we can hear the sound of the audience as it reacts to Samantha Bruce removing the red silk cloth on Tytus's glass display box holding his life's work. We can hear the horrified gasps of the audience that ripple from Row A all the way to Row Z. People howling. A woman wailing. Men screaming in shock and outrage.

'What's happening, Eli?' Mum asks.

I turn to her.

'I found him, Mum.'

'Found who?'

I can see the police officers rushing down the central aisle now. Other officers close in around Tytus Broz from the east and west sides of the auditorium. August and I share a glance at each other. *Your end is a dead blue wren. Your end is a dead blue wren.*

I see it all unfolding in my mind's eye from the perspective of the people still sitting in Row M.

Captain Ahab is drowning in a sea of Queensland Police. The sky-blue cops dragging Tytus Broz away, taking his old and frail arms by the sleeves of his white suit. Placing those arms around his back. Audience members shielding their eyes with their cupped hands; women in cocktail dresses gagging and screaming. Tytus Broz dragged from the stage as he looks, looks, looks in befuddlement at the glass box on stage, wondering how in the world and in this puzzling universe his life's-work silicone super limb was replaced with the warped and macabre and plastinated severed head of the first man I ever loved.

*

Time, Slim. Do your time before it does you. It slows now. Everybody moves in slow motion and I'm not sure if I'm making them do it. The police lights, flashing red and blue and silent. That slow and deliberate nod of August's that says he's proud of me. That says he knew it was going to happen exactly like this. That it was going to all unfold in this busy City Hall foyer, with people rushing to leave the building, clutching their purses and umbrellas and tripping over their long evening dresses. Important men barking their dismay and trauma at event organisers. The woman with the evil eye in tears, overwhelmed by the pandemonium caused by that severed head on stage. August's knowing smile and his right forefinger pen writing me a message in the air.

August walks away, shuffles elegantly and calmly towards Mum and Dad, standing to the side of the hall's entry doors. They're giving me some space. They're giving me some time. Time with the girl of my dreams. She stands before me, a metre from me, police and audience members and officials zipping back and forth around the bubble of us.

'What just happened?' Caitlyn asks.

'I don't know,' I shrug. 'It all happened too fast.'

Caitlyn shakes her head.

'Were you really talking to someone on that telephone?' she asks.

I think about this for a long moment.

'I don't know any more. Do you think I was?'

She stares into my eyes.

'I need to think on that some more,' she says. She nods to a huddle of police officers.

'Cops want us down at Roma Street police station,' she says. 'You wanna come with me?'

'Mum and Dad are gonna drive me down,' I say.

She looks out from the foyer to Mum, Dad and August, now waiting at the edge of King George Square.

'I thought they'd look different, your mum and dad,' she says.

I laugh. 'You did?'

'They're so nice,' she says. 'They just look like any normal mum and dad.'

'They've been working on normal for quite some time now.'

Caitlyn nods. Hands in her pockets. She bounces on her heels. I want to say something else to stay in this moment, freeze it, but I can only slow time, I can't stop it yet.

'Brian's gonna want me to write all this up tomorrow,' Caitlyn says. 'What do you think I should say to him?'

'You should say you'll write it, every last bit of it,' I say. 'The truth. All of it.'

'No fear,' she says.

'No favour,' I say.

'You want to write it with me?' she asks.

'But I'm not a crime writer.'

'Not yet,' she says. 'Joint byline?'

Joint byline with Caitlyn Spies. Dream stuff. A story in three words.

'Caitlyn and Eli,' I say.

She smiles.

'Yeah,' she says. 'Caitlyn and Eli.'

Caitlyn shuffles back towards the huddle of police. I walk to the entry doors of the auditorium. The space is almost empty of people. A police forensics officer is on stage carefully inspecting Tytus Broz's glass box, now with the red silk cloth covering it. I look up to the moon-shaped white ceiling, like four white beach shells, four quarters of a circle coming together to form a whole moon. I see the beginning in that ceiling and I see the end. I see my brother, August, sitting on the fence in front of the Darra house, the full sun behind him, writing those air words that have followed me through my short life: *Your end is a dead blue wren.*

*

I turn away from the auditorium and walk towards the front hall exit but a figure stands before me. Tall and lean and old and strong. I see the figure's shoes first, black leather dress shoes, unpolished and worn. Black dress slacks. A blue button-up shirt with no tie and an old wrinkled black jacket. I see the face of

Iwan Krol and it's the face of death. But my spine knows him first and so do the teenage bones in my calves and they help me move. I spring sharply away but not sharp enough to miss the blade hidden in his right fist that stabs into the right side of my belly. It feels like a tear. Like someone tore open my belly and stuck a finger inside, wiggled it around like it was searching for something I shouldn't have swallowed. Something I swallowed long ago, like the universe. I stagger groggily backwards, staring at Iwan Krol as though I still can't believe he would do such a thing. That he could be so cold, despite everything I know about him, despite everything I've seen. That he could stab a young man on a night like this, this electric night when Caitlyn and Eli saw the future and they saw the past and they smiled at them both. I'm dizzy and my mouth is suddenly dry and it takes me a moment to realise Iwan Krol is coming towards me for a second blow, a final blow. I can't even see the blade he stabbed me with. He's hiding it somewhere. In his sleeve, maybe. In his pockets. Run, Eli. Run. But I can't run. The wound in my belly makes me keel over in agony. I try to scream but I can't because screaming uses the muscles in my gut and my gut muscles have been stabbed deep. All I do is stagger. Stagger left. Stagger away from Iwan Krol. And I pray to be seen by police gathering beyond the hall doors but they have not seen me in the movement of the audience members gathered in the foyer, discussing the horror of the severed head while missing the horror of the boy and the blade-wielding beast unfolding among them. Iwan Krol got me with a perfect prison yard stabbing, an accomplished porridge shiv. Quick and quiet. No big scenes.

My right hand grips my belly and I see it painted in blood. Stagger to the staircase to my left. A grand marble and wood staircase sweeping in an arc to the hall's second floor. I pull myself up each step and Iwan Krol staggers behind me, dragging his severed left foot, evidently bandaged now and stuffed agonisingly into a black leather shoe. Two cripples playing cat and mouse, one more accustomed to physical pain than the other. The word is 'help', Eli. Say it loud. Just say it. 'H ...' But I can't get it out. 'Hel ...' The wound won't let me scream it. Three audience members descend the stairs from the second floor, a suited man and two women in cocktail dresses, one wearing a fluffy white scarf like she's shouldering a white wolf. I burst through them, clutching my stomach. They see the blood now over my hands and across the shirt beneath the old black jacket I took from the newsroom's emergency coat rack.

'Help!' I say, loud enough for them to hear.

The woman wearing the white scarf howls in fear, reels away from me like I'm on fire or diseased.

'He's ... *knife*,' I spit at the man in the descending trio and this man makes a dot-to-dot connection between my blood-stained belly and the man waddling after me with the look on his face like a thousand fires from a thousand hells.

'Hey, stop,' demands the suited man, bravely standing in front of Iwan Krol who promptly stabs the brave suited man in the top of his right shoulder with a lightning-swift and masked downward stabbing motion that leaves the man collapsed instantly on the marble staircase.

'Harold!' howls the woman in the white scarf. The other woman in the trio banshee-screams then runs down the stairs and across the foyer in the direction of the gathered police officers. I stagger on, reach the top of the stairs and turn a sharp right into a hall space and I burst through a nameless brown solid wood door and then another hall space that curves around through sky-blue walls for twenty metres and I look behind me to see the drops of blood I'm leaving in my wake, blood crumbs for the beast whose rabid old-man wheezing tells me he's slower than me but hungrier. I burst through another nameless door – no people, nobody around to save the boy – and this door opens to a staircase zig-zagging up to another level still and I know this level. I know this white wall space and I know this elevator. I know this, Slim. This is the room from my youth. This is the room where we met the maintenance man who showed us how the city clocks work and how the clock faces look from the inside out.

I stagger to the old yellow steel clock tower elevator and I try to open the cage door but it's locked and I can hear Iwan Krol bursting through the doors behind me, so I stagger to the door of the maintenance stairs. Your friend Clancy Mallett's secret stairs, Slim, the ones he showed us years ago, around the corner and through the door running off the elevator room.

Total darkness in the secret stairwell. I'm fading now. I can't breathe right. My belly doesn't even hurt so acutely any more because my whole body aches. Numb now. But still moving. Up and up and up the secret stairs. These concrete stairs zig-zag upward, eight or nine steps going up sharply, then I bang into a wall I can't see, then I turn and step up eight or nine more steps, then I bang into another wall hard and turn and go up another eight or nine steps. I'll do this until I drop, Slim. Just keep going up. But then I stop because I want to lie down on these steps and close my eyes but maybe that's called dying and I don't want to do that, Slim, not when there's so many more questions to ask Caitlyn Spies, so many more questions to ask my mum and dad about how they fell in love, how I came to be; about August and the moon pool and all those things they were gonna tell me when I was older. I've got to get older. My eyes close briefly. Black. Black. The long black. Then my eyes open because I hear the door to the secret stairs open below me, a shaft of yellow light flooding the entry then vanishing as the door closes. Move, Eli Bell. Move. Get up. I can hear Iwan Krol below me, wheezing and sucking in the dank stairwell air. His crippled psycho legs and his crooked heart driving him up the stairs in search of my neck and my eyes and my heart, all of which he wants to stab. Frankenstein's monster. Tytus's monster. I drag myself up another cramped flight of stairs, then another, then another. The woman with the white fox around her neck. She screamed on the curved staircase. She bellowed so loud the police had to hear her. Keep walking, Eli. Keep going. Ten flights of stairs. I'm ready to sleep now, Slim. Eleven flights of stairs. Twelve. I'm ready to die now, Slim. Thirteen.

And then a wall with no more stairs zig-zagging up. Just a thin door with a handle for turning. The light. The room with the lights that shine at night through the four clock faces of the Brisbane City Hall clock tower. The north clock. The south clock. East and west. Illuminated from here for the city of Brisbane. The sound of the clockwork. The machinery of the clockwork. Rotating wheels and pulleys working into themselves, not beginning at any point but not ending at any point either. Perpetual. A polished concrete floor and a caged elevator shaft in the centre of the engine room. Four grand ticking clock faces on each side of the tower, engines at the base of each clock encased in protective metal.

Both hands clutching my stomach now, I stagger along the square concrete path around the elevator shaft, past the east clock face, blood dripping on my shoes and on the concrete, past the south clock face and the west clock face. Eyes closing. So thirsty. So tired. Eyes closing. I come to the north clock face and there's nowhere else to go, the concrete path ends here, blocked by a tall wire protection gate giving access to the elevator. I fall to the ground, push myself up so I'm leaning against the metal casing of the engine that pushes the long black steel minute and hour hands of the north clock face. The minute hand moves up a notch and, cupping my stomach, holding my hands over the blade wound to stop the bleeding, I mark the time on the clock from the inside out. Time of death. Two minutes to nine o'clock.

I hear the door to the engine room open and close again. I hear Iwan Krol's footsteps. One foot steps and the other foot drags. And I see him now through the wires and steel beams of the elevator cage. He's on one side of the engine room and I'm on the other. The elevator shaft between us. I just want to sleep. I'm so lifeless now he doesn't even scare me any more. I'm not afraid of him. I'm angry. I'm furious. I'm vengeful. But I can only channel that rage into my heart, nothing else. Not my hands to pull myself up or my legs to stand.

He limps past the east clock face and the south and the west and turns a corner into my path, my body spread out before the north clock face, my useless punctured flesh and my weak bones without any marrow.

He limps closer now. All I hear is his wheezing and his left shoe dragging along the concrete. Up close he seems so old. I see his wrinkles, the lines in his forehead like dry desert gullies. His face is covered in farming sunspots. Half his nose has been cut away surgically. How could he be so filled with hate at such an old age?

He steps closer. One step, drag. Two steps, drag. Three steps, drag. And he stops.

He stands over me now, studies me like I'm a dead dog. A dead bird. A dead blue wren. He kneels down, placing his weight on his right foot, relieving the pressure on his cut left foot. Then he prods me. He feels for a pulse in my neck. He spreads open the flaps of my black jacket to study the wound in my belly clearly. He lifts my shirt up to study the wound. He pushes my shoulder. He squeezes my upper left arm in his hands. He's squeezing my left bicep. He's feeling my bones.

I want to ask him what he is doing but I'm too spent to speak. I want to ask him if he thinks he's a good man but my lips don't move. I want to ask him what moment in his life preceded his heart turning so cold and mechanised and his mind so mad. Then his hands return to my neck and he's feeling the bones in my neck and his forefinger and thumb squeeze my Adam's apple. Then he cleans his knife on my pants, wipes each side of it. And he breathes deep and I can feel his breath on my face. And he brings his clean blade to my neck.

Then the door to the engine room opens. Three police officers in sky-blue uniforms. They scream things.

My eyes closing. The police screaming.

'Step back.'

'Step back.'

'Drop the knife.'

The cold blade on my neck.

An explosion. A gunshot. Two gunshots. Bullets bouncing on metal and concrete.

The knife momentarily released from my neck and I'm standing now, hauled to my feet by Iwan Krol. My vision blurs. I know he stands behind me and I know his blade is touching my Adam's apple now and I know those shirts are blue in front of me. Men in blue with weapons raised.

'You know I'll do it,' he says.

Then go ahead, I cannot say, I'm already dead. My end was a dead blue wren.

He pushes me forward and my legs move with him. And the movement of feet moves my jacket and something inside my jacket moves. I reach inside my jacket pocket with the four fingers of my right hand gripping something made of glass. Something cylindrical. A jar.

'Back,' Iwan Krol bellows. 'Get back.'

The blade presses hard against my throat. We're so close together I feel his breath and his spit in my earhole. And we stop because the police can't go back any further.

'Put the knife down,' one officer says, trying to calm things. 'Don't do this.'

Time stops, Slim. Time does not exist. It is frozen in this moment.

Then it starts again because it is given something human to understand it, something we built to remind us of ageing, a deafening bell that chimes above us. A bell I did not see above me when I entered this engine room. A bell tolling nine times. Clang. Clang. Clang. The sound clogs our eardrums. Stifles our minds. And temporarily clouds Iwan Krol's sense of awareness because he does not defend himself from the glass specimen jar holding my severed forefinger which I smash against his right side temple. He reels back and the knife is momentarily lifted from my neck, long enough for me to drop to the ground hard, a dead weight drop, landing on my arse and rolling over like a party-trick dog playing dead.

I don't see where the bullets go from the guns of the officers. Just my perspective through a dead man's eyes. That's my perspective on this moment, Slim. Face flat on concrete. The world turned on its side. The black polished shoes of police officers moving to something behind me. A figure running through the door to the engine room. A face leaning down into my view.

My brother, August. My eyes are closing. Blink. My brother, August. Blink.

He whispers in my right ear.

'You're gonna be okay, Eli,' he says. 'You're gonna be okay. You come back. You always come back.'

I can't speak. My mouth won't let me speak. I'm mute. My left forefinger scribbles a line in the air only my older brother will read before the line disappears.

*Boy swallows universe.*

# Boy Swallows Universe

This is not heaven. This is not hell. This is Boggo Road prison
yard Number 2 Division.

It's empty. Not a soul alive in the place, except ... except
for the man kneeling down, tending the prison garden in his
prison clothes with his prison-issue spade. A garden of red and
yellow roses; lavender bushes and purple irises under full sun
and cloudless blue sky.

'Hey, kid,' the man says without seeing me.

'Hey, Slim,' I say.

He stands, dusts soil from his kneecaps and his palms.

'The garden's lookin' real great, Slim.'

'Thanks,' he says. 'If I can keep them bastard caterpillars off
it, she'll go all right.'

He drops his spade and nods his head to the side.

'C'mon,' he says, 'we gotta get you outta here.'

He walks across the yard. The grass is thick and green and
swallows my feet. He walks me to a thick brown brick wall
skirting behind Number 2 Division cell block. A knotted rope
hangs from a wedged grappling hook high above us.

Slim nods. He tugs on the rope hard, twice, to ensure it
holds taut.

'Up you go, kid,' he says, handing me the rope.

'What is this, Slim?'

'It's your great escape, Eli,' he says.

I look up at the high wall. I know this wall.

'This is Halliday's Leap!' I say.

Slim nods.

'Get goin',' he says. 'You're runnin' outta time.'

'Do your time, hey Slim?'

He nods. 'Before it does you,' he says.

I climb up the wall, my feet pressing up from the thick knots in Slim's rope.

The rope feels real, burning my hands as I climb. I reach the top of the wall, lean my head back down to Slim, standing way down there on the thick green grass.

'What's over the wall, Slim?' I ask.

'The answers,' he says.

'To what, Slim?'

'To the questions,' he says.

I stand on the thick edge of that brown brick prison wall and I see a yellow sand beach below me, but that beach does not run to ocean water, it runs to the universe, an expanding black void filled with galaxies and planets and supernovas and a thousand astronomical events occurring in unison. Explosions of pink and purple. Combustive moments in bright orange and green and yellow and all those glittery stars against the eternal black canvas of space.

There's a girl on the beach, dipping her toes in the ocean of the universe. She turns her head and she finds me up here on the wall. She smiles.

'C'mon,' she says. 'Jump.' She waves me to her. 'C'mon, Eli.'

And I leap.

# Girl Saves Boy

The Ford Meteor speeds down Ipswich Road. Caitlyn Spies'
left hand drops the gear stick down as she yanks the steering
wheel too hard and fast into the Darra turn-off.

'And you think that was me standing on the beach?' she
asks.

'Well … yeah,' I say. 'Then I opened my eyes and my family
were there.'

It was August I saw first. He was looking over me just as he
was looking over me in the clock tower engine room. I thought
I was back there until I saw the drip sticking into my hand.
Felt the hospital bed. Mum rushed to the bedside when she saw
me awake. She told me to say something so she would know I
really was alive.

'Gr …' I said, wetting my dry lips to talk.

'Gr …' I said.

'What is it, Eli?' Mum asked, anguished.

'Group hug,' I said.

Mum suffocated me in a hug and August threw his arm
around us. Mum slobbered tears and spit on me and turned
to Dad who was sitting in an armchair in the corner of the
room.

'He means you too, Robert,' Mum said. And that was a kind invitation to many things for Dad, starting with a hug he tried to pretend he didn't want.

'And that's when you walked into the hospital room,' I say to Caitlyn.

'And that's why you think I brought you back?' Caitlyn asks.

'Well, it's kinda obvious, isn't it?' I reply.

'Sorry to spoil the magic, mate, but it was RBH Emergency who brought you back.'

The car hits a bump on Darra Station Road. The knife wound in my belly howls for attention. It's only been a month since City Hall. I should be in bed watching *Days of Our Lives*. I shouldn't be in this old car. I shouldn't be working.

'Sorry about that,' Caitlyn says.

The RBH doctors say I'm a walking miracle. A freak of medical science. The blade hit the top of my pelvic bone as it went in. And that bone stopped the knife going deeper.

'You must have strong bones!' the doctor said.

August smiled at that. August said he'd told me I'd come back. August knows things because August is exactly one year older than me and the universe.

Caitlyn turns into Ebrington Street and we pass Ducie Street Park, with the cricket pitch and the playground I once followed Lyle across on his midnight walk to pick up drugs from 'Back Off' Bich Dang. A lifetime ago. Another dimension. Another me.

The car pulls up in front of my old house in Sandakan Street. Lyle's house. Lyle's mum and dad's house.

We're retracing the story. Brian Robertson wants it all. The rise and fall of Tytus Broz, the man every newspaper across Australia has had splashed across their front pages for the past month. Brian's going to turn our story into a five-part crime series, with special first-person accounts from the boy who saw some of the story up close, through his own eyes, from his own perspective. Joint byline. Caitlyn Spies and Eli Bell. Caitlyn will handle nuts and bolts. I will handle colour and detail.

'Details, Eli,' Brian Robertson said. 'I want every last detail. Everything you remember.'

I said nothing.

'What do we call it?' Brian asked at the editorial meeting. 'What's our headline for this whole insane saga? Give it to me in three words.'

I said nothing.

*

I knock on the door of the house. My old house. A man comes to the door. Mid-forties. Deep black skin of an African man. Two smiling girls around his legs.

I explain why I've come. I'm the boy who was stabbed by Iwan Krol. I once lived here. This is where Lyle Orlik was taken away. This is where the story began. I need to show my colleague something inside my old house.

We walk down the hall to Lena's room. This room of true love. This room of blood. Sky-blue fibro walls. Off-colour paint patches where Lyle once puttied up holes. It's a girl's bedroom now. There are Cabbage Patch dolls on a single bed with a pink quilt. My Little Pony posters on the walls.

The African man's name is Rana. He stands at the entry to Lena's old bedroom. I ask him if he would mind me looking inside the room's built-in wardrobe. Rana nods. I slide the wardrobe door along. I push against the back wall of the wardrobe and the wall pops out. Rana is puzzled by this secret door. I ask him if he would mind if Caitlyn and I slid down into the secret void built into his house. He shakes his head.

Our feet meet the cold damp earth. Caitlyn clicks on her small green flashlight. The little circle of white torchlight bounces off the underground brick walls of Lyle's secret room. The circle stops on a red telephone resting on a cushioned stool.

I look at Caitlyn. She takes a deep breath, stands back from the telephone, like it might be a thing of witchcraft, a thing accursed by dark magic. I move closer to it because I feel compelled to. I stop on the spot. Stand in silence for a long moment. Then the phone rings. I turn back to Caitlyn, confused. She gives no reaction.

*Ring, ring.*

I move closer to the phone.

*Ring, ring.*

I turn back to Caitlyn.

'Do you hear that?' I ask.

I move closer.

'Just leave it, Eli,' Caitlyn says.

Closer.

'But do you hear it?'

*Ring, ring.*

My hand reaches out to the phone and I grip the handset and I'm about to raise the handset to my ear when Caitlyn's hand rests gently on mine.

'Just let it ring out, Eli,' she says softly. 'What's he going to tell you' – she puts her other hand behind my head, her perfect and gentle hand sliding down to the back of my neck – 'that you don't already know?'

And the phone rings again as she moves into me and the phone rings again as she closes her eyes and presses her lips against mine and I will remember this moment through the stars I see on the ceiling of this secret room and the spinning planets those stars surround and the dust of a million galaxies scattered across her bottom lip. I will remember this kiss through the big bang. I will remember the end through the beginning.

And the phone stops ringing.

# Acknowledgements

*With them the seed of wisdom did I sow,*
*And with my own hand labour'd it to grow:*
*And this was all the harvest that I reap'd —*
*'I came like water, and like wind I go'*

*Into this universe …*

*The Rubáiyát of Omar Khayyám*

Arthur 'Slim' Halliday was a brief and unique friend from a brief and profound chapter of my childhood. Two wonderful books on Slim's extraordinary life helped fill in some factual blanks for this book: *Slim Halliday: The Taxi Driver Killer* by Ken Blanch, and *Houdini of Boggo Road: The Life and Escapades of Slim Halliday* by Christopher Dawson. Thanks, as always, to Rachel Clarke and the library staff at the *Courier-Mail* archives.

Catherine Milne built this universe with the most assured and encouraging nod of her head. She believed from the start and so did all the extraordinary people at HarperCollins Australia, from James Kellow to Alice Wood to hawk-eyed genius Scott Forbes. Thanks also to copy editor Julia Stiles and proofreaders Pam Dunne and Lu Sierra for your sharp, tender and invaluable work.

The editor of *The Weekend Australian Magazine*, Christine Middap, is the best magazine editor in the world and she had no clear reason to believe in me a long time ago but she did and this book exists because of her. Deep and eternal thanks also to Paul Whittaker, Michelle Gunn, John Lehmann, Helen Trinca, Hedley Thomas, Michael McKenna, Michael Miller, Chris Mitchell, Campbell Reid, David Fagan and every last glorious and dogged and inspiring mag mate, pod buddy, super sub-editor, snapper brother, byline sister and generally brilliant colleague at *The Australian, The Courier-Mail* and *Brisbane News*, past and present.

There have been several creative angels on my shoulder throughout this particular endeavour and I am forever indebted to Nikki Gemmell, Caroline Overington, Matthew Condon, Susan Johnson, Frances Whiting, Sean Sennett, Mark Schliebs, Sean Parnell, Sarah Elks, Christine Westwood, Tania Stibbe, Mary Garden, Greg and Caroline Kelly, and Slade and Felicia Gibson for all the right words at all the right times. Three genuine lifelong cultural heroes of mine – Tim Rogers, David Wenham and Geoffrey Robertson – made the whole book worthwhile just by reading it.

Eli Bell and his full beating heart would like to thank Emillie Dalton, Fiona Brandis-Dalton and every last dear Dalton, Farmer, Franzmann and O'Connor.

Special thanks to Ben Hart, Kathy Young, Jason Freier and the Freier family, Alara Cameron, Brian Robertson, Tim Broadfoot, Chris Stoikov, Travis Kenning, Rob Henry, Adam Hansen, Billy Dale, Trevor Hollywood and Edward Louis Severson III for being there then.

And, finally, thanks to the three beautiful girls who always save the boy. They got it wrong: the universe begins and ends at you. My left shoe.